THE HIDDEN LIFE OF ASTER KELLY

THE
HIDDEN LIFE
OF
ASTER KELLY

A NOVEL

KATHERINE A. SHERBROOKE

PEGASUS BOOKS

NEW YORK LONDON

THE HIDDEN LIFE OF ASTER KELLY

Pegasus Books, Ltd.
148 West 37th Street, 13th Floor
New York, NY 10018

Copyright © 2023 by Katherine A. Sherbrooke

First Pegasus Books edition April 2023

Interior design by Maria Fernandez

Library of Congress Cataloging-in-Publication Data is available.

ISBN: 978-1-63936-353-7

10 9 8 7 6 5 4 3 2 1

Printed in the United States of America
Distributed by Simon & Schuster
www.pegasusbooks.com

To my mother, Sandy,
and my sister, Barbara
This is for you

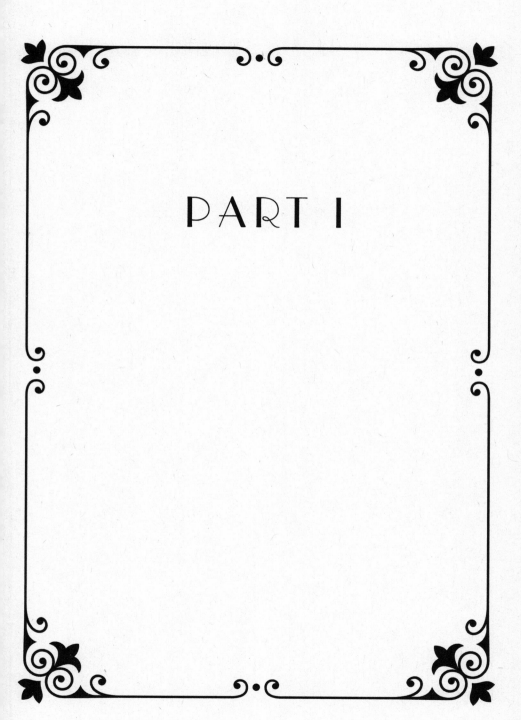

PART I

1948
LOS ANGELES

CHAPTER ONE

S tanding outside Fernando's Boutique on Wilshire Boulevard, Aster took a moment to compose herself before adjusting her glasses and opening the door. A saleswoman, wearing a luxurious silk and organza dress with pumps so pointy they pinched Aster's feet with the thought of them, glanced up hopefully and then with confusion when she noticed the worn suitcase Aster carried.

"I'm here to see Fernando Tivoli?" Aster clutched her purse, the train ticket inside a niggling reminder of just how far she'd come and how little she had to show for it.

"I'm not sure he's available." The woman eyed Aster with suspicion.

"He's expecting me. Aster Kelly."

The woman told her to wait and disappeared behind a long panel of green velvet.

Aster tucked her suitcase out of the way and surveyed the limited yet stunning selection of gowns for women and dinner jackets for men on display. To the uninitiated, Fernando's looked like any other small boutique, but Fernando was a couturier, and Aster knew well how the system worked. Anyone who lingered after taking in the jaw-dropping prices, inquired about different sizes, or asked to try something on, would be whisked away to a back room—likely behind that green curtain—offered a glass of champagne, and seated around a runway. There, models would take turns walking, turning, and twirling various dresses down the runway, hoping the customer would find something to her liking and place an order. Fernando was one of the youngest designers in Beverly Hills but was already a darling among LA fashion critics. He was also Aster's last chance to break into the world of design. If she didn't land an apprenticeship with him, she'd be forced to make the long trip back to New York, the first Fashion Guild Contest winner not to secure a promising position in the industry.

The velvet shimmered as the woman stepped back into the room.

"He'll see you, but he has a client coming at three o'clock."

Aster glanced at her watch, which said 2:50 P.M., certain her appointment had been scheduled for three. She'd arrived early and yet would have less than fifteen minutes with him. She told herself to stay positive and calm, then followed the woman behind the green curtain.

Fernando's back room was a smaller space for couturier shows than Aster was accustomed to in New York, but careful attention had been paid to every detail. Instead of musty wall-to-wall carpet, colorful area rugs suggested a living room. Similarly, the couch and two chairs arranged for customers were upholstered in fine linen, not the scratchy wool herringbone that generated static in every New York season. And the runway, usually black with scuff marks, gleamed with a polish that somehow hid the well-trodden path of the models.

On the far side of the room, a man squatted over photographs strewn across the floor, his back to Aster. He cut a slim figure in gabardine trousers, his Oxford sleeves rolled up to the elbows. A pencil rested on his ear and disappeared into a thick mane of jet-black hair. Aster could tell he wasn't particularly tall, but he carried himself with the strength of a dancer, his back muscles flexing as he reached for various photos, flipping them over to examine the backs before returning them to the pile.

"I'm sorry to be rushed," he said, without turning around. "I'm on a tight deadline. I see that you were in the book, but remind me why you're here?" He took the pencil from his ear and jotted something in a notebook.

Aster tightened her grip on her suitcase. She'd spent the previous two days sketching more dresses, rethinking the order of the samples she'd show and perfecting the stories to go with each one. He was her last hope, and he didn't even remember why she was there?

"The Fashion Guild Contest?"

He gave an almost inaudible grunt, a dismissive "hmm" suggesting the award didn't mean anything to him.

"You signed up looking for an apprentice?" she added.

"Oh, Greta convinced me to do that. She's a doll." Warmth infused his voice, which had the lovely baritone vibration of a piano. "It's always worth meeting anyone Greta sends."

He stood and swiveled toward Aster with his hand outstretched, all in one grand movement. When he finally looked at her, he stopped midmotion.

"Wait, I thought . . . are you one of Greta's models?"

Aster swallowed, trying to tamp down her dismay at the question and the flush rising in her cheeks. How to explain that yes, but no, not anymore. Yes, she'd suffered through the humiliation of walking the runway, the steady ache of starvation, the constant cornering in a back room by some client's husband who wanted a "closer look" at what his wife wanted to buy, the smells of cigarette smoke and bourbon the only relief from the stink of his sweat, desperate for one of the seamstresses on hand to come swat him away. Only Greta could be counted on for a brisk interruption. Greta had saved her in so many ways, first allowing her to take home abandoned samples because she couldn't afford any decent clothes of her own, then helping Aster when she wanted to disassemble them and rearrange the parts into new garments that would communicate more power, less sex appeal. It was Greta who'd spliced together the new creations for her. And Greta who'd convinced Aster to enter her best pieces into the design contest, to show the world what she could do.

"I used to work with her," Aster said. "I'm here to show you my designs."

He studied her for a moment, looked at his watch, and said, "Well, you've come all the way out here. Let's see what you've got."

Aster hitched in her breath as a rush of adrenaline surged. She clicked open her suitcase and felt her way through the silk and cashmere to the garment on the bottom. She'd intended to show it to him last—it was nothing like his designs—but it was her favorite, and she didn't have much time. She pulled out the black velvet tunic with sable fur sleeves cropped to three-quarter length. He reached out to touch it.

"The cut of these sleeves looks almost like Dior," he said.

"They were . . . once."

He laughed. "Really? And the tunic?"

"Off the rack, but I added the edging at the neckline from the piping of a Turkish pillow."

"Interesting. I hate to ask, but do you mind putting it on for me so I can see its hang? I gave all the girls the afternoon off."

"What about your three o'clock?" she asked tentatively, worried there wouldn't be time to show him anything else.

He smiled apologetically. "There is no three o'clock, but I am under a different sort of deadline, so that part's true. Anyway, I'm intrigued. I'd like to see your work in motion."

Aster's heart ricocheted in her chest like the little orb in a pinball machine. She coaxed her shoulders to relax.

He showed her into the dressing room, a familiar place with a rack of heels in different sizes, hooks with backless bras, strapless bras, girdles and slips, and a robe for cover between changes. Aster took off her prim silk blouse and pulled the tunic over her head. She wished she was wearing something other than a brown pencil skirt—it didn't exactly work with the tunic—but she'd been determined to dress as demurely as possible for her interviews. She appraised herself in the narrow mirror and decided she needed a little more flair to show off the piece. She released the twist of her bun, letting soft ringlets fall to her shoulders, and took off the thick-rimmed glasses perched on her nose. They were purely for effect and weren't right for the outfit. Finally, she switched her flats for a pair of black patent leather heels. She thought their shine would contrast nicely with the soft fur of the sleeves.

When she came out of the dressing room, she found Fernando sitting on the couch sketching in his notebook. She took it as a cue to step up on the runway and give her creation a proper viewing. Before she thought better of it, old habits kicked in and she strutted away from him, turned slowly, and walked back on a tightrope, each step exactly in line with the one before.

"So you are one of Greta's girls," he said, smiling.

She wanted to curl inward, furious at herself for veering from her plan, but saw only kindness in his eyes. And she did adore him for calling the models "Greta's." Like so many women in fashion, Greta was the power behind several great designers but never got any of the credit. She'd been summarily demoted to seamstress on her sixtieth birthday and sent back to the dressing room to await tailoring assignments.

"I knew her from my time in New York. Another lifetime ago," Fernando said.

He looked too young to have had another lifetime—was he even thirty? Aster reminded herself of her mission and stepped off the runway.

"I have other things to show you." She took a step toward the suitcase.

He caught her arm and gestured for her to sit.

"Miss. . . . ? I'm sorry, your name again?"

"Aster Kelly. Please call me Aster."

"I have to be honest with you, Aster. I have no money for an apprentice right now, and even less time, but I see you've got some talent. Tell me why you're here."

Hadn't she made it perfectly plain? Her brow reflexively furrowed, all while her mother's admonishment rang in her ear. *Don't snarl your face like that. No one's interested in what goes on inside a woman's head.*

"What I mean is," Fernando continued, "I get the gist—design contest, see the country, meet with designers along the way, *questo e quello*. But you're a long way from home. Tell me. Why are you here?"

The question unmoored her. Her mind went blank, or rather was crowded with all the things she shouldn't say: that she wanted to prove her mother wrong, to show her that people did want to know what she thought; that winning the design competition had given her such a false sense of prowess she'd been sure she'd be offered at least one job before the trip was half-over, and the idea of going back home having failed turned her insides sour; that she'd stupidly broken the heart of a man she loved because she needed to be free to take one of the opportunities that would surely be coming her way, no matter which city she might have to call home; that she would happily move clear across the country if that's what it took to get away from scouring bars late at night in search of her mother, finding her courting a circle of liquored men, her father's head hung low in the car; that she was here, in Fernando's studio specifically, because the other eight designers who had interviewed her dismissed her after only a cursory glance at her designs; that if he didn't give her a chance, she would have no professional prospects beyond secretarial school.

"I want to do something that matters." She barely kept her voice from quavering.

"Okay then. Maybe you can help me with something."

He moved to the arm of the sofa closest to her, suddenly animated.

"I have the opportunity of a lifetime. I wasn't kidding about having no money to hire you, but all that could change later this month. Sid Sawyer himself—do you know who that is?—he has invited me to audition, if you will, for an exclusive contract with Galaxy Studios to outfit his most important actors when they're off-screen. As he sees it, how his stars look moseying about town is just as important as how they look on the big screen. He's looking for a designer to run a regular series of private runway shows on the lot to pick out the right getups for their biggest stars. And I've got the first shot at it!" Fernando leapt up and clapped his hands together.

Aster quickly absorbed the enormity of the opportunity. Galaxy had one of the largest stables of stars under contract in Hollywood. Outfitting them for key off-set moments would be a boon to any shop. That kind of opportunity, plus all the press sure to come with it, could turn Fernando's into an empire overnight.

"The challenge," Fernando said, pacing now, gesticulating, "is that they want me to tailor for each actor in advance. The publicity people apparently have very little time and even less imagination, and this way they can see each selection on a model who is the same build as the actor and the outfit will be ready in no time. This whole thing is the kid's idea. Sid Sawyer may control the money, but Sam definitely has the brains."

Aster understood the challenge. Most designers in couturier worked with one "fit model," making all samples to that one size. Pieces were custom-made for each client's specific measurements after they'd placed an order and paid for it, not before.

"There are four actors I know I need to prepare for: Gary Cooper, Rita Hayworth, Bogey, and Bacall."

Just hearing those names made Aster dizzy. This man, standing in front of her, might become the personal couturier for all of them? The whole idea of it boggled the mind. But why was he telling her all this?

"The men are easy enough. I've just got to get the build right. The women are the bigger challenge. I feel sure the girls I pick for this need to not only have the right figure, but the right attitude. They need to mimic the demeanor of the actress in question, or the publicity people won't be able to imagine them in my clothes. One of my models is a dead ringer for Hayworth—sassy, buxom, a natural ginger to boot. But Bacall is a challenge. Come over here and tell me what you think." He waved her toward the river of photos he'd been looking at when she arrived. "Here's what I have to choose from. You know this business. Who would you pick?"

Aster relished the chance to show him her instincts, demonstrate her awareness that fashion went far beyond the clothes. It was a tool to amplify an attitude already resident, enhance an image without trying to manufacture it. You couldn't be a top-notch designer without first understanding the kind of person who wanted to don a particular look. And you couldn't be a first-rate model without acting the part. Walk the walk, as Greta would say.

She knelt in front of the photos. It was a difficult task given that she had never met any of these girls. Personality played a critical role, and all she had to go by for each woman was one photograph with a name and measurements scribbled on the back.

"How tall is Bacall?" she asked.

"Five nine."

Common enough among models, but Bacall was unique. She was lean yet had curves in the right places, radiated elegance yet moved with a certain determination, as if she thought a few steps ahead of everyone else. And even though her cheeks and chin line were soft, her eyes smoldered. Aster considered her both feminine and strong, the kind of gal who wowed in a pantsuit just as easily as in a bathing suit.

Aster put aside two girls who were too petite, a few who were too buxom, one whose hair was too dark. She felt Fernando watching her every move, gauging her aptitude.

"This one . . ." Aster flipped over the photo. "Jenny has the right figure." She tentatively raised the photo, but sensed something about her wasn't quite right. "Christine here, though, has better coloring, and I get the sense she's got more confidence." She cocked her head to the side to consider Christine's full stature more carefully. "Yes. It should be Christine." She held the photo out to Fernando, hoping she had chosen wisely.

"Definitely not."

Aster's heart plummeted. She'd blown it.

Fernando crouched in front of her and waited until she met his gaze. Something crystallized in his eyes.

"You're the one," he said.

"Me?" Her lungs seized with a familiar constriction of air. "No. I'm done with all that."

Tears welled up, and she cursed herself for thinking he'd actually wanted her opinion. She was wrung out by the roller coaster of misplaced hope and abject failure she'd been on for weeks—four cities, nine interviews, more than enough opportunity to impress, to earn a chance. But no one had cared much for what she had to offer, most of them barely paying attention. And now Fernando only wanted to use her body.

"I need this, Aster." He sat down on the edge of the runway. "This place could be the next Balenciaga, the future Jaques Fath with an opportunity like this. You could be part of that. Help me win Galaxy, and I'll help you. I promise."

He looked ready to kneel at her feet. He needed *her*. But he wanted her to do the one thing she swore never to do again. And if he won the contract—which she had no idea if he could—she would surely be expected to continue as the fit and display model for Lauren Bacall. But might she find a real mentor in Fernando? Could this stranger be taken at his word?

Or should she pack it up and head home? She was being asked to stay in this strange town—for how long did he say? A month?—with no guarantees. After the last three months of disappointment, the idea of running back into Graham's arms, if he would still have her, was tempting. Although, if she went home now, she could picture her life exactly, and it would include a secretarial pool and too many nights searching the streets for her mother. If she stayed, maybe realizing her dreams was still possible. But could she trust Fernando?

As if reading her mind, he said, "Let's call Greta. She'll tell you all about me."

Greta again. Just her name spread warmth through Aster, a rush of maternal comfort and protection she'd never gotten from her own mother. Greta was the one who'd protected her during those horrible years on the runway in New York, had for some reason adopted Aster as her own. If Greta trusted this man, surely Aster could too.

Years later, Aster would picture this scene in her mind and think of it as the moment before: before she met the man she would marry, before the fangs of fame dug into her, before her life became defined by lies.

"Okay," she said. "I'll do it."

CHAPTER TWO

Walking from her taxicab to soundstage number three on the Galaxy lot was more complicated than crossing Fifth Avenue in New York at rush hour. The flow of traffic was entirely unreliable, with whole façades of buildings moving on rollers, golf carts crisscrossing at odd angles, and stacks of equipment rumbling up from behind. It suggested a temporary existence, one in which any streetlight, apartment building, or even an entire town could be disassembled and carted away at a moment's notice. It was all a bit distracting. Aster forced herself to focus. This was the most important day yet in Fernando's career and would determine her future as well. Its success or failure would literally hang from her shoulders.

Fernando had worked feverishly over the last month to create the perfect selection of gowns for Bacall. Aster had stood for him for hours on end as he tried out new fabrics and countless variations on traditional designs—strapless, mermaid, bell-shaped, full-length, midcalf—nipping and tucking with chalk and pins until she thought she might keel over. He relied on Aster to tell him how a certain cut felt on her hips, or if it pulled on her knees as she navigated stairs. He wanted his designs to not only look good, but to feel good. He wanted Bacall to love them if she ever wore them and come back for more.

Watching Fernando's creations take shape around her, Aster learned basic technique and also understood she was witnessing extraordinary talent in motion. He could alter the entire bearing of a gown with the smallest adjustment in the height of a ruffle or angle of a hemline. She hoped she might absorb some of that genius.

And while he worked, they talked. They swapped stories about Greta the unflappable, and she told him about her brother, Teddy, how he used to call her Pip—short for pip-squeak because she was the younger sister—and how he was killed at Guadalcanal. Fernando told her about his early days in LA and described his banishment from New York after his father, a formidable figure in the garment district, learned he was gay. There was an easy give-and-take to their conversations, and as time went on, Aster found herself looking forward to work. She wanted to learn from Fernando, build fundamental design skills, and make a life here on her own terms. But they needed to win the Galaxy business first.

When Aster finally entered the soundstage, she discovered another landscape of seemingly disconnected parts, but on a smaller scale. The activity revolved around two sets, one designed as a formal living room and the other a street scene outside a brick building. A cacophony of lights crowded the space—in black cans on a mesh of tracks on the ceiling, on rolling poles with wire tails, and in huge drums that glowed like hazy sunshine. Crew members, all dressed in black, adjusted and readjusted various wires and props. They shared a silent camaraderie, one fellow tossing a role of tape to another who caught it without even looking.

Three canvas chairs faced the living room set, each tagged for its intended occupant—Director, Director of Photography, and Bogie. Would Humphrey Bogart be there today? Her hand shook as she reached up to smooth her hair, the sticky surface reminding her not to fiddle. She and Louisa, her best friend from home, had snuck into *Casablanca* three times back in junior high. They couldn't get enough of the story and crunched their popcorn just as anxiously during the second and third showings, as if the ending might change and Bergman and Bogart would choose to stay together after all. Louisa, disappointed every time, decided the film was simply a political statement, designed to suggest that romantic love should never eclipse duty. Aster saw it differently, moved by the beauty and tragedy of choosing the greater good over one's own personal desires, a signal of how strong love could be. She contended that love wasn't about the grand gestures sweeping across the screen as the credits rolled but was something much deeper. Rick and Ilsa never stopped loving each other, even after being apart for so many years, and they never would.

It made her think of Graham. She hoped he'd found a way to forgive her, might even keep a small space in his heart for her as they went on to lead their separate lives. It pained her to think he still might not understand why she'd chosen to leave.

As she approached the set, the idea of coming face-to-face with Humphrey Bogart himself was enough to catch Aster up short. She located her breath and reminded herself that she would not be expected to converse with any stars, nor would they have any interest in her. She just had to do this job and do it without faltering. Fernando was counting on her.

She found him behind the street corner set, examining a rack of dresses.

"There you are, *amore mio*." He deposited a kiss on both of her cheeks. His warmth had started to remind her of her brother, which both put her at ease and pinched her with grief. Had she hugged Teddy tightly enough before he shipped out? She'd never imagined that he wouldn't come home.

"William should be here any minute. Let's get you into your first gown before the studio people get here," he said.

Fernando took her gently by the arm and steered her behind a curtain hanging from a lighting apparatus. Unlike the tight changing quarters Aster was used to, this space was uncomfortably cavernous, and a door on the far wall looked like an exit to the outside. She couldn't help but wonder if someone might come charging in without warning and find her half-clothed.

Fernando unzipped a stunning white chiffon dress with ruching around the bust and at the hips, leaving a teardrop of smooth fabric at the abdomen. Aster raised her eyebrows.

"Sexiest one first?"

"Need to show them what we're capable of right out of the gate." He winked, turned the dress around, and held it out for Aster to step into.

Aster glanced at the door behind her again before letting her tulip skirt fall away. She had learned the trick of wearing nylons with no underwear to avoid unsightly bumps and wrinkles and had long since stopped worrying about disrobing in front of Fernando. It all went with the trade. But the looming specter of the back door was hard to ignore.

"All the action is on the other set this morning," Fernando said. "The crew won't be coming back here, don't worry."

She stepped over the dress's zipper, careful not to let her heels catch on the fabric inside, unbuttoned her Oxford, and tossed it onto the chair with her skirt. Fernando positioned the gown properly before she turned so he could zip her up. Fernando eyed each seam, tugged a bit at her left shoulder, and stepped back for a full appraisal.

"Zeew," he whistled. "We are going to knock them dead."

"How's my makeup?" She worried the heat of the taxi ride might have left her flushed. "My bag's on the chair."

As Fernando powdered her forehead, William appeared at the edge of the curtain. His stature echoed Bogart—small by the standard of male models Aster was accustomed to—and with an arrangement of features neither traditionally handsome nor unpleasing, just like the actor.

"I think the publicity folks are right behind me," William said.

"Pinstripe double-breasted suit on the double, Willy. I'll go get them situated. Come out when I call you, Aster on your arm, just like we practiced. Let's make this count. You're going to be *molto bene.*" Fernando ran his hands through his hair before stepping around the curtain.

"Ready to make a splash, William?" Aster turned her back so he could change in privacy.

When Fernando raised his voice to introduce the first suit and gown, Aster and William strode out onto the wooden studio floor, careful to maintain matching strides while making it all look as natural as possible.

In two director's chairs about thirty feet in front of them sat a man with a gray bowler pulled down low on his forehead and a woman with black cat-eye glasses and a clipboard on her lap. A cigarette dangled from the man's mouth, a cloud of smoke hovering below the brim of his hat. Fernando stood to the side so he could see both his models and his clients while narrating the show. "You'll notice a long slit up one side of the gown, which will showcase Ms. Bacall's lean legs nicely. We're showing a double-breasted suit here for Mr. Bogart, which we think will be a nice tip of the hat to the Chicago crowd during his appearance there in April . . ."

Aster always felt strangely invisible in these initial moments, aware that the garment made the first impression. She imagined the client taking in the color of the dress first, then the fabric and its overall proportions, before forming an opinion about what a particular style suggested, what it might say about the sort of person who would wear it in public. Aster knew it was only after she walked right up to the clients, turned to reveal the back of the gown, moved all the way back to the starting point, and spun around to face them again that they would notice her—her hair, her eyes, the way she held her head, or the expression on her face. If she could embody the person they wanted to be in the dress, or in this case, who the studio wanted their actor to be, that's when the ensemble would be considered a winner.

Unlike the clients in the shop, this Hollywood pair conferred in secret. The woman leaned over and whispered into the man's ear. He nodded his head and puffed again on his cigarette before saying something else too quietly to hear. They shared several exchanges, the woman making notations on her clipboard before he spoke.

"Promising. What's next?" he asked.

Fernando's chest visibly expanded, and Aster realized he might actually have been holding his breath.

"We'll be right out," Fernando said, following his models behind the curtain. While choosing which gown to show next, he whispered, "You two look great. William, blue suit with the vest this time while I help Aster."

Aster and William repeated the same steps with each outfit, the clients only occasionally making a closer inspection of something, once asking Aster to demonstrate maneuvering on and off a chair—simulating, she supposed, what it might reveal while leaving a table at a restaurant or getting out of a car. No detail that might be caught on camera and printed in newspapers across the country was too small to consider.

Back in the dressing area after the fifth set of outfits, Fernando had just unzipped a strapless navy gown—Aster's favorite of the bunch—when the door she'd all but forgotten lurched open. Two men strode into the space with such unabashed confidence she almost didn't have time to clasp the dress against her body to stop it from slipping to her knees.

"Mr. Sawyer." Fernando fumbled with the zipper at Aster's back. "Good to see you."

"Mr. Sawyer's my old man. Call me Sam."

Sam and his colleague were both tall, six feet two, Aster surmised, and both blond, but there the similarities ended. Sam's fair complexion complemented striking hazel eyes that bore into her with an intensity she couldn't quite interpret. He either wanted to know everything about her or simply wondered what she of all people was doing there. He smiled and held out his hand.

"This must be our Lauren Bacall double," he said.

Aster switched hands to make sure her dress stayed in place and held hers out to him.

"Aster Kelly."

Sam took Aster's hand the way one might hold a bird—gently at first, and then, once certain it wouldn't struggle, wrapping it in a comfortable cocoon. His eyes locked on hers for a beat before he unfurled his fingers and released her. She hadn't returned such an intent gaze from any man other than Graham in a long time.

"Fernando, allow me to introduce you to Christopher Page, Galaxy's next big star. I want you to dress him too."

Given his bright shock of hair, Christopher's skin tone surprised with an olive tint that went beyond a Southern California tan, and his eyes were such a dark brown it was difficult to find pupils in their deep pools. His eyebrows, equally dark, made Aster wonder if his hair was naturally light or if the publicity people had invented the stunning combination.

Fernando finally zipped Aster's dress back up and stepped out from behind her to shake Christopher's hand.

"What a pleasure," Fernando said.

"Christopher debuts next month in *Ransom*, and we're quite sure he's going to be our next hot property. Have we missed the whole show?" Sam leaned closer to Fernando and lowered his voice. "What do Tweedledee and Tweedledum have to say about your selections here?"

"We have one more set to show them."

"Splendid. We'll head out front and continue this after." Sam appraised Aster again before walking through the curtain with Christopher.

As Fernando helped Aster into the last gown—a siren red, deep V-neck with a swath of satin at the waist and a flowing skirt—she caught herself wishing she was getting back into the long white gown instead. It flattered her narrow hips and offered a more subtle flirtation than the red dress's blatant call to be noticed. More her style. Her hands were suddenly clammy, and she forced herself to keep them off her waist lest she splotch the satin.

"You didn't say anything about Sam Sawyer being so gorgeous," she whispered.

"Not my type." Fernando snapped the closure at her back and then said into her ear, quietly so William couldn't hear, "But that Christopher? I hope dressing him includes a chance to undress him too, *mio Dio*."

Aster laughed and spun to face him. She'd been modeling long enough not to be shocked. Fernando's lifestyle was a kind of open secret at the boutique, embraced by those who adored him, quietly hidden from those unwilling to tolerate it. Aster was grateful to be considered worthy of the truth.

"Didn't you teach me never to mix business with pleasure?" she asked playfully.

"Which is why you're always safe with me. Okay, last one, and then we get our verdict. Keep doing exactly what you've been doing. No distractions." He wagged his finger at her.

He was right. She needed to bring to the runway the cool and mysterious persona Lauren Bacall had made famous if they were going to win the studio's business. She took a deep breath, pictured herself as a sleek panther who needed only to eye its prey to subdue it, and waited for Fernando to introduce them one last time.

⚜

Back at the studio that afternoon, Fernando opened a bottle of champagne, which was not something Aster had ever seen him do without a client present. He handed out glasses to Aster, William, Shirley, and two other models, Masie and June, who were regulars on Fernando's runway. He raised his glass.

"Kids, we had quite a day today. They decided on the spot that Fernando's will be the couturier of choice for all Galaxy stars!"

In between cheers and clinks, Fernando praised Aster's excellent work and told William he was like the perfect partner to a prima ballerina. Aster watched everyone's faces, particularly Masie's and June's, hoping the opportunities imbedded in the new contract would soften a little of the resentment she feared they harbored given that she'd swooped in and gotten what they considered a starring role at the boutique.

"And our gal Shirley will be on the runway next. Rita Hayworth, here we come!"

More whoops and clinks.

Shirley was one of the few people who didn't think Aster's dream of pursuing design was misplaced. "Brains don't droop as fast as boobs," she liked to say. She'd been modeling for more than six years and told Aster, in her Oklahoma twang, that at twenty-eight years old, she was an overripe peach soon to be tossed in with the rest of the slop. She was sure her job at Fernando's would be the best and last she would ever have as a model, and this latest opportunity put her over the moon.

"I think I might cry." Shirley's hand fluttered at her throat. "Me and Rita Hayworth walking in the same shoes, for real. My mama will be so proud."

Aster saw the joy on Shirley's face and wondered what that might feel like. When she'd told her mother she was temporarily working as the stand-in for Bacall, her mother had scoffed. "And you actually fell for his nonsense about wanting you for anything else?"

"What did they buy today?" Masie asked. On top of her modeling responsibilities, she kept the accounts for Fernando and always said the most beautiful gowns are the ones that sell.

"The white and blue gowns for Bacall, the navy three-piece and the pinstripe suit for Bogey. And . . ." Fernando paused and tipped his glass toward Aster. "Sam Sawyer himself bought the red dress for Aster."

The bubbles went dry in her throat. "What?"

"He wants you to wear it. Tonight. He's picking you up at eight o'clock."

She froze.

"Only if you agree, of course," Fernando said, and then looked pained. "You will agree, won't you?"

The other girls eyed her with awe, but something like shame enveloped Aster. She would never forget what her mother said when she took her first modeling job: "Watch out for any man who tries to grab you off the runway. It's no better than being picked out of a lineup at a brothel."

"What about mixing business—" she started.

"*Mia stella*," Fernando interrupted. "As long as your pleasure brings me business, mix away!"

Everybody laughed, but Aster could see resentment building again. The new girl in town had not only gotten the top job but now had a date with one of Hollywood's most eligible bachelors.

"I don't know . . ."

"Don't be a fool, honey," Shirley said. "What could be the harm in one date?"

CHAPTER THREE

Aster considered her reflection in the mirror before choosing two sequin-tipped combs to hold her hair off her face, leaving the rest to curl gently at her collarbone. Deciding the dress was worthy of her grandmother's pearl-drop earrings, she retrieved the box from the back of her panty drawer and clipped them into place. She left her neck and arms bare.

"Looks like someone's got a date." Her roommate, Ria, stood at the door, a cigarette dangling from her hand. "It's about time."

"It's kind of a work event." Aster concentrated on applying her mascara.

"No one dresses like that for a work event." Ria plopped onto Aster's bed. "Who's the lucky guy?"

Aster hesitated. Ria worked for a casting director at Paramount, and one of the first things she ever told Aster was that there were no secrets in Hollywood. "Tinseltown is the smallest town in the world," she'd said. Aster already worried about socializing with

Fernando's newest and most important client. Creating any gossip at a competing studio wasn't advisable. Then again, Ria did seem to know something about just about everyone in Hollywood, and dipping into her font of knowledge might not be such a bad idea.

"What do you know about Sam Sawyer?"

"You mean beyond the Sophia Green debacle? Wait, you're going out with Sam Sawyer?"

"What debacle?" Sophia was arguably the biggest star in the country, if you liked movies with a bombshell at the center.

"You really don't pay attention to trade gossip, do you?" Ria waved her cigarette in the air as she spoke. "Sophia was new to Galaxy maybe three years ago? By the time *Lonesome Rider* came out, she and Sam Sawyer were already engaged. But three months later, she was on loan to Warner Bros. and the engagement was off. Word on the street was that Sophia got a little too friendly with Brian Tiller when they did *Slingshot* together. Sam eventually took her back, but then she went on location with Rex Williams, and it happened all over again. Daddy Sawyer shipped her off to MGM on permanent loan after that to keep her away from his son—I'm sure he made some good money from the deal—but the rumor is that Sam is still her go-to."

"Her go-to?" Aster fumbled with her lipstick. What in the world was she doing going on a date with the former fiancé of Sophia Green, a woman her own brother had called "the real American dream"? A pinup photo of her still hung in his room, her full lips puckered just so, her shirt a tad too tight at the bosom. Her mother couldn't bear to put his things away.

"There's a rumor she needed a stint in a dry tank about six months ago, and he's the one who delivered her there."

"So he's a good guy then? Reliable?" Aster needed to hear something reassuring. He would be there in less than ten minutes.

"What man would ever turn down a call from Sophia Green?"

Aster watched Sam closely as they drove to the restaurant. From his warm greeting at her place to his ease guiding the Chrysler around tight turns, she took him to be a man of confidence yet one who preferred company to being alone. She decided to project her own sense of independence, to be welcoming of his attention without being awed by it, no matter who he might be. She was going to make the red dress her own—it was technically hers now anyway—and prove to herself that she didn't have to hide behind fake glasses and flats to be taken seriously and considered a woman of substance. As her first signal, when they pulled up to the curb, she would wait for him to help her from the car. But before he had even closed his door, hers swung open, and a gloved hand appeared at the ready. A valet. Of course. Stars didn't park their own cars, and Sam Sawyer lived like his stars. Once she was safely deposited onto the sidewalk, Sam tossed the man his keys.

"Keep it up front, if you would, Garrison." Sam slipped his hand around the back of Aster's waist. "Ready?"

She wasn't sure what she should be ready for, exactly. But she did know how to walk into a room.

"I don't see why not." She reflected his smile back at him.

The short hall curved sharply and ended at a maître d's podium. In a white dinner jacket and black tie, the man looked rather like a captain standing at the prow of a ship, the oval dining room behind him his vessel.

"Welcome back, Mr. Sawyer. Ma'am." He bowed his head in Aster's direction. "Right this way."

The warmth of Sam's hand on the small of her back helped her slow her step and soak in the moment. Sam greeted several patrons by name as they made their way through the room. When the maître d' paused beside an empty table, Sam slid his hand down the length of her arm and guided her into a crescent-shaped booth. Two martinis arrived before Aster even had a chance to adjust the crinoline of her dress around her.

"Thank you for joining me tonight," he said.

"This is lovely." As much as she'd promised herself not to be fazed by any glitz she might encounter, the beauty of her surroundings dazzled. The booth, built of solid mahogany, was covered in velvet cushions the color of sapphires. A flock of exotic birds soared across the wall, painted in shimmering tones of ruby, emerald, and gold. Every table glowed with candlelight and crystal glasses, all the women glittering with diamonds. The tablecloth and napkins were crisply starched, and pink roses gushed from a silver vase, their extravagant blooms timed perfectly. Had Sophia Green sat in this very seat? Aster touched one of her grandmother's earrings to reassure herself this was all real.

"Have you never been here before?" he asked. When she shook her head, he continued. "Then welcome to Romanoff's, a place almost as gorgeous as you are." He held out his glass for a clink. His broad smile sent a flywheel through her abdomen. It had been a long time since she'd registered such internal commotion. She sipped her martini, welcoming the cool burst of liquid followed by a warm rush down her throat. She needed to relax.

"Let me give you the rundown on this place," he said in a low voice, leaning in conspiratorially close.

He pointed out several industry titans with small nods of his head. "That's David O. Selznick over in the corner. He was responsible for *Gone with the Wind*. The table with six men and one woman behind us? That's Gloria Rubenstein—the most important movie critic at the moment. She always has a gob of producers vying for her attention. I don't think she's paid for a drink in years. And the long table on the other side of the dance floor? B-list actors looking for their big breaks.

Don't let anyone tell you they're just out for an evening of fun. No one ever stops auditioning in this town."

Aster didn't know what to say to that. She supposed she had arrived in LA to audition for Fernando in a way, but certainly not for Sam.

"How about you?" He leaned back against the booth.

"What would you like to know?"

"What's your Hollywood dream?" He pulled a silver cigarette case out of his breast pocket and offered her a Lucky Strike. He lit a match from the tiny box on the table, and she inhaled deeply before answering.

"No Hollywood dream. I'm studying fashion."

"A woman as beautiful as Bacall, and you have no designs on getting onto the big screen? I find that hard to believe."

"Not if you'd seen my tenth-grade rendition of Desdemona." She laughed at the memory.

"Not a fan of Iago?"

"I could never make all those long speeches seem natural." Not to mention how oppressive she found Desdemona's obedience to the men around her.

He smiled into his cocktail.

"Do I detect relief, Mr. Sawyer?"

"Actresses are . . ." He paused and took another long pull from his cigarette. "Actresses are complicated. My father warned me, but I had to learn that one the hard way."

"That bad?"

"Let's just say it can be difficult to tell what's real." He crushed his cigarette in the ashtray. His eyes lingered there for a contemplative beat before turning back to Aster. He looked older to her in that moment. She guessed he was hardly more than thirty years old, but something painful had left tiny etchings at his brow. The lines evaporated when he spoke again.

"So if it's not acting, what are you after?"

She felt surer of her answer now than when Fernando had first asked.

"I want to be known for being good at something." She blew a ribbon of smoke over his shoulder without losing track of his eyes.

"From what little I saw today, you are already very good at something." His eyes slid down the V-shaped edges of her dress.

The lure of him surprised her, her reflexive flinch at such overt attentions supplanted by a tantalizing thought. Couldn't she be seductive and, at the same time, be much more than the sum of her body parts? Why not both?

"I'm talking about being good at something that requires skill." She kept her tone light.

"I think you're taking your talents for granted. Very few people know how to move like you do, how to telegraph elegance as well as intention."

"Ballet training. It was my dream when I was little. But I woke up one day and was suddenly too curvy." It still hurt to recall the moment Madame Bouchard told her mother she would no longer train Aster. The first of many failures in her mother's eyes.

"Your body is capable of getting you into all sorts of trouble, it seems."

She willed herself not to be too distracted by that smile. His lips. He was just so stunning, and damn if he didn't know it. She pushed the conversation back onto solid ground.

"I think I loved ballet because it could tell a story without words. Fashion is like that. Every design tells its own tale. Being the author of the story, so to speak, is compelling to me."

"Okay, but why come all the way out here? Plenty of fashion's going on at Bendel's."

How did he know where she'd worked in New York?

"Don't look so surprised. We're in the business of vetting people. It was pretty easy for my team to come up with that one."

"That was strictly a modeling gig. No interaction with the designers whatsoever." She didn't mention that the models were treated no better than bait pulled from a bucket and flung out on a line.

He waited.

"I won a contest put on by the American Fashion Guild. They gave me the opportunity to explore design trends in Chicago, San Francisco, and LA for three months, with interviews in each city. That's how I ended up out here."

One of his eyebrows came to a point, suggesting both surprise and annoyance at his "team" for missing that bit of information. As much as Aster enjoyed throwing him off kilter, she didn't want some poor research assistant flogged for it. She filled him in on the rest.

"I entered the competition as AJ Kelly, so they wouldn't know I was a woman. You should have seen the looks on the judges' faces when I walked up to the dais!" She laughed at the memory, the annual awards ceremony a ritual among established and aspiring designers alike. The three men and two severe-looking women who made up the judging panel kept looking over Aster's shoulder, even while shaking her hand, to see if a man was going to appear behind her to rightfully claim his prize. Greta clapped loudly enough to make up for the sputtering applause from everyone else. It took almost the entire trip across the country for Aster to realize that the joke had been on her. None of the designers who had signed up to interview the winner had expected a woman either.

"On the last day of my tour, I met Fernando. He offered me a chance to study him at his trade. You've hired a genius, you know."

"He found you, didn't he?" Sam's eyes locked on hers.

All the glitter and glamour of the room threatened to disappear around the edges of him, and Aster imagined what it would be like to be taken in this man's arms and kissed.

"Congratulations on landing Christopher Page, Sam." A gravelly voice dissolved the haze that had momentarily obscured everything else.

"Roger." Sam tipped his head in the interloper's direction.

"Of course, it helps when you make such a hefty offer."

"As I told Sid, it'll come back to us in spades."

When Sam made no move to introduce Aster, Roger glanced back and forth between them and took the hint.

"I'll leave you to it. But give me a ring in the morning. I might have a proposition for you," he said, then stepped away.

Sam sipped his martini and leaned back as if settling in for a long and lazy train ride.

"Where were we?" His eyes fell to her lips.

A dangerous urge spread through Aster's body, a primal pull. She had never been forward with men before, certainly not on the first date. She'd mostly played defense, carefully positioning herself beyond the reach of roaming hands. But she wanted Sam's hands on her. Why couldn't she be the one to make that choice?

"I was about to make a proposition of my own." She leaned in.

"Is that right?"

When Sam took Aster back to his house, he hadn't needed to ask or even tell her where they were going. He just steered the car high up into the Hollywood Hills. Aster tingled with a mix of anticipation and nerves and what she could only name as desire.

She barely registered the long winding driveway, the sleek house with windows on all sides, the marble foyer, the claw-foot table in the hall where he dropped his keys. He didn't say a word before he pulled her to him, his hands cupped behind her. He kissed her below her right ear and worked his way down her neck with his tongue. She bit her lower lip.

"I wanted you the moment I saw you," he said into her hair.

And she wanted him to have her, take her. She'd never done this without trusting a man, without fully knowing him, but there was something thrilling about acting purely on desire. What could be more freeing than surrendering to it? Besides, if she didn't, she thought she might burn up from the inside.

He kneaded her skirt and pulled it up high enough to caress her inner thigh.

"Do you have something?" It was as much of a sentence as she could formulate.

"Don't worry," he said. "I'll take care of you. I can take care of you."

Before she knew it, they were in his bedroom, his hands everywhere, clothes coming off like paper torn from a parcel. He laid her back on the bed, his body hovering above hers as he kissed her deeply.

And then, something unexpected. Sam began to move ever so slowly down her body, first kissing the length of her neck, then the base of her throat, the tender curve of each breast, the spaces between her ribs, the soft of her belly, the edges of her hip bones, the insides of her thighs. She clutched the pillow under her head as he trailed down the length of her, the longing intense, her body instinctively arching to meet his. His lips moved like a whisper back up the inside of her thigh, and then, as she gasped, his tongue was on her in only one miraculous place, each of his tender touches a brushstroke on a map of her with a direct line to her molten core. His slow coaxing opened an endless river in her, a shiver of excruciating pleasure. She pulled him into her then, their hips undulating together and apart. As she shuddered and contracted around him, she clutched him and held him there until his tremors echoed her own.

She brushed her fingers down his back as their muscles slowly uncurled, his body relaxing over hers like a blanket. He smoothed the hair from her face and smiled at her.

"Well, I'd say we've discovered another natural talent of yours," he said.

She let out a bright laugh. He chuckled and hopped off the bed.

"I do like your style, Aster Kelly. I'll be right back."

As he left the room, she sat up and pulled the crisp white sheet over her and marveled at what had just happened. She didn't know her body was capable of so much anticipation, electricity, and satisfaction. It felt like something of her own to keep rather than something she had given away. Strangely empowering. And surprisingly freeing. She was quite sure Sam had no outsized expectations based on this one act—although she did hope it might be repeated.

Was this her new style? Was she a woman who could simply enjoy herself, rules be damned? Follow her own impulses wherever they may lead?

One thing was for sure. It was a hell of a way to start.

CHAPTER FOUR

Fernando's bustled. As soon as the first photo of Bogie and Bacall wearing Fernando's clothes at the premiere of *Key Largo* hit the papers, everyone in Los Angeles wanted one of his creations in their closet. Customers were often waiting when the shop opened at ten and were visibly annoyed whenever he had to close because of a runway show at the Galaxy lot or when he left to handle a final fitting for an actor. Not that fittings took long, but Fernando always went to the most convenient place for the star in question. He'd even driven all the way to Ventura to fit Rita Hayworth on location.

Whenever the store was open, customers came in droves. With spring fling season around the corner, the elite of LA needed new party dresses. Just as one runway show for a mother of the bride ended, a Getty or du Pont would arrive in search of gowns for a weekend of galas. Aster had taken on a full modeling schedule so all the other girls wouldn't be worn to the bone, and they had found a steady rhythm in the rotation. They appreciated her willingness to jump in the dressing room and put on whatever gown needed to be shown next, and everyone was pleased with the sales that came from her efforts.

A lull finally materialized one afternoon, and Aster nestled into the couch in the studio with her black sketchbook. She'd been noodling a particular design and hadn't had the chance to wrestle the idea from her imagination onto the paper. She was so focused on getting various lines right, she didn't notice Fernando looking over her shoulder until it was too late. She slapped the book shut.

"Don't hide it." He held out his hand for the book. "I told you I'd help."

"It's not ready." Aster hugged it to her chest. She'd waited so long for his attention, she wanted to present him something more polished.

"I have a few minutes just now." He pried the book from her grasp and then handed it back to her. "Show me."

The spine was well-worn and easily opened to the last page she had used.

"Okay, so imagine I'm invited onto a lovely yacht for a luncheon."

"Are we lunching on yachts now?"

She swatted him.

"Shush or I'll lose my nerve." She couldn't deny that Sam had taken her to more fancy restaurants in the last few weeks than she'd been to in her entire life, but no yachts. She was trying to think like Fernando's best clientele. "Let's say I need something to wear that's not too casual, not too dressy, and works in the middle of the day. Other than a sundress—which can be tricky in the wind—there's no good option for something between shorts, which would be too casual, and long pants, which seem too heavy for a boat or a picnic."

"And?"

"I was thinking about something like this." She turned the book around for him. "These are essentially pants, but they don't go below the ankle. They're less formal—more fun, really—and cooler, but they can still carry the style of a nice pair of slacks."

He tilted his head and examined the drawing.

"What fabric did you have in mind?"

"Cotton? Maybe a poplin?"

"Yes, poplin, I think. Better hang. And what kind of closure?"

"Back zipper to keep the front smooth, complement a svelte line?"

"Side zipper, I think, to keep it in line with the seam." He retrieved a pencil from his drafting table. "May I?" He held the pencil in the air as he sat down on the love seat beside her.

"Please."

"I think you need to bring the line in at the bottom, the way a pencil skirt narrows below the knee." He swiftly drew two diagonal lines cutting into one of the pant legs. "This way, it follows the contour of the leg. Otherwise, see how the one with the open bottom just looks like it's too short?"

Of course. His altered version was elegant, while her drawing recalled pants on a kid who had grown six inches overnight, knickers covering a pair of stilts. She burst out laughing.

"Have I misunderstood what you were going for?" He sounded uncharacteristically sheepish.

"That's exactly what I was going for. Which is why you're the master and I am your lowly apprentice." She kept her tone light while realizing just how very far she had to go.

"Nothing lowly about it. It's a good idea. Keep it up."

She closed the book and caressed the cover. Maybe she was onto something after all.

"Now I have a favor to ask you." He popped off the couch and glanced at his watch. "I have a last-minute fitting in the Hills at noon. I'll be back by two o'clock. Can you put the sign out front and let the girls know?"

"Of course. Whose fitting?"

"Christopher Page's first suit. He asked me to meet him at his house."

Aster raised her eyebrows.

"Oof, don't get me thinking that way. I have to keep my head on straight. Wish me luck." He grabbed his keys and hurried out the door.

It was past three o'clock by the time Fernando finally returned. Aster, Shirley, and Jane huddled in the back to avoid the knocks of frustrated customers—they'd changed the note on the shop door no less than four times.

"So sorry to be late, girls. There are two ladies out front. Shirley and Jane, would you mind doing the honors? One of them already has a gown in her sights. Aster, let's get you dressed."

Aster eyed him. Not one hair was out of place, and his clothes were as neatly pressed as always, but he was unusually calm considering he was over an hour late and had come back to waiting customers.

"How'd it go?" Aster watched him sort through various dresses on the long rack behind his drafting table, his back to her.

"It went well. I didn't expect it to take that long, but there was a lot to do."

"Was there a problem with the suit?"

Fernando was famous for taking meticulous measurements. He would be mortified to present a client with a suit that needed anything other than minor adjustments.

He handed her an emerald gown with an embroidered bodice.

"No. It fit him to a T." His face broke into a boyish grin.

Aster's hands flew up to her mouth.

"How exciting!"

"Our secret."

"Of course," Aster said over her shoulder on her way to the dressing room.

"I mean it." Fernando's tone made her stop and pivot back toward him. There was no playful lilt in his words, no splash of humor. He put his hands on her shoulders—were they shaking?—and spoke quietly. "This isn't some out-of-town businessman or cute waiter we're talking about. If your Mr. Sawyer ever heard about this, Christopher's career would be over."

"Sam couldn't possibly care about such a thing." Would he?

"You don't know how Hollywood works, love. It would be over for Christopher."

"You like him."

Fernando looked happy beyond measure, and yet she thought something like sorrow clouded his eyes.

"I get it," she said. "I promise."

CHAPTER FIVE

Aster began to spend Sunday afternoons at Sam's house—the one day Fernando closed the boutique. She enjoyed lounging lazily by the pool, snapping small oranges off the trees in his backyard when she was hungry, and floating on her back in the cool water. She relished the freedom from pantyhose and heels and the relative quiet of Sam's company.

Sam rarely stopped working, even when out on the sunny patio. He used Sundays to scour the newspapers and magazines that had steadily arrived at his house all week, from the *Daily Examiner* and the *Los Angeles Times* to *Life* magazine and *Women's Wear Daily*. He read every article about stars in the Galaxy stable and those at competing studios, trying to gauge the public's rising fascination with one star and their loss of appetite for another. Aster was beginning to understand what an important part public opinion played in the casting of each role.

She also understood how hard Sam was working to prove himself, still trying to dispel the notion that he hadn't earned his position at the studio, and maybe even remind his own father of his capabilities. He couldn't afford to make any mistakes or give anyone reason to question his judgment if he was going to run the place with the level of authority required to maintain Galaxy's success.

Whenever she managed to coax Sam to take a break, they usually retreated to the delicious shade of his bedroom, the wide windows above his bed thrown open to the breeze. Thanks to Ria—who had discreetly referred Aster to her doctor—there was no need to pause their mesmerizing dance while Sam got situated, leaving nothing but pure enjoyment. She occasionally wondered if she was becoming addicted to the pleasure, but quickly decided there were far worse afflictions.

"Look at this." Sam handed her a profile of Rita Hayworth from *Look* magazine one afternoon. It featured a photo of Hayworth holding her infant son up in the air, arms outstretched, her face aglow.

"The PR people thought showing a wholesome side of her was a good idea, but I don't know what I think about her as the mother figure. That's not what the men go to the movies to see. What do you think?"

Aster considered the photograph. Rita's smile was worthy of a toothpaste ad, her lips a shiny Revlon red.

"She just raised the bar of what a mother is supposed to look like at home, that's for sure."

"Hmm. Good point. Maybe women will admire her for that."

Aster smiled to herself. Men so often missed the point.

While Sam focused on Hollywood stories, Aster relished the photographs. She discovered that she gravitated more toward the casual clothes than the elaborate gowns on red carpets or at the Stork Club. She began to notice how one pair of shorts might emphasize the athletic shape of someone who played a lot of tennis, while another might reveal a set of knobby knees, suggesting a more delicate person. She became as interested in the forms beneath the clothes as in the clothes themselves and started to pay extra attention in her own sketches to the bend of an arm or shape of a calf. The detail felt integral to the verity of her designs.

"This is impressive coverage of Robert Strong's marriage." Sam tilted the paper he'd been reading in her direction. "Hard not to believe those photos, right?"

In one photo, the bride beamed under her lace and rhinestone tiara, the satin bodice and tulle skirt of her wedding dress any young girl's dream. Robert Strong looked as dashing as ever in white tie. The second photo showed them kissing in front of the small plane that would apparently whisk them away to a secret destination for a weekend honeymoon. He would be back on the set of *Sunset* by Monday.

"They make a gorgeous couple."

"Gorgeous, yes. Couple, no. Strong's just lucky his box office receipts came in before the MGM folks figured out his true colors. No one can afford to lose the public favor of an asset like that."

Robert Strong was gay?

"Who is this woman then? Why would they marry?" Aster looked at the photographs again. They looked genuinely happy.

"She'll do just fine. One, maybe two years from now, they'll find him a mistress who will supposedly wreck the marriage, and they'll get divorced. She'll walk away with a tidy sum of money, and he'll further increase his reputation as the playboy who couldn't resist other women even with such a beautiful wife. Everybody wins. But it's hard work for the studio. And expensive. Much harder than some starlet who gets herself knocked up. That's an easy fix."

"An easy fix?"

"Sure. I mean, pregnancy out of wedlock is a dealbreaker, of course, but it's easy enough to make it all go away before anyone knows any different. It happens all the time."

The irony of that burned. The success of so many of Sam's films, of all of Hollywood in truth, depended on the portrayal of women like Sophia Green not as merely sexy, but sexual, not just sultry but daring enough to indulge passion. A wife personified drudgery and responsibility, but a mistress, a lover, was a woman worth watching. And yet the same people who flocked to the theaters for the raciest of films were scandalized if that same woman dared act on those passions in real life. The ultimate double standard.

"But Strong's case requires vigilance for the long haul," Sam was saying. "If the press ever exposed the truth, the public would revolt. No one would ever go to one of his pictures again."

"And if he hadn't already been a big star before MGM figured it out?" She tried to sound as casual as possible but heard Fernando's voice in her head, his warning.

"His career wouldn't have gotten out of the gate. People will put up with a faggot if they're a proven money machine. But no one's going to take that risk without a solid track record."

Heat flashed under her skin. She needed to change the subject before he sensed her discomfort.

"I have some exciting news. Fernando's going to take me to his production facility next weekend."

Fernando had told her that understanding the actual construction of garments, how certain fabrics responded to a pattern while others resisted it, made designing considerably easier. And now, he was going to use one of his precious days off to teach her himself. He was taking her seriously, encouraging her in a way no one ever had before.

"He likes some of my ideas. I'm finally getting a chance to try my hand at design." She shaded her eyes and looked over at Sam, intently reading a profile of one of his newest acquisitions.

"Sam?"

"Sorry, what do you need?" He didn't look up.

"Never mind," she said, then dove into the pool.

A week later, Fernando unlocked the door of his magic factory, as he called it, which occupied one corner of a brick warehouse five stories tall and the length of two city blocks. The room was five times the size of the studio at the boutique. Countless bolts of fabric piled onto long metal shelves obscured the brick of the back wall. An enormous butcher-block table dominated the center of the room. A muslin dress pattern covered one end of the table, a design in process. Below the windows six sewing stations stood at attention, each fitted with a black Singer. Aster realized for the first time how much labor it must take to turn out Fernando's never-ending line of formal wear.

"How many people work here?"

"I have five full-time dressmakers and another four gals who handle beadwork, lace, embroidery, that sort of thing." He surveyed the room like a conductor with no orchestra at the ready, not quite sure what to do with his hands.

It was an impressive operation, especially for a relatively new label. He'd worked under his father, the great Vincenzo Tivoli, in New York since his teens, but at twenty-nine years old, he'd moved west and struck out on his own, quickly making a name for himself designing evening wear as comfortable for women as it was stunning. For the men, he had sourced a fabric from Italy as structured as wool but cool as linen, a godsend to the high-steppers of Los Angeles. The rumor mill claimed that Christian Dior himself offered Fernando an ungodly sum of money for the source, but Fernando turned him down. "If there's no secret in the sauce, why bother with the Bolognese?" he liked to say.

"Come over here, this is what I wanted to show you." He pulled three bolts of fabric off the back wall, each a different shade of sand.

"Now, which do you think would work best for the knickers you sketched? The gabardine hangs wonderfully but might be too heavy. Feel the weight of it? The twill here has a lovely bias grain cut. If you went in that direction, the fabric itself might inform the angle you choose for the tapering below the knee."

Aster touched each piece of cloth, trying to picture it in the shape of the pants in her sketchbook. Her only real experience creating garments thus far relied on fully formed pieces she could take apart and put back together to create a new shape, 3D to 3D. This was altogether different, taking something as flat as paper and converting it into an object with curves and angles. She tried to envision the transformation, suddenly overwhelmed by the enormity of the task. She hadn't properly contemplated the complexity of the entire process.

"Where do I even begin?"

"At the beginning. You experiment, and you learn."

He dragged a barrel from the corner of the room over to the table.

"This is all scrap material. So is that stack of larger pieces over there." He pointed to the back shelves. "I want you to pick out any material you're drawn to. Don't make assumptions about what will and won't work for a particular design until you play with it a little."

Aster placed a pile of remnants on the table and began to examine them, feeling the differences in weight and texture in her hands. Her absorption in the materials was interrupted by a loud *clunk*.

"My first sewing machine." Fernando stepped back from the table. The black hunk of metal gleamed. "You're going to borrow this and practice on various fabrics until you find the right one."

"Your original machine? It must already be a collector's item. I couldn't possibly." Aster rang her fingers over the letters stenciled across the arm.

"It's not worth a dime if it's not making clothes. It would give me endless pleasure to know it's being put to good use."

The bright light from the windows revealed the puffiness around Fernando's eyes, tender pillows of skin touching his lashes. No wonder, given the double duty of working for Galaxy while running his shop.

"I should have let you have your day off today. You're exhausted."

"Is it that obvious? I haven't been getting a whole lot of sleep lately." He ran his fingers through his hair, and a boyish grin crept onto his face.

"I trust it's worth it?" Aster grinned back.

"Truthfully, Aster, it's beyond anything I ever let myself imagine. He's working so hard to prove himself at Galaxy right now, but you wouldn't know it when we're together. When I complain about being on my feet all day, he massages them. When I mentioned my penchant for towels made of Egyptian cotton, he had a stack of them delivered the next day. He even made homemade meatballs for me the other night. As good as my nana's. It's like a dream." He shook his head, as if jolting himself back to reality. Aster saw something else in the lines around his eyes, something beyond physical exhaustion.

"What is it?" Aster reached for his arm.

He leaned against the table as a streak of sunshine cut across his shirt.

"My life will never be completely in the open, I do understand that, but for me, it's always been about knowing who I need to let look the other way, who not to offend. But this is different. Christopher's entire life is a performance. There's no one he can tell. It's exhausting. On top of it, I'm not sure he doesn't actually enjoy it a bit, having beautiful women on his arm during the day, with me to come home to at night."

She didn't know what to say to that. She didn't know anything about Christopher.

"He wants it all so badly, and I can't be what destroys it for him. That would devastate me. But it doesn't stop me from wishing it could be different."

He sank into the table, his gaze in a far-off place. Aster wanted to tell him he was being paranoid, assure him there was no risk of causing Christopher's downfall, but she knew it wasn't true. She thought of Sam's comments by the pool and shuddered.

"I had to do a fitting for him on set the other day while Sid Sawyer's assistant rattled off a list of appearances he had to attend, and the lighting people circled around organizing the next shot. I cuffed his pants without letting my hands graze his ankles. I had to stand in front of him and chalk the angles of his lapels without being able to stroke his cheek. I could barely look him in the eye for fear of what they'd all see."

Aster's heart bunched like a ball of yarn pulled too tight, and she realized just how much she took for granted—her ability to walk into a room with Sam's hand on her back, to throw the top down in his convertible without a moment's worry about being seen together, all because they fit the part. And yet Fernando and Christopher might be planting the seeds of a true relationship, one that deserved water and light.

"Forgive me for going on. I know it's worth it. I've never felt this way about anyone, and he is so good to me."

"You deserve love like that," Aster said.

"Did I say love?"

"I think you did."

⊗

That afternoon Aster made a rare phone call home. She'd been excited to show Ria the sewing machine, but when she found the bungalow empty, she picked up the phone. Her father was a craftsman. He would surely understand the lure of the process, the desire to make something out of nothing, much like how he welded sheets of steel into floating vessels.

Unfortunately, her mother answered, and no, her father wasn't home.

"Have you met Cary Grant yet?" This was her mother's most common question, part of why Aster had stopped calling with any regularity. As far as her mother was concerned, the only way for Aster to prove she lived anywhere near Hollywood would be a sighting of Cary Grant. Aster opted not to tell her mother anything about Sam—it would make her questions even less tolerable. That she was dating the head of a studio was bad enough, but the man formerly engaged to Sophia Green? Out of the question. Her mother would undoubtedly try to impress bartenders with that tidbit, as if it said anything truly interesting about her or her daughter.

"My boss thinks I have an eye for design. He just gave me his sewing machine to practice making clothes."

"Well, that's a start."

Aster's chest filled with an unfamiliar warmth. A distant memory flashed just then, of her mother teaching her as a girl how to sew on a button. She hadn't said much when Aster won the design contest beyond asking why she insisted on barking up the wrong tree, and reminding her the committee would never have considered her entry if they'd known she was a girl, so why did she bother? But maybe the simple act of sewing could give them a point of connection.

"Good skill for a wife," her mother continued. "When are you coming home? You need to settle down before you throw away your youth and no one wants you."

Aster hung up the phone, grabbed a swath of poplin, and started to make her first pair of pants. By the time Ria got home, Aster was tangled in a clump of thread and fabric she didn't know how to fix, her mother's scowling voice ringing in her ears.

CHAPTER SIX

W hy so fidgety?" Ria asked Aster as they laid on towels in their tiny backyard. Aster normally relished the downtime on Saturday afternoons between what they called the "gown rush"—the shop was always busiest right before it closed at three P.M.—and whatever borrowed dress she would strap herself into for a night out with Sam. But tonight would be no ordinary night out.

"You haven't been able to sit still since you got home. What's up?" Ria pressed.

"Sam's taking me to a party at Judy Garland's house."

"What? When were you going to tell me this?"

"He mentioned it so casually last night. I've been trying all day to pretend it's normal." Aster pulled her hat down lower on her face. She needed to be more careful of her skin.

"This is not even close to normal! Who's going to be there?" Ria sat up and crossed her legs under her.

"I have no idea. He said it was a casual party. Drinks around her pool. He's picking me up at six o'clock."

Casual and *Judy Garland's house* did sound like an impossible combination. She wished she'd succeeded by now in making a pair of her sophisticated short pants. They would be perfect for the occasion. Was this actually happening? Aster Kelly lying in the grass, considering what to wear to Judy Garland's house?

Aster felt Ria watching her now and propped herself up on her elbow.

"Why are you looking at me like that?"

"Sounds like Mr. Sawyer is getting serious about you."

"What? No, we've talked about this. Neither of us is interested in anything serious. He just needs a date."

Aster and Ria had spent many afternoons on the patch of scrubby grass outside their kitchen door discussing the merits of an exciting physical relationship. Why had men been allowed to indulge in such arrangements since the beginning of time, while women were only supposed to acquiesce if the pairing included true love and the promise of something permanent?

Ria had told Aster about a long-standing fling she enjoyed with a bartender in West Hollywood. She would perch herself on a stool near closing time whenever she pleased. He would either apologetically tell her he was on duty to close up for the night, or he would call down the bar to his partner, "Hey Bobby, leaving you to it," ring the bell above the register reserved for recognizing particularly excellent tips, and pull her out the door. "Ring the bell indeed!" Ria said with a laugh.

The two roommates agreed it was a relief not to have family and friends asking if they were "committed" or when they might take "the next step." There was only ever one next step, and from Aster's point of view it was twenty feet tall and too high to scale. She had way too much to accomplish in her life first.

Her apprenticeship with Fernando was finally beginning. The promise of what lay ahead made her heart accelerate like a stone skipping on a pond, immune to gravity. She was eager to discover the outer limits of her creative talents. Maybe she would beat all the odds and have her own label one day, a sister boutique to Fernando's, a sign with her name on it. His specialty was evening wear, the gowns. She would focus on leisure wear and resort fashion. And fun with Sam didn't get in the way of any of her dreams, as wild as they might be. Their relationship was less about an emotional connection than it was a tantalizing physical one, new territory for her.

These thoughts inevitably crashed into the section of her heart still reserved for Graham, the man she'd left behind in New York. She'd met him one rainy day after dashing into the Whitney Museum to escape an unexpected summer storm that had turned West 8th Street into a river. She'd found refuge admiring the soft lines of Georgia O'Keeffe's *The White Calico Flower* and didn't notice the man standing next to her until he leaned sideways and said, "Ma'am, I think you're dripping." She could hear the smile in his voice.

Aster looked down to see a circle of water surrounding her feet and growing, apparently coming from the hem of her skirt. She suddenly heard the *tic, tic, tic* of it as loud as a grandfather clock and started to laugh—the kind of giggle she would struggle to suppress as a kid in church, which only made it worse. Within seconds, neither of them could contain the cackles erupting from their throats like popcorn in a kettle. When an old man with unruly eyebrows turned around to glare at them, Graham grabbed her hand and pulled her back out into the storm. They ran to the café next door where they could laugh properly, without constraint.

They sat at the café until dinnertime, him telling her about how much his grandmother loved art, had introduced it to him at a young age to the dismay of his father. Aster told Graham about how she came to the Whitney sometimes to stare at the Calder sculpture on the second floor. Something about the slow movement of the geometric shapes and the balance maintained among them gave her a sense of peace.

She learned that Graham had eschewed his father's steel business to learn about curation and taught art on the side to make ends meet. He asked her countless questions about her life, her parents, her career. She told him about Teddy, how he'd gone down on the *Juneau*, a ship her father had helped build, about her mother's unending depression after his death.

"My father was so proud of Teddy being on that ship, and my mother used every ounce of that against him, as if its sinking was somehow his fault." Aster shook her head. "Ted even wrote home once about five brothers he'd met on board. He thought they were lucky to be on such a big adventure together. That's how he actually put it. The papers made a huge deal about that family, how one mother had lost five sons on one day."

"I remember that." Graham reached across the table.

"My mother could never understand how her grief was supposed to be considered less because she had lost only one."

They talked through two cups of coffee and then dinner at a cozy trattoria. Most evenings after, Graham met her at the door of Bendel's, and they would spend a few hours together before she boarded the train back to Newark.

Looking back now, she tried to remember when she first knew she was in love with him. Had it taken more than one cup of coffee?

In the six months they were together, she spent only one night in Graham's bed. He told her he wanted to take her to a special dinner with a night of dancing afterward. The trains would stop by then, and he didn't have a car to take her home. She understood what he was really asking and told her parents a story about staying with one of her modeling friends in the city. He was gentle and loving with her, tentatively peeling back each layer of her clothing, slowly revealing new sections of skin, turning off the light before either of them was completely naked. An entirely different experience than with Sam. With Graham, it was less about the act itself, Aster realized now, than about the vulnerability of two people baring themselves to each other, removing all pretense, showing themselves completely.

Graham proposed to her over breakfast the next morning.

"I want to spend my life with you, Aster Kelly."

The words stunned her. She adored him—no, she loved him—but marriage was a step she hadn't contemplated yet. And it didn't fit with her plan.

"But I applied for the Guild award."

Ever since Greta had talked her into submitting her work for the contest, had convinced Aster her creative eye was as worthy of being developed as anyone else's, the whole idea of becoming an artist had taken on critical importance to her. She craved the chance to stand out based on talent alone. Surely Graham of all people could understand that. Every day she waited to hear the judge's decision only deepened her desire to buck the constraints binding her. She had a racehorse's urge to run and had been held in the paddock for too long. She needed to test her full stride.

"But if you win, you'll be able to get whatever job you want right here in New York." His face glowed just like it had the night before, when the candles between them sparkled with anticipation.

"It doesn't work like that. Fashion designers don't take on untested underlings with no design school credentials, not when they have their pick of the crop in New York City, and definitely not when that person is a woman. The designers who signed up for the award agreed to give the winner a look even if they have no experience. That's unheard of."

"But those jobs are all in other cities. What about us?"

Aster swallowed. He sat back in his chair.

"You want to leave?"

"It's not like that," she started, and then wasn't sure what to say. She didn't want to leave, but she couldn't possibly pass up the opportunity to burst through a new door, into a new realm that just might offer a future of her own making. How could he understand that while she loved him, she also knew with certainty that if Nathan Morris offered her a job in St. Louis or Chandler LaRouse hired her in Chicago, she would accept and wouldn't come back? Graham would carry on with his career at the Whitney. That's how it worked.

The first-place notification came in the mail the following week. It included an invitation to the awards ceremony and a train ticket to depart New York ten days later.

As her time in LA stretched into something permanent, her love for Graham crystallized, like an artifact to be visited in a pocket of her heart, only to be taken out when she needed comfort most. It lived in the past, and she was determined to enjoy every moment of the present. She was finally getting a chance to study design under a true talent. And she had the freedom to indulge in a mutual attraction with someone who asked for little in return.

"I think you're missing how big a deal this is. Any party at Judy Garland's house is a major studio event, no matter how casual everyone makes it out to be. Do you know how many of those Sam must go to by himself, shaking hands, buttering up young stars he might want to sign, checking in with old hens he wants to make sure he hasn't pissed off? The last thing he needs is a date. He's bringing you for a reason. He's trying you out."

"I'm sorry?" Alarm mixed with the anxiety already buzzing through her body at the idea of coming face-to-face with Judy Garland.

"He's in his early thirties, right? A guy like Sam doesn't stay single forever. Just doesn't happen. And you've had a lovely time for, what, a few months now? Either the relationship moves on, or he does. And this is the opposite of him moving on."

Aster shifted uncomfortably. She couldn't deny that Ria's point made a certain amount of sense, no matter how differently Aster characterized their relationship in her own mind. On their first date, she'd told him matter-of-factly that she had no interest in anything serious. But that was before they'd started spending several nights a week tangled up in the sheets together. And men like Sam Sawyer expected people to bend to their wills. Especially women.

What if Ria was right? Aster wasn't in love with him, but the idea of having to turn down a proposal made her queasy. What sort of fallout might such a rebuke create for Fernando?

No. Ria was wrong. Aster needed her to be wrong. And she had a good reason to think so.

"I'm not so sure he's over Sophia." Aster thought back on how long Sam had lingered over the latest profile of her in the *Saturday Evening Post*.

"He may never get over her. That doesn't mean he isn't ready to move on with you." Ria rolled onto her stomach and pulled at a dandelion weed. "He's quite a catch by most measures. Good-looking. Great sex, by the sounds of it. Why not him?"

Now even Ria couldn't understand that not all round pieces were comfortable being neatly slotted into a round hole?

"Are you ready to marry Mr. West Hollywood?" Even as Aster said it, she knew the two relationships were entirely different. Ria's bartender didn't even know where Ria lived, while Aster and Sam spent more time together than most couples in the windup to marriage. Ria's question ran to a deeper level. She wanted to know what was missing.

Aster sighed. "We don't really talk. The first night we met, he asked lots of questions. That was sexy in its own right." She remembered the glitter of Romanoff's, how he'd asked her about her dreams. "But it's like he already knows all he needs to know, or all he'll ever want to know. What kind of life would that be?"

There was also the part she could never tell Ria, that she worried Sam wouldn't accept a relationship like Fernando and Christopher's, even outside the confines of Galaxy. She was beginning to consider Fernando a true friend. How would that work if she stayed with a man like Sam? If she always had to keep such an important secret?

"Anyway, I don't think that's what Sam's after." Aster believed it a little less than she had just five minutes before. And now that she'd admitted to the deficiency in her relationship with Sam, she knew it would niggle at her like a snag in a new pair of nylons, which always presented only two choices: ignore it and hope it didn't cause an unsightly bump, or pull on it and risk a complete unraveling.

CHAPTER SEVEN

There were at least fifty people at the party, women as young as Aster, men as old as her father, all flitting between a pool house and the stone patio that surrounded the inviting rectangle of blue in the middle. Judy's house, an enormous Tudor with balconies on every window, stood removed beyond the vast backyard, clearly off-limits. Multiple tables around the pool were laden with platters of cocktail shrimp, tiered displays of caviar, and enough barbecue for a bus full of Navy recruits. Of course, among this constellation of guests, only those who made their living behind the camera would dare go anywhere near the food.

The men wore polo shirts or short-sleeved Oxfords neatly tucked into pleated shorts, with an occasional sport coat and long pants, but the women's outfits ran the gamut from silk crepe de Chine dresses to short shorts. A few daring beauties even perched on the edge of the pool in their swimsuits, legs dangling in the water. One woman's sheer sari cast her curves in stark relief against the sun. Aster touched her hair, hoping that riding with the top down hadn't pulled too many strands loose from the bun at the nape of her neck.

She recognized a few faces—they could be actors she had seen in her comings and goings from the Galaxy lot or out with Sam—but she couldn't put names to any of them. Sam snatched two flutes of champagne off a tray but made no move to wander toward the crowd, perhaps taking an inventory of his own.

"I don't see Judy," Aster finally said.

"I don't suspect we will."

"At her own party?"

"This is really an MGM affair. See him over there?" Sam pointed with his elbow to a burly suited man, sitting in the shade on the other side of the pool and gnawing on a sticky chicken thigh. "He's the boss. Judy has become unreliable of late, you might say, and he's trying to rehabilitate her image before her next picture tanks."

Aster relaxed into Sam's familiar banter. He wasn't rushing to introduce her to anyone and would probably leave her in a moment to talk up a newly acquired actor. He'd brought her here for fun, nothing else.

Sam went on. "This whole thing is designed to get the right people talking about being at Judy's lovely party at her lovely house. No one will admit to not having actually talked to her."

"She's working on another movie already? Didn't she just have a baby?"

"Hollywood waits for no one. She was back on set within two weeks. Another reason you're smart not to want this life, Aster." He clinked his glass against hers. "Someone like you deserves to be properly focused on motherhood, no distractions, with someone to take care of you."

His words from that first night—"I can take care of you"—came back to her with an erotic rush of heat at the memory. But it was quickly doused by the ease with which he could conjure domesticity in her future. Was Ria actually right?

"Will you excuse me for one moment? I need to have a quick conversation." Sam flashed a cheerful smile before heading toward the far end of the pool.

She took a long sip of champagne and surveyed the crowd again, searching for a friendly looking group to join. By the pool house, which looked more like a summer beach cottage than a shed, she spotted Christopher Page—"Fernando's Christopher" was how she thought of him now—talking with a stunning brunette in a bright green sundress. The level of flirtation in their conversation was plain, the tilt in the woman's head, the way he leaned in close to her when he laughed, the lock their eyes had on each other. Aster wished she could unsee what she was witnessing, but she couldn't stop staring. Fernando was in love with this man. But Christopher's reality might be far different, just as Fernando had feared. He would be crushed.

The woman put her hand to Christopher's cheek, said something brief—maybe that she needed to use the powder room?—and left him leaning on the porch railing. As soon as she turned away, Christopher's smile fell from his face, as if a director had just yelled "cut." Aster almost laughed out loud. She had fully believed his interest in the woman, the playful dart of his eyes around her face, his coy grin. But the change in his demeanor after she left was complete, a taught string gone slack. Sam's description of his relationship with Sophia came back to her, the difficulty of separating reality from invention.

"You might want to hide your relief a bit more," she said, joining Christopher on the porch. Aster saw his eye twitch ever so slightly as a flicker of panic crossed his face and then dissolved into studied nonchalance.

"I work with Fernando. You and I met briefly on the lot a while ago." She held out her hand.

His expression softened, a hint of recognition in his eyes.

"Aster, right? How lovely to see you." He clasped her hand warmly. "Fernando raves about you."

"And he you." Aster tried to broadcast with her eyes that she understood.

"Enjoying the party?" He gestured beyond the railing.

"I only just arrived, but I'll confess to being a bit overwhelmed. Do you ever get used to this sort of thing?"

"Not yet. Everyone looks so casual, but we're all posing."

Exactly what Sam had said. How did people live like that every day?

"Fernando told me you're up for a starring role. Is any of your competition here?"

"The chap in the blue swim trunks over there." He tilted his head toward a lean man in sunglasses sitting on the steps of the pool, flanked by two blonds in bikinis. "But I hear Clark Gable is the man we really need to beat out."

"Not to worry. Fernando says you have the perfect proportions to carry off a top hat and tails, so you should be a cinch for the part."

"He would focus on the attire, wouldn't he?" Christopher leaned back and smiled. She fully understood Fernando's attraction to this man, beyond his obvious physical appeal. He exuded confidence, but his eyes were soft and probing, his smile broad and utterly natural. It was a disarming combination.

"He also told me he ran the lines with you, and you'll be impossible to resist."

"Did he?" Christopher didn't try to hide his pleasure at the compliment. "Does he always tell you this much about his clients?"

"No. Just you." Glancing over Christopher's shoulder, Aster saw the woman in the green dress coming their way.

"I want you to know that I would do anything for him." Aster spoke quietly into his ear before stepping back and playfully swatting Christopher's chest.

"Stop. You're too sweet, you'll make me blush," she said loudly, laughing and sending Christopher a doe-like wink. He raised his eyebrows.

"I mean every word of it, darling." He leaned in close. "Let me know when I can stop whispering into your hair."

Aster did her best rendition of a coy giggle and watched the woman change course, sweep her wounded expression back up into a sparkling smile, and join a conversation on the other side of the porch.

"Green dress averted."

"Thank you." Christopher let his relief show again. "You're as much of a peach as Fernando said you were."

"Does he talk about all his models to you?"

"No. Just you." He smiled and clinked her glass.

"I think I'll take this as my chance to escape the masquerade party. I'm sure you understand."

"Of course." She was sorry to see him go.

Not sure where Sam had gone, Aster stepped into the pool house in search of more champagne.

"Miss Kelly, is it?" a man said, intercepting her route to the bar. "I've been looking forward to meeting you today."

Surprised that a second person at this gathering knew her name, she waited a beat before responding.

"I heard you were Bacall's body double, but I had to see it for myself to believe it." His eyes ran the length of her body while she took in the contours of his face. He was an older man with gray hair, a bulbous nose, and narrow-set eyes that were not unkind but darted about, first in appraisal of her and then past her, as if on the lookout lest he miss something important. His tortoiseshell glasses and silk jacket distinguished him as a man of means, but Aster imagined he could just as easily pass for the local butcher if he put on a bloody apron and carried a knife.

"Sammy wasn't kidding," he added.

She felt the familiar flare of annoyance and wondered if Sam had mentioned anything about her other than her measurements.

"Mr. Sawyer, I presume." Aster held out her hand. He didn't look anything like Sam, or how she imagined Sam might look in another thirty years. He was shorter, for one, with an ample midsection. And his cheeks were unchiseled, unless the extra weight on his face simply obscured the indents of youth. Mostly, this man seemed aloof, all business, the opposite of her interactions with Sam, which from the start had always been playful.

"We appreciate the opportunity to work for Galaxy."

"We?" His eyes flicked over Aster's shoulder as if trying to spot whom else she might mean.

"All of us at Fernando's Boutique. It's a wonderful opportunity."

"Indeed. Makes for good husband shopping, eh?" He winked at her.

"Don't let him get to you." A woman appeared at Mr. Sawyer's side in a blue halter top with sapphire earrings to match. She had to be ten or fifteen years younger than Sid Sawyer, her hair pulled back tightly, her taut cheeks bronzed and flawless. She held out her hand to Aster, who took it gratefully.

"Sid's always looking out for Sammy's interests. The first wife is always the most important, isn't that right, dear?"

Aster's relief at the interruption evaporated quickly.

"Wilma Sawyer. Wife number three." She smiled broadly.

Aster fumbled around her mind for something charming or witty to say but came up empty. She pictured a flawless walk down a runway despite a broken heel to restore some sense of calm.

"Fetch us some drinks, would you, dear?" Wilma said to Sid. To Aster's surprise, he didn't hesitate and excused himself.

"I can see it." Wilma appraised Aster.

"Pardon?"

"Sid has been wanting Sammy to settle down for years. You know the saying: 'Any decent executive needs work in front of him and a wife behind him.'"

No, that saying hadn't been thrown around Aster's kitchen table. Wilma angled a long strand of smoke over her own shoulder before continuing. "Sammy hitched his wagon to a ticking time bomb last time, but I see he may have finally found what he needs."

"Is that right?" Did this woman think she was waiting to be snatched off a hanger by whoever liked the fabric of her? A familiar annoyance roiled beneath Aster's ribs.

"Sid has always counseled Sammy against actresses. Too complicated from a professional perspective, too needy personally. Even Sid made that mistake the first time."

"Sam's mother is an actress?" As much as Sam loved to talk about the industry, he'd never mentioned this before. She knew almost nothing about his family, not even that his parents were divorced—his father twice, apparently.

"Not anyone you would have heard of. But she was on the rise and gave it up for Sid. Four kids later, she could never quite accept that she was the one at home while he was out with other actresses." She leaned in close enough for Aster to smell the smoke on her breath. "Something to consider. Holding out, I mean. I've got the lifestyle, but don't have the burden of having to give him kids, and I don't have to be the only one to entertain him, if you know what I mean."

Aster tried not to appear shocked lest she be labeled unsophisticated somehow, but she couldn't quite imagine adopting such a cynical view of relationships.

"Thank you for the advice, but Sam and I haven't known each other for long."

"Time has nothing to do with it. But if it's not for you, take what you can get and run for the hills."

Before Aster could gauge if Wilma was serious or making a joke, the air shifted with the arrival of both Sawyer men.

"Champagne for the lovely ladies." Sid held two flutes in one hand and a rocks glass in the other.

"I see you beat me to the introduction," Sam said.

"I'd be careful leaving this one alone at a party for long, son. Someone else might snap her up."

"I'd like to think she'd have something to say about that." Sam beamed at Aster.

"Do choose wisely, love," Wilma said, holding her glass out toward Aster. Aster attempted a clink and a smile. When she put the flute to her lips the liquid tasted sour, tinged with something Aster was no longer sure she wanted to swallow.

CHAPTER EIGHT

C hristopher told me you were a love yesterday." Fernando unzipped Aster from a sleeveless black gown and took it to the rack to swap it for the next contender.

They were back at the Galaxy lot finishing up a runway show, this time featuring Aster and Shirley in gowns under consideration for the Oscars. Taking turns on the runway with Shirley brought a certain normalcy and comfort to the day, which Aster welcomed. She'd been a bit off since the Garland party, and suspected it had everything to do with the unpleasant taste that had lodged in her mouth when she met Sam's father and Wilma.

"I can see why you're so enamored of him. He's a sweetheart." Aster pulled on a light silk robe while she waited for Fernando to make his pick.

"That he is. Although he failed to remember what you were wearing. Tell me."

Aster laughed. Always fashion first. She described the sundress with its simple bodice and pale pink accents she thought suited her skin.

"Next time, we'll get you in a backless bathing suit with a wrap skirt. That would turn heads." He unzipped a strapless gown that shimmered with sequins and held it up for her to step into.

"It's a shame you're otherwise involved. We'd make a great couple," she said.

"Only because we're not trying to be, darling." He peered at her more closely. "Do I detect trouble in paradise with Mr. Sawyer?"

"Oh, I don't know. I'm just not so sure I'm cut out for his world." She felt Sid Sawyer's eyes crawling over her again, Wilma's flippant commentary.

Shirley came around the curtain in a ravishing velvet mermaid gown, tight down to her calves with a satin flare at the bottom. The deep hue complemented her fair skin.

"Shirley, love, will you help Aster into this last one while I kowtow out front?"

Aster turned so Shirley could zip her into the trumpet-style dress that hugged her hips before sloping gently to the floor. The bodice was a gorgeous sky-blue with a lace overlay running down the center. Aster sucked in as the zipper rose and groaned. Too many meals and drinks out with Sam were starting to take their toll. She held her breath as the dress locked around her ribcage, glad she had packed a grapefruit in her handbag for lunch.

"Miss Kelly, Mr. Sawyer would like to see you in his office when you're finished," a woman's voice said from behind the curtain. "I'll take you there when you're ready."

Shirley raised her eyebrows. "That's a bit bossy."

"Well, he is the boss," Aster whispered, although she did wonder at the summons. It seemed an odd mix of business with their personal relationship.

Ten minutes later, the show complete, she whizzed across the Galaxy lot in a golf cart with Sam's assistant, Jean—an attractive but bored-looking young woman with a perfect ponytail—at the wheel. She gave Aster a tour as they drove, narrating and pointing to various structures.

"The gray building on the corner is interior set design. The bigger stuff, exteriors and landscapes, happen in the industrial shop on the far west end of the property. Film cutting, editing, sound mixing are in that brick building. The one next door is for the writers."

While the sheer scale of the Galaxy lot had struck Aster on her first visit, she hadn't considered all the different specialties that went into each film. A vast ecosystem, all under the control of the Sawyers.

"Here we are." Jean parked the cart in a reserved space in front of a wide, white A-frame. It squatted lower than the other buildings, but the substantial portico commanded attention. Double doors protruded between two oversized windows, each adorned with black shutters.

Beyond a square entryway decorated with nothing but a bench on each side, a center hall receded deep into the space, movie posters covering the walls on both sides. They walked past the original artwork for *Spellbound*, *The Big Sleep*, and photographs featuring Lana Turner in *Slightly Dangerous* and Gary Cooper in *The Pride of the Yankees* before turning into a small room on the right. Aster assumed it served as the anteroom to Sam's office.

"Mr. Sawyer is finishing up a meeting and will be with you shortly." She motioned to the couch beside the closed door before arranging herself at a small wooden desk with rows of filing cabinets behind.

As soon as Aster sat down, the door opened and the muffled voices inside became clear.

"Thank you, sir. I won't let you down."

She recognized the voice: Fernando's Christopher.

Aster stood and held out her hand as he came through the door. "Hello, Christopher."

"Well, hello, you." His smile broadened upon seeing her. "What a lovely surprise."

"How do you two know each other?" Sam came around a huge double-sided desk that backed up to one of the large windows she'd seen from outside.

Aster glanced at Christopher. "The first fashion show we did here." She tried to adjust her face to hide the sudden nervousness enveloping her. How to explain their instant friendship?

"And we got acquainted at the party yesterday." Christopher gave off no hint of discomfort.

"Is that right? Well then, perhaps you are due some of the credit, Aster. Goldwyn walked away convinced by how attractive our newest star is to the young ladies." Sam's voice had an edge to it.

Aster mustered a smile. Christopher thanked Sam again and shook his hand. He tipped his hat at Aster before briefly stopping at Jean's desk, causing color to rise on her cheeks. Fernando was right. Christopher never stopped performing, and he was exceptionally good at it.

"You two are friendly." Something bitter tinged Sam's voice. Was he jealous? He gestured to one of the leather chairs that faced his desk. "Have a seat. I just need to make one phone call, and then we can be on our way. Since you're all the way out here, I thought we could have lunch."

Aster felt the weight of the grapefruit in her purse as she sat, her attempt to return to her regular routine already under siege. She knew full well that even two extra pounds showed. She needed to cut back, not add more.

"It's settled, Dad. Four films for us at seven-fifty a week," Sam said into the receiver. "Assuming MGM still wants to borrow him for *Gentlemen's Bet* after that, we'll be able to get a grand a week for him easy, and then he comes back to us with a hefty raise that's actually still a hometown discount."

Aster calculated the math in her head. Seven hundred fifty dollars a week? Three thousand a month? That was almost as much as she made in a year. She already lamented the taxi fare it would cost her to get all the way back to work instead of the free ride she could have gotten from Fernando.

Sam shook his head while his father said something Aster couldn't make out. "No, the timing is perfect. Two months from now it will feel like a bargain. You've seen the rough cut of *Baby Face*. And the dailies of *The Last Tycoon* are incredible. Buy the horse before he wins the derby, right? Trust me."

Sam hung up the phone and fixed his eyes on the receiver for a long moment, saying, "It'll work out. It'll be fine." Aster wasn't quite sure if he was speaking to her or trying to convince himself.

"I'm sorry to interrupt, but Edna is here," Jean said from the door.

Sam glanced at Aster.

"She says it's ur-gent." Jean broke the last word into two equal syllables, as if it were code for something else.

Before Sam could reply, a woman swirled through the doorway like a swath of unfurling satin. She rushed to the desk, and Sam stood.

"Edna, this isn't the best time—"

"They can't make me do this." She held out a script to Sam. "They say if I refuse it, I'll be suspended. You have to fix this."

So *Edna* was her real name. Everything in this world really did rely on deception. Aster shrunk in her chair as she took in the full presence of the woman known to the rest of the world as Sophia Green. She looked like she had been crying, but the mist around her face only increased her beauty. Her chestnut hair hung in a perfect wave, her pool-blue eyes set off by luxurious eyelashes. She wore a sleeveless top the color of sunshine that disappeared at her tiny waist, tucked into a skirt embroidered with tulips. She managed to make the modest outfit look wildly sexy.

Sam ignored the script and put his hands on her arms. He spoke quietly.

"You already turned down the last three roles. They're not going to pay you not to work."

"They want me to play opposite Vaughan, Sam. You know I can't do that." Desperation filled each word.

His thumbs caressed her bare shoulders. Aster glanced at the door, the room suddenly too small for the three of them.

"Okay, I'll ring Marvin this afternoon," Sam finally said.

"No, you have to come with me now. They want me to sign on before the end of the day."

Sam nodded and grabbed his keys from his desk.

"I'm sorry, Aster. I have to take care of this. I'll have Jean call you a cab."

Sophia followed Sam out of the office, walking past Aster again without registering her presence. Then Aster was alone. She sat for a moment in the reverberating silence and tried to decipher what about the interaction unsettled her. After all, she had no official claim on Sam. But his obvious discomfort at having them both in the same room suggested a man whose wife had intercepted his mistress. Which of those was she meant to be? Or maybe it was the ease with which Sam could demand her presence one minute and then summarily dismiss her the next.

Sweat pricked her forehead with a rising sensation of being caught in a world she didn't want to inhabit, as if a deceptively spacious room she'd wandered into was about to become a cage. She heard Wilma's warning in her head and felt the urge to get out.

Aster found her feet, her bag still heavy with the grapefruit, and pressed a smile onto her face. She summoned her most confident strut and walked off the lot.

CHAPTER NINE

Three days later, a rush of nausea sent Aster flying into the bathroom. She knew with dread in her heart what it meant. The queasiness had started the day of the Judy Garland party, which she'd easily attributed to nerves but couldn't explain away afterward. Then Fernando's dresses had become a smidge too tight. As panic swelled inside her, she refused to believe what she already knew. She had used the sponge exactly as instructed, hadn't she? It wasn't possible to utilize it religiously and still be pregnant, was it?

As she emptied the meager contents of her stomach into the john, she knew she couldn't avoid reality. Kicking the door closed, she crumpled to the floor and stared in mute shock at a piece of wallpaper at the edge of the doorframe. It curled off the wall, the lime-green flowers arching back to reveal the sticky mess beneath. She was undeniably pregnant.

The tears rushed down her face as she thought about the future having a baby would erase. She would stop working with Fernando. She would never start her own clothing label, as ridiculous as the aspiration may have been. She would no longer be able to earn her own way, to prove herself worthy of her own dreams. She would never again walk into a room as an independent woman, at the ready to surprise those who measured her on the wrong criteria, to prove them shortsighted for not recognizing her as an intelligent and talented person who would make something of herself one day. All of it was lost.

And her mother. Aster began to sob. Her mother never did think she would amount to anything. Teddy had always been the favorite. It wasn't a matter of debate, just a fact. Only Teddy could be trusted to spin the ice-cream maker, only Teddy had hands gentle enough to braid her mother's hair, even though Aster had to teach him how. Teddy was handsome and smart, and Aster's mother never wasted an opportunity to tell him so. In contrast, Aster was never groomed well enough by day—"We're only as good as we look," her mother would say after pointing out Aster's too-light eyelashes or too-pale skin. But after a few drinks, Aster was suddenly too beautiful, her mother's words turning sour. "Don't go around thinking you're better than anyone just because the boys fall all over you. They're only after one thing."

Whenever Aster found her mother in one bar or another in Newark, the routine would be the same. Her mother would angrily eye Aster, empty her glass with one gulp, and then politely, if not gracefully, excuse herself from whatever group of men she'd been talking to. She would storm past Aster while slinging a nasty comment her way—"Can't stand for me to get the attention, can you?"

And now this. To raise this child on her own, Aster's only choice would be to return home and live with her parents, ask for their help and support. But she could already envision the lack of joy under their roof, judgment oozing from the walls, every meal tasting of shame. No, she couldn't allow her child to be treated as a horrible mistake. She would never go home an unwed mother.

No, she would have to marry Sam. Anguish burned her throat as she hiccupped tears. Not that he was a bad man—there were certainly worse to be bound to. But she knew in her bones that she didn't love him, not the way she considered worthy of spending a life together. And even if she could reverse the clock a few days, take back what she had said to Ria, forget Wilma's warnings, erase what she'd seen between Sam and Sophia, something would still be missing. Being together by choice was a luxury no longer afforded to either of them. They were now linked first and last by obligation.

Her life as she knew it was over. She wept as quietly as she could, then threw up again in the toilet.

Ria found Aster on the floor before she could wipe the spit from the side of her mouth the second time, before she could mop up the mess of her tears. Ria handed her a wet washcloth and sat beside her on the bath mat.

"Bad night last night?" Ria asked.

Ria had been out late the night before and didn't know Aster had done nothing but nurse a lemonade in her slippers all evening. But Aster had never suffered debilitating consequences from a night out before. Ria was probably just giving her cover, the opportunity to avoid making a horrible truth more real by speaking it aloud. Aster loved her for it. Avoiding all words, she rested her head on Ria's shoulder and let her remaining tears pour into the washcloth, Ria rubbing her back without saying more.

That night, Aster was halfway through her cocktail when a waiter at the Mocambo brought a phone to the table. She and Sam had agreed to meet at the restaurant. It was on the same block as Fernando's, so Aster slipped into yet another borrowed dress and walked over after work. Despite arriving alone, the maître d' recognized her—was this her third time there or fourth?—and had escorted her directly to a booth in the corner. A chilled martini arrived moments later. The burn of the liquor helped quell her nausea and smooth her nerves. She dreaded telling Sam her news and everything that would come after.

"You have a phone call, Miss Kelly." The waiter placed the phone in front of her, its long cord snaking back to the bar.

"I'm so sorry," Sam said on the line. "The dailies came in late today, and my father needs me to review some contracts for him after. Maybe a nightcap instead?"

Aster told him not to worry. She didn't feel well anyway.

"You're a doll. Dinner at my house tomorrow night, then?"

Aster lingered over her drink after hanging up with Sam. It was already paid for, after all; it would be added to whatever endless tab Sam kept at the restaurant. And she wanted to indulge, for a few minutes more, the relief of not having to face reality quite yet.

When she did leave, she tried to meet the sheepish look of the maître d' with confidence and nonchalance, not wanting him to assume her stunning aquamarine gown and matching shoes signified high hopes some man had dashed. She fought the urge to tell him she wore ten dresses like it every day, that it was simply on loan to keep up appearances.

"Your car, Miss Kelly," the doorman said. Aster noticed he was looking at her expectantly, before she was able to reapply the serene expression she had offered the maître d'.

"Pardon?"

"Mr. Sawyer sent it for you."

She instantly realized Sam had choreographed his cancellation, had waited to call the table until he could be sure the driver would be there. He'd probably been certain the appearance of the shiny chariot would replace any annoyance she might feel, as if she were a peasant who should be nothing but grateful for being treated this way. Was she already living her future?

"I'll walk, thank you." Aster turned back toward Fernando's. At least she could rid herself of the confining dress and be in the comfort of slacks and flats for the ride home, even if it cost her cab fare. And this way, she wouldn't have to worry about carting the dress back to work in the morning on the bus.

She fished the boutique's key from her clutch. Given his unpredictable schedule of late, Fernando had made her a copy so she could open or lock up as needed. She liked the weight of the metal in her hand, imagining what it would feel like to unlock the door to her own boutique, to see her own designs displayed on the racks, something she now knew she would never actually experience.

When she let herself in through the back door of Fernando's, she was surprised to find him and Christopher sitting on the couch drinking champagne.

"I'm sorry, I didn't know you were here." She reflexively backed up toward the door.

"Don't be silly," Christopher said. "Come join us. We're having a bit of a celebration."

Aster felt anything but celebratory but was touched by how quick he was to include her.

"Christopher got the lead in *Moonlight Sonata*!" Fernando beamed. "He'll be playing opposite Laraine Day. He'll be on the red carpet and accepting a statue in no time."

"Only if you make me look worthy." Christopher tilted his head toward Fernando.

"Congratulations." Aster tried to match their jovial tone but doubted they could hear anything beyond the confines of their tête-à-tête anyway.

"You don't need a thing from me, darling. You'd be the talk of the town in overalls and bare feet." Fernando lightly touched the rim of his glass to Christopher's.

Christopher smiled, and their eyes locked on each other. Aster decided to make herself scarce, let them enjoy the moment without interruption. She slipped into the dressing room and quickly changed. With any luck, she would be in a taxi within five minutes. When she walked back into the studio, though, Fernando held up a third glass of champagne.

"Come and sit with us. What happened to your date?"

"Caught up at the office. But I really should be going. I don't want to intrude."

"I'd be insulted if you didn't stay," Christopher said.

She knew by now how convincing Christopher could be no matter his true feelings, but she saw earnestness in Fernando's expression too. And staying for a short while would give her less time at home to wait for sleep to come while dreading her future.

Their trio of glasses met in a clink, and Aster sat in the chair nearest to the couch. As Fernando asked questions and Christopher told them more about the film, Aster watched their dynamic closely. Fernando was clearly in awe of Christopher, already having enough stake in their relationship and Christopher's talent to feel protective. He seemed determined that the studio ought to properly value the caliber of his performance. Christopher looked amazed, perhaps humbled by knowing he need not perform for Fernando at all. They had a generous give-and-take—each comment, each gesture molding the shared creation of their relationship.

She felt grateful to be included in this moment, to be witness to this love affair blooming before her. But watching this pair pinched her heart with a yearning that doubled as despair. She'd always assumed she would be an essential part of a duo one day, when the time was right—that she would be one half of a whole, not some meager slice, not a mere accessory to someone else's busy life. But these were old thoughts. She no longer had a choice in the matter. She would become Mrs. Samuel Sawyer. Aster Kelly would disappear.

"What's wrong, love?" Fernando asked.

"Just tired." She forced herself to sit up taller and take another sip of her champagne, but she failed to gulp down the full sweep of her emotions with the bubbles. She thought she might cry.

"Did you two have a fight?" Christopher leaned forward, his brow furrowed with genuine concern.

Aster shook her head and suddenly knew she could trust these two people more than any others. Even though she barely knew Christopher, her instincts told her they would both be on her side.

"I'm pregnant."

"*Mio Dio*." Fernando's hand flew to his forehead.

Aster hadn't gone back to Ria's doctor for confirmation yet, but she had no doubt. The tenderness of her breasts, the tightness of Fernando's dresses, the undercurrent of nausea running through her all signaled a major shift in her body, and there could only be one explanation.

"Sam's a good man. He'll do the right thing. You'll elope and then when it's time, you'll just claim the baby came a little early," Christopher said.

It struck Aster anew how quickly he jumped to making appearances fit expectation. While she would have considered such scheming the reflex of a disingenuous person a year ago, she now fully appreciated what an important survival technique the ability to adapt to any situation was for him.

"It's not what I want." Aster found little relief in saying the words out loud. In fact, it simply gave the truth weight and shape, like a bunched-up girdle that ruined the line of a dress no matter how gracefully she moved.

"You don't love him." Christopher put his hand on hers.

"I'm sorry." Aster tried to gather herself. "I don't want to ruin your night. I'm just going to grab a taxi."

"No, no. Let us help you."

"Listen, I know a few actresses who have been through this before. I could discreetly ask them for a recommendation. It happens all the time," Christopher said.

Aster looked at Christopher squarely and saw no judgment in his eyes: only a sincere desire to help her. She desperately hoped he wasn't acting.

"That's not an option." This truth had surfaced with surprising clarity. While being pregnant was devastating in every logical way and would surely upend her entire future, she was already attached to the being growing inside her. She'd assumed an unwanted pregnancy would feel like a painful splinter that would be a relief to have removed. But now, she knew ending it would be as devastating as removing her own bones. She had no logical explanation, but this new life had already become integral to her, and she had an overwhelming desire to protect it. It was as if she'd unexpectedly come across a tiny bud in an otherwise barren field, and while she had no interest in living in such a desolate place, she wanted desperately to care for the young seedling. She needed to.

"I didn't want it to be this way. Sam and I . . ." She couldn't say the rest—that she didn't think love was something that could be manipulated, that a union forced by obligation would more likely sprout resentment than partnership. But what choice did she have? She had no way to support herself as a single mother, would never be able to face her parents. And she couldn't live with herself if she chose to burden her own child with a lifetime of shame. Bastards suffered the consequences of their mothers' indiscretions. It was a truth as old as time.

She put her head in her hands, a tempest of emotions swirling, and began to cry. Her old self, her old dreams poured out of her. Her limbs became heavy, almost useless, and she wondered if she would even be able to rise out of the chair. Instead, she wanted to curl into the smallest shape possible and disappear.

Fernando knelt beside her and rubbed her back, the warmth of his hand like a balm on her frayed nerve endings. She found comfort in their silence, their patience, and knew they would wait all night for her to gather herself if that's what it took.

She slowly matched her breath to the steady rhythm of Fernando's touch and decided she needed to stop feeling sorry for herself. Sam was a good enough man. He would do the right thing, and he could provide. She was luckier than most women in her position. Their relationship might not be the stuff of a grand love story, but it could be enough, couldn't it?

She finally raised her head and wiped her face.

"What a fun party guest I turned out to be." She attempted a smile.

"Let us drive you home."

"Thank you, but no. You should be celebrating. And I just need to be alone. I'll be fine."

The men stood in unison with Aster and opened their arms to her. Their joint embrace made the perfect cocoon, and she instinctively knew how completely she could count on them both. She breathed in the familiar musk of Fernando's cologne, felt the soft linen of Christopher's jacket on her cheek, and wished she could stay there forever.

CHAPTER TEN

Aster arrived at Sam's for dinner and settled into a chair on his patio, her carefully chosen yellow skirt already wrinkled from the ride over. Gazing up at a cluster of oranges close enough to pluck off the tree, she recited in her head the order of events as she had envisioned them all day. She would wait for Sam to finish his work. They would trade niceties over a cocktail, after which they would sit for dinner. She would share her news with him, tell him she wanted to keep the baby. He would offer marriage, and she would accept with as much delight as she could muster. Simple as that.

She concentrated on steadying her breath and did her best to push aside more complicated thoughts—that this was the last moment she could call her own, that after tonight her new reality would begin to harden in place, that nothing would ever be entirely in her control again. She didn't want to think about it anymore. Wallowing in the truth wasn't helping.

"Champagne?" Consuela asked, walking across the patio with a silver tray in her hand, the flute already fizzing. "Sammy will be right with you."

Never before did Aster think she could tire of champagne, but the thought of sipping it made her stomach turn. Even so, she accepted the glass from Sam's cook, grateful for the distraction.

"How's Bobby?" Aster asked.

"He's back to work, thank the lord. He was only out for two days." Consuela's husband worked construction and gave them both a scare when he wrenched his back a couple of weeks earlier. Aster wondered how old was too old for such a physical line of work. He was probably only in his fifties, but Aster now understood how the body can betray your ability to do the job you had been hired to do. What would become of her once her waist began to expand in earnest?

"I'll be right back with some nibbles." Consuela returned inside.

Consuela had been a fixture in Sam's world, originally as his nanny, then eventually as his house cleaner and cook. She always wore the same blue housedress, an ill-fitting garment Aster had the urge to tailor for her. A tapered waistline and slightly shorter skirt would better flatter Consuela's small frame. Aster wondered if service uniforms were designed to degrade at some level, to make the individual disappear behind a badge of inferiority. The simpler explanation was cost. They were cheap garments that came in only a few sizes and fabrics with little regard for the variation in body type and skin color of those wearing them. But wasn't that the same thing?

Aster gazed into her glass, the tiny bursts of carbon bouncing on the surface a mini festival that felt wrong in her hand. She tried to envision this house as home, the oleander bushes her responsibility to tend, Sam's favored goose liver her job to track down and stock. Or would he keep the gardener and Consuela, and it would become Aster's job to manage them? What would she do all day? She could keep sketching and sewing, but to what end? Wives of Hollywood moguls didn't have careers. She supposed she could make new slipcovers for the chairs in Sam's den, make curtains to block out the midday sun. The idea of it left her hollow, like an orange peel after all the good stuff's gone.

❧

As Consuela served the coq au vin, Aster's stomach clenched. She needed to tell Sam about the baby before the evening went much further. And she had decided not to say, "I'm pregnant," but rather, "I'm going to have a baby." Pregnancy sounded too much like a state of altered being that could be fixed like so much in Sam's universe. This was a living being she planned to usher into the world and nurture, protect. She hoped being in the privacy of his house would make it easier to tell him, maybe even create a moment of joy between them, but she hadn't yet been able to bring herself to say the words. She almost marveled at the power this one piece of information contained. Sam had no internal signal to alert him to the existence of this child. It was entirely up to her to tell him.

She sucked in her breath and tried to picture sitting at this table every night, greeting her husband after his workday, scrounging for something interesting of her own to say. The scene would include a baby who would become a toddler, and there would inevitably be more than one. They would be a family. She looked across the table at Sam. Could she picture them as family? Could he?

"I've told her for a long time that women in this business need tough skin to get on with the show, but her acting treads very close to the real thing. Too close." Sam spoke around mouthfuls of bird and fingerling potatoes.

In an attempt to talk about anything but the one topic on her mind, Aster had asked about Sophia Green's visit to his office earlier in the week. She hadn't meant it to spur a ten-minute diatribe.

"She just couldn't put herself in that position with Vaughan Stevens, which no one else but me seems to understand. It's complicated."

Aster nodded her head, feigning interest, and took a long sip of water. The glass cooled her palm. The frost hovering above the ice cubes misted her lip. Sam went on.

"Anyway, it's all been a mess, but I think I convinced Marvin that he can find plenty of actors to take Vaughan's place. She's the bigger draw."

"She always will be." Aster pushed a clump of rice across her plate.

Sam wiped his mouth and looked at Aster with surprise.

"You're not sore at me for having to cancel lunch the other day, are you?"

Was she? Of course, he'd practically ordered her to appear at his office and then proceeded to pack her off in a cab. But would she still be thinking about it if she weren't in her current bind?

"And dinner last night." Her words were sharp with a level of anger she hadn't expected. Did being pregnant make a person testy? Or was she already protesting a lifetime of being his second or third priority? She shook her head. He was an important businessman, with a very demanding father. She didn't want to be the sort of woman who begged for assurances.

And yet, something had changed. Everything carried more weight, more importance. Would any of it have bothered her two weeks ago, back when she was free to walk away the moment the relationship no longer suited her? It struck Aster that a person with no strong ties to another wouldn't be jostled by their unpleasant gyrations. But once firmly tethered, uncomfortable tugs are impossible to ignore. She and Sam were bound now, even though he didn't know it yet.

"I'm sorry about that. Sophia panicked again last night. She got it in her head that Marvin set the whole thing up on purpose to upset her. She was threatening to walk off the film again, and I had to talk some sense into her."

Aster bit down on an ice cube, replaying in her mind his brief phone call to the Mocambo.

"You told me your father needed you to review contracts after the dailies last night."

Sam's face drew a blank. She couldn't stand to watch him squirm, so she turned her attention out the window. A flock of starlings landed on one of the orange trees like a wave rippling onto the shore. She thought of summers with her brother. What would he have made of Sam, of all this nonsense?

Tears pricked the edges of her eyes. She detested how she sounded: doubtful, questioning, jealous. Was this how the rest of her life would feel? She remembered how Wilma had described being married to Sam's father. Would Sam become like his father? Had he already?

"Edna's very demanding. I didn't want to worry you."

Edna. He was talking about the person now, not just the movie star. She needed to change the subject.

"Wilma told me your mother was an actress. You never mentioned that before."

"Ancient history by the time I came along. She started as a vaudeville singer. I guess she was something in the day. But I never thought of her that way. She was just my mother."

Kids never do get to know their parents as young people with a life ahead of them, Aster thought. *Only as caretakers, or impediments, or both.*

"The divorce must have been hard on you."

"Honestly, it was a bit of a relief. We didn't have the happiest household. I suspect my parents only married because my mother was pregnant with Margaret—the math never quite worked otherwise—and I can tell you firsthand it's no way to start a marriage. I mean, I'm sure they tried to make it work—they managed to have four kids, after all—but I don't think they were ever truly suited to each other. It made for a pretty dismal childhood."

Aster put down her fork and stared at her plate. She tried to center herself by picturing the boutique, the steady movement of one foot in front of the other, twirl and repeat, the shared camaraderie with Fernando and the girls. She tried to breathe.

"Are you all right, doll? What's wrong?"

The tenderness in his voice surprised her, and it threatened to unleash a flood of tears. This was the moment to tell him, for better or worse. Her heart tripped on itself as it clambered up into her throat. She closed her eyes and tried to compose herself. But before she could formulate the right series of words, Consuela rushed into the room.

"There's a call for you, Sammy. They say it's important."

Sam returned to the table, took a long swig of his drink, and attacked the bird on his plate without saying a word. Aster watched him carefully, wondering how long it would be before he remembered that they'd been on the brink of an important conversation. As each second ticked by, she felt herself pulling back, the taut line between them stretched to the point of unravelling. Any connection to him would snap if she didn't find a way to inch closer.

"Goddammit!" Sam slammed down his knife and wiped his mouth.

"Are you going to tell me what's going on?"

"That was Bruce Garner." The reporter from the *LA Times*. Aster knew they had a deal. Garner would tip Sam off if a scandal was brewing to give Sam a chance to fix it before it exploded into a real story. In return, Sam gave him exclusives. On more than one Sunday afternoon, Aster had heard Sam working the phones to get charges dropped or invent a scheduling conflict to hide someone's black eye for a few days.

"One of his beat reporters has seen the same car coming and going from the house of my biggest investment, lately arriving at night and not leaving until morning. Which wouldn't be a problem, except Garner has reason to believe it's a man. Dammit!" Sam slammed his fist on the table again.

The percussion of Sam's anger reverberated in her chest.

"Whose house?" She steeled herself for the name she knew was coming.

"Christopher Page."

She forced herself to take a tiny bite of chicken, hoping that chewing would help her control the muscles of her face.

"That's impossible." Aster's neck blazed like a sunburn.

"Nothing is impossible in this town." He got to his feet and began to pace.

"No, I mean, I should know." Aster pushed words out of her mouth as quickly as she could. She needed to put him off the trail. "He's been quite forward with me."

Sam stopped pacing and turned to her with an almost hopeful expression. "I thought you two looked awfully cozy in my office. Did he make a move on you at the party?"

"Nothing I couldn't handle."

Sam's eyes narrowed, considering this new information.

"Hopefully the reporter made a mistake," he said. "But I have to see for myself, talk to Page face-to-face. I need a counter story to offer by tomorrow if there is one. I'm sorry." He was already turning away. "I'll be back soon. He doesn't live far from here."

"Can't it wait?" Her mind raced. "We haven't finished dinner."

Sam's shoulders dropped. He labored back to the table and leaned on the top of his chair.

"Garner can only control so much," he explained, his impatience evident. "Reporters follow gossip, so other reporters could be snooping around too. Page is a huge investment for us, and my father trusted me on this one."

"But if by some wild chance it's true, you'll figure out how to cover it up, right?" Aster tried to sound as nonchalant as possible. This kind of thing happened all the time, didn't it?

"My father will never sign off on it. Too risky for someone with no real box office yet. The only hope is that Garner's got this one wrong. It wouldn't be the first time. I'll be back within the hour."

She needed to slow him down.

"I think I'll just go home." She folded her napkin and stood. "You might have a long night ahead. Before you go, would you mind asking Troy to take me home?"

Troy lived in the cottage on the back of Sam's property, mostly as a groundskeeper, but he was at the ready for errands or the occasional livery job. He had driven Aster home on a few Sundays when too much unexpected business elbowed its way into their day. She hoped the small errand of going to fetch him would delay Sam long enough to give her the time she needed.

Sam didn't hesitate.

"You're a doll. Thanks for understanding." He kissed her on the forehead.

"I just need to go to the loo. Tell Troy I'll meet him in the driveway."

As soon as Sam headed for the back door, Aster hurried across the foyer. She turned on the light in the powder room and closed the door before slipping into Sam's study. She'd heard him make plenty of calls from behind the gigantic mahogany desk, and it didn't take long to find his leather address book. He told her once that the book itself would probably be worth a few thousand dollars given how many direct numbers of stars it contained. She turned to *P* and found no listing for *Page*—only *Peggy*, *Paul*, and *Pamela*. All first names. She quickly flipped to *C*, but still no Christopher.

The front door closed—Sam on his way out—and the press of time increased her anxiety. She didn't have long—perhaps seven minutes before Sam pulled up to Christopher's house? Five? She was sure this was the right book, its burgundy cover deeply worn with Sam's initials on the front. But his newest and most expensive star wasn't in it? Then something occurred to her. She turned to *E*, and there it was: *Edna*. Sam used actors' birth names to shroud his list of contacts from the uninitiated.

She willed herself to remember what Fernando had said about Christopher's real name. They both still referred to him as Christopher—all the better to keep up the illusion of a professional distance—but Fernando told her not long after he'd started seeing Christopher regularly that it wasn't his given name. Her mind homed in on her memory of the conversation—Fernando fitting her for a new gown, a maroon sequined bodice and flowing satin skirt, the hemline dripping with tiny beads. He had just started to pin the sleeves. She searched for Fernando's face in the memory, his reflection slowly coming into focus in her mind.

"He asked me to call him Benny. Isn't that sweet?"

"Benny?"

"Benedict Horowitz is his real name. I think Benedict is lovely, but it wouldn't do for the studio."

Aster turned to *B* and ran her finger down the page. She saw *Bette*, which would be Lauren Bacall, *Bruce*, *Barbara*, and then *Benedict*.

After the phone's sixth ring, Aster started to lose hope. She had taken too much time. Shoes scuffed across the marble foyer in the direction of the den. Someone finally picked up.

"It's Aster. A reporter has seen you. Sam is on his way."

"What?" Christopher asked.

Aster lowered her voice. "Get Fernando out of your house. Now."

She placed the receiver gently in its cradle, then hurried out of the room, almost bumping into Consuela as she turned the corner.

"Is everything all right?" Consuela glanced over Aster's shoulder.

God, she hoped so. Had Christopher understood? Would Fernando be able to move fast enough and safely exit Christopher's driveway before Sam came charging in?

"I just had to powder my nose before heading out. Thank you for the lovely dinner. So sorry to leave in a rush, but you know how business gets." She attempted a smile and strode toward the front door as casually as possible.

Only after the car rolled out of Sam's driveway with Troy at the wheel did Aster realize she had forgotten to open the door of the powder room and turn off the light.

CHAPTER ELEVEN

Aster skipped the bus in favor of a cab the next morning to get to the boutique as early as possible. She had barely slept, and her body hummed with exhaustion and anxiety. Fernando was already there, lying on the couch in the studio.

"What happened? Are you all right?"

Fernando kept his eyes trained on the ceiling.

"I can't stop thinking about this thing from when I was little, maybe ten years old. A group of boys a couple of years older than me nabbed this other kid's lunch box on the way to school. This poor kid was always getting his sandwich stolen, but this time they took his whole lunch box. He loved that thing. It had Peter Rabbit on it and these special designs. They asked me to bring it back to him in the lunchroom, and I was so amazed this group of cool kids even knew my name, I did it without thinking. And he was so excited to see it, like I was his hero. And then he opened it, and it was filled with bugs. He shrieked and then started to cry, and the whole room laughed at him. A teacher had seen me bring over the box. A letter was sent to my home, and I got a whooping. No matter what I said, the teacher never looked at me the same way again. Neither did that kid. That's how I felt last night, ashamed and embarrassed, needing to run away without having done anything wrong."

Aster lowered herself into the chair beside him. She waited. He eventually sat up and ran his fingers through his hair. His shirt was creased in odd places, his face stubbled.

"I got out of the house before Sam got there, thanks to you. Christopher called me a couple of hours later. Sounds like he managed to convince Sam the reporter made some kind of mistake—made up something about an affair with a woman who always borrowed her brother's car. Thank god he's such a good actor." He paused and leaned his elbows on his knees, his eyes tilted toward Aster. "But they won't stop watching, will they? What kind of way is that to live?"

"If the next few pictures do well, the studio will help you. They'll have no choice. But he has to be a bankable star first."

"Did Sam tell you that? Does he know?" Fernando's eyes widened as if seeing a second wave of danger just behind the first.

"I don't know what he thinks, but you need to avoid each other for a while. Sam will drop him if he can't control the story."

Fernando nodded. "That's what Christopher said."

"I can't believe I'm dating the man you need to hide from."

How had this become her life? Last year at this time, Aster had nothing more to do with Hollywood than buying an occasional ticket to see a show.

"You're a bit beyond dating, darling." His voice sounded small, the claustrophobia of their world pressing in on them both.

"I didn't tell him last night. I couldn't bring myself to do it." Aster's emotions bounced between the relief of being able to keep her news, her baby, to herself for one more day, and worry about the cost of with-holding it. Would it become harder for her to feign surprise, impossible for them to pretend it was what they wanted?

"Eventually, you and I are both going to have a hard time hiding what's real," he said.

Aster looked across the gleaming runway at Fernando's latest work in progress, pinned to a canvas dummy. So many times, she had envisioned the thrill of presenting one of her own designs to a client sitting in a chair not unlike the one she occupied now, a smile blooming as the customer imagined herself in one of Aster's creations, the growing list of clients that would follow, the joy of making a living by offering something original to the world, her gratitude for it all. She shook her head as the images faded.

"I've got to make myself presentable. Would you mind opening up the front?" Fernando dragged himself over to a rack of perfectly starched shirts, the stiff white collars and cuffs at the ready for his daily performance.

Thirty minutes later, the bell on the storefront jangled. Aster heard Sam's voice before she saw him.

"Where is he?" Sam stormed past Aster.

"Who?" Aster hurried to follow as he pushed through the velvet curtain. He marched right up to Fernando and pointed at his face.

"It's you, isn't it? I hired you for the studio, gave you your big break, and this is the thanks I get?" Sam was practically spitting.

"Slow down. I don't know what you're talking about." Fernando held his hands up in front of him as if to block Sam's assault.

"Like hell you don't. Do you know what my father told me this morning? He got a call from a reporter too. This one said he saw

Page sneaking out of the back door of this store the other night. Late at night. I swear to god, neither of you will ever work in this town again."

Time slowed as Fernando stepped back, a look of horror on his face. He was no actor. Fear and guilt and shame contorted his face.

Aster had never seen Sam so angry. He was used to being the one in control, from handpicking his actors to doling out leading roles, to placing the chosen few in front of the right flashbulbs, all carefully designed to create the next darling for American audiences. If there was a detour on the path to stardom, it was supposed to be Sam's choice: his calculation that the actor wasn't ready, his opinion that their particular style wasn't resonating with the public. This was different entirely, and it infuriated him. He told Aster once that the hardest thing of all was watching an actor who embodied everything Hollywood wanted self-destruct. There were some things he could fix, but only if they were worth it. And Christopher Page wasn't yet worth it, especially not in the eyes of Sam's father. He might never be.

Everything began to play out in slow motion for Aster, the way she had always imagined the moment before a car crash—the split second when the driver needs to swerve or stay the course, knowing the move will determine everything. With no time to decide, is the choice ever logical? Or does it come purely from instinct? As if removed from the situation, she watched herself teetering on the precipice of a decision, unsure which path was less fraught, less dangerous. But there was no time. She swerved.

"It was me." Aster could barely hear her own voice over the thrumming in her head, but both men whirled in her direction.

"Excuse me?" Sam still seethed. Veins bulged at his neck and sweat beaded on his forehead. Fernando stared at her, the shock evident on his face.

"I'm so sorry, Sam. The night you didn't come to the Mocambo, I came back here, and Fernando was just finishing up a fitting for Christopher. He and I stayed after Fernando left."

"What are you saying?"

"That wasn't the only time, Sam." She was freewheeling entirely now. Fernando's eyes grew wide.

"You told me he hadn't made any moves on you." Sam's voice sounded eerily flat.

"I told you it wasn't anything I couldn't handle."

Sam backed up from Fernando and leaned against the couch, his jaw twitching. He didn't say anything for what might have been less than a minute, but to Aster it felt like an hour. She tried to imagine his various reactions, what would happen next. She was effectively blowing up her relationship with him, demolishing her escape route. It felt like the right thing to do and the biggest mistake she could possibly make, all at the same time. She braced herself for his anger, his fury at her betrayal, the pain that would surface from holding something broken—the harsh edges that would wound them both.

Instead, he straightened up and tugged on his lapels to smooth his jacket. He stepped close to her, blocking Fernando from their interaction.

"I thought you were different, Aster." Sam glared at her.

The accusation burned. She remembered the first time he ever looked at her, how he'd drunk her in as if deciding whether she would please the palate of his world, as if the choice was his alone. But this time she saw a glimmer of something else. Was it confusion? Regret? He had been kind to her, yet she was tossing him aside. Some part of her yearned to explain, to help him understand, but none of it would make sense to him. She said nothing.

Eventually, Sam blinked. Then he left.

Despite the swirl of emotions threatening to engulf Aster, one thought prevailed. She had to get to Christopher before Sam did.

※

Fernando dropped Aster off on the corner closest to soundstage six. As she dodged a moving crane and cut a wide path around a Christmas tree covered in fake snow, her body buzzed with adrenaline. Her limbs seemed disconnected from her brain—a jumble of confusing thoughts with one bright spot of clarity.

Fernando had agreed to her plan almost immediately, but the silence between them in the car during the long drive to Burbank crackled, as if they were both in shock from something that hadn't happened quite yet.

Aster slipped onto the soundstage through the back door and snuck toward the light and action filling the northwest corner. Christopher was in the final days of filming *Man in the Crowd* and was deep in an emotional monologue, cameras rolling. She had never seen him work before and almost didn't recognize him in his role as a dock worker, his shoulders hunched in despair, his absorption in the scene complete. Aster marveled again at how he could transform into someone else entirely and understood Sam's confidence that he could be Hollywood's next big star. He wasn't just an attractive face to put on movie posters; he was a truly gifted actor.

She positioned herself a good distance behind the main camera, hoping he would see her when the action broke and before someone questioned her presence. As soon as the director yelled "Cut!" Christopher straightened his spine and came back into himself. She gave a small wave to catch his eye. He asked for a moment, hurried over to her, and led her off the set.

"What's wrong? Is Fernando okay?"

Aster filled him in on everything as quickly as she could, including what she had discussed with Fernando.

"I know it's a lot to absorb." She tried to catch her breath.

He took both her hands. "Are you sure?"

Was she sure? She had no way to know if it was a good plan or a terrible mistake, but it was the best idea she could think of, for all of them.

"We can't afford to lose any time," she said. "We have to tell Sam today."

"Tell me what?" Sam was less than ten feet away, striding toward them with purpose.

Aster's legs threatened to fail her. She assumed she'd have at least a few moments to gather herself, to find the right words, before having to face Sam. As if it were a practiced dance maneuver, Christopher spun Aster in place and pulled her back toward him, his arms cinched around her waist. She leaned into him, grateful for the support. Sam came to a halt and waited, his expression suggesting impatience or annoyance at an inconvenient interruption even though he was the one doing the interrupting.

"We're getting married. We thought you should know," Christopher said.

Sam crossed his arms over his chest. Aster clenched Christopher's sleeve and tried to avoid Sam's glare. She didn't know how she would answer him if he asked how long they'd been together, or why she continued to come to his house, take meals with him, and sleep in his bed if she was falling in love with someone else. Would he tell her she was making a mistake, that she should marry him instead? A new thought struck her. Could this all backfire? Would Sam be so angry with Christopher for stealing her away that his career would be ruined anyway? She hadn't thought of that.

"You must be joking." Sam scanned Christopher's face, then Aster's. "And I just introduced you to my—" Sam stopped himself from finishing the sentence. He shook his head.

"Sam, I—"

Sam held up his hand, cutting her off.

"Page, see me in my office after you wrap for the day." Sam flicked his hand at the air as he walked away.

Aster felt the slap of the dismissal from his life, the demotion to someone no longer worth his time. The momentary euphoria that had sparked when she realized she had the power to help her friends and solve her own dilemma at the same time threatened to dissolve. As much as she'd orchestrated the situation, the ease with which Sam acquiesced stunned her, as if she were a pawn to be handed from one man to another. And he would be gone from her life with one flick of his wrist. She closed her eyes against the rebuke.

Christopher spun her slowly back around and held her shoulders gently.

"Are you okay?"

Aster nodded, not trusting her voice.

"I'd better get back to the set. Will you tell Fern I'll call as soon as I can?"

Aster nodded again.

"You are a wonder, Aster Kelly. Thank you." He kissed her cheek.

She watched him walk back toward the cameras, less sure than when she'd arrived of where the movie sets stopped and real life began.

1975
NEW YORK

CHAPTER TWELVE

Lissy stood in front of the casting room door and ticked through her mental checklist: *Show them you have a spine; keep their attention; you've got what it takes.*

This is it.

She took an extra moment to calm the staccato of her breathing, then imagined herself sashaying from the wings of a stage into the spotlight.

"Horowitz?" asked a petite woman with enormous glasses.

Lissy nodded, her reverie temporarily interrupted. She handed over her paperwork and the headshot she'd splurged on, knowing it was an important part of the impression she would leave behind. The photographer had caught her grinning at something beyond the reach of the camera. Lissy hoped it would add to the intrigue of her profile, if anyone read those things.

She immediately recognized the two men sitting behind a folding table as Hal Zimmerman and Rudy Gray, the can't miss duo of

Broadway. Zimmerman and Gray—they were always referred to together—had written the book and score for four of the biggest hits of the last ten years and had taken home Tonys for three. They were on a winning streak, and the power of their partnership lit up half the marquees in town. When she saw the open casting call for *Happily After Ever*, which highlighted the need for a young cast, Lissy knew it was meant to be. She just needed to show them the promise that was part of her DNA, inspire them to give her a chance.

The woman handed Lissy's paperwork to Zimmerman, who looked the part of the disheveled professor: too wrapped up in the workings of his mind to bother with something as inconsequential as pressing his blazer. Rudy Gray, on the other hand, radiated command, like a principal dancer and TV talk show host rolled into one. His Yul Brynner–like bald head and chiseled features made him almost too beautiful to look at, but Lissy knew the best way to hold his interest was to maintain eye contact until the part demanded otherwise.

Zimmerman studied Lissy's bio, raised his eyebrows, and passed it on. Gray didn't bother with the paperwork and tilted his head to scrutinize Lissy from a different angle. She delivered a friendly smile, careful not to blink. Auditions turned on quick judgments. There was no time to warm up the audience. Every movement had to be worthy of a grand finale.

"Okay, Horowitz. Let's see what you've got."

Back in her apartment, all she could do was wait for the phone to ring, and she hated waiting. If she'd been on shift at the diner, at least she'd have the distraction of ferrying hamburgers and fruit cups from kitchen to table. She could forget for a few spare moments that two men with the power to confer stardom were evaluating her talent in a smoky room somewhere. Normally, by the time her shift ended, the callback list would be decided. She would stand outside her apartment door for an extra beat to ready herself for the verdict, then peer into the living room to find it either suspended in morbid darkness or pulsing red with the glorious blinking light of the answering machine.

Instead, she fretted from her vinyl couch, willing the call to come. Lissy's roommate, Bae, had taken the evening shift at Al's Diner. The two of them split just about everything—the studio apartment hardly big enough for one person but barely affordable for two; the bath salts Lissy's mom sent to help soothe their aching muscles; the home-cooked meal Bae's brother delivered every Sunday on his way back to NYU; and the answering machine, a huge splurge even though Bae's dad sold it to them at cost. Splitting the waitressing job at Al's made it easy to cover for one another for any auditions, and god willing, any rehearsals. When they were both free, they divvied up the shifts based on who needed the money the most. Hence, Bae was working dinner. She'd been on an impressive run of callbacks during the last month, which Lissy would have happily traded for the ones and fives piling up in her sock drawer.

She wished she could call her friend Georgia, but it would tie up the line. Talking to Georgia calmed her like the lapping waves on the beaches at home. Though she rooted for Lissy whenever she auditioned and let out great whoops of congratulations when Lissy got even a small part, Georgia didn't really care about things like starring roles or the possibility of fame. She wanted to know whether Lissy was having fun, if she was happy. She always knew when Lissy forced a cheery tone. To get Lissy's mind off the latest rejection, Georgia would inevitably bring up their fourth grade Christmas show, the time they'd turned "All I Want for Christmas Is My Two Front Teeth" into a hilarious duet that left the small auditorium in stitches, or the night before graduation when they convinced all sixteen seniors to go skinny-dipping together. "Now that was fun," Georgia would say.

The kettle whistle broke the silence and pulled Lissy into the tiny kitchen. She was careful not to place her mug on the warped section of the counter before filling it and adding a dollop of honey for her throat. She put her nose to the edge of the cup to let the steam moisten her cheeks. It reminded her of the humidity of the heated pool at her high school, a strange comfort for someone who grew up on the ocean. Something about bobbing between liquid silence and the surface of the bright turquoise water of a pool always made her feel content, as if she already had everything she needed in the world.

When the phone rang, she raced back into the living room, hot water spilling onto her hand.

"BaeJin Kim, please," a woman's voice said on the other end.

"She's not here. Can I take a message?" Lissy tucked her disappointment inside a practiced, professional voice, infused with indifference.

There were two pads next to the phone used exclusively for this purpose. Bae's was yellow and almost down to the cardboard. Lissy's was thick with white pages. She dutifully scrawled the particulars for Bae: *Callback for the role of Connie, ten A.M.*

Lissy hadn't put her name in for that show. Hamlisch wrote great music, but mostly for film, and the cowriters of the book were complete unknowns. Besides, the casting call emphasized the need for hard-core dancers. Perfect for Bae.

Lissy wiped up the trail of water and honey she had splashed across the floor and flopped onto the lumpy couch. The adrenaline the ringing phone had pushed through her evaporated, leaving her spent. They lived for callbacks, each round getting them closer to the real thing. Lissy always performed better the further along in the process she got—she needed the time to develop the character, to feel her way into the script—but those chances were rare. She feared she would never rise above company parts, those no-name roles awarded based on the size and color the director needed in his bouquet of extras.

Lissy eyed her mattress, tucked under Bae's neatly made bed, and wondered if it was too early to pull it out, cover her head with her trusty daisy blanket, and forget all about the day. Was it worth it, all the hoping, all the rejection? Unless or until she got a sizable role, she'd never know if her efforts were adding up to anything. Sure, she'd gotten a few small roles Off Broadway, and even a company part in a larger production, but nothing she could make a profession of yet. She had no way to know if a real career would ever materialize. It was like being in a never-ending maze with no map to tell her if she was one turn away from success or still stuck somewhere near the beginning. Would turning back be the safer bet or a foolish decision after the strides she'd already made, no matter how small?

After graduating from college, she'd given herself three years to make a career of stage acting. She'd been doing this now for almost five. Maybe the endless twists and turns, the incessant second-guessing about whether she was going in the right direction had gone on long enough. She decided right then, staring into her cup of tea, that if the phone didn't ring again, that would be her sign. She should put her time toward something else. She had a Vassar degree, after all. She had other options. That lesson had been drilled into her since grade school: work hard, get a good education, and by all means, go for your dreams—but make sure you have options.

There was a lot she would not miss if she gave up trying to make it on Broadway, like the ride on the M train into the city: the stench of men with empty nips in their pockets, always standing too close and threatening to topple into her. She wouldn't miss the walls of steam pouring out of manhole covers on every street, smelling of dirty water and hot pretzels. The closer she got to audition sites, the tighter she clutched her bag against ever-present pickpockets, the streets littered with advertisements for peep shows and live porn, XXX movie houses with their blinking signs and the con men who tried to talk her into the building, most of them hopped up on drugs they hustled on the side. She counted herself lucky whenever she made it all the way to Midtown and back without being accosted, whistled at, or jostled. Those were the good days, the rare days.

But what if the phone *did* ring? That would be the surer sign. Giving up now would only prove she'd wasted all those years chasing the wrong thing, confirm that her ambitions were misplaced, that she couldn't hack the long climb up to the Broadway stage, couldn't stomach waiting for her turn in the golden spotlight. Only a small percentage of hopefuls ever made it, but she reminded herself that she still held the best poker hand in town, the royal flush no one knew about. Well, almost no one.

Zimmerman and Gray were unique as directors in many ways, from the kinds of stories they tackled through musicals to their reputation for treating hopefuls not as poker chips in their high-stakes game but as human beings worthy of respect. Even their requested submission materials had a human touch. On top of the standard bio requested at all auditions—essentially a rundown of previous acting credits—they asked one key question to be answered in no more than three lines: "What is your motivation for wanting to perform?" Lissy had never been asked that before. She considered the stock answers she could provide: *Disappearing into a character is like oxygen for me*; or *Performing in musical theater makes me feel alive.* Instead, she decided to tell the truth, to admit she'd always been driven to live up to her father's exceptional talent, to be considered one of the greats. She'd never traded on his name before but was running out of time to catch a break. She just needed to get this callback, and then she'd earn her spot.

When the loud trill erupted, her heart pirouetted in her chest.

This is it.

She took a sip of warm honey water to settle her voice.

"Hello?"

"Hi, honey. It's Mom."

CHAPTER THIRTEEN

Lissy pulled off her lunch shift apron and decided to treat herself to an afternoon of nail polish and music so she could consider her future. She'd told herself the night before that the time had come to pack it in and leave Broadway behind. But was she really ready to do that? She often turned to her record player to help her think. Music was her balm. It calmed her, gave her a sense of balance when the world spun too fast. She picked out a Janis Ian album, her register a perfect match for Lissy's.

She blew on her nails in between verses, admiring her work. Lissy's mother always marveled that she could paint her own nails—her skill, her patience, her exacting standards about the shape of each nail and the barely visible brushstrokes of the thick lacquer. Of course, her mother's hands were beyond help, dried bits of sculpting clay stuck like cement to her cuticles and in the creases of her knuckles. A proper manicure wouldn't last on her for one day.

By the time Bae reappeared after her callback, Lissy had managed a near-perfect manicure. She was belting out the lyrics to "Stars" while coaxing the ruby red on her fingernails to dry. Lissy hadn't heard the keys jangling in the lock but couldn't miss the familiar thump of Bae's dance bag falling from her shoulder and hitting the floor, out of syncopation with the song.

Lissy waited for Bae to vent. Choreographers could be the cruelest sort. Quick to call out a misstep, they would bark at you to start again, only to declare that if you couldn't get such a simple step right you might as well leave the stage. The humiliation factor was high, even worse than a director's typical midscene interruption: "Thank you, I think we've got what we need." Lissy could usually wedge a sliver of hope into those words—maybe they loved her immediately? Sometimes she made it all the way home before facing the harsh reality of the rejection. She certainly wouldn't miss all the judgment and coming up short.

Bae threw herself onto the couch, her legs splayed out. If her body was exhausted, the message hadn't been relayed to her face.

"That was unreal."

"It went well then?" Lissy turned down the volume. Encouraging stories gave all aspirants a rising tide to enjoy, if only until another rejection sucked it all dry.

"I've never experienced anything like it. The audition mimicked the show. There must have been two hundred dancers to start."

Lissy pictured all those bodies, stretching in the halls, eyeing the competition. Women splayed out in splits, elbows on the floor, trying to stay loose while surreptitiously picking at the edges of their leotards to stop them from slipping into unsightly territory. The men generally danced in something close to street clothes—loose pants with tank tops accentuating taut abs and biceps—but the women bared as much skin as possible without letting anything pop out during ronds de jamb and pirouettes. The shape of a girl's thigh might win an admirer on the casting staff. Perfect cleavage won easy points. And hairdos had to be carefully considered. A ponytail might not fit the part, but finishing a sequence with a bird's nest on your head didn't work either. Bae usually secured her glossy black mane with a small barrette on each side, leaving just enough hair around her ears to add softness to her face. The look ensured no stray locks would fly across her face and block her vision, or worse, destroy the illusion of complete control over every inch of her body.

"The script, have I told you about it? The whole show's about an audition." Bae's words tripped over each other. "We all performed sequences in small groups. Lots of sequences. I mean, first it was jazz, then ballet, then traditional cancan stuff. The choreographer would cull the line, put us in different groups, and ask us to do it all again, which is exactly how the opening number goes. I don't even know if he was the real choreographer or if that part has already been cast."

It wasn't unusual for Bae to describe her auditions in detail, but she normally recounted her failings, how her voice had splintered, how she'd come out of a pirouette too soon and blown it. Today, every word crackled with excitement.

"In the end, there were about forty of us left on the stage when we were finally released. Six hours later! I've gotta get something to drink. Do you want something?" Bae bounced off the couch and brought two Frescas back with her.

"Forty people for how many parts?"

"Eight female, nine male, I think. And then there are a few smaller roles for dancers who only appear in the beginning before getting cut from the show."

Lissy was carefully pulling the tab off the can so as not to nick her nails when the phone rang. Bae's eyes went wide.

"That was fast." Lissy felt the wave of something important curling toward her friend. Why did it put so much pressure on her own chest?

Bae lunged for the phone. Lissy prepared herself to cheer the news, to be gracious, not to let any glimmer of jealousy ruin this moment. She reminded herself that Bae had worked even longer and harder than she had. While Lissy tried to be discriminating about the parts she auditioned for, Bae went after everything, whether it included dance or not. And Bae had pushed aside everything else for this, including college—still a point of contention with her parents—and she was still waiting for her big moment too. Bae deserved this.

No matter how strongly Lissy made these proclamations in her head, though, they did nothing to stop the buildup of tears. Why would watching her friend succeed make her own failure hurt so much more? She hated herself for it.

"It's for you." Bae held the phone out for Lissy, the curly cord stretching to the far side of the couch.

Lissy didn't have her notepad in hand and didn't at all expect what the woman on the other end of the line had to say. She offered a lengthy explanation about taking an extra day to decide on the full callback list for *Happily After Ever*. Lissy struggled to keep track of the specifics given the percussion of her heart. But she heard the important part loud and clear. They wanted to see her again. Tomorrow. Noon. West 44th. *This is it.*

"They want me back for *Happily After Ever*!" Lissy tangled Bae in the cord as she jumped off the couch. "For Melanie! The lead!" A bona fide chance at a part. On Broadway. In a Zimmerman and Gray show. *Holy shit.*

Bae let out a joyful shriek and wrapped her arms around Lissy. They bobbed up and down like twin pogo sticks. Guilt pricked at the edge of Lissy's conscience, her jealousy of moments before drowning in Bae's genuine excitement.

"It's just a callback," Lissy said, a little out of breath. "Just a callback." But her intuition told her this would be her moment. Hard work always produced success for her, and more than four years of auditions in New York was enough.

"I have to prepare! Can you take the dinner shift again tonight?"

The phone clamored again. Bae and Lissy looked at each other. Could they both be on their way at the same time? Now that would be something extraordinary. Lissy watched Bae's face carefully as she nodded her head and thanked the caller. She prepared to be genuinely excited for Bae this time, but Bae's face was hard to read, not obviously elated or disappointed. She moved in what looked like slow motion as she put the receiver back in the cradle. Lissy noticed a slash of red stuck to the contracting spiral of cord.

"They want me back at West 44th too."

"You didn't tell me you tried out for it. When did you even have the time?" Lissy's singular moment had just been rendered ordinary.

"I didn't think it went very well." Bae still looked flustered or confused, like she was trying to swim toward the memory of yesterday's audition through the froth of today's excitement.

Lissy fast-forwarded in her mind, as she often did. She believed visualizing the future not only pushed it closer to happening but helped her to wish for the right things. This could be good. She pictured sharing the stage with Bae, keeping the exact same schedule, rooming together during out-of-town previews. The scene she had long imagined—the spotlight blinding her from everything but the dust particles swirling around her as the audience jumped to their feet—had never included another person, let alone a familiar face. But maybe having Bae beside her would make the experience more fun, more satisfying. She told herself to be generous. Her mother had frequently warned her against becoming the cliché of an only child, unaccustomed to sharing and unwilling to start. She would do better.

"This is great." Lissy hoped she sounded sincere.

"They want me to read for the part of Melanie too."

Lissy's eyes fell to her hands to confirm what she already knew. Her manicure was ruined.

CHAPTER FOURTEEN

Zimmerman and Gray ran parallel auditions for three or four hours each afternoon, one focused on scenes, the other on songs. It became clear by the second day that the book still needed work, and the auditions served a dual purpose for Zimmerman, who honed the story while choosing the best cast for the evolving script. Gray was more precise, his focus squarely on finding the right voices to make his songs soar.

Like most musicals, a few songs immediately stood out as anthems, the ones audiences would forever associate with the show, and all three hovered right in Lissy's range. And whenever Zimmerman handed out an updated version of a scene, it better fit the contours of her performance, which gave her hope in having a chance at the part.

As usual, the lyrics came faster to Lissy than Melanie's lines. The chosen key of a song, the rhythm and flow of the melody, filled each piece with an emotion Lissy embodied as naturally as getting wet by stepping into the ocean. She stood at Gray's piano, sheet music scattered on top, the paper stained with coffee rings, and effortlessly merged the lyrics with the notes flying off the keys.

Transforming a flat, typed page of dialogue into something with breath and life, on the other hand, felt more like trying to squeeze water from driftwood. Zimmerman's method of constant iteration, though, allowed her to help shape the words in some small way, to mold the character into a shell for her to inhabit, exactly what she needed. Belting out lyrics might be her forte, but depth of acting was the real achievement. Throw in solid dance moves, and she would make her mark.

The casting team clearly liked Bae, but luckily for Lissy, they began to favor her for Trudy, Melanie's best friend, which called for a heavy Bronx accent. Somehow Bae pulled it off with ease, but she wasn't pleased.

"Typical. *Asian* and *leading role* don't ever go in the same sentence." Bae took off her shoes and chucked them into the corner.

Lissy wanted to believe directors wouldn't factor such a thing into their decisions, but what else could she say? That Bae's performance didn't cut it? Lissy wasn't sure which was worse.

"Trudy's a great part." Lissy pulled an afghan over her legs.

"But not the lead. Don't worry about it. I'm used to it." Bae went to run a bath.

Auditions continued every day from noon until the casting team decided to shut them down for the day. A handful of actors were asked to stay behind and given quick notes by the casting director, and then asked to either read for a different part or go on their way, usually the latter. Treating actors like actual humans and sharing tips for improvement with those being sent home was integral to the Zimmerman and Gray brand, and it was no small part of the loyalty they engendered with legions of aspirants.

As auditions continued and the number of players dwindled, the final cast started to come into focus around the edges. The role of Melanie was coming down to Lissy and one other actress, a brunette who wore too much blue eye shadow. Bae appeared to be a near lock for Trudy, but Lissy worried she might run out of steam since she was also still trying out for the dance-heavy musical. How she managed auditions for both at the same time, while still handling an occasional shift at the diner, boggled the mind. Bert, a guy with a rough-and-tumble look, was faring well as Sal, the overdeveloped and undermatured sidekick, and JoJo, a wry jokester, transformed herself magically into the demure and wholesome role of Debbie, described in the casting list as "the mother hen." The part would not likely go to anyone else. The talent in the room was impressive. But Lissy found no other actor as compelling as Noah. He was in the running for Cassidy, the male lead—a struggling musician and Melanie's love interest.

Noah slipped into the room every day with a guitar case in hand, his denim shirt rolled up past his elbows, his forearms strong from strumming. He sat quietly, leaving the nervous chatter and pre-audition posturing to others. As unobtrusive as he tried to be, his presence blazed—and Lissy barely noticed anything else. When he sang, his voice carried the resonance of home, a ballad she was meant to share. Of all the wonderful songs in the show, Cassidy and Melanie's duet, "Stay with Me," was the one people would sing to themselves as they left the theater and for days afterward. Her mezzo-soprano and Noah's alto melded so naturally the first time they sang together she could have sworn the song had been written just for them.

"Hey, that was nice," he said as they retreated to the standby room to let the next pair audition. Lissy hadn't heard him say anything other than his lines until then.

"Thanks. You too." She searched around for something else to say to keep him talking. "Do you bring your guitar with you everywhere?"

He still had the strap around his back, as if he were reluctant to put the instrument back in its case. He laughed, and she noticed a dimple on his cheek.

"It's my security blanket and steadiest friend rolled into one."

"We need to find you some better friends." She took an extra moment to appreciate the ebb and flow of blue in his hazel eyes.

Despite how well the duet had gone, the brunette stubbornly reappeared the next day and read more scenes with Noah than Lissy did. She worried she might be relegated to understudy. Not the worst way to break into Broadway, but not the stuff of legends either. She reprimanded herself. Compromise could not enter her thoughts. This was the role for her.

And Noah.

When he asked her if she wanted to grab a drink one afternoon, she readily accepted, ignoring her rule of only eating and drinking at Al's or inside the apartment. New York City was unaffordable otherwise. But each day of auditions could be her last, and if she got cut from the show, she might never see him again.

By nine o'clock they were lounging in his bed, sharing a pizza, and laughing about whether their sexual tension onstage would get better or worse now that they had explored each other thoroughly.

"I say we keep it a secret. No touching in front of anyone unless we're doing a scene. That should make it interesting." Noah's dimple reappeared, and she pulled him back under the sheets.

Later that night, he brought his guitar into the bed. She quipped that the bed wasn't big enough for her and his best friend at the same time, but she fell silent as soon as he began to play. She closed her eyes, swept up by his voice and the soulful chords.

"What's that song?"

"I don't have a name for it yet."

"You wrote that?" She wanted to hear the lyrics all over again.

"Yep. Failed musician, just like in *Happily After Ever*."

Lissy pushed herself up higher against the pillows.

"Not failed, just not discovered yet."

"I don't really know what I'm doing auditioning, to be honest, but the *Village Voice* said the show called for a strong guitarist, so I thought a job like this might tide me over."

Lissy laughed, though part of her wanted to cry. Noah had so much talent, acted circles around her, and might get the lead in a Zimmerman and Gray musical—but it wasn't even what he most wanted.

"Have you ever thought about singing in a band? You have an incredible voice," he said, propping his guitar against the side of the bed.

"Are you offering me a gig?"

"Nope. No girls in my band. But seriously, there's lots of bands looking for good singers. You should give it a shot."

"Are you saying I'm not about to make it on Broadway?"

"I guess I don't get the appeal. Reciting the same lines over and over, singing the same songs in the same way night after night . . . I mean, I'll do it if it pays the bills, but it's nothing like a live concert where the crowd is just as much a part of it as the band. Nothing beats letting the sound evolve by responding to the energy in the room, you know?"

She had experienced the sensation in a small way when she'd sung at the farmers market. Seeing a bobbing head or a full-blown smile in the crowd infused her voice with extra power. Live theater worked differently. The audience was crucial, of course; great actors didn't exist without onlookers who bought what they sold in the moment, and a scene could only be considered moving if it elicited strong emotions. But the audience ultimately played a passive role—validation of the play's existence, judge and jury of its value.

Ironically, live performances were Lissy's least favorite part of theater. She most enjoyed the hard work of cast and crew turning a stack of pages and an empty stage into a coordinated illusion. Dress rehearsal was her favorite, a chance to see the perfectly timed moments in full motion, her castmates collaborating like blind-folded trapeze artists throwing and catching one another out of the air. But opening night brought nothing but anxiety. Every time the curtain rose, Lissy feared the audience would see straight through the façade of her recited lines and collectively gasp as she plummeted and crashed.

"Anyway, I'm just saying you've got the goods for singing."

She appreciated Noah's compliment given his level of talent.

"I suppose I got my first chance in theater because of my voice, that's true. You know how it is in high school, even college. Anyone who can sing gets the big parts. But great acting is something else altogether. To be able disappear into someone else's skin and make an audience believe you are that person. I want to prove I can do that."

"Prove to who?" Noah propped his head on his elbow and brushed his fingers through her hair. Her toes tingled.

The answer to his question would make no sense to anyone, so Lissy kissed him instead and asked him to play her another song. One more and then she would go. She needed sleep.

Given their audition schedules, she and Bae had swapped the lunch shift for the morning breakfast rush at Al's for the week, and Lissy was working all of them so Bae could go to morning tryouts for the dance musical. Whichever one of them got out of Zimmerman and Gray auditions early enough in the afternoon to get back to Queens by four thirty took the evening shift, which was becoming increasingly difficult to pull off. Al's patience was being tested to no end. He'd already made an exception by letting them share the job and work out shifts between them—a payroll complication he didn't appreciate—and he didn't really care that they might be on the brink of something big. He just needed his pancakes and grilled cheeses delivered with speed and a smile, and he regularly reminded them how many other pretty girls would be happy to have the job. If auditions didn't wrap up soon, he'd surely tell them both to take a hike. Worse, if Bae got a part and Lissy didn't, she would quickly have to become a full-time waitress to keep the job. Then she really would have to pack it up and go home.

CHAPTER FIFTEEN

During the second week of auditions, Noah coaxed Lissy to go out to hear live music. She wanted to stretch out on his bed and doze off early, but Noah had other ideas.

"This place reopened over a week ago. We've gotta get there. And tonight, man, these guys are good." Noah hopped down the subway stairs.

"It's called Max what?" Lissy gripped the railing as she tried to keep up.

"Max's Kansas City." He pushed through the turnstile. "You haven't been?"

Lissy hadn't even heard of it. Her nonexistent reserves of money and energy prevented her from going out much at night. Sometimes she scored free or highly discounted tickets to the theater on a night off, but she rationalized those outings as furthering her education.

On the 6 train down to Noah's loft, he told her all about the place, how it was an old-time restaurant and nightclub that served as a home base of sorts for singers like Iggy Pop and Lou Reed. Noah spoke of the place with reverence, like one might describe the Grand Ole Opry. He rattled off the artists who hung out there and band after band that had gotten started on its stage. Among many famous and not-so-famous names, none of them struck a chord with Lissy until he mentioned Joni Mitchell and Emmylou Harris. Lissy thought Joni Mitchell was a masterful songwriter, and she particularly loved Emmylou's duets with Gram Parsons. She started to pay more attention to his excited descriptions.

"Anyway, the Ramones won't go on until at least eleven." Noah hopped up the stairs to the street and walked backward down Bleecker, practically skipping. "First I'm going to make you dinner at my place. And we can even have a nap before we head out."

He winked, and his adorable dimple sealed the deal.

Max's was a world unto itself, each room a mix of crazy art on the walls, cups and bottles scattered on tables, and so many burning cigarettes that the spotlights were nothing more than gray streaks of smoke dead-ending in darkness. The crowd lived by a different set of rules, if there were any at all. Someone dancing on a table or grinding broken glass into the floor barely registered given the spectacle of everyone else. Lissy felt out of place, her ordinary jeans and T-shirt rendered prudish. But none of it mattered once the band came on. She didn't listen to much punk, but watching Noah in that atmosphere was like seeing him for the first time.

He didn't sit down, didn't go to the bar for another drink, and barely moved from his spot near the stage for the two-hour set. He was mesmerized, his eyes either closed in reverence as he listened and soaked in the music, or trained directly on Lissy, looking for the connection they might find in the rhythm. The songs sounded nothing like Noah's, at least the ones he played for her, but his appreciation for the band's artistry, his absorption in the energy of the room, was total.

Back at his place, Noah flumped onto the bed. "Can you imagine anything better than being in a band like that?" Fortunately, his apartment was only a few blocks from Max's, so they got home by three.

"Just one thing," Lissy said, then rolled on top of him.

As the next day of auditions ended, Rudy Gray asked Lissy to stay for a few extra minutes. Thankfully, none of Trudy's scenes had been on the docket, so Bae was taking the dinner shift at Al's, but that did little to quell Lissy's anxiety at being asked to remain behind. It couldn't be good. She shouldn't have stayed up so late the night before.

While the remaining players packed up their things, which took an excruciatingly long time, she stared at her black Capezio shoes. They were standard in the trade, and she hated how the black straps across the tops made her ankles look fat. It was the one physical trait she didn't inherit from her mother—pencil-thin ankles that even made sneakers look elegant. Noah's guitar case appeared at her feet, and she raised her head just enough to meet his eyes, which seemed to say, "Don't give up yet." He rested his hand on her shoulder for a moment—the situation must've been as dire as Lissy feared—before following the rest of the crew out the door.

She wished she could be somewhere else, anywhere else, so she pictured riding her bike down the sandy lane at home. Back there, she often played the game of trying to get through a full stanza of "Unchained Melody" or "My Girl" while she pedaled down the road without a bump or rut causing a hiccup in the song. She would either break out laughing, or on occasion, find she could keep the notes steady all the way to the house, her voice rising above the crunch of pebbles, the maple trees waving their approval.

"I'm going to level with you, Lissy." Rudy jolted her back to the rehearsal room. "Obviously it's come down to you and Tammy for the part. Your voice is perfect for my score, but Hal's not as convinced. He feels your performance is a little guarded. I suppose I see it too."

Lissy braced herself, unsure how this interaction was supposed to go. On the one hand, Rudy Gray, Broadway god, was taking the time to talk to her—by name!—about her performance: what would have been an improbable dream two weeks ago. On the other hand, this was likely a preamble to being sent home. She badly wanted to retain her dignity and not dissolve into a blubbering fool in front of him, but she doubted she could keep it together. The last two weeks had been nothing short of exhilarating, especially singing for this man.

"Hal's willing to go out on a limb here with me if you can show me you can do this. Let's run through the scene right before the duet. No blocking, just the lines." He twirled a chair around and mounted it backward less than a foot away from her. His bare ankles poked out between his jeans and loafers, smooth and the color of caramel. She decided he must be a runner. Everything about him was taut and lean.

"I'm not sure you ever believed in me." He spoke Noah's line, transforming himself into a desperate man on the brink of losing his wife.

They were actually going to do this scene. He was coaching her, not firing her. She dug for the line, for the moment when Melanie roiled with turmoil.

"You know that's not true. I always wanted what was best for you, for us."

Rudy leaned back.

"What were you thinking about just then?"

She was thinking she needed to impress him, needed to fill the ordinary words with emotional depth. But she had tapped into nothing but anxiety.

"Remember, what she says is different from what she feels. We need to see on your face and hear in your voice the anger and despair over everything she gave up for him, the challenge of having barely enough money to survive replaced by the boredom of being married not to a promising musician, but to an office wonk in a dead-end job. She feels the loss of the artist she fell in love with and worries it all may have been her fault."

Lissy nodded her head. She knew all of this. She needed to give herself over to the role.

"Let's keep going."

In the moment before they began again, she pictured the day her grandmother had died. Her mother had crumpled onto the rug, her grief confusing and frightening. Lissy remembered wanting to comfort her but not knowing how, her ineptitude gouging an uncrossable trench of fear and sadness and shame into her heart. She searched for those emotions within herself now and tried to combine them with longing for the man seated in front of her. He cupped the side of her cheek, continuing the scene. A shudder ran up her legs and into her chest.

"Stay with me." His words overflowed with intimacy, desperation.

"What if I've already left?" She maintained his gaze as a charge crackled between them. Everything inside her tightened, a push and pull between wanting to show him how well she could finish the scene—which ended in a passionate kiss—and not wanting to kiss him or worrying she shouldn't . . . she wasn't sure which. But hesitation would lead only to failure. *This is it.*

"Then come back." He leaned in close.

Lissy closed her eyes when their lips met. There was no orchestra to cue the duet, no resounding piano to signal the end of the scene. He kissed her deeply before finally pulling back.

"Okay, that's better. Did you feel it? That's what I needed to see." He pushed off the chair and walked over to the piano.

Lissy felt wobbly, unsure if she had just experienced an acting lesson or something else. Was he telling her what he wanted on more than one level, or was he simply trying to improve her performance?

"Tomorrow's our last day. Hal wants to try a new scene between Melanie and Trudy he just finished. Work on it." He took stapled pages off the piano and handed them to her, then rested his hand on her shoulder. "I'll let Hal know you're my pick, but you need to nail it tomorrow."

Lissy nodded and slipped out from under his grasp.

Lissy read the new pages over at least five times on the subway but couldn't quite absorb them. She was Rudy Gray's pick for the role! He wanted her voice to immortalize his songs as part of Broadway lore. But she couldn't shake the buzzing in her bones from running through the scene with him. Could she chalk it up to adrenaline? Her desperate need to prove herself? The unexpected thrill of performing it with him of all people? Or was it a test of her attraction to him?

She shook her head as she trudged up the steps to her door. No use in overreacting. It all came with the territory. She forced herself to focus. She had work to do to earn the role, to infuse Zimmerman's dialogue with the same kind of energy she brought to Gray's lyrics. She couldn't afford distraction.

She heard her phone ringing from out in the hall as she fumbled with her keys. Once inside, she picked up the receiver.

"Oh, hi, Mom." She dropped her bag to the floor and sat on the couch. "What's wrong?"

Lissy considered how much to say. Her mother was of the opinion that people in show business were ruthless. She decided not to mention anything about the coaching session with Rudy—only that she had one last shot at the part.

"And Noah?"

"I think he'll get the lead, yeah. At least I hope so." She felt a rush of guilt for allowing herself to be drawn in, even for a moment, by the magnetism of Rudy Gray. Enough women fawned over him, and she had no interest in being one of them. But she desperately wanted to play Melanie and wanted to play her opposite Noah. It had to be him.

"Are you being careful?"

"Of course, Mom." Her mother always asked this question. Lissy had been sheepish when her mom proactively took her to an ob-gyn for a diaphragm after she turned sixteen, even though the furthest she'd gotten by then was fumbling around in Jack Newman's jeans. Her mom had probably gotten the idea from one of her younger women's libber friends. But Lissy was grateful for a mother who'd evolved with the times and recognized that Lissy's generation operated differently than her own.

"You're smitten, aren't you?"

Lissy heard her mother smiling on the other end of the phone.

"He's amazing. And what a voice."

"That's what I called you about. I went to the Barn last night. They had a fantastic duo; you would have loved them. Anyway, they announced they're going to start doing open mic nights again. When you come, you should play. You and Noah could sing together, even. Wouldn't that be fun?"

Lissy sometimes wished her mother had other kids to worry about, siblings who could share the burden of her mother's attentions.

"Mom, I just told you I might finally land a starring role. On Broadway. If that happens, I won't be going anywhere for a long time." Lissy immediately regretted the irritation in her voice. But her life would no longer accommodate long stretches at home during the summer.

"I know, honey. But if you don't get it, why don't you come home for a while. Take a break. We can take long walks on the beach, and I'll make you grilled cheese for lunch every day."

Lissy could almost taste her mother's open-faced sandwich of home-made sourdough bread with a roasted tomato and dripping cheddar, always served on a handcrafted blue ceramic plate. The ritual did bring Lissy instant comfort. Her friends thought her a little odd for craving a hot sandwich that needed to be eaten with a fork and knife on a summer day, but Lissy loved it like no other meal.

A sigh escaped Lissy. It would be lovely to slip back into that nonper-formative space, knowing she wouldn't have to do much beyond pulling a few weeds from her mother's raspberry bush bed and Windexing the back door to keep the sea salt from building up on the glass to earn her mom's homemade everything.

Her mother had this way of making life almost annoyingly comfort-able, as if the possibility of Lissy failing terrified her and she would rather her daughter just put her feet up now and relax. As if she saw the disappointment coming and wanted to provide a soft cushion in advance. But Lissy didn't go in much for cushions.

"Wish me luck, Mom. I'll call you as soon as I find out."

CHAPTER SIXTEEN

Lissy got to Al's near the end of the dinner rush. She slipped into a booth in the corner farthest away from the kitchen and Al's sight line. A smattering of customers lingered, but Bae and Carmen, the other waitress on shift, were already pulling receipts out of their aprons and starting to add up their tips.

Lissy played with the flip-top on the sugar dispenser while she waited. She was eager to get started, to take advantage of her leg up on the competition. With the new script in hand, she and Bae could rehearse all night to perfect the scene if needed. The extra work didn't faze Lissy. And tomorrow would be her last chance to show Zimmerman she had the goods to be Melanie.

She was all but certain Noah would get the part of Cassidy. The only competition left was Jake Barnes, a talented performer to be sure, but whenever Lissy read with him she found his performance to be a little campy—nothing close to Noah's easy fluidity with the character. Plus, she had no chemistry whatsoever with Jake. No, Noah would get it. And Bae would be Trudy. Lissy very badly wanted to be the third member of the triad. She shook her head at the wonder of roommates being cast in the same play but refused to believe it couldn't happen.

Lissy'd hit the jackpot when she met Bae in a hallway full of hopefuls auditioning for *Hair*. Bae was hanging up flyers, hoping to find a roommate. If she didn't move into her uncle's rent-controlled apartment within the week, she would lose it. Lissy was in desperate need of permanent housing at the time—sleeping on the couches of employed college friends while flitting from one audition to the next could only last so long—but she worried she would never be able to afford anything that wasn't a hovel. And in walked a fellow actress in need of a roommate with a below-market rent apartment on offer.

Lissy decided that meeting Bae was fated, a sign she should continue the pursuit of her Broadway dream. And on top of finding an almost-affordable place to live, Lissy lucked into making a true friend, someone navigating the same precarious path, someone willing to put aside getting a "real job" for a shot at the stage. Her Vassar friends couldn't quite comprehend such a risk. There was a lot they didn't understand about her.

She never told anyone at Vassar who her father was, even her friends in the theater crowd. Growing up, Lissy never had to think about it. In her hometown, people either knew or didn't. It was neither common knowledge nor a secret, and the fact didn't seem to matter one way or the other. Once she stepped onto the Vassar campus, though, her connection to him weighed on her like an invisible obelisk strapped to her back, equally momentous to acknowledge or ignore whenever she met someone new. Confiding in anyone felt as dangerous as conjuring an ocean liner in the middle of the cafeteria. The potential fallout might be impossible to control. So she stayed silent on the topic.

But she would never forget the night she went with her girlfriends to see *Cabaret* in Poughkeepsie. They all grew up with *The Wizard of Oz* as kids, sitting cross-legged in front of the television every year. Watching Liza Minnelli on a huge screen, not only hitting the high notes like her mother but also strutting around in sequins and fishnets, astounded them. Lissy's friends couldn't stop talking about how Judy Garland's talent had obviously been passed down directly—Liza's stage presence, voice, and gentle vibrato in "Maybe This Time" remarkably reminiscent of her mother's.

"Talent like that does not come from nowhere," Lissy's friend Allison declared. "It's definitely in her blood."

Lissy remembered listening quietly that night, so tempted to tell them that she also carried a second generation of rare talent. But she knew it would sound empty until she had the goods to go with such a major declaration. She first had to rise to a place of distinction on her own, be whispered about as one of the greats before connecting those dots.

Lissy lost touch with most of her college friends after moving in with Bae. Their corporate jobs meant knocking off work after she donned her apron at Al's, and meeting up with them late night was a dumb idea if she wanted to be sharp for an audition the next day. Her friends thought she took life a bit too seriously. Lissy thought they didn't take it seriously enough.

She did enjoy long conversations with Georgia on those rare nights they were both off. Her medical path was proving as grueling as Lissy's climb toward the stage. Lissy found comfort in talking to someone she'd known all her life, who shared the same memories, the same longing to return to the beaches of their childhood whenever their schedules and bank accounts allowed. She and Georgia would never lose that bond.

But Bae quickly became the friend Lissy relied on the most. And they made a good team. Lissy's pragmatism coupled with Bae's blind faith kept the larger dream alive on the many nights rejection followed one or the other of them home. Bae had given up far more than Lissy for the chance at Broadway and was possibly more determined than Lissy not to let the dream slip away. Lissy made it her job to focus on the more practical elements: the best path to getting an Equity card, dance studio fees versus acting lessons, the opportunity to keep a waitressing gig by splitting shifts. Now they were on the brink of making it together—as long as Lissy could prove her worth to Zimmerman.

Bae poured Lissy a cup of tea behind the counter and hurried over to the booth.

"Did you hear?" Bae's face flushed with excitement.

"Hear what?" Did Lissy miss a phone call?

"I got cast! It's one of the smaller roles—a dancer who gets cut after the second scene—but I'll also be the understudy for the part of Connie. Rehearsals start on Monday. Can you believe it?" Bae looked ready to jump onto the red seat and dance across the table.

"Wow. Congrats."

Clearly Bae was on her game, and this other show offered a viable plan B. But she was about to do better than understudy.

"Thank god double auditions are over." Bae rubbed the back of her neck. "And this place. An entire softball team walked in at six. The poor Humphreys came in right on the heels of that massive order. Mrs. Humphrey waited half an hour for her bowl of soup. I won't miss Al's fits of rage, that's for sure! Get me into a bath and into bed."

Bae didn't sound remotely tired. Even her complaints overflowed with energy. A hopeful sign. They needed stamina tonight.

"Listen, Rudy told me tomorrow's the last day of auditions for *Happily*, and Zimmerman has a new scene. You're going to kiss me when you see what I happen to have a copy of in advance." Lissy slid the script across the laminate tabletop, its swirls of tan and white meant to mimic marble.

"Lissy, I just told you I got a part in the other show." Bae didn't touch the stapled pages.

"And you're going to get this one too."

"After all these years? Two?" Bae's voice weirdly mixed disbelief and dread.

"No one else has read for Trudy all week. You're definitely going to get it."

What a godsend that the casting for *Happily* wouldn't be delayed any further. Turning down a part without another firm offer would be hard for anyone to stomach, but a bit part and a spot as understudy couldn't compare to a major role in a Zimmerman and Gray show. One more day, and Bae would have the role in hand.

"I should do the other one. You have no idea how wonderful it is. The music—oh my god, it's amazing. Being involved in any way feels like a once-in-a-lifetime kind of deal. I can't quite believe it."

Lissy smiled. Unlike her own vision of Broadway success, the solo turn in the spotlight, Lissy was certain Bae imagined the entire cast welcoming the thundering applause together, the accolades showered on them equally. Bae didn't think her individual part mattered as much as the success of the whole. It was her job to help Bae see the reality of the thing.

"Trudy's a principal role." Lissy pointed at the pages in front of Bae. "No way you don't take this. That's the goal. To be a principal, right?"

Bae didn't even nod in agreement, which dumbfounded Lissy. No one shrugged off a role like Trudy, and certainly not in a Zimmerman and Gray production. She kept her frustration at bay by reminding herself she almost always won Bae over with sound logic. She would eventually respond to common sense.

"Besides, the writers of the other show are unknowns," Lissy continued. "Do you know what percentage of shows with first-time writers succeed on Broadway? Only 27 percent. That means the show folds 73 percent of the time. So you'll have a job for a couple of months and then be back to working here for scraps. Zimmerman and Gray don't have that problem."

"But Marvin Hamlisch just won multiple Oscars—"

"Music for film is completely different from music for the stage."

"Gotta cash out table nine. I'll be right back." Bae walked toward the counter with a defeated slump in her shoulders rather than the exultant stride of a soon-to-be Broadway star.

Lissy knew Bae loved to dance, but Broadway careers were made by originating characters and ushering them into theatrical history, by being on the stage every night so theatergoers got to know *your* name, not by hoping for someone else to catch a cold so you could be announced by the little slip of paper in the Playbill that made audiences groan with disappointment at the *real* star's absence. Sure, it didn't hurt to have an understudy role to put in your bio for the next audition, but Bae was about to get a major role of her own. She didn't need five more years of waiting in the wings. Lissy couldn't fathom why she would ever consider turning down this opportunity. She had to make sure Bae didn't make a colossal mistake.

When Bae returned to the booth, she kept her gaze tilted toward something in her periphery, reminding Lissy of the day Bae told her she couldn't make rent for the month. Lissy'd immediately signed them both up for triple shifts for the next week, and they pooled their money to pay the landlord. She knew Bae would do the same for her if she ever needed the help. This could be fixed too.

"Okay, here's the thing. I have concerns about *Happily After Ever.* The script is confusing." Bae fidgeted with her apron.

The show had an unorthodox setup, to be sure. It opened with Melanie and Cassidy in their forties, unsatisfied with their lives, considering divorce. Every scene moved backward in time by two or three years, until the final scene showed them in high school, full of dreams. The script still needed some work, but Zimmerman and Gray were known for taking theatrical risks that paid off. No one predicted a show about cults would make it as a musical comedy, but then they created the blockbuster *Manson Mania*. These guys were mavericks, and they had a way of turning almost anything into Broadway gold.

"He's still working on it, obviously." Lissy gestured to the scene Bae still hadn't touched. "He'll figure it out. He always does."

"It probably wouldn't even cross my mind if it was my only choice—"
Lissy's spine stiffened of its own accord.

"I'm sorry, I didn't mean it that way. You'll be great as Melanie. And I'll probably regret not taking the part of Trudy for all my days. It's just that I have a gut feeling about this other show. Did I tell you the entire script is based on an all-night conversation between a group of stage actors?" Bae's face glowed. It sounded dreadful to Lissy. But debating the merits of two scripts, neither of which they'd seen in their entirety, would get her nowhere. She needed another angle.

"I think JoJo will probably get Debbie."

"And?"

"You saw Gray's interview last week in the *Village Voice*, right? He said Broadway has always been too white, and trotting out only one nonwhite actor at a time won't fix the problem. He wants to lead the charge in giving audiences more interesting casts. Isn't that important to you?"

Bae scowled, and Lissy couldn't tell if she'd tipped the scales in the right direction or toppled into dangerous territory.

Anxiety buzzed in her blood, threatening to blur her vision. She needed Bae to audition with her. She wasn't sure she could win over Zimmerman if she read with someone else completely cold. Not to mention how furious he'd be if Bae disappeared after they thought they'd found their Trudy. It would make him even less likely to take a chance on Lissy. Auditions would need to be extended. And Zimmerman and Gray would have more time to find someone they agreed on for Melanie.

"Listen, here's what I think you should do. You said rehearsals start on Monday, right? There's no need to decide right now. Let's do this scene together tomorrow. Find out if you get the part. Wouldn't that be something to brag about? Getting two roles?"

While Bae rarely talked about it, Lissy knew how much her parents' disapproval weighed on her. They fully supported her ballet ambitions when she was a young girl, but when American Ballet Theatre and New York City Ballet turned her down, there were only two acceptable paths for her: working in the family electronics store or college. Where she came from, she explained to Lissy, family came first, always, which meant being useful to her father's business or using education as a bridge to the kind of career that would bring honor to the Kim name. Being a no-name actor with only minor stage credits and no college degree wouldn't cut it. But Lissy imagined landing a named role in a Zimmerman and Gray show might change all that.

"This is a major part, Bae."

"I know. But it wouldn't be right to go back tomorrow if I'm pretty sure I'll—"

"As I said, there's no need to decide now," Lissy interrupted. Her future depended on getting Bae to the audition. Both of their futures. "You've worked your butt off for this. Don't you deserve the choice?"

Bae tilted her head as if to consider the point. Lissy felt the calm of a slack tide, the moment when the ocean momentarily stopped, shifted, and began to pull in the opposite direction. She reached across the table and put her hands over Bae's, looking her straight in the eyes.

"I need you there if I have any chance at this part, Bae. I need to show Zimmerman I can do this. I can't do it without you."

"Okay. I'll get out of here as soon as I can, and we can rehearse at home." Bae stood.

There it was, the tide turning back in her direction. Relief washed over Lissy. Now she just had to stay afloat long enough to survive.

CHAPTER SEVENTEEN

O n the last day of auditions, Lissy flopped into a chair like a flimsy trading card in an unwieldy deck. The twenty or so actors still under consideration nervously paced the edges of the standby room or huddled in small groups on folding chairs, waiting to be called in for different configurations. Lissy and Bae read the new scene together but were dismissed from the room halfway through. Noah sat with Lissy while Bae went back in with Tammy, ostensibly to perform the same one. All the while, Mrs. Magnum—Lissy now knew the name of the woman with the huge glasses—scratched notes on her clipboard and tossed papers around like a general designing an invasion. She had more say in all this than Lissy had originally assumed.

"This is awful." Lissy couldn't stop her heart from tap dancing inside her chest every time the audition room door opened. "How many times do they need to see the same people?"

Noah broke their rule and took her hand in his.

"Whatever happens, stay with me, okay?" He hummed the chorus in her ear.

Lissy leaned her head against his shoulder. The song was custom-made for them, and the idea of him singing it regularly with someone else crushed her. But she adored him for making it clear that his interest in her had nothing to do with her success—whether her star was on the rise or about to sink below the horizon, out of sight.

Mrs. Magnum read the next list of actors to be summoned, twelve in all. Noah and Lissy walked in together and stood beside Bae, who was already inside. Gray handed out sheets of music before sitting down at the upright piano and stubbing out his cigarette in an overflowing ashtray.

"This is a song you haven't seen yet. It's mostly a company number, but there are a few small groupings, a few solo lines. The part I want you to sing is on the top of the page."

Lissy, Noah, and Bae glanced at the headers on each other's sheets of music: Melanie, Cassidy, Trudy. Gray's hands flew across the keys with his usual flair, the opening bars suggesting a bighearted number, possibly the show's finale, called "What's in a Dream?"

They hadn't yet sung as a group—the focus had been on solos and duets until then—and as soon as all twelve voices belted out the first stanza, the uneven spring floor and the rusted edges of the rehearsal mirrors fell away. The space transformed for Lissy into a grand stage, the windows out to 44th Street becoming a proscenium, the metal chairs scattered about the room turning to lush velvet seats. Two stanzas in, Lissy knew the song was another surefire hit. She sang her solo line perfectly, and a full stanza of harmony with Noah came off as if they'd practiced it.

As Gray banged out the final chords, the players were breathless. The collective experience had knit them together in a way Lissy had only previously experienced after weeks of rehearsal with a group—never as a first run-through. This, she supposed, was the power of professional talent.

"That sounded great," Bae whispered to Lissy.

Gray pivoted on the piano bench and nodded at Zimmerman. Zimmerman stood.

"We have a few things to cover with you. First, the good news. This is the cast of our show." He allowed his face to break into a grin for the first time since auditions began.

Lissy's hand flew up to her mouth as Noah wrapped her in a hug. There were wild whoops and cheers, kisses and handshakes and hugs between people who barely knew each other. Gray and Zimmerman looked on with pride, knowing they were adding the most important ingredient to the ink on the page: the people who would make Zimmerman's characters real and cement Gray's songs in the hearts of audiences for years. They had constructed another company of players to deliver their next groundbreaking show.

"Listen up." Gray raised his voice just enough to be heard above the racket. "I know I speak for Hal when I say that we are thrilled to be working with all of you. A few quick things. Mrs. Magnum has contracts for you to sign. Pick yours up before you leave, and please return it by Friday. Rehearsals will begin one week from today. Previews start ten weeks later. Plan on full days, sometimes nights also. We trust you will organize your lives accordingly. We expect two things: for you to work your tails off and be kind to each other. You're going to be spending a lot of time together, and as you all know, the unity of the cast can make or break any show. Oh, and please, no dating."

Nervous laughter rippled through the room. Lissy glanced at Noah.

"I know, I know. But I'm serious. It's such a cliché, and it never turns out well. Trust me. Hal?"

Zimmerman adjusted his glasses and clasped his hands behind his back.

"You're part of our youngest cast ever—important, obviously, to the conceit of the show, and we're certain you're up to the challenge. We're going to create something magical together. Mrs. Magnum will give you each a copy of the script along with your contract, but it's not in final form yet. So spend the next week thinking more about the internals of your character than memorizing lines. I plan to have the book ready on our first day of rehearsals. We'll do a full table reading then. That's it. You all have your marching orders. Congratulations, and we'll see you back here in a week."

More hoots and claps filled the air as the reality of it all sank in. Bae looked shell-shocked, the chaotic hugging and cheering happening around her, her tiny frame unmoving. Lissy squeezed her with delight before JoJo came over and offered high fives. Lissy reveled in looking at the assembled group. They would become like family over the next three months—Lissy's favorite outgrowth of any production. Strong hands fell on the back of her shoulders, and she was about to remind Noah to at least attempt to keep their relationship quiet when she turned to find Rudy Gray pulling her into a hug.

"I knew you could do it." He shook her a little after kissing her cheek, winked, and walked toward Noah with an outstretched hand.

Lissy stood motionless, like she did whenever an express train hurtled through a station without stopping, the violent rush of metal sucking all the wind in the tunnel with it, threatening to snatch her off the platform. But as she watched him greet her fellow castmates—she had castmates!—the shine of him returned, the glitter of success, and she knew she would never turn down a chance to hitch herself to his Broadway train.

"Let's celebrate." Bert, the boyish one with curly blond hair, went group to group with his invitation. "Beers at the Clover?"

"Sounds good." Lissy spotted Bae across the room changing her shoes, her head down, positioned to avoid any more celebratory gestures. She started toward her when she heard Zimmerman's voice behind her.

"Congratulations, Lissy."

She turned to face him. "Thank you so much for the opportunity." She still couldn't quite believe she was going to spend the next who-knew-how-many months with this man as her director!

"I'm a huge fan of your father's work. I figured, if you can bring one ounce of his genius to this show, you'll be terrific." He patted her shoulder and turned away.

Heat rushed to Lissy's face, and she quickly smiled to cover it, relieved no one else was close enough to hear the comment. She'd entirely forgotten about including her father's name in her bio. Sure, she figured at the time it might help her stand out among the throngs of hopefuls, adding a little stardust to their first impression of her. But after hours and hours of evaluating a narrower and narrower set of actors, getting to know their quirks, and settling into their strengths, a detail like that would never influence their final casting decision, would it? She heard her mother's voice in her head, her insistence that people did strange things when they associated you with fame, that it made it hard to know what was real and what was gratuitous. The edges of Lissy's elation blurred with confusion.

"Game to go to the Clover with everyone?" Noah bumped her shoulder playfully.

"Let me just make sure Bae's coming."

Lissy stood in front of Bae as she stuffed her dance shoes into her bag.

"Coming to the bar?"

"Thanks, but one of us has to take the shift tonight."

"What's Al going to do, fire us? Seriously, we're going to quit anyhow. Let's go celebrate."

"You go ahead. Working the shift will help me think."

"What's there to think about? Come on, let's cut loose a little. It's going to be intense once we get started on the show."

Bae didn't move.

Lissy lowered her voice. "You're not still seriously considering taking the other job, are you?"

When Bae said nothing, Lissy couldn't help herself. "Those other guys will understand why you had to turn down their offer for this. But no one turns down a principal role with Zimmerman and Gray. You'd have a target on your back in every future casting call if you did. You do know that, right?" *Bae must have understood that when she agreed to come today*, Lissy thought.

Once Bae allowed herself to enjoy the celebration and the bonding that would begin at this first gathering—comparing audition jitters and prior rejections was so much more fun with a job in hand—she wouldn't question her choice. Maybe she'd realize there had only ever been one choice to make. This was their future, starting now.

"We'll call Al from the bar," Lissy said.

Ten minutes later, the cast strolled down 7th Avenue in small clusters, heading toward the tavern. Lissy was tempted to break into a run. She was going to be the star of a musical. On Broadway. A Zimmerman and Gray show. *This is really it!*

"Does art imitate life, or life imitate art?" Lissy linked her right arm with Bae's and entwined her left hand in Noah's. "I still can't believe I get to do this with you two."

"Doesn't this show end with unfulfilled dreams?" Bae asked.

"BaeJin Kim. Hal Zimmerman and Rudy Gray just handed you the keys to the kingdom of Broadway. What could possibly be unfulfilling about that?"

"Not to mention a steady paycheck," Noah said.

Lissy would have taken this job for free.

She didn't notice the man on the corner until he'd bumped into Bae and shoved a flyer in her face. "You three look cozy. Come on in. Hot girls. Asian bang-bang. Best show in town."

Lissy held her breath for a step or two, trying not the let the man's sour smell invade her nostrils. She pulled Noah and Bae in closer and forced herself to look past the grimy storefronts and clumps of litter hugging every curb. She peered at the thin streak of sky she could see between the buildings and reminded herself that no one came to Times Square for the atmosphere. They came for the dreamscapes found inside its hallowed theaters, for a release from reality and a connection to something better imagined than the world around them. And now she would be part of creating exactly that.

She raised her arms and twirled away from her friends, picturing just how fantastic life was about to be.

"Watch it." Noah pulled her back onto the curb right before a taxi barreled past.

1950
LOS ANGELES

CHAPTER EIGHTEEN

Everything about the home Aster shared with Fernando and Benny—she'd stopped calling him Christopher as soon as they'd announced their engagement—looked more like a movie set than a real home, with its slick white couches and the wall of sliding doors leading out to an impossibly beautiful pool. Palm trees stood at attention on all sides of the lawn, waving their fronds like cheerleaders waiting for the star quarterback to take the field.

Despite its movie-star veneer, it was a happy home, a place where Aster had enjoyed the last two years, the second of those immersed in the fog of motherhood and trying to learn the secret language behind each of her daughter's squawks and coos. She'd created soft places in every marbleized room and spent hours each day bicycling Lissy's chubby legs, making her giggle with raspberry explosions in the palms of her hands.

Thankfully, at the tender age of one, Lissy was immune to the extravagances—the fireplace mosaic imported from Sicily, the champagne flutes designed by Baccarat, the shiny rugs skinned from Kenyan beasts. Her world encompassed whatever she could grasp, most often her mother's soft cheeks or a spoon of oatmeal held out to her lips. She shrieked with delight whenever the cool of the lawn touched her toes, and she liked to raise her fist toward the sky as they lay on their backs in the grass, punching the shapes of bunnies and dogs into the clouds. Aster adored nothing more, though, than the look of wonder on Lissy's face when she was lowered into the crystal blue of the glorious pool. Mother and daughter would sit for full afternoons on the wide white steps of the shallow end, Lissy slapping the water at her feet while Aster held onto her scrumptious belly, making sure she didn't tip over.

Lissy's favorite game, though, was being passed back and forth between the arms of her bouncing mama and Fernando's steady hands, bobbing in and out of the water up to her shoulders, watching the primary colors of her life dip in and out of view. Such a simple game, played most evenings, and for hours on Sundays—whenever the sun was up and Fernando wasn't at work, which wasn't as often as anyone would have liked.

After Aster sang Lissy to sleep each night, she would join Fernando and Benny for a cocktail and then sit with them for a proper meal for three. Nothing extravagant—both men watched their figures almost as much as Aster had during her modeling days—but enough to give them time to share important news of the day: Fernando's fitting with a Getty, the latest script change to *Falcon Rising*, Lissy's new penchant for smushed bananas.

By now Christopher Page's star was firmly etched into the firmament of Hollywood. *Man in the Crowd*, *Moonlight Sonata*, and *The Last Tycoon* all smashed box office records. *Falcon Rising* and *Doll Face* were coming out within the next six months. Everyone thought he would have at least two more Oscar nominations to go with his win for *Moonlight*.

They still protected their secret like spies, but Aster sensed a lessening of the worry in the air with each of his successes. The ghost of anxiety and sadness in Fernando's expressions seemed to be fading. He allowed himself to more actively envision a world in which they wouldn't need to be so guarded. The public could never know the truth, of course, but Christopher Page's value to Galaxy had just about reached that incalculable point of no return. If the studio execs found out now, she felt sure they would perpetrate any charade needed to protect him. And the rest of Hollywood, from the moneymen to the makeup artists, would never alienate a man with his level of star power over something as trivial as his sex life. No small percentage of actors and journeymen might applaud it, hopeful to be afforded the same treatment one day.

Motherhood had so far allowed Aster to escape most of the Hollywood circus swirling outside their door, although it hadn't started out that way. Being introduced to the world as Christopher Page's wife brought a level of interest and intrusion she somehow hadn't considered before making such a drastic decision. At the time, she'd only envisioned their private arrangement, a perfect safety net for all three of them. But that safety net, she understood as soon as their announcement was heralded by the papers, also involved the public at large.

She was renamed Pip Kelly, now Pip Page, to the press. Sam had demanded the name change. "Anything German-sounding isn't such a big hit right now," he said. Benny suggested she choose something she would be comfortable responding to when the press or a stranger wanted her attention. Otherwise, she might come off as aloof.

She chose Pip, her brother's nickname for her. He was the one who'd always advised Aster to have a long-term plan, to think ahead, to take charge of her own life. She wished she hadn't rolled her eyes at his lectures. How she would appreciate his counsel now. She missed everything about him—his teasing, the way he used to chase her into the cold waves at the beach at Avalon, even his overprotection. Every time she heard the name *Pip* it would be a tribute to Teddy, a reminder to keep her eye toward the future.

The elopement created a tsunami of attention for Fernando's, but the dramatic increase in browsing customers didn't translate into sales. Droves of women came solely to get a glimpse of Christopher Page's wife. The typical runway show of four models became an exercise in futility for Shirley, June, and Masie, who increasingly felt in the way, and it rankled Fernando to no end. Aster knew him well enough to detect the slight distortions in his expression each time a group of women cooed over how lucky Aster was to be chosen by "a hunk like him," slathering her with the kind of reverence usually reserved for a bona fide star. It humiliated Aster. She had become an exhibition animal in a crinoline cage, undeserving of any awe or praise.

Within two weeks, Aster quit the business. She didn't have long before she would start to show anyway, but she didn't relish the idea of those many months away from the studio. The girls would manage the rushes without her; someone else would stand in for Lauren Bacall. Most discouragingly, she would lose the daily tutelage of Fernando in motion. His commentary about every alteration he made was a master class in design. Aster would miss all of it. She'd been a key part of the team, and it was difficult to watch it all go on without her, no matter how much it was a situation of her own making.

Of course, the pause in her career coincided with a period in which everyone recognized her, from maître d's to magazine editors to the grocery clerk who never let her wait in line. She did her best to accept the attention gracefully, all while detesting it. She had done nothing to deserve it. She often wondered what those same gawking strangers would make of her if they knew even half of the truth. She began to avoid leaving the house unless absolutely required.

The loneliness of her pregnancy was compounded by isolation from her girlfriends. Shirley was busy modeling all day and had a claim on her time every night, having recently taken up with the owner of the jewelry store across the street from Fernando's. Whenever Shirley suggested a double date—they had an implicit understanding to pretend at all times that Shirley didn't suspect what was going on—Aster feigned pregnancy exhaustion, unwilling to ask Benny to put on any performance in public not required by his job. Aster missed Shirley, her constant encouragement, her certainty that nothing couldn't be solved with a glass of bourbon and a bath.

Aster also found herself missing those simple evenings when she could come home from work and sit with Ria on the back steps of their bungalow. Packing up had been a painful process, with Ria's playful inquiries as to why Aster had never mentioned her relationship with Christopher Page turning toward concern. The more Aster avoided her questioning, the more Ria wanted to know why Aster didn't seem wildly happy. Had she gotten into some kind of trouble? The closer her questions got to some version of reality, the fewer words Aster attempted in reply. Ria finally said, "If you're going to shut me out, there's no point," and left the house. She was right. There was no point. Aster couldn't risk Ria ever knowing the truth.

Despite eventually settling into what became the lifestyle of a recluse, Aster did put in some important appearances as the dutiful wife. After all, the ruse wouldn't hold its luster if the happy couple wasn't seen just enough to satisfy eager gossip reporters and hungry readers. They showed off the emerald engagement ring ("A costume befitting your role, my dear, except you're too wonderful not to have the real thing," Benny told her), and Fernando dressed her to the nines. The press referred to her as the Runway Wife, which was ironic given that the start of her career as a wife was the end of her career on the runway.

The *LA Times* broke the story: "Christopher Page first saw this ravishing beauty in a stunning red dress during a Galaxy fashion show and knew immediately that she was the one for him." With only an innocuous reference to the fact that she'd been seen out on the town before with a studio executive or two, the paper claimed that "as soon as Page laid eyes on her, they were instantly inseparable." Page had gushed to Bruce Garner, who had been dispatched for the exclusive, that they "just couldn't wait to get their life started together," and had quietly eloped. After making this pronouncement he gave Aster a made-to-be-photographed passionate kiss, the flashbulb glamorously popping as he held her face in his hands. His impeccable acting made the kiss look very real, and it almost could have fooled Aster. She worried she was betraying Fernando somehow in these moments. As much as they had all agreed to the plan, she imagined it was hard for him not to feel discarded every time she and Christopher Page were trotted out for public consumption.

She was perhaps most surprised by the reaction of her parents. She fretted for days that they would wonder why she had made no mention of the relationship earlier, be suspicious about the decision to elope, or be angry at being left out of such a major milestone in their daughter's life. Figuring it would be better to play the giddy young bride rather than offer too much unnecessary explanation, she sent the article from the *Times* to them along with a simple note that said, "I know you'll think this is sudden, but Christopher is a wonderful man. We're very happy."

Aster's mother phoned her at Fernando's before the letter even arrived, breathless and giddy.

"I went to the picture show last night with Betty and saw you in the newsreel. I practically leapt out of my seat. How adorable that he calls you Pip, darling. The people sitting around us could hardly believe that was my girl on the screen. Oh, Aster, you've really made something of yourself after all!"

Aster had never felt more invisible.

A week later, Aster received a package, a wedding gift, from her mother. As soon as Aster felt the weight of it, she knew it was her mother's prized crystal vase. On good days, Aster's mother would fill it with fresh flowers and speak to her about the importance of family heirlooms, that it wasn't so much about the quantity of items one owned as it was about cherishing something of meaning and value. On her bad days, she invoked the vase as the kind of thing she should have been showered with on her wedding day, if only she hadn't married an ironworker. She ranted that she deserved settings of china and silver and crystal wineglasses. Instead, she would be eating off simple ceramic with tin forks the rest of her life.

"For a life befitting Hollywood royalty. We are so proud," the note said. Aster had finally won her mother's approval for something that was pure illusion. She packed the vase back up and stored it in her bedroom closet.

Three months after their elopement, Aster appreciated being able to pour authentic emotion into a letter home announcing her pregnancy. She told them about the deep attachment she already felt to the baby and how excited she was to welcome this little life into the world. She warned them not to be worried if they read anything in the papers about it being a difficult pregnancy. She simply intended to preserve as much of her energy as possible and needed the press not to badger them about her reduced public appearances. In reality, she felt more energetic than ever, but she didn't have the acting chops to make convincing small talk with other Hollywood wives at cocktail parties.

She did, however, attend three different movie premieres, as not appearing would have raised questions. Fernando made special gowns that flattered her growing belly and her rosier-than-normal complexion. He took his usual pride in the work, but she could tell how much the outings pained him. Fernando was the one who should have been at

Benny's side, beaming at his partner's performances. And he certainly deserved to enjoy a close-up of the red carpet ablaze with his own gorgeous creations. Instead, he heard about it all secondhand, and would only ever see the spectacle in miniature on the printed page.

After the premiere of *Moonlight Sonata*, Fernando was waiting for them when they got home. Aster had barely taken off her stole before he began asking about the details of the night—who had come, what they thought about the movie, how Laraine Day looked in Fernando's sequin gown. As Aster took her heels off to free her pinched toes, a deep weariness coursed through her. Never before had standing on her feet been so exhausting. But as tired as she was, she would stay up as late as necessary to tell Fernando every detail.

"Can Aster fill you in tomorrow, love? I'm bushed," Benny said, beckoning Fernando toward their bedroom. He was always more exhausted by public performances than by whole days on the set. He admitted it was much easier to play a character when everyone knew that was what he was doing.

"The sequins on Laraine's dress rivaled the chandeliers," Aster said, giving Fernando at least one important detail of the night. Then she retreated to the other side of the house and fell gratefully into bed.

On other nights, the three of them would stay up dancing together. Fernando would put "Tuxedo Junction" or "King Porter Stomp" on the record player, and the two men would take turns spinning Aster around the room, laughing at how her growing bump changed her center of gravity. Aster would eventually plop down on the couch and watch her friends fall into a slow sway together as "It's Always You" crackled through the speakers. She adored watching them, imagining the glow of their love infusing her unborn child with something magical, much like she believed happy words filled the womb with positive thoughts.

On a cloudless night in March, Bella Tivoli Horowitz finally arrived—two weeks late, but an entire month early as far as the press was concerned. Aster was immediately smitten. So was Fernando. He took one look at her and insisted on calling her "Bellissima," for beautiful—which everyone else quickly shortened to Lissy. After months of playing the part of wife, Aster discovered in an instant that Lissy tethered her to reality, introduced her to a level of unconditional love unlike anything she had ever experienced. It softened all she had lost.

Her long and brutal labor had ended with bleeding that couldn't be controlled. At the hospital the doctor told Benny, ever playing the part of the doting husband, that Aster had needed an emergency hysterectomy to save her life. It was Fernando who gently broke the news to Aster. Welcoming this new baby and navigating the intricacies of motherhood while trying to comprehend the loss of the very thing that had rendered her Lissy's mother was overwhelming. The only way Aster knew to survive it all was to dive headlong into life with Lissy. Thankfully, she found she didn't want to be anywhere else. Hours would race by in a day that Aster couldn't account for later, other than to recount how Lissy learned to make bubbles from her own spittle or discovered her big toe and gripped it like the rudder of a boat.

Fernando and Benny were like loving uncles who couldn't get enough of the littlest member the household. Fernando doted on her. He brought home bolts of cozy fabrics, encouraging Aster to sew blankets or little jumpers for Lissy. Aster wasn't sure if his goal was outfitting Lissy with lovely things or making sure Aster didn't lose her interest in creating. She guessed it was both. But as much as she tried, anything overly complicated left Aster in a tangle, and she ended up converting more than one attempt at a jumper into a soft rag doll instead. As soon as Lissy started to walk, she rarely pushed off without one of the fuzzy creatures in her grip. Aster did manage to produce one perfect blanket, a double-ply pink flannel square with three daisies embroidered on the edge. When Lissy slept on her back, her chubby fists unfurled to the sky on either side of her head, Aster would tuck the blanket around her and imagine those flowers as the three adults who would always keep her safe.

≈

The three of them settled into a steady rhythm after Lissy was born. Fernando came to the house as soon as he closed the boutique each day. It never took him long to jump in the pool with Lissy, bouncing her up and down the length of it to her unbridled delight. By the time Benny arrived, Fernando, Aster, and Lissy were usually bundled in terrycloth, Fernando playing with the baby on the couch while Aster made a round of cocktails.

Benny did most of the cooking, which he said relaxed him after a long day on set. Aster suspected it had more to do with not wanting to make her feel she had to play the part of a wife in private, so she found no need to protest. Besides, he seemed to relish the praise when he made something delicious, particularly if he perfected an Italian dish. Benny beamed when Fernando pronounced his chicken piccata better than his own nana's and declared his cacio e pepe as good as any Roman restaurant's.

In many ways, the arrangement was ideal. The three adults were well-suited roommates, the men helping Aster with Lissy as much as possible, Fernando and Benny grateful for every day they could be together under the cover of their ruse. A friendship blossomed between them all that felt essential to Aster. They easily shared the small details of everyday life—Benny's frustration with the director of his latest film, or Fernando's excitement about a new silk from India—to more difficult issues, such as a report from Aster's father that her mother had gone missing again, or Fernando's parents ignoring yet another birthday.

Aster remained attentive to the fact that she was the interloper. She would sometimes pad back into the living room after checking on Lissy to find Fernando and Benny holding hands on the couch, deep in a whispered conversation, their foreheads touching or Fernando stroking Benny's cheek. She would retreat as quietly as possible and slip onto the side terrace to watch the palm trees sway in front of the moon or return to her bedroom to read. She was always grateful when she managed to sneak away unnoticed by them, having successfully preserved the sanctity of their personal moment. But it did have a way of throwing her situation into stark relief—the perfectly tucked sheets on the other side of her bed, the empty patio chair beside her. The lack of her own partner to love became its own presence in the house.

She wondered more than once if she'd made a mistake in not at least trying to make things work with Sam, and if she'd made a huge moral misstep by hiding Lissy from him. But she didn't have it in her to pretend she wanted to make a lifelong commitment to Sam. The arrangement with Benny and Fernando, by contrast, was temporary, and while it was based on a lie, she wasn't lying to any of the people involved.

More often than not on those lonely evenings, her thoughts turned to Graham and the relationship she had willingly left behind in New York. She realized now how much first love could be taken for granted, how often it was assumed to be a fleeting experience likely to be supplanted by another of greater import. But she could think of nothing lacking in that relationship—and no one she would rather sit with on that patio, watching the rippled reflection of the palms in the pool.

In those moments, she would gaze at the ring Benny had given her, a three-karat emerald flanked by glittering diamonds, and remind herself to appreciate all she did have in her life. The ring was gorgeous in its own right, but she adored it because it symbolized the relationship the three of them had knowingly formed, a deeply important partnership that moved well beyond convenience. Unlike so many gems that attempted to place a claim on a person, this was about mutual independence. They'd made the active decision to support the lives they each authentically wanted, willfully ignoring the confines of what society at large thought best. They were bound to each other by that choice in ways most people would never understand.

And watching Fernando and Benny's relationship evolve taught Aster something about love—how complex it is, how strong it needs to be to overcome inevitable challenges. The one argument that surfaced regularly was Fernando's desire not to stay hidden away forever. The longer they were together, the more Fernando pressed Benny to commit to eventual retirement from the spotlight—not immediately, but within some reasonable time frame that would allow them to enjoy each other more freely while they were still relatively young men. Whenever Benny cringed at the idea, saying how unrealistic it was, Fernando challenged Benny's willingness to constantly choose inauthenticity, the image of what Hollywood wanted from its leading man over an honest life with him.

"William did it. He quit. He chose Jimmie. He chose love," was one of Fernando's familiar refrains.

William Haines was an A-list actor before his studio delivered him an ultimatum: continue to make movies or continue on with Jimmie Shields. Haines chose the latter. The two had since started an interior design business, and Fernando knew them well. As much as Haines's former costars had lined up to hire the duo to decorate their homes, the press didn't drop the scandal for months. The public couldn't get enough of sneering in disgust, and Haines's movies were relegated to the dustbin. While it was a happy love story in Fernando's eyes, it served as a grim warning to Benny.

"I'm not Bill Haines," was Benny's most common response. Then a door would get slammed, keeping Aster from hearing the remainder of the argument.

Aster knew her presence postponed any real reckoning. Benny could continue to build his filmography while enjoying a homelife that suited him. But she also knew it couldn't last.

⚌

The tenuousness of their situation surfaced all at once on the day Lissy spoke her first word. Fernando beamed when he described the scene to Benny at the dinner table.

It had been a glorious afternoon, and Fernando had jumped into the pool to join Aster and Lissy as soon as he got home. They were playing their usual game—Fernando holding his hands out to Lissy, saying, "Come to Fernando," and Aster saying, "Here we go to Fernando"—when Lissy reached out her chubby arms and said, "Naddo!"

"Isn't that something?" Fernando said at the table. "Our sweet Bellissima picking *Naddo* as her first word!"

Aster had suspected for weeks that Lissy was rolling unformed vowels around in her mouth, getting ready to put them together into something coherent. "Mama," she had hoped for, of course, but Naddo was adorable. A perfect name for her favorite friend. Benny usually cheered Lissy's developmental milestones, but this one left him looking pale.

"What is she going to call me?"

Quiet fell over the table as the reality of it sank in. Lissy would not call him *Daddy.* That wasn't a word used in the house. But what else could she call a man the rest of the world saw as her father?

Aster knew all along, of course, that their days together were numbered, but she thought they'd have more time. The arrangement still benefited all of them greatly. But it was one thing for the three of them to live safely inside the illusion they had created for the rest of the world. Aster had no intention of bringing her daughter in on the scheme. It was understood from the beginning that before Lissy formed lasting attachments, Aster and Benny would divorce, she and Lissy would leave, and Lissy would have no memory of her early days. Aster would become nothing more than a footnote in the life of movie icon Christopher Page, an early but failed marriage. Within a few years, the public would forget she was ever part of the picture. But the longer they waited, the more of Lissy's childhood would need to be essentially erased. The more the world around Lissy came into focus, the more images and words would be cemented in her mind, memories Aster wouldn't be able to explain.

Aster swallowed and excused herself from the table. She quietly closed the door to her room, careful not to wake Lissy, and buried her face in her pillow. She knew it was the beginning of the end.

CHAPTER NINETEEN

"T he only way for this to work is for it to be a bitter divorce." Aster
disliked the words even as she spoke them. "You'll need to have
cheated on me."

She and Benny were sitting in the shade by the side of the pool while
Fernando bounced Lissy in the water. Lissy's predictable glee made
their grim task all the more unbearable. But their plan had worked. In
the nearly two years since they announced their marriage to the world,
Christopher Page had become one of the biggest stars in Hollywood,
his box office receipts eclipsing even the likes of Cary Grant. He and
Fernando had been able to enjoy a relatively normal life, at least inside
their own house. And she had focused on her pregnancy and her baby
without the dark shadow of unwed motherhood or a loveless marriage
hanging over her like a curse. She would now be free to move on with
her life with her beautiful daughter. They had pulled it off.

What she hadn't counted on was how Fernando and Benny would
become her family, and how horrible it would be to lose them. She

dreaded it like an oncoming tornado they all knew would rip through their happy little home.

Without Lissy in the picture, of course, they could have set up an amicable divorce. But the only way to explain to the world, and eventually to Lissy, why Christopher Page wasn't in her life as the doting daddy, was to be estranged, irrevocably.

"We'll have to sow the seeds of a custody battle in the papers. We'll move back to New York, and that will be that." She knew she was oversimplifying.

She wasn't ready to acknowledge the pain of separating from these men she adored, but she understood they needed to snuff the lie burning bright in the center of Lissy's life. Keeping Benny in their lives in any way would only give it more oxygen. And while moving back East made sense on many levels—it would make the lack of interaction between father and daughter even more believable—it meant they would lose Fernando too. Once she was old enough to understand, Lissy would be told that her mother and father were estranged. She would remember nothing of her first year and wouldn't carry it as a loss. They would be secure in a new life by then, surrounded by a new reality based on different relationships— ones they could kindle and tend in the long run. Christopher Page would be nothing more than a figure on a screen, out of reach in daily life.

"Wait," Fernando said. "How will this actually work? Benny becomes a lowlife of a father who doesn't even acknowledge his kid anymore? What does that say to Bellissima?"

Fernando sounded shell-shocked. He hadn't thought much about how this would all unravel either. Benny's face settled into painful resignation, the exhausted expression of someone who'd beaten back a lifetime of chronic pain. His own father had abandoned him as a young boy. And now she was asking him to do the same thing.

"How about Benny sends her a Christmas present every year, and a birthday card?"

"No." The vehemence in her own voice surprised her. "She can't be tugged on every few months, asked to pine for someone who won't be there. It has to be a clean break."

"She's right." Benny's brow furrowed, creating a dark shelf above his eyes. "Hating my father was just about the only way I could cope with the fact that he left us."

Aster watched Lissy happily splash water on Fernando, having no idea they were architecting the blueprint of her life. It pained her to admit how little she'd thought through the undoing of their scheme before she made the snap decision to suggest the marriage. At the time it seemed like the perfect solution to their collective problems. While divorce carried its own stigma, it was by far the lesser of the evils she'd imagined would befall them all.

But back then, Lissy wasn't a whole human. She was a piece of Aster, like a new digit requiring a different set of gloves. Aster had failed to consider the separate person Lissy would become. And now she would grow up with an absent and disinterested father as part of her origin story.

Fernando handed Lissy up to her mother and pulled himself onto the side of the pool. Water puddled where he sat.

"We should wait until *Falcon Rising* comes out. If I'm going to be portrayed as the bad guy here, it wouldn't hurt to have another success under my belt."

"He's right. We might as well get as much as possible out of *Falcon*. That will make eight movies and more money than you know what to do with. Proof you've made your mark." Fernando sounded almost pleased.

"Made my mark? Next you're going to tell me I should be done. Are you satisfied, Fern? Have you made enough dresses? What if I told you

I wanted you to give up designing?" The anger in Benny's voice made Aster wince.

"I would give it up for you. You know I would."

Aster could feel the argument building momentum in the silence that followed. It had become a common refrain in the house—the spoils of Hollywood versus a life of living freely, of loving freely, at least outside the media lens. She wanted to duck away and leave them to work out their future on their own, but she had no right to abandon the conversation. This was of her making too. She wrapped Lissy in a towel and held her tight.

"I just signed with Galaxy for another three years," Benny finally said.

"What? Three years? What are you talking about?" Fernando asked.

"Sam said he'd find me another wife."

Now it was Aster's turn to be shocked. "Sam knows?"

Benny looked confused. "Of course he knows."

Aster's arms tingled with numbness, as if she'd taken a sleeping drug and the world might soon go black. How much did Sam know?

"Another wife?" Fernando jumped up and furiously paced. "You told me when Aster was ready to leave, you'd quit."

Aster didn't know that. Benny had promised to quit? Like William Haines?

"I said I would quit when the time was right. But I don't want to walk away. Not yet."

Fernando sat down next to Benny. He lowered his voice, pleading with him.

"You can't expect to just replicate this situation. It will never work with some stranger. I'd have to hide in our own house. Do you know how exhausting it already is to sneak out before dawn every morning so I'm not seen leaving here? Do you ever think of that?"

"Trust me. There are plenty of women who would do anything for the boost in fame they'd get by marrying Christopher Page." He said his own stage name with contempt. He was tired of the ruse too. He just didn't want to give up his life's work to be rid of it. "The new wife will sign up for whatever we want."

"But this is not what I want. Not even close, and you know it." Fernando stormed into the house and slammed the sliding door behind him, leaving a trail of water in his wake. Benny put his head in his hands.

"How long has Sam known?" Aster was still trying to digest the implications.

Benny looked up again, distress crumpling his features.

"He's always known. His father was the problem."

Anger scorched the back of Aster's throat. She'd questioned her decision to hide Sam's own child from him a thousand times, afraid she'd acted selfishly, immorally. She'd spent hours wondering if she'd had the right to orchestrate the scenario for her benefit, even worried she might have wounded Sam in the process. But maybe she'd simply served up a convenient way for him to protect his most valuable star. Had he actually been relieved to be rid of her? Why did that hurt so much?

Aster hugged Lissy tightly as the edges of the table began to blur, the water in the pool no longer a crisp blue, the person sitting next to her a smudge of color. Nothing felt stable or real. Nothing except Lissy.

"Why didn't you tell me?"

"Tell you what?" Benny strode across the patio. "I need to talk to Fern."

Fernando stopped playing with the baby in the pool. After work, he would instead sit in his full suit in the shade and miserably watch Aster and Lissy splash in the water.

"Naddo!" Lissy would call out every so often, her arms outstretched.

"Not today, my Bellissima. Naddo is tired." He seemed to be preparing himself for the emptiness that would exist after they left.

Their evenings no longer included happy cocktails and leisurely dinners. They spent their time over the next week working out the terms of the divorce they would ask the studio lawyer to formalize, the story that would be told. The more the plan solidified, the more somber the house became.

"It's going to be Lana Hope," Benny said as he walked into the house one night. "Sam says she agreed to it."

"Do I even get a say in this?" Fernando asked.

Lana Hope starred with Benny in *The Last Tycoon*. Benny complained about working with her, and tensions on the set ran high. But the movie did well and earned her top billing in two more, including *Falcon Rising*. Her career was decidedly on the rise.

"She doesn't need a high-profile marriage." Aster felt oddly defensive for Lana, or maybe she was just angry with Sam. What made him think his newest star needed a famous husband to succeed? But mostly she was furious for Fernando, for the insanity of his having to live this way.

"She has her own reasons." Benny let the unsaid say it all—why Christopher Page's trademark charm hadn't worked to spark the kind of chemistry he normally created on set. But they'd fooled the cameras, both of them. And the public loved an affair between two lead actors. Not to mention the extra boon the studio gained from heightened interest in their newest film. The timing was perfect. Sam was a marketing master.

The idea of Benny marrying a recognizable star did carry some amount of relief for Aster. The news would allow her to fade that much faster into the background, to be dismissed as nothing more than Christopher Page's starter wife, the one he naïvely picked before his own fame rose to epic heights.

"I'm going to head home." Fernando stood. "I have a big day tomorrow."

Aster couldn't remember him ever leaving before the wee hours of the morning. Aster and Benny were rarely in the house alone together, making Fernando's absence all the more acute.

Benny quietly sliced the roasted chicken he had prepared with garlic and rosemary, one third left miserably on the butcher block. He plated the meat with sautéed spinach and absentmindedly drizzled red currant sauce over both before sitting down with Aster. Fernando's empty place setting glared at them. Aster took a few bites but had no enthusiasm for chewing, for swallowing. Benny stared at his plate and didn't even make an attempt. Eventually he threw down his napkin, pushed back his chair with a mumbled apology, and walked out to the patio.

Aster cleared the table to give him a minute, then joined him outside.

"I'm ruining his life." He leaned forward with his elbows on his knees.

Aster rubbed his back. She worried about the same thing sometimes herself. Not that Benny was intentionally trying to hurt Fernando, but the situation felt untenable.

"He knows how much you love him. That has to be what matters most."

Benny looked unconvinced.

With nothing left to say, they padded off into their separate bedrooms, like any couple on the brink of divorce.

As they tried to sort out the exact timing of the "scandal," Benny grew more agitated by the day. Sometimes he insisted on particular details regarding the divorce. At other times, he questioned if the details mattered at all. He often seemed anxious, unable to find calm in his cooking routines. He even let a temper flare that Aster had never seen before, snapping at her for leaving Lissy's toys underfoot or suggesting Fernando hadn't tailored one of his suits correctly. The mosaic of their life together began to crumble into disconnected shards, and it broke Aster's heart.

On one of their last evenings before the rumors would be planted with the press, Benny was working late, wrapping up shooting for *Tycoon*. After putting Lissy down, Aster joined Fernando on the patio. She took his hand as they watched the moon rise between the trees.

"I'm going to miss you." Her voice cracked. She briefly imagined an alternate world, one in which she'd kept her head down as Fernando's anonymous young apprentice, worked hard to apply his teachings, and eventually mastered the craft. She opened that sister boutique beside his, and they remained lifelong friends. Her choices had made that vision impossible.

"I've been thinking. Why don't you stay here? You and I were pals before all of this. There's no reason why I couldn't pop over and visit you two. I could still be Bellissima's Naddo, watch her grow up."

A knot tightened in Aster's heart, threatening to squeeze out tears.

"I'm going to apply to Parsons." It was the best design school she knew of, and she still had some friends in New York, including Greta.

There was one enormous downside to moving back East, of course. She would be back under the storm cloud of her mother's constant disapproval. Once she found out about the divorce, including the fact that Aster's movie star husband had cheated on her, her mother's scorn would be profound. As much as Aster had hated finally winning her mother's approval for something fake, she dreaded the additional layer of disappointment her divorce would create. Her mother would now see her only as the woman Christopher Page tossed aside, the woman who couldn't even hold her husband's attention, an embarrassment.

"Have I ever really thanked you?" Fernando squeezed her hand, still laced in his. "This has all been *la roba dei sogni*."

"I owe you the same thanks." She let her head fall onto his shoulder, like old times. He had thanked her many times before, and every time he used that phrase to describe their unusual life together: *la roba dei sogni*, the stuff of dreams.

Just as Aster's eyes began to droop, Benny clattered through the front door. He raised his voice toward the open sliding doors to the patio.

"Lana says she'll only do it if I move to her house in Malibu." His car keys missed the edge of the hall table, and his steps toward them wavered.

"Obviously that won't work," Fernando said.

Driving to his apartment from Malibu every morning would add at least thirty minutes to Fernando's predawn routine. But the problem far exceeded extra lost hours of sleep. Fernando might feel like an uninvited—maybe even unwanted—guest in someone else's house.

"I told them it was okay by me." Benny flopped onto a lounge chair.

"Are you kidding?" Fernando's voice trembled. "Where am I in this?"

"It'll be fine. Don't make a big deal of it." Benny rubbed his face.

"Have you been drinking?" Fernando asked.

While they shared cocktails every night, Aster had never seen Benny overindulge. He was a consummate professional who needed to be sharp on the set every day. Even when he didn't have a shoot, he rarely had more than two drinks. This was a different person.

"You don't run my life," Benny mumbled.

"And I don't know what makes you think you can run mine." Fernando was already out of his chair. Moments later, the front door slammed behind him, the second such exit in less than a week.

The idea of this couple disintegrating before her eyes pained Aster to her core. And she struggled to shake the worry that it was all somehow her fault. She had actually congratulated herself more than once for giving Fernando and Benny a chance to be together. But her leaving seemed to now be their undoing. Their blissful two years as a trio made the tearing apart of what they had created so much harder to bear.

"I have to go after him." Benny pushed himself off the chair and caught his balance.

"No." Aster stood with him. "You shouldn't drive."

"If I don't, I might lose him forever. Love has to matter most, right?" Benny strode toward the door. His determination blazed, and she tried to calculate if she should convince him not to go at all, or to find another way to get there. She would have driven him herself, but she couldn't leave Lissy in the house alone. He could call a cab, but that carried its own risks. Someone like Christopher Page calling a taxi near midnight wouldn't go unnoticed. She decided to try to talk him out of it altogether.

"Wait until morning. It's so late. Nothing good will come of an argument at this hour."

He wasn't listening. He scooped the keys off the floor and stumbled out the door. She begged him not to go, her words bouncing off his back as she followed him out to the driveway. He surprised her by wheeling around and pulling her into a hug.

"I'm so sorry for all of it." He sounded desperate, like a man about to jump off a tall building.

She clutched him, breathing in the familiar pomade on his hair, the hint of cologne that still lingered on his jacket. She tried to hold on long enough for him to calm down and think better of leaving, but her grip couldn't contain him. He peeled her off and folded himself into the driver's seat. She rushed to the side of the car, pleading with him to stay home, telling him it would work itself out, that Fernando would be back. Then she watched with horror as he skidded down the driveway, the wheels of the car screeching, leaving behind a trail of smoke.

✦

The call came at 3:45 in the morning. Aster hadn't slept. For the last four hours, she'd listened to the night sounds around the house, waiting for Benny and Fernando's return. She clung to every distant bark of a dog or whoosh of air against the windows as a hopeful precursor to the rumble of Fernando's car, the happy noises of the couple banging through the front door, back home, safe. Each time, as the gust of wind abated and the driveway remained empty, she told herself that Benny was simply at Fernando's apartment. Of course they would stay there for the night. They had made up, and the worst that would come of it would be the challenge of sneaking Benny out in the morning, and the awful day on set he would suffer while nursing a hangover. But she never managed to hold onto the invented relief for long, instead returning each time to her vigil of listening and waiting and worrying.

When the trill of the phone shattered the silence, Aster snatched the receiver off its cradle to stop the noise but couldn't bring herself to raise the cold plastic to her ear. She wasn't ready. She wanted the silence back. If she could just go on waiting until the sun came up, it would erase the dark dread in her heart. The warmth of her life would return, everyone would be fine, everything could be fixed.

"Aster? Are you there?" The caller's voice was muffled.

Reluctantly she raised the receiver.

"I'm here."

"It's Sam. There's been a terrible accident."

Aster began to shake uncontrollably. *Please no. Please say he'll be all right.*

"Christopher's dead."

She wanted to throw the phone across the room, away from her, but she couldn't move. Her breath escaped her body entirely, her lungs no longer functioning. She mouthed the air for oxygen. It couldn't be. It just couldn't be.

"Listen, the press is going to swarm your house tomorrow. They'll want a glimpse of you and the baby. There will be no talk of divorce, all right? You're a grieving widow now."

A widow? What about Fernando? What was he? His life as he knew it had just ended too—crumpled, destroyed.

"Aster? Are you hearing me?"

Aster hung up the phone and fell to her knees beside the couch. Sobs erupted from her, animallike sounds that frightened her. Her head swarmed with visions of Fernando and Benny holding hands, whispering cheek to cheek, Benny proudly donning one of Fernando's suits and mimicking Aster's runway walks, Fernando beaming as he read out loud the review of Benny's performance in *Moonlight Sonata*, the way they looked at each other with so much love.

He was gone. It was all gone.

The whole world would hear the news by daybreak, the grim details crackling over the radio—collective gasps spreading across factory floors, department store makeup counters, college campuses, and rural sewing circles. But there was one person who couldn't learn of it that way. Aster had to be the one to tell Fernando.

CHAPTER TWENTY

The week after Benny died blurred into a jumble of logistics and phone calls and visitors Aster could barely remember. She wanted only to comfort Fernando but hadn't been able to see him since that first horrific night. She would never in her life forget the devastation she'd wrought when she told him the news, a memory so painful she locked it away deep in the recesses of her heart. Since then, she'd moved through each day in a state of complete numbness, afraid that going anywhere near the sharp knife of grief would rip open a portal to that moment and bury her.

The only emotion Aster allowed herself to access entirely was anger—a growing fury at Sam, bordering on hatred, for his cold and calculated approach to the whole situation. Benny was a person who had died, a person Sam worked closely with, and yet he orchestrated the fallout like a PR exercise. He kept talking about Christopher Page's legacy, about Aster's need to show her grief, how she needed to give

Christopher's fans something to hold onto. Did he not realize how real her grief was? And how little she cared about all the strangers out there who idolized the manufactured version of him up on the screen? They knew nothing of Benny, of his gentleness, his longing to be accepted, his lifelong battle to conceal his real being—all to please them, so they would swoon over the kind of man they thought he should be. They didn't deserve anything else from him.

But she went through the motions, not for Sam or for Galaxy, but because she wanted to mourn Benny properly, because he deserved it. And she did it all for Fernando, the man who couldn't outwardly share his devastation with the world. He wasn't allowed to sit in the first row at the service and let tears fall without constraint. It wasn't his cheek stranger after stranger brushed with a kiss to express how much they adored Christopher—how wonderful he was on set, how generous toward the crew. He wasn't the one invited to place the final mound of dirt on the coffin before it sank into the earth.

Instead, Fernando went through his own motions. He kept his shop open, he zipped up his models, he poured champagne for his guests. But Shirley said he was a ghost of himself, wandering through the boutique like a person who could barely hold up the suit hanging from his shoulders. When talk among the customers inevitably turned to the horror of the accident—the disbelief that a car could so completely disintegrate and then the rumors about Christopher Page's heavy drinking—Fernando would excuse himself and slip out the back door. Shirley said she found him in the alley more than once holding an unlit cigarette, staring at nothing, like a man who'd forgotten where he was.

A few days after the service, Aster finally managed to get to Fernando's unnoticed. At closing time, she let herself in through the back door with her key. When the other girls saw her, they cleared the room and locked the front to allow her to be with him alone.

He fell into her and wept. She held him tightly, this time not as the grim reaper, bringing the news that would alter his life forever, but as the only friend who truly understood what he had lost, the lone witness to a deep and abiding love now gone. There were no words to speak, nothing to do other than try to hold some small part of his bottomless grief.

❧

In his only show of decorum, Sam waited a full week after Benny's funeral to summon Aster to Galaxy to clarify legal arrangements. Outside of premieres and awards ceremonies—crowded affairs that made it easy enough to avoid him—she hadn't been in a room with Sam since the day she and Benny announced their decision to wed two years earlier, the day Sam so quickly dismissed her from his life. She considered what she had learned since then. He knew the marriage was a ruse all along and hadn't even tried to dissuade her. He'd chosen the value of his business over any feelings he may have had for her. She was never gladder not to have shared Lissy with him. He didn't deserve her.

She was further annoyed that the press had served up a photograph of her daughter to the public. In her numb state, Aster had failed to properly shield Lissy from the snapping cameras outside the church. The picture ricocheted around the country, the caption reading: "The Next Bella of the Ball?" as if they were on their way to a party. Had they no decency? Aster worried how long the photograph would follow them, follow her daughter, her name now caught up in this mess.

In the conference room with Sam was Granger Honeywell, the attorney who'd been drawing up the terms of the divorce and would now handle the estate. Like so many young and immortal stars, Benny apparently didn't have a will, so his wishes were anyone's guess. But Aster thought she had a pretty good idea.

"As his lawful wife, you of course are entitled to 100 percent of his assets. This includes his home and all personal property within it, all funds in his various banking accounts, and future royalties." Honeywell's red nose bulged below his reading glasses.

"Royalties?" Aster had been around the business long enough to know that contract actors rarely received royalties against their movies.

Sam cleared his throat. "In Christopher's new contract, he negotiated a lower salary, but a portion of all net profits from his films, including the three movies in the can that haven't yet been released. Of course, he is no longer just a bona fide star, but his death makes him a legend. The future income from royalties could be worth more than his entire estate."

The lawyer pushed a document across the table to her detailing the value of his current assets. The number was enormous, but far smaller than what she would have guessed. She briefly wondered if these men had siphoned off some of Benny's funds before showing her the numbers. And she didn't know if the royalty percentage stated on the page accurately represented what Benny had negotiated, but neither was a fight she would ever win.

"Congratulations, Aster. For a gal with no designs on Hollywood, you sure managed to make yourself a rich woman," Sam said.

Molten anger bubbled. She willed herself to stay calm lest she erupt and reveal something she would regret.

"In the terms of the divorce we drew up, the one-time payment I was to receive looks to be about one quarter of this bank balance. Is that right?" She addressed her question to the lawyer, doing her best to ignore Sam's presence.

"Yes, but—"

She held up her hand.

"I would like to receive that same amount, and one quarter of future royalties. The rest I would like you to put in the name of Fernando Tivoli."

"We can't do that."

"Of course you can."

"Well, the legality of what you're asking is a bit complicated," Honeywell said.

"You people find ways to hide anything you want to hide. I'm quite sure you can figure out a way to make it work. It's what he would have wanted." She dug her spiked heels into the carpet below her chair, appreciating the power of her uniquely feminine weapons in a new way.

"You have a daughter to think about now." Sam eyed her coldly.

She closed her eyes against the specter of all he might know and its implications. She willed herself to ignore it. It would only increase her ire.

"That's precisely who I am thinking about. Otherwise, I would refuse all of it. I'm done with this town."

Sam pushed his chair away from the table and stood at a long plate-glass window, surveying his empire of make-believe.

"I'll do it under one condition." He faced her again. "If you so much as breathe a word about Fernando, about any of this, to anyone, at any time, I will stop the royalties. Christopher Page's legacy depends on it."

And so does your studio's bank account, she wanted to say.

"Fine."

He looked smug, pleased with himself for successfully securing her silence. Aster couldn't believe how daft he was. Of course she would never speak the truth. It would only lead her daughter to question who her father really was, something Aster was surer than ever she never wanted Lissy to know.

Aster finished packing up the trunks she would take with her on the train—mostly toys for Lissy—and went to Fernando's apartment to say goodbye. He answered the door dressed in slacks and a white undershirt. He was unshaven and looked as though he hadn't slept in days. But he did manage a half-smile upon seeing Lissy, then opened his door to them.

To Aster's relief, the living room and kitchen were tidy, likely the work of a housekeeper. Keeping an apartment clean was one thing; restoring Fernando to his previous self would be a much harder task. Aster wondered if he would ever again be that dashing man she'd met on her first day in LA—the creative genius, the vibrant soul who'd been so generous to her in every way.

They sat on his balcony overlooking a small garden, Lissy playing with one of her fabric dolls. The peonies and begonias below were in full bloom, hopeful reminders that life has a way of rejuvenating. The tenderest sprout finds a way to push through the soil and share its bounty. Aster needed to believe Fernando would eventually find his way back to his former self.

"When's your train?"

"Four o'clock." Five hours more and she would leave Hollywood forever. But she didn't want to leave this friendship behind. She leaned into him and gave him a nudge. "You should come with us. To New York. Fashion center of the world and all."

She had allowed herself to picture the scenario. It would be like erasing the last two years and starting again, only in New York. Fernando with a bustling business—it wouldn't be hard for him to establish himself in the city—with her as his apprentice. In this version she would study at design school and ask for his help on the side. And Lissy would grow up with his presence in her life. No lies punctured that picture.

"New York is my father's territory. I'm not welcome there."

Aster nodded. She had forgotten all about Vincenzo Tivoli, the fountainhead of Fernando's design genius. The well-heeled in New

York had filled out their wardrobes at Vincenzo's for more than forty years. Vincenzo had served as Fernando's first mentor, and father and son became a fashion duo extraordinaire. That was until Vincenzo discovered Fernando and one of his tailors in a dressing room after-hours. He'd banished his son from the business and the family. Los Angeles was about as far away as Fernando could get.

"What a fool I was," Fernando said, practically in a whisper. "I really thought Benny was going to give it up. That's why I got so furious. He told me we would be together. He said I just needed to be patient. And then he went and signed that damned contract. Why couldn't I have been patient? Three years feels like nothing now." He stared into space, his face slack, his eyes dry. Aster wondered if his well of tears was simply empty.

There was so much Aster wanted to say, but she didn't manage to voice any of it: that the last two years had made her feel part of a family unlike anything she had experienced before; that watching Fernando and Benny together gave her hope in the existence of unbridled love; that they showed her how passion can be effortlessly joined with caring and kindness and partnership; that she couldn't bear to see Fernando's misery but knew the world needed a heart as generous as his, a heart she believed would heal one day. It would have been all too easy for her to say. She hadn't just lost the love of her life. And she had Lissy. Fernando was alone now.

"You did try to stop him, didn't you?" Fernando's voice almost disappeared in the gentle wind blowing across the balcony.

Aster's gut constricted. She'd played the scene over in her mind, reliving the image the way one might watch the scariest part of a horror film: not able to look away, yet terrified by what she might see, a different angle that would reveal a way she could have stopped him. Continually coming up empty didn't lessen the horrible guilt she felt for not finding a way.

"I begged him not to get in that car." Her voice cracked.

Her guilt often sparked anger, a powerful cocktail of emotions she couldn't seem to get out of her bloodstream. She was furious with Benny for being so reckless, so careless with his life, for shattering Fernando's world. And she hated herself for allowing it to happen. She'd had him in her grasp. How could she have ever let him go?

Fernando nodded his head and swiped at his eyes. "I know, I know you did. I'm sorry."

They embraced with Lissy squished between them. Aster thought her chest might explode from the sorrow trapped there, but she kept it in. Fernando didn't need the weight of her sadness on top of his own.

"I'm so sorry, Fernando."

When he finally pulled back and released her, Lissy started to cry, perhaps sensing the gravity of the moment, understanding they were about to say goodbye.

"Naddo!" she wailed, reaching out her chubby arms to him.

Fernando kissed them both and then, unable to speak, walked to his bedroom and quietly closed the door. With that, Aster knew the remaking of her daughter's memories had begun.

CHAPTER TWENTY-ONE

Aster hid out at Greta's apartment on the Lower West Side for weeks after arriving from LA. Greta opened her door without hesitation, never questioning why Aster and Lissy weren't staying with her parents in Newark, and never pressing for details about life on the red carpet with Christopher Page. "Grief deserves a sacred kind of silence," Greta had said. She did, however, want to hear everything about Fernando.

"I hope life is easier for him out there. Has he found someone?" she asked one night over her homemade meatloaf and tomato soup. It didn't match Benny's cooking, but Aster appreciated the comfort of the warm food, and Lissy liked anything mushy.

Aster blew on her spoonful of soup and shook her head, taking a moment to compose her face so as not to give anything away.

"It can be as hard for him out there as it was here. He has a pretty high profile now that he works for Galaxy." She slurped and swallowed. "There's no one in his life right now."

"That's too bad. Isn't he the loveliest man?"

"I'm going to miss him dearly." Aster put down her spoon, unable to say more.

She struggled to find normalcy after losing Benny and saying goodbye to Fernando, and she hadn't expected how excruciating it would be to reunite with people she cared about and not be able to tell them the truth. As much as she adored and trusted Greta, once she opened that door, it might be too difficult to ever properly close it. She needed to practice the cover story, inhabit it with every fiber of her body, so by the time Lissy started to ask questions it would be second nature.

Fortunately, Greta still worked full-time, and Aster and Lissy had the apartment to themselves for most of the day. When Lissy got fussy or bored, she cried for Naddo and the pool. Aster did her best to distract her with finger paints and by making up plays starring her cast of fuzzy rag dolls. She did get out for a walk every day, a hat pulled low over her forehead even when there was no rain in sight. Nonetheless, it was rare to look anyone in the eye without being recognized from the photos still plastered across every magazine rack in the city. She hadn't before understood that New Yorkers were almost as invested in the goings-on of Hollywood as those in LA. If Aster hadn't traveled the three thousand miles between the two cities herself, she would have thought them to be in neighboring counties.

The day of Aster's interview at Parsons, the woman from apartment 2B who had agreed to babysit called an hour before Aster's appointment to cancel because of the stomach flu. With no other options, Aster brought Lissy, now fourteen months old, to the meeting. Miss Crumb—she would never forget her name—glanced at Aster and gasped. "You're

Pip Page!" At first, she wanted only to fawn over Aster, talk about the tragedy of Christopher Page, and gossip about Hollywood. Despite Aster filling out her application as AJ Kelly—intent on making the connection with the Fashion Guild award from a few years earlier—Miss Crumb said she'd seen photos of Aster in the papers and would "know her anywhere."

Aster finally persuaded Miss Crumb to consider her small portfolio, and she proudly showed off the design for the short pants she had worked on so diligently in her early days at Fernando's.

"Oh, capris," Miss Crumb said, and informed Aster the new fashion was already making the rounds in New York boutiques, thanks to the inventive genius of European designer Sonja de Lennart. She flipped past Aster's studies on the piece from multiple angles.

"What else do you have?"

Aster showed her several other sketches: a high-waisted skirt with an angled hemline, gabardine slacks with tuck pleats, and a midthigh raincoat belted at the waist, meant for casual outings. She'd spent hours on those drawings, getting the bend of each elbow just right, making sure the body looked realistic beneath the clothes, but she could see by watching Miss Crumb's unchanging expression that the designs themselves weren't very interesting. Sure, the capris, as she now knew they were called, had been a good idea, but she didn't have much else.

She'd pushed Lissy's stroller down Bleecker Street and Waverly Place, through Central Park or down Fifth Avenue every day looking for inspiration, a new concept, a fresh idea, but she'd found herself more interested in the people than the clothes. As she sat down to draw after Lissy was asleep, her mind replayed the motion of a young girl hopping through the spray of a hose, the stoop of an old man's shoulders, the grace of a bicyclist swerving around the monument at Washington Square. The clothes were inconsequential to the scene as she remembered it.

As Miss Crumb flipped past the last sketch, Lissy started to fidget—causing Miss Crumb to do the same. Aster considered turning up the charm, describing the kinds of gowns she wore as Lauren Bacall's stand-in to make up for the shortcomings of her portfolio. But as she lifted Lissy onto her lap, the image of what life might be like at the school gave her pause: long days trying to impress the likes of Miss Crumb, Lissy placed in the hands of unreliable caregivers, their money dwindling by the minute. And for what? To create clothes? She realized right then that a life in fashion wasn't at all what she wanted anymore.

She closed her portfolio and left Miss Crumb and Parsons behind.

Aster stood outside Parsons, wondering where to go next in every sense. Perhaps New York City wasn't the best place for her to raise Lissy—too expensive, no room for Lissy to roam, too much focus on fashion and stardom and all the things she wanted to put behind her. There were too many people here who breathed in magazines and newsreels and knew exactly who she was.

But was she ready to leave New York again, this time with no plan for her future? There was one thing she needed to do before she decided for sure.

She took Lissy to Washington Square Park so she could organize her thoughts, and as she watched a man in a frayed peacoat methodically lay bread crumbs at his feet, she considered all that had transpired in the last three years and what others thought to be true. How would she find a comfortable place between those two things? Had she just finalized a nasty divorce, she could've played off the marriage as a hasty mistake, a foolish girl falling for a movie star—who wouldn't?—claimed it wasn't worth talking about, and moved on.

Instead, she was a grieving widow in everyone's eyes—a woman who had lost a great love. Something about Hollywood made everyone assume all love stories involving stars were epic. As far as the rest of the world was concerned, she had already summited, given herself to a man no other suitor would ever want to be measured against—a man who, ironically, had just been rendered immortal.

But living with Fernando and Benny had taught Aster a lot about the subtleties of love, the strength of a bond built on small gestures. Being with them often made her think of Graham: the ease she'd felt around him, how much she'd looked forward to seeing him at the end of her busy days back then, how his way of listening to her made her feel valued, made her want to absorb all the details of his days too, merge their lives into one vessel the way Fernando and Benny had done so willingly, so effortlessly. And she knew Graham to be a man who made principled choices, like turning down the opportunity to run his father's business, willing to cast aside the wealth and power of that position in favor of pursuing a life in the artistic world. She now knew just how rare such a man could be. And Aster was sure they could have built something together had she stayed, maybe something lasting.

Of course, this was all probably a moot point. Graham was likely married with a baby of his own by now. He'd always been a romantic—a charming, smart, and warm man any woman would be delighted to call her husband, any child would be lucky to have as their dad. Aster winced at the thought and stroked Lissy's head. She couldn't help but long for the time before everything became so complicated, before she started hiding behind a patchwork of lies.

When the last crumb disappeared into a pigeon's beak, Aster rose from her bench and walked to the Whitney Museum.

Aster held Lissy's hand and slowed to a waddle as they approached the small reception desk.

"Is Graham Wingate here, please?"

The woman behind the counter stared at Aster blankly.

"Sorry, what department?"

"Curation?" Aster felt suddenly unsure of herself—the museum wasn't very big—and squatted down to pick Lissy up so she could see over the counter. The woman closed a three-ring binder on her desk and asked Aster to wait.

A few moments later a tall, bearded man appeared. His expression was both kind and unsettled. Aster got the impression he was practiced at projecting calm but was nervous for some reason. He smiled.

"Good afternoon. I'm Mr. More, the director here." He offered his hand, his eyes boring into hers as if communicating a secret message. "As I'm sure you can appreciate, we don't usually give out any information about former employees."

She nodded her head. Former employee?

"But I think it's fair to make an exception in this case. We were sad to see him go, but he left us over a year ago for a job up north, in Martha's Vineyard."

"Martha's Vineyard?" Aster tried to place it.

"I know. I was surprised too. A young single man headed to an island like that? Felt kind of crazy to me, but there you have it. I don't have any other information, but I hope it's helpful to you."

Aster noted that this man hadn't asked her name, yet he had broken his own rule before she requested anything. She'd never get used to being treated as an exception. In fact, she'd do just about anything to make it stop. But she did appreciate the information he'd offered, and if her being instantly recognized was the reason, then she'd take it. Especially the most important word he'd uttered in all of it.

Single.

CHAPTER TWENTY-TWO

Aster found the words Haven Art Gallery carved into a drift-wood sign above a white door on Main Street in Vineyard Haven. She could see the entirety of the tiny gallery through the mullioned windows. The walls were full of framed sketches and paintings, mostly landscapes and seascapes, some featuring boats, others of beach grass or the foam of an incoming wave. Painted buoys and carved seabirds crowded the windowsills, every inch of the place filled with little pieces of Martha's Vineyard.

And there was Graham, flipping through a set of prints propped up in a wooden crate. He wore Levi's and a white T-shirt, his feet bare, his hair longer than Aster remembered, the brown curls at his neck soft enough to touch. He was whistling. She'd forgotten how much he loved to whistle. She watched his lips and tried to guess if it was "The Old Lamplighter" or maybe "Once in a While."

He looked entirely at home in this place, on this island, the sun shining through the windows onto the honey-colored floor. The moment the ferry had rounded the corner toward Vineyard Haven, she remembered Graham's story about the first painting to capture his attention as a boy, Hopper's *The Lighthouse at Two Lights*. He said he'd never seen anything so beautiful, the simple white house on a hill, the lighthouse protruding into the deep blue sky, how he could almost smell the saltwater just off the edge of the painting. Aster had never been to New England before, had never been on an island other than Manhattan, and immediately felt the draw of it. He'd chosen to live in that painting.

A rush of excitement rippled up her spine as she pictured stepping into the store, his look of surprise, then delight. How he would take her hand and walk her out the door and into those paintings, show her his favorite corners of the island, introduce her to its sunrises and sunsets. How he might even kiss her right here, envelop her in his arms, like he had so many times before, a familiar refrain. A rush of relief and gratitude washed over her. The nineteen-year-old girl who'd captured his attention that first day at the Whitney would get a second chance. She closed her eyes for a moment, willing herself not to let it all unspool too quickly in her mind, and opened the door.

When he saw her his whistling stopped. Time shifted, as if they were both caught in a sphere of amber, momentarily unable to move, the air too solid to breathe. He regained movement first.

"Aster." He closed the gap between them. He put his arms around her, but the embrace felt stiff, almost formal.

"My god, what you've been through," he said, pulling back.

She stared at him blankly, having forgotten momentarily the story of her life as he knew it. She hadn't considered where to begin, hadn't decided what she should tell him. She clutched his forearms. She might fall over if she let go.

She took in his square chin and slightly crooked nose, a deep tan softening the angles, his narrow hips, warm eyes. The familiarity of him created the sensation that time hadn't moved as fast here as it had in California, that what felt to her like a lifetime of opportunities and disappointments, decisions and consequences, the joy of birth and devastation of death, had occupied only weeks for him, just enough time to take the tension of the city out of his shoulders. She was a different person, and he was the same.

She suddenly burst like a water balloon, tears streaming down her face before she could stop them. Graham went into motion again. He flipped the sign on the door to Closed, pulled her into a tiny annex that barely had room for two stools, and gestured for her to sit. He rummaged in a small desk, handed her a handkerchief, and waited.

"I'm sorry." She wiped her eyes, noting a streak of black on the white linen. She sullied everything she touched, it seemed.

"How did you find me?"

She told him about the gawking strangers in New York, how Greta had been a great comfort, but she couldn't stay with her forever, about going to the Whitney, how she didn't know where else to turn.

"I'm babbling." She couldn't read the confused expression on his face. She was trying to tell him everything but in the end was telling him nothing.

"Is your little girl here with you?"

She hadn't brought Lissy—why not, exactly, she now wondered. Maybe as an unconscious attempt to slip back into the past as they had left it? Then she understood with sudden clarity that her daughter's temporary absence would never change that Aster was a mother now, a woman who had given birth to someone else's child. She was no longer the girl Graham had known.

"She's with Greta, at her sister's house in Hudson Valley for the weekend. It's where she's going to retire. I convinced her to get a little practice."

He laughed. "She's still running Bendel's then?"

Aster relaxed into his laugh, realizing how tense every muscle in her body had been, maybe for weeks.

"She's finally going to put the last pin in the cushion at end of the year. I don't know what the girls will do without her."

Graham nodded, and Aster knew she didn't need to say more. He understood exactly why Aster hated the place, and the spark Greta had ignited by helping her create clothes of her own. She regretted how little she appreciated back then the intimacy that came with sharing the minute details of their lives with each other, the exciting and the mundane. How Graham used to hang on her every word, and how much she enjoyed hearing about his day at the museum or with his students in the art room, how he would light up with excitement as he described coaxing self-portraits from his third-graders, or how the idea of perspective clicked for a fifth-grader. Then he would stop himself midsentence, turn the sparkle in his eyes toward her, and say, "But here you are. Let's talk about you instead." Being here, she knew her reservoir of love for him had never run dry.

"So you finally have a gallery of your own." She wiped her eyes again and tried to smile.

"Just in the summer months. I teach during the school year."

He told her he'd learned about the opening for an art teacher who could handle elementary school through high school, how he thought the island might be the kind of place he could live on a teacher's salary and afford to try his hand at running a small gallery on the side.

She was too distracted by her swirling thoughts to follow what he said next. She sensed an unnatural pause in the conversation, but he pushed on.

"Where are you staying?"

"Just over at the Seaside Inn."

He told her about the Granger family who owned the inn, but she still wasn't listening. The tension she was certain had vibrated between them when she first walked in had slackened, as if each word they spoke rendered their interaction more ordinary and would eventually reduce it to something meaningless. That was not what she wanted.

"I'm sorry I never wrote. Things moved so fast out there, and . . ." Her words faded.

"The newspapers kind of filled in the blanks for me." He attempted a smile that didn't last. She heard the pain in his voice.

"There's so much I need to explain." She reached for his arm.

He stood and walked over to the box he'd been sorting through when she arrived, his back to her now.

"You don't owe me any explanation." His hand shook as he pushed a print back in the stack.

Aster studied his back. Had she been crazy to come here, to think he could possibly understand what had really happened, to hope he might still burn for her in spite of it all? She needed to explain her past foolishness, her appreciation now for the demands of love, the moments of joy it could spur, and the heartache it could withstand. She badly wanted to touch him, tell him she was ready to commit to that kind of love now, ask if he still wanted it too. She was almost desperate for it.

She positioned herself beside him and took in the watercolor painting beneath his hands, a lighthouse beacon barely visible through thick fog.

"That's exactly how I feel," she said.

He tilted his head toward her, almost imperceptibly, but she knew the gesture. He was listening.

"I'm lost, Graham. I didn't appreciate the steady light you offered, back when my future seemed, I don't know, like something I had to go searching for, something I'd find somewhere else. I was a fool. And now I'm flailing. I'm trying to find my way back to what matters, to what's real."

She still didn't know how much she should say, what part of the story mattered, how to best communicate that the world had it wrong. Christopher Page wasn't her great love, nor would he be her greatest loss if she couldn't find her way back to Graham.

He ran his hand up her arm and searched her eyes before letting his gaze fall to her lips.

A bell rang and the door of the gallery swung open. Graham jumped back as a woman flipped the sign on the door and swept into the space without looking at them, saying, "You have the Closed sign out, silly," and dropped her purse on the counter.

Graham cleared his throat.

"Marcia, this is my old friend Aster."

Marcia hesitated before turning to face them. "Oh my gosh," she said, her hand pressed to her chest as if trying to stop herself from gasping.

Time stuttered again.

"Graham has told me so much about you." Marcia was clearly trying to strike a friendly tone, to keep the confusion and awe out of her voice. "I'm so sorry for your loss."

"Thank you." Aster took an awkward step sideways to increase her distance from Graham.

Marcia was a petite woman with striking features, thick eyebrows and full lips that gave her an alluring Mediterranean look. Were she of larger stature, she could have been a stand-in for Sophia Loren but without the makeup. She wore short linen shorts that flattered her slim legs and a butcher boy top. Her casual bearing made her all the more stunning. But what really caught Aster's eye was the ring on Marcia's left hand.

Marcia noticed. She held up her hand, diamond out, and wiggled her fingers.

"I'm sure Graham shared our exciting news?"

A fist clamped over Aster's lungs, depriving her of air.

"That's wonderful." Aster pushed as much enthusiasm into the words as she could muster. She glanced at Graham, who had turned to stone.

Marcia seemed not to notice this and filled the void by talking about the wedding, only two months away—everything on the island was cheaper in September, otherwise they'd be married already—how wonderfully local it would all be, clambake and all, except of course her dress. Even though she wanted something simple, she'd still been forced to go to the mainland to find it.

When Aster didn't comment on any of it, Marcia's expression grew somber.

"I'm so sorry. Going on about our wedding when you just . . ." Marcia shook her head. "What a shame. If there's anything we can do . . ."

Aster eyed the door, then the floor, planning the best route of escape between the two sets of feet that stood in her way.

Marcia started talking again, which at least kept some oxygen flowing in the room and gave Aster something to listen to beyond the banging of her own pulse. Marcia said something to Graham about needing to meet with their Realtor at five and dinner at her mom's house right after.

"Sounds like a plan." Graham's voice was still stiff.

"Oh, and Mary Flemming came into the bookstore today. She said Charlotte can't wait for school to start so she can get back to the art room. Isn't that adorable? For a seventh-grader to be excited for summer to end? You can't imagine how much everyone loves Graham here. He completely reinvigorated the art program. I don't know how we survived before he came."

Graham visibly softened, as if his blood had begun to circulate again, warming him from the inside.

"It was lovely to meet you." Marcia picked up her bag and placed an index finger on Graham's chest. "You, I'll see at five. Miss you until then."

This last part sounded to Aster like a familiar refrain between them.

Marcia tilted her head up to Graham, and he kissed her. Then she was out the door.

What an idiot Aster was, thinking she could come here and step back into Graham's life. Of course he'd found a beautiful young woman who adored him, a woman who, Aster was certain, hadn't hesitated to accept his proposal. And who was Aster now other than a broken person—used up, already a mother, widowed. There would be no going backward.

"Aster, I—" Graham moved toward her.

"No explanations needed, like you said. I'm sorry, I shouldn't have come."

A swirl of heat gathered under Aster's ribcage and threatened to break her open. She didn't look at Graham again before pushing through the door. She headed in the opposite direction as Marcia, having no idea where she was going.

Aster was sitting in a rocking chair on the front porch of the Seaside Inn when bright headlights swept across the lawn, slicing the darkness. She'd never been to a place where the stars overpowered man-made glow. Manhattan glittered with a riot of light. Even LA maintained an undercurrent of luminescence at night, as if the city teetered perpetually on the edge of sunrise. But Martha's Vineyard, perched out in the ocean, wore the night like a blanket pulled over a fort, the only light coming from tiny pinpricks in the fabric. Aster wondered how long it might take to count every star.

She'd been thinking about what she should do next, where she and Lissy could find the anonymity she felt under that expansive sky. She knew she couldn't be anywhere hemmed in, where she would worry about whispers and sidelong glances, where Lissy's life would be defined by the residue of fame. If it ever took hold, it would grow like mold.

She wanted more than anything for Lissy to enjoy a carefree and simple childhood, and Benny's death did give her the chance to remake Lissy's origin story once again. Lissy no longer needed to be the daughter of an estranged father who couldn't be bothered with her. Instead, she would grow up being told she'd been adored and well-loved by a man named Benedict Horowitz. It was as close to the truth as Aster could get. She wouldn't hide Benny's stage name or profession from Lissy when the time came for more detail, but she would hear about a loving father first. When the time came, the fact of his stardom would be entrusted to Lissy for safekeeping, a story the rest of the world wouldn't need to know. Aster knew all too well how strangely any whiff of fame made people behave, and Aster wouldn't allow it to cloud Lissy's life. If Aster could give Lissy one thing, it would be this.

The car lights went out as the car sputtered to a stop.

"I'm glad you're still here." Graham walked up the steps and sat in the chair beside hers. After rocking in unison for several long moments, Aster decided she owed him some closure.

"I'm happy for you, Graham. You seem at home here." She turned toward him. She wanted him to know she meant it and hoped it might serve as an apology for bursting back into his life, for trying to drag him back to where they'd left off, for ever thinking he wouldn't have moved on by now. "Marcia seems lovely."

"She'll make a great mom. She's already picked out the perfect house for a gaggle of kids. We want the same things."

A gaggle of kids. She remembered now his familiar refrain about the wonder of big families, lots of brothers and sisters, the fun of a chaotic household. Aster reflexively put her hand on the hollow of her stomach.

"Even with all those children around you every day, you still want more?" Aster tried to locate a teasing or sarcastic tone but realized in the same breath how much she cared about his answer.

"It makes me want kids more, I think. I adore my students, but I doubt it comes anywhere close to having children of your own. You would know."

She did know. And no, it couldn't possibly compare.

They continued to rock in their separate chairs, the insistent thrum of the crickets emphasizing a growing silence between them. And then his chair stopped moving.

"I want you to know that I waited for you, Aster. Probably longer than I should have. Or maybe I didn't wait long enough." He spoke toward the distant trees, as if the words were less likely to be captured permanently if he sent them out into the dark. She waited. "I know you've been through a lot, but is there room in your life for a bigger family? Is that what you want too?"

Aster's heart surged like a burning star—brightness, heat, a rush of light. She understood what he was asking. If she was still in love with him. If she had come to the island to be with him. If she wanted to create a family with him. The answer to all those questions was yes, except the one she could do nothing about. How ironic that the extraordinary gift of motherhood had been given to her and snatched away at the very same moment. There could be no more children for her. Telling him this would present an awful choice—rejecting her because of her body's limitation or choosing her over having a family of his own. If he made the wrong choice, he might never forgive himself, or her. She had already mangled too many lives. She closed her eyes as the trail of light arced through her heart and dimmed.

"I already have my family," she said.

He leaned forward in his chair and gazed at her across the lamplight spilling from the windows of the inn.

"Why did you come here?"

Aster heard no accusation in his voice, just confusion laced with something close to sorrow. She kept her chair rocking. There was too much she could never explain, she understood that now. The burden of the truth would be hers to carry alone. But there was one part of it all she could be honest about.

"I think I'm looking for some sense of normalcy. I have this beautiful child to raise on my own, and I want her to have a normal life. I want to have a normal life. But I have no idea how to do that."

"What's normal?"

Just like she remembered. Graham actually wanted to understand her thoughts. And she could think of no one she'd rather talk it through with. She laid out her worries and hopes—how she wanted to find a job she could be proud of but didn't want to leave Lissy in the care of anyone else; how she knew she had creativity to offer but wasn't good enough at anything to make a living; how she wasn't sure she deserved any of it.

He listened, gently asking questions to clarify, validating her feelings by not trying to talk her out of any of them. She desperately wanted to stroke his cheek, pull his lips into hers, admit she did still love him, but it was now out of the question. The opening had been there for an instant, and she had closed it off. Instead, she would remain behind the veil of the heartbroken widow, and he could get on with his life.

"You should stay here. Work for me."

"What?" She didn't try to hide the shock in her own voice.

"Hear me out. I've been wanting to test if the shop can make it in the off-season, but I teach all day. You could work at the gallery, and you could bring Lissy with you. I can't pay much yet, but it would be a start."

"And what would your fellow islanders make of me?" She hadn't felt the same glaring eyes on her since arriving on the island, but would it last?

"The people here aren't much interested in magazine stories or gossip. They care about making an honest living and building a strong community. Christopher Page's wife is called Pip to the world. You're Aster. My old friend. Put on a pair of oversized overalls and sneakers, become a shopkeeper in a town in need of more shops. No one will know you as anything else."

"And if that doesn't work?"

"This island is like one big family. They will protect your child like their own. And if that means conveniently forgetting your past, they'll do it."

"What about Marcia?" This treaded close to treacherous ground, but before she could seriously consider his offer, she had to ask.

"This is her idea."

Aster didn't know what to say.

"Marcia's boyfriend drowned in an accident in high school. All she wanted was to get away from the constant memory of it, from everyone looking at her with pity all the time. It lasted for years. But she never did leave the island. She said over dinner how much she worried for you, such a public loss. That what you need more than anything is somewhere to go to be able to forget, start fresh. Plus, I can test the gallery without us having to give up her income at the bookstore. She's already thought it all through."

He angled toward her and spoke slowly.

"And then she asked me if there was any reason why it wasn't a good idea."

He was testing her resolve one more time. If she stayed, she would be accepting more than a suggestion of a place to live and an offer of employment. She would also be accepting a silent agreement to ignore any lingering feelings for each other, to forget that Graham momentarily offered a life together, or that she rejected it. Instead, they would occupy the space of friendship. Could she do that?

Aster breathed in the scent of pine trees mixed with the brine of the ocean and Graham's soft musk. A live wire still connected them, and she suspected stepping over and around it would be a daily struggle for her, maybe for him too. A stronger person, a better person would tell him she had other plans, there was somewhere else she had already picked to start up a new life with Lissy, someone else she could turn to. But she had nowhere else to go. She certainly wouldn't return to her childhood home where her mother obsessed over a glittery status that had been irrevocably tarnished, or even to Greta, who was a constant reminder of Fernando and all she had lost.

The island already felt like a sanctuary where Lissy could run free and enjoy an unfettered childhood, a place where Aster could disappear inside a new persona and start over.

As she rocked in her chair, she told herself that the quiver racing up her arms, the electric draw of Graham would surely fade with time. There was real friendship here. It was what fed her love for him. She would make this work.

She finally looked him in the eye.

"No reason at all. I think it's a great idea."

1975
NEW YORK

CHAPTER TWENTY-THREE

L et's go back to Morty's." Noah rolled over on his towel and shaded his eyes from the sun.

With a week off before the start of rehearsals, Noah had brought Lissy out to his parents' house on Long Island. They only used the house on weekends, which meant Lissy and Noah were blissfully alone for two nights and three days.

Lissy had fallen asleep to the sound of the waves and slipped into her favorite dream—bobbing up and down in bright blue water, the sun and her mother's smiling face never too far from the surface. The ebb and flow of the water didn't create foam like the ocean, the tiny waves more like splashes in a bathtub. And the prevailing sensation was of being held safely in someone's arms, someone she could never see, all laughter and bouncing and bright. Lissy had no idea why the dream recurred, only that it came to her whenever she felt content in her life.

She rubbed her eyes and got her bearings, Noah's beautiful face looking at her expectantly.

"Are you trying to make me fat? We went yesterday."

Morty's was Noah's favorite ice-cream shop on the planet. She couldn't deny the superiority of the maple walnut, which tasted even better when Noah licked the dripping cream off her wrist. But lying in the heat with Noah beside her now, the waves crashing in time with her breathing, had sent her into a trance. She didn't want to move.

"Then we'll ride bikes there and back." His body blocked the sun as he reached down to pull her up.

She'd never been to Long Island before and found the beaches to be remarkably similar to Martha's Vineyard's, the sweeping dunes, the long beach grass. And of course, the same ocean crashed on both shores. The size of Noah's house was a different story, a rambling shingled structure with at least five bedrooms—she and Noah had already made use of three of them—a huge patio with outdoor dining, a hot tub, and a fieldstone fireplace inside big enough to walk into. The fact that it wasn't the Hoyts' primary home boggled Lissy's mind.

Noah didn't seem to notice the grandeur of the place. Either he somehow didn't consider it particularly grand, or he didn't care about such things. He spent most of his time beyond the dunes anyway, sunrise a treasured time, only to be outdone by sunset. He attended both symphonies of color with guitar in hand, strumming in the changing light.

When she asked him to play a few Carole King songs their first night there, he said he didn't know her work beyond a song or two on the radio but managed to find the right key and the right chords almost without misstep. Lissy closed her eyes and belted out the lyrics into the salty wind, feeling as content as she could ever remember. Picking their way back through the dunes in the dark, the way Noah held his guitar in one hand and hers in the other, made her feel wanted, safe, a linked part of his world.

Looking up at him now, an inviting breeze wisping across her body, she decided the least she could do would be to pedal to Morty's and back to indulge his love of ice cream. She'd consider it a delicious break from the hot sand and steady sun.

Sitting together on the bench outside Morty's, Lissy finally asked Noah the question that had been bothering her for days.

"Do you think I was really better than Tammy?"

"Who?"

"Tammy. The other one auditioning for Melanie. Blue eyeshadow?"

Noah took a bite of his ice cream, considering the question in earnest.

"You definitely have a better voice."

"But the acting. You read with her. Do you think she's better than me?"

"What is this about?" Noah turned away from his cone to look at her directly.

What *was* it about? Did she want pat assurance or his true opinion? Or maybe she simply needed to voice her fear.

"I would hate to have gotten this role because of my father."

"Your father?"

"He was pretty famous back in the day. I mentioned him in my bio—which I've never done before—just to help me stand out enough to make it through to callbacks. I didn't think it would matter in the end, but Zimmerman definitely remembered."

"What's his name?"

Noah didn't recognize the name, which made Lissy laugh.

"What?" Noah joined in her in laugher. "I told you I wasn't a theater kid."

"He was in the movies, Noah. You don't follow any of it, do you? I still can't fathom how you just got cast on Broadway."

"Thanks a lot." He grinned into his cone. "He's not in movies anymore?"

"He died when I was a baby."

"Oh. That's rough."

"It was really hard on my mom. She won't talk about it."

Any discussion of that time caused her mother too much pain, a visceral reminder of losing the man who had been proven to be irreplaceable. Of course, men had come and gone, a date here and there, but no one who captured her mother's imagination enough to eclipse Lissy's father.

Lissy saw it firsthand on those nights she begged to stay up late to watch one of his movies on TV. *Moonlight Sonata* was her favorite, although she loved the ending of *The Last Tycoon*, watching the townspeople of Chattanooga lift her father up as a hero. Her mother would watch for a few minutes and then leave the room, disappearing behind a wall Lissy could never quite penetrate. Lissy surmised at an early age that it was simply too difficult for her mother to be within reach of him and yet be nowhere near him, too painful to hear him speak without being able to respond.

And it had all made Lissy's mother a hopeless romantic. She told Lissy countless times that the only thing she wished for her was to find her one great love and hold onto it tightly. Her mother would look off wistfully then, seeing something beyond the reach of Lissy's vision, and add that love like that should never be taken for granted.

Could Noah be that person?

"Wanna switch cones?" Noah asked, making Lissy laugh. Apparently it was some kind of summer ritual for him. He told her about the time his friend Scooter first suggested the idea when they were ten—two flavors for the price of one, he'd said. Noah didn't know Scooter had pushed a worm into his cone with a straw first.

"How did that not kill your love of ice cream?" She peered at the chocolate scoop she'd just inherited.

"That's nothing. I used to eat just about anything if I could make a quick buck off someone who dared me."

Lissy loved Noah's ease in the world and adored him even more for barely registering the fact that she had sprung from a movie star. It didn't impress him in the least. An enormous sense of relief rippled over her, like a summer shower that left the world gleaming. She let out a breath she didn't realize she'd been holding for years.

✍

Full of ice cream, they lazily steered their Schwinns down the shaded lane back to Noah's house. Turning into the sandy driveway Lissy heard Noah swear before she saw the Buick parked at the end.

"Shit. My parents." They were a day early. Lissy's utopia cracked from the inside.

She hopped off her bike and pulled at the edges of her cutoffs, wishing she could wash the salt out of her hair before having to meet his parents.

A tall woman in creamy linen shorts and a navy blouse pushed through the screen door.

"There you are. I'd begun to worry you'd been swept out to sea. And who have we here?"

Noah introduced Lissy as his costar. While Lissy loved the sound of it, she realized how much she would prefer to be described as something else. Mrs. Hoyt insisted Lissy call her Renada.

"And where's your other friend?" Renada asked.

"Who?"

"The other guest. I noticed that three bedrooms are in use."

"Oh. Bae, another cast member," Noah said quickly. "Sorry. I didn't expect you until tomorrow."

Noah's easy demeanor seemed to evaporate, or at least wilt a bit in front of his mother, a woman as stunning and prickly as the rosebushes Lissy's mother grew at their house, known for their hearty response to harsh ocean winds.

"Where's Dad?"

"He's having a rest before dinner, which I need to get back to."

"Can I help with something?" Lissy asked.

"I have it well in hand. You go freshen up. Cocktails at five." She disappeared back through the screen door.

❧

"Noah says you're in a play together?" Mr. Hoyt chose a swordfish steak from the platter Renada held at his side. He didn't offer a first name to Lissy, and she wondered if she should revert to calling Noah's mother Mrs. Hoyt.

"It's a musical. A Zimmerman and Gray show?" Lissy said.

Mr. Hoyt shrugged. Though Renada maintained a carefully staged appearance, Lissy surmised that no one in Mr. Hoyt's life had the guts to recommend he order his khakis a size or two larger or consider loafers that didn't list so badly to one side.

"It's going to be on Broadway, dear." Renada held out the platter for Noah and Lissy. "We can go see it."

Mr. Hoyt peered into his rocks glass and took the swig of a man who knows where the bourbon is stashed.

"I was brought up to believe a man needs steady work."

"Not now, Dad." Noah clenched his jaw, his fork clinking off the china plate.

"What's the harm in a discussion, son? We're all adults here. Anyway, as I was saying, I realized early on, even more important than steady work is leverage. The thing to do back in my day was to become a doctor or a lawyer. But you know what those professions are missing? Leverage." He chewed around a forkful of green beans and kept talking. "Every dollar you make depends on providing a service in person, no better than a high-priced plumber. So I decided on finance. Now there's a profession with leverage. At least Noah's brothers understand."

Noah asked his mother to pass the wine, and he filled his and Lissy's glasses with healthy portions. The gurgle and swish of his pouring temporarily drowned out the sound of Mr. Hoyt's chewing. Everyone waited for him to swallow and continue.

"Now, live performance seems worst of all, don't you think? You have to show up at an appointed time and spin like a top for coins in the hat. I told Noah . . ." He paused for another gulp of bourbon. "If he insists on music, the least he can do is get a recording contract. Then he might have some leverage. A few hours in the studio and some disc jockey can sell the hell out of his record. He doesn't have to actually be there. Am I right?"

Lissy wished her mother were at the table. Noah's parents weren't so different from many of the folks who came to the gallery every summer and went home with one of her mother's sculptures, sometimes year after year. Lissy's mom never confused them for friends—her friends were the other artists who reveled in the quiet of fall after all the tourists left, the farmers who loved the stone walls of Chilmark just as much against the snow, the fishermen who braved the sea even when they couldn't feel their fingers pulling at their nets—but she knew how to talk to them. She was never put off by their wealth, how easily they wrote checks in the thousands to take part of the island away with them. Lissy had watched her mother's graceful interactions for long enough to know how to play along.

"As the original cast, we'll get to record the show. *Godspell* was one of the biggest selling albums last year," Lissy said.

"Really? Well, there's something," Renada said.

"We sing an amazing duet. Wait 'til you hear Lissy's voice. She's a knockout."

It was one thing for her to humor them, but it pained Lissy to hear Noah ingratiate himself to his own parents while being unappreciated for his work. He'd sent out a slew of demo tapes to record labels that winter. Worse than the "rejection letter days," as he called them, were all the days when he heard nothing, all those music executives not even interested enough in his sound to bother sending a response. The persistent silence was what drove him to audition for the show. He was determined to prove to himself—and to his father, Lissy now understood—that he could make a career from music, in whatever form it took.

"Do they pay you by the hour for recording, or do you get a cut? You need to read the fine print on these things." Mr. Hoyt stabbed his fish with his fork.

"You should tell my parents how you got involved in acting, Lissy." Noah clearly wanted to redirect the conversation.

"It all started with singing, just like Noah." Lissy doubted they were particularly interested in her history in the theater. "May I just say how beautiful your house is? Thank you for having me here."

"No, I mean about your dad. Maybe they've heard of him."

Lissy stared at her crystal glass, her surprise at the topic rendering her temporarily mute. It hadn't seemed important to him earlier. And the word *dad* jolted her. A dad was someone you knew, someone who raised you. She had never thought of the ghost of her past as anything other than her father, the source of half her biological code, half of her built-in attributes.

Mr. and Mrs. Hoyt looked at her expectantly. Noah's eyes implored her to fill in the blanks—apparently he had forgotten her father's name already—and the only way now not to make it an even bigger deal was to simply blurt it out.

"No kidding." Mr. Hoyt leaned back in his chair. "Christopher Page?"

Renada clapped her hands together at her lips. "Wow."

Noah looked rather amazed at his parents' reaction.

"Now there's a man's man for you." Mr. Hoyt swirled the ice in his glass. "And movies? There's leverage in movies. Just what I was saying before. A few hours in front of a camera and millions of people can pay to watch."

"You're from California then?" Renada stepped on the end of her husband's commentary.

"I grew up on Martha's Vineyard."

"Really? Year-round?" Renada deflated. "There's something about snow on the beach I find so bleak."

There was rarely ever snow on the beach. What the warmer-than-snow ocean wind couldn't take care of, the high tide always did. She and her mother loved to bundle up and walk under the spires at Lucy Vincent Beach in the winter. They considered it their own private cathedral. But Lissy decided not to correct her.

"Are you trying to break into movies?" Mr. Hoyt's sudden interest in her made her queasy.

"I prefer musicals. Hollywood doesn't make them anymore."

"Your father never did musicals anyway, did he? Too good of an actor for that."

Noah put down his napkin and pushed his chair back from the table.

"Thanks for dinner, Mom. There's an open jam at the pub tonight. Lissy and I are going to go down and check it out."

This was the first Lissy had heard of it but was grateful for the excuse.

"What are your plans for the weekend?"

"We'll be leaving in the morning."

"That's a shame. The Baxters would have loved to meet Lissy. They're such movie buffs," Renada said.

Noah took Lissy's hand and linked his fingers through hers as they walked away from the table.

CHAPTER TWENTY-FOUR

The table reading on the initial day of rehearsals marked the first time anyone in the cast had read the script from start to finish. Lissy relaxed slightly during the third or fourth scene, remembering that no one expected a spectacular performance. It was simply a way for everyone to familiarize themselves with the entire story and each other, and for Zimmerman to hear his words out loud, which would help him further refine the script.

The flow of the show was a little unusual to be sure. Time moved in reverse throughout the show, which required a continual resetting of perspective. By the third act, the declarations of each character as their younger selves would be heard by an audience that already knew how their lives had turned out. It created opportunities for even simple lines to be rendered as comedic or tragic, demanding considerable nuance from the cast so as not to turn the entire show into a satire of itself.

Lissy counted on Zimmerman to help his young actors find their rhythm. And the talent around her was impressive. She particularly enjoyed watching Bae in action after so many years. She infused the role of Trudy with heaps of sass one minute and surprised with raw emotion the next, like a chameleon whose changes were undetectable until they suddenly manifested an entirely different color. And the pivotal scenes with Noah were high points for Lissy, moments she knew she could bring home to the audience.

Rehearsals took place in the same building in Midtown that had housed auditions, but a warren of rooms was now in use. The original audition room functioned as a dance studio where the cast studied the choreography of the group numbers under the tutelage of a taut package of a woman named Tully who donned her wrap skirt and leotard like a matador wielding a cape. Only her face gave away how far removed she was from her last stage appearance, her dancers falling to the floorboards whenever she allowed them to take five.

A larger room was marked up with tape, delineating the edges of the stage and the eventual location of doorways and other structural elements of the set. This was Zimmerman's domain, where he blocked each scene, and the actors honed the dialogue utilizing dimension and space, gestures, and movement. An old Yamaha upright commanded the south corner of the room where all the early vocal rehearsals took place. They huddled around the piano in twos and threes to refine the syncopation and harmony of Gray's music without concern for the confines of the taped-off area. Gray insisted each song be learned to perfection before it be put in motion.

A converted storage room with dueling desks behind the marked-up stage functioned as a makeshift office for Zimmerman and Gray. A folding table between them displayed a 3D rendering of the set, which they tweaked during breaks as the blocking for the show began to take shape. Once it was sent to the shop for full-scale production, it couldn't be changed.

Rehearsals ran from nine thirty every morning until at least six at night, a whirlwind of singing and dancing, collapsing in laughter when someone missed a line, stern silence when it happened the third time in a row, repeating the same kick-ball-change into a twirl until the timing was precisely right, and tweaking the pitch of the group songs until their collective voices created a vibration of perfect harmony in the room.

The energy coursed through Lissy all day. She felt like a race car perpetually revving at the starting line, until she would finally run out of fuel. Then she would sputter over to one of the benches along the mirror and peel off her Capezios. Lissy's favorite part was leaning on Gray's piano and singing his signature songs, the cigarette smoke slowly curling toward the ceiling as each stanza progressed toward the crescendo, Gray breaking into a wide smile every time. The acting proved harder.

Lissy struggled to fully inhabit the skin of Melanie. The character evolved from a driven teenager determined to succeed in the world—something Lissy could relate to—to a grown woman whose life experience left her uncertain, questioning all aspects of her life, including the validity of her own marriage. Everything about the older Melanie—her tone of voice, her posture, her facial expressions—was foreign to Lissy. Emotions like dejection, insecurity, and loss of hope in the future occupied territories Lissy had avoided all her life lest she get stuck in them. And because the story was told in reverse, the unsure and unsteady version of Melanie opened the show. Lissy knew all too well that the opening scene was the moment when the audience would or would not accept the world being presented by the actors on the stage. They would either relax into the illusion or observe every gesture through a lens of uncomfortable skepticism. She had to get it right.

She thought of Mrs. Delano, the director of every show she'd been in on Martha's Vineyard. She'd given Lissy her first big part because of her voice, of course—no one else in the junior high could carry a tune—and Mrs. Delano had spent extra time working with Lissy on her lines and choreography.

"With your voice, if you work extra hard, one day you could be a triple threat," she'd said. Mrs. Delano was demonstrating how to pop open an umbrella and close it in time with a box step. Lissy was only twelve at the time.

"A triple threat?"

"Singing, dancing, and acting. You'd be amazed how many professionals only do one or two well and try to fake the other." Mrs. Delano performed in summer stock "back in the day," as she put it, so she knew what she was talking about. "Excellence in all three is rare."

"My mother was a good dancer when she was young," Lissy said hopefully.

"Was she? Well, in that case, you've got all three in your bones. But never forget, even those who inherit gobs of talent still have to work for it." Mrs. Delano winked.

It marked the first time—maybe the only time—an adult other than her mother acknowledged who her father was. She sounded certain that Lissy had inherited her father's acting chops, and given her vocal strength—assuming she could learn the choreography—it would simply be a matter of putting it all together. Lissy had never before considered the possibility of inheriting talent. Her mother's physical features had obviously been passed down to her—people always commented on how remarkable their similarities were, calling Lissy a miniature version of her mother—but she hadn't realized that she might be a carbon copy of her father too, from the inside. If she could fuse his acting gift with her mother's natural grace and her own voice, maybe she truly could be exceptional. And maybe that braiding of talents would bring her mother happiness, make all the heartache worth it somehow. She grabbed the umbrella and worked the latch. Open. Close. Open. Close. Step, cross, back, side. She danced until her feet gave out, then spent the night poring over her lines.

Lissy applied the same ethic to the *Happily* script, convincing Noah to rehearse one of their scenes at home every night, or Bae if she was back at the apartment. During the day, she watched her fellow actors closely, hoping to absorb something of their craft. JoJo, in particular, astounded Lissy.

JoJo arrived each day chomping on a stick of Doublemint gum, then she spit it out into the garbage can next to the piano before disappearing into her demure character. Her high-pitched laughter at her own jokes infected everyone, and she was the first to break out of a scene to suggest an edit to Zimmerman. "Wait a minute. This line makes no sense. It's gotta be something more like: 'Doing the right thing can be the hard thing,' not this crap about 'I hope you're happy with the choices you made.' That just sounds mean," she said one day, shocking Lissy with her directness, not to mention Zimmerman's acquiescence to her point. But as soon as the scene started again, JoJo cast aside her crusty shell and exposed a soft and pliable creature, its tiny tentacles waving in the light.

"How do you do it?"

They were sharing one of the deli sandwiches brought in for lunch every day. Lissy and JoJo made a pact to always share a sandwich lest they gain ten pounds before the show opened.

"Do what?" JoJo picked a stray piece of pastrami from her teeth.

"Transform yourself so completely into Debbie. No offense, but she's the kind of person I can't imagine you having patience with in real life. She's so accommodating, so . . . I don't know. Bland, maybe?"

"No. She's not bland. She wants everyone around her to feel good. My father's like that. When I get home from rehearsal every night, he'll say something like, 'The creole's on the stove and ready to go, but you let me know if you need a long bath before we sit.' And I feel this glow inside, you know? Like he just wants me to be happy. So when I step onto the stage as Debbie, I basically picture myself as a mirror of my father, shining light on everyone else."

Lissy understood part of what JoJo was saying. The romantic scenes with Noah came naturally to her because she had experienced the emotions attached to them. But she wasn't sure she knew anyone like the older Melanie, so disillusioned. Even after suffering through tragedy, her mother had a positive outlook, always finding the best in everyone around her.

"But what if you didn't have a father like yours? What if the character represents something you don't know well? What do you do then?"

JoJo scratched at her wild mane. Zimmerman told her it would need to be tamed for previews. She told him she needed an extra twenty-five dollars each week, so she could go to her local salon and get it done right.

"Don't overthink it. You know how they always say there are only five basic characters in any story—or ten when you include their foils?" Lissy hadn't heard this. "The giver and the taker; the commander and the rebel; the lover and the siren; the innocent and the sage; and the joker and the straight man." JoJo ticked these off as easily as one might say that sand went with sea, something everyone already knew. "I pick out which one my character is from the pack and exaggerate it. The theater is all about exaggeration, right? Our gestures need to big enough to be seen by the back row, and the songs have to be dramatic enough to be sure the audience gets the point. This one's easy. Debbie is giver, giver, giver, giver!"

Lissy nodded her head and mentally ticked through her scenes, trying to fit Melanie into one of the buckets, unsure she could narrow it down quite so easily. As a teenager Melanie radiated bravado, the burgeoning activist determined to change the world, but the role of wife and mother dulled her confidence, leaving her wistful, questioning the ingredients of a fulfilling life. Could one character be both a rebel and an innocent?

JoJo slapped Lissy on the back. "You're doin' great. Don't worry so much."

Bert, on the other hand, either never broke character or was the same person in real life. His role of Sal, Cassidy's goofy sidekick, was burly but gentle, funny in a self-deprecating way. In JoJo's list of characters, he was definitely the joker, the comic relief. Of course, the comic relief often brought a fair bit of wisdom. Maybe she *was* overthinking it.

"Okay, everyone, lunch break's over. Let's take it from the top of act two in five. This is the last time before full run-throughs, so let's make it count." Gray flashed his electric smile.

Act two. Lissy tried to come up with something in between rebel and innocent to represent Melanie in those scenes. Lost wanderer? Could she make up her own archetype? At least the act opened with "Go Time," one of her solos. She pulled a lozenge from her bag and breathed deeply into her diaphragm. She didn't have long before the audience would be let into the cocoon of their world for the first time. She had to get it right.

CHAPTER TWENTY-FIVE

The producers decided early on to run the *Happily After Ever* previews in New York, on the same stage as the eventual grand opening. It was an unconventional choice. Previews were normally performed in a smaller market like Boston, which allowed the show-runners time to gauge an audience's initial reaction and hear feedback from less important critics before letting the curtain go up in front of a proper Broadway crowd. If there were changes to make, songs or scripts to alter, Manhattan theatergoers would be none the wiser, treated only to the final version of the show. But Zimmerman and Gray had done this so many times before that the underwriters saw out-of-town previews as an unnecessary expense. They saw no need to cart sets to another city or pay for the travel and board of a cast in another town, not when *Happily* would be welcomed with open arms in New York.

The afternoon of the first preview, Lissy woke to a streak of sun glaring at her like a spotlight through Noah's flimsy shade. Her mind waded through the murk of deep sleep and scrambled for purchase until the present came into focus. Tonight would mark the first time they would perform in front of an audience. There would be two weeks of previews, six nights a week. Then the grand opening.

The last seven days had been a whirlwind of walk-throughs and final tweaks, the cast finally able to rehearse at the theater with the full set intact. Stepping onto the stage of the Majestic Theatre for the first time, Lissy took several minutes to stop staring dumbly out at the rows of red velvet seats in the orchestra, the gilded woodwork of the mezzanine, and especially the private boxes on the sides, each one looking like a royal carriage suspended in the air. Lissy had watched countless curtain calls, the actors beaming from the stage, raising their palms in the direction of those little boxes, handing up their gratitude before the heavy curtain cascaded down with a satisfying *thump*.

She had always imagined the actors retreating backstage to luxurious dressing rooms, lounging with fellow castmates, or receiving visits from luminaries in town to see the show. Now she knew the dressing rooms to be hardly bigger than closets. She shared hers with JoJo and Bae, who had ultimately decided to take the part of Trudy, although Lissy could still feel the doubts hanging on her like an ill-fitting costume. The narrow space had just enough room for a counter with three makeup stations, each barely wider than the metal stools tucked beneath. The radiator on the opposite wall relentlessly competed with a standing fan at the far end of the room, the one window blocked by a costume rack.

The intensity of rehearsals plus the powerful mix of excitement and anxiety in the run-up to opening night had left Lissy exhausted. After telling Noah she just needed to close her eyes for a few of the 236 minutes remaining until the first preview, she had apparently slipped into a deep sleep.

She looked at her watch before pushing herself up on one elbow and rubbing her eyes. She located Noah across the room, hunched at his small kitchen table, a mug in one hand and a letter in the other. His eyes weren't moving, suggesting he had read the contents of the page but continued to look at it anyway.

"Noah?"

"It's from RCA. They like one of my songs."

She didn't know he'd sent out any demo tapes recently.

"But it's not me they want." He sat next to her on the bed and handed her the letter.

Lissy sat up and squinted against the sunlight reflecting off the page.

> *While we don't feel your solo work is a good fit for our label, we have a band under contract that is very interested in the song entitled "Resurrection" and would like to purchase the rights and produce it as a rock ballad. Please contact us at . . .*

Lissy threw her arms around Noah's shoulders.

"That's incredible! Any idea who it could be?"

How exciting it would be to have one of Noah's songs recorded by an established band. She could already hear Casey Kasem introducing it as a new arrival to his countdown, or better yet, hearing it sung aloud by a stadium full of voices.

His arms stayed at his sides.

"That's my best song." His tone suggested he took their praise as an insult somehow. "Maybe I'm crazy, but I don't think I can give up that song. It feels like giving up on *me*."

Lissy understood the pain of this kind of half-chance, like being cast as the understudy, which could cut deeper than a flat-out rejection. To be impressive enough to be seriously considered but failing to fully capitalize on the opportunity. Close, but just not good enough.

It would probably be easier to think some jerk in a suit had tossed his tape into the trash without playing it, rather than imagine a recording executive with his feet up on his desk saying, "I don't care for the kid, but the song's not half-bad."

Of course, other songwriters would kill to sell their work.

"It's a validation of your songwriting. And there could be a lot of money involved if it becomes a hit."

"It's not about the money."

Noah took the letter back, threw it into the trash can beside the bed, and slipped the business card from RCA under the lamp perched on the nightstand. Lissy shook herself back to reality. Two hours from now, she'd be debuting on Broadway.

She took Noah's hand in hers and kissed it, feeling doubly blessed to have found him at the same moment as she was finally getting her start in professional theater. Noah was the first guy she had ever dated who knew the whole truth of her, one of the only people in her life other than a few friends on the Vineyard, who understood where she had come from. She'd never even told Bae, fearing it might throw their friendship off-kilter somehow. But telling Noah the truth—seeing how little it fazed him—felt like edging the top off a boiling kettle, the steady release of steam an incredible relief. And she was surprised by how much she wanted to talk to him about it all: everything she did and didn't know about her father, about her parents' love affair, her mother's determination to make their mother-daughter duo a happy one—which was occasionally a little suffocating. Noah listened to her patiently, never pushing her to say more or rushing her to move onto another topic. It made her feel fully seen, perhaps for the first time in her life.

"Big night tonight, kid." Noah squeezed her hand. "You ready?"

"Only one way to find out."

Lissy, Noah, Bae, JoJo, and Bert took their places behind the heavy curtain as the hum of the tuning violins and oboes faded and the crowd welcomed the conductor with ravenous applause. It was easy to hear how full the house was, all those clapping hands. She looked at Bae and smiled. They had actually done it, made it all the way here.

All her years of performing in countless school plays on Martha's Vineyard and then at Vassar came back to her, that young girl onstage who needed to find her mother in the audience before she could begin. Lissy thought of Graham, who helped her rehearse lines on so many afternoons in the gallery after school, playing every part she ever asked of him; of Mrs. Delano, who introduced her to *Grandstand*, her first Zimmerman and Gray musical; and of Georgia, who regularly told her she could succeed at anything she really wanted. Lissy hoped they would all be proud of her now.

Especially her mother. She'd always been supportive of anything Lissy wanted to try, from letting her take surfing lessons to driving her to the animal shelter up-island every Saturday morning back when Lissy was convinced she wanted to be a vet. And she didn't blink when Lissy began to express an interest in the theater, even though Lissy sensed there was more at stake for her mother in this arena. She might as well have been the child of Muhammad Ali trying to float and sting with the same power as the original. Lissy suspected her mother held her breath every time she stepped onstage, willing her not to fall too far short. Lissy knew better than to raise the topic. Once, when she'd asked her mother if there was anything about her that reminded her of him, her mother stiffened and fell silent, as if afraid to admit that no, there were no similarities, that fate's cruel whims had failed to leave some bit of him behind in their daughter. But if Lissy could shine on Broadway, it would be like giving her mother back a piece of him, proof that he did live on in her. And what a miraculous way for it to manifest.

This is it.

The first chords of the overture rumbled in Lissy's chest. She planted her heels firmly on the stage, reminding herself to keep a slight bend in her knees lest she keel over. She took as deep a breath as she could muster. As the orchestra transitioned from "Roll It Back" to the crescendo of "Stay with Me," Noah squeezed her hand. She took one last inhale and lifted the sides of her mouth into a stage-worthy smile in time with the rising curtain. The audience applauded all over again as the velvet wall ascended, their excitement at being the first to see a brand-new production palpable. The applause soothed the rough edges of Lissy's nerves. The crowd loved them already, and they had yet to utter a line.

The stage lights came up, and it all felt effortless, like a sailboat catching the wind, moving in concert with the waves, catapulting across the sea. The full company transformed into a single unit, everyone hitting their marks perfectly, the harmonies flying off the rafters. The triumph of the opening number created a high unlike anything Lissy had ever experienced.

It didn't last.

While Lissy couldn't make out the faces of the audience past the stage lights, the shifting in seats and disapproving murmurs became increasingly distracting by the third scene. The applause after "Life's Too Short," the second large number, was lackluster, and at the end of the first act, Lissy saw a dark mass the size of an elephant moving through the audience. It took her a moment to understand that she was watching the backs of ten or fifteen patrons push past their seatmates and walk out.

When the lights came up at the end of the show, the house was only half-full. Lissy raised no palms to the empty boxes. There were no shouts of "Brava!" or bouquets showered on her. The cast took the briefest of bows before trudging off the stage.

Zimmerman and Gray gathered the cast after the theater emptied. Their expressions were grim but not hopeless.

"This is why we do previews. We need audience reaction so we can get the show where it needs to be. No point in getting overly upset about tonight. It happens." Gray stuffed his hands into his pockets and paced as he spoke. "Hal and I are going to work up some changes. We'll need everyone here at eleven A.M. tomorrow so we can walk through anything that's new. We'll hold off on any other notes until then. Go get some sleep."

Every day from then on, Zimmerman presented changes to the script, sometimes an entirely new scene to be memorized, blocked, and rehearsed. The main feedback centered on the progression of time in the show, which baffled the audience. They didn't understand that the cast, who all looked young enough to be teenagers, were presenting their future, middle-aged selves in the opening scene, with each subsequent scene moving backward until they were, in fact, in high school. It was a daring conceit requiring a nuanced script and subtle acting. Lissy thought it was Zimmerman's greatest achievement. Preview audiences didn't yet agree, but Lissy trusted the men at the helm to figure it out.

Zimmerman spent most of his efforts rewriting the openings of each scene, finding ways to more clearly signal how many years in reverse the action had moved. Some of the best lines of the show emerged through this work, and Lissy began to look forward to the new script handed out each morning.

Gray rethought the costumes. He hit on the radical idea, which Lissy thought particularly brilliant, of each character wearing a T-shirt throughout the show with a one-word description of their persona printed on the front. While accessories would signal significant changes in age—a skirt with pantyhose and pumps for Melanie when she was middle-aged versus short shorts in her youth—the T-shirt would stay the same. Cassidy's shirt said "Rock Star," while Melanie's said "Activist." This alone gave the opening scenes greater depth as the audience took in the words and gestures of the adult through the lens of who each person originally hoped to be—the disillusioned housewife and the bored banker trying to put on a brave face all while unable to escape, quite literally, the pronouncements they'd made about themselves in their youth. As the show progressed, the audience would better grasp the unfolding of the past and understand they were witnessing the same person, moving back in time, coming into their own as the young person with a sincere dream for the future intact. The point was that the teenager was still in the adult, the adult was always in the teenager.

As the alterations to costumes, scenes, and songs unfolded, the curtain went up every night. Sitting in the dressing room between Bae and JoJo before each performance, patting on base, rubbing in her rouge, and lining her eyes in charcoal with blue eyeshadow above, Lissy envisioned increasing levels of success—first no uncomfortable murmurs from the audience, then the entire house filling again after intermission, and eventually the sound of all those velvet seats springing up in unison as the finale hit its last chord, the audience jumping to their feet with resounding applause. They were getting closer and closer every day.

After each show, Noah flopped onto his bed and drank a beer while Lissy ticked through a daily list of improvements—beats the audience had responded to, why the show was leaps and bounds better than the first night. Noah nodded along with each point or sometimes disagreed, all while flipping the business card of the RCA executive from finger to finger like a card shark. He'd told RCA he wasn't interested in selling his song, that if they wanted it, they needed to sign him too. But his attachment to the card made Lissy wonder if he regretted it. The exec told him to give them a call if he ever changed his mind.

On a rare afternoon off, Lissy went back to her apartment to scrounge for some clean clothes. She called her mother to tell her previews had been extended so they could continue to tweak the show, pushing opening night back by two weeks. Her mother wanted to come to New York as previously planned anyway, but Lissy convinced her to wait until opening night. Once the script was finally locked down, all remaining wrinkles smoothed away and the timing between new lines tightened, the ease of repetition would be restored. The show wouldn't be ready until then.

"I want you to see the best version of the show."

What she didn't say was that she also wanted to perfect her own performance before her mother came to watch. She was on the verge of a Judy Garland and Liza Minnelli moment—even if only she and her mother would know it. Lissy wanted to share it with the only other person on the planet to whom it really mattered.

After hanging up the phone, she realized Bae had been in the bathroom for an unusually long time. Lissy put her head to the door to ask if she was all right.

After a pause, Bae let out a small, "I'm fine." Lissy heard the tears in her voice.

"Bae?"

Lissy pushed through the door to find Bae sitting on the floor, her face swollen with crying, a half-crumpled newspaper at her side.

"What is it?"

Bae looked up as if to say something, but then brought her fingers to her quivering lips as another tear careened over her cheek.

"I'm sorry. I promised myself I wouldn't do this. But everything's such a mess."

Lissy sat on the pink bath mat next to Bae and leaned against the ceramic tub. Bae picked up the newspaper and handed it to her. Lissy scanned the smudged page of the *New York Times* and followed Bae's index finger to the article in question, a review of *A Chorus Line*, the show Bae had passed up. Lissy's chest tightened as she read the glowing words of Clive Barnes, the most important critic in all of theater. He spoke of the show as if he had just attended a coronation. Not only did he call it a moment of pure joy, a groundbreaking event that would change Broadway forever, but he gushed that it was the kind of musical you would "sing to your grandchildren for years to come."

"Oh, Bae." Lissy let the paper fall to her lap.

"Read the end."

In the final paragraph, Barnes praised the entire cast as spectacular— "the perfect ensemble"—and admitted he was loathe to call out any one performance in particular, but he needed to offer a special shout-out to Baayork Lee. She had stepped into the role of Connie only three nights before the opening due to a freak accident in which the original actress broke her ankle. "If this show has a heart, she just might be it."

Bae had been cast as Connie's understudy. Barnes could have been talking about Bae.

All Lissy's self-assurances that *Happily After Ever* had finally improved enough for a rousing opening reception broke into a thousand pieces, like a crusty layer of sand that looks solid until you try to pick it up. No matter how many changes they made, even if *Happily* went on to a respectable run, she knew it would never reach the rarefied air of *A Chorus Line*. If Barnes was right—and he was always right—it would have the kind of staying power that was every showrunner's dream, maybe even surpassing previous Zimmerman and Gray hits.

"You said this wouldn't happen." Bae's voice was hoarse from crying.

"I didn't know anything about *A Chorus Line*—"

"No, when you said Hal and Rudy couldn't possibly miss, that their show was guaranteed to be a hit. Why did you insist on dragging me into that? This is what I gave up." Bae gestured to the paper. "For what?"

"No matter what happens, playing Trudy will be good for your career."

"You still don't get it, do you? They tell me all the time that I'm too small to play a leading lady. First my legs aren't long enough to be a principal dancer, and then I'm not tall enough for a leading role. But do you know what they're really saying? I'm not white enough."

Bae never let her anger show. Not even when her father said she shouldn't come home until she made something of herself.

"Bae—"

"Don't. Do you know how tall Sandy Duncan is? Five feet two. Your beloved Judy Garland? Four feet eleven, Lissy. Not even five feet. You don't have to be tall in this town. You have to be white!"

Bae's voice reverberated off the tile.

"I don't quite understand what that has to do with this show." Lissy tentatively picked the paper up off her lap.

Bae didn't try to hide her frustration and sighed like she was giving directions for the third time to someone with a perfectly good map at their disposal.

"Listen to what I'm saying. Connie only exists in *A Chorus Line* because it's a story of misfits, frustrated actors, including the Asian who never gets the part. Baayork Lee is showing everyone that people like us can hold their own onstage, in the most important musical of our time. And now, in ring number two"—Bae swept her arms out to the sides, imitating a circus announcer, her voice thick with sarcasm— "short Asian number two, Miss BaeJin Kim, is going to demonstrate what total failure looks like."

Lissy had no response. For the first time, she considered the unthinkable, the possibility that the show she had convinced Bae to choose, her own Broadway debut, might flop. Her big break might crumble into a thousand grainy pieces and disappear with the tide.

Bae pulled herself up and stepped over Lissy's legs. Lissy couldn't move.

"Where are you going?"

"We're supposed to be best friends in this show, remember? I'm gonna need some space to get into character."

Bae slammed the door, leaving Lissy alone on the cold tile floor.

CHAPTER TWENTY-SIX

The phone next to Noah's bed rang at an unacceptable hour—at least for anyone slogging through previews—jarring Lissy out of a deep sleep. *Who calls before nine A.M.?*

After postperformance notes were given each night, makeup was removed, and cabs were hailed, it was always past midnight before she and Noah got back to his place. It took another hour before leftover adrenaline could be extinguished enough to contemplate sleep. The only saving grace was the ability to cocoon in until at least ten every morning. And on this particular morning, with no eleven o'clock rehearsal to attend, Lissy had intended to stay in bed until noon. Zimmerman had declared the script finished the night before, the audience had stayed in their seats, and the show was finally ready.

"It's Rudy." Noah stretched the phone across the bed to her.

Rudy? Lissy jerked herself upright. How did he know to call her at Noah's?

"Hello?" Despite trying to sound awake, her first word of the morning was a croak. She pulled the sheets up to her throat as if Rudy could see her naked body, as if Noah could intuit the passionate kiss she'd shared with Rudy during auditions. Nausea gripped her.

"I'm sorry to wake you, but I was hoping you might be able to come into the office this morning. There's something I'd like to discuss."

Lissy's skin went numb and cold, akin to a too-early-in-the-season jump into the Atlantic. She robotically agreed on a time to meet and handed the phone back to Noah so he could hang it up. One looming question took shape in her mind.

"Are they going to fire me?" Saying it out loud frightened her, like opening the cage of a beast and encouraging it to attack.

"What? Of course not."

The enormity of the responsibility she'd been carrying pressed in on her, and her head started to ache. Since the start of rehearsals, she'd feared she was the weak link in the show. She'd heard her castmates collectively groan whenever it took her a third round of running through a new scene to get it right. Zimmerman often gave her more postperformance notes than the other actors, which she told herself was normal for the lead. But in truth, unlike her experiences in high school and even college, when her voice alone put her performances leaps and bounds above her castmates', she'd felt insufficient from the moment she got this part. She didn't fully embody Melanie, didn't always feel what Melanie should be feeling, even after all those hours of trying to become her.

"I'm not cutting it," she said, more to herself than to Noah.

The admission fractured something essential in her. She'd believed for years that she'd been granted something special at birth, a rare talent she would eventually be able to access with the help of experts like Zimmerman and Gray. But she'd failed to fully unlock her father's gift for acting, failed to transform her performance into something extraordinary. She was no triple threat. Maybe a dual dud, or a single sham. She'd have no salve to offer her mother after all.

"Lissy, the show opens in a week. No way they make a change now."

She flinched at his words. He didn't say they'd be crazy to swap her out because she was incredible in the role, only that he thought it was too late.

"It happens more than you think. We all have understudies ready to go at a moment's notice. A week is plenty of time to prepare." She picked up a pair of shorts from the floor and put them on. "And if they want to make a change, they have to do it now. Doing it after the show opens definitely wouldn't look good." She knew it to be true.

Embarrassment ballooned in her chest. She had failed in the worst kind of way, letting down her castmates, the crew, the whole team.

Noah grabbed her hand midgesture and kissed her palm.

"You're working yourself up for no reason. Just go talk to him."

"What if I'm right?" She needed to know. What would she do then?

"If you're right, you'll come back here, and you'll crawl right back into bed with me. I'm not here for Melanie. I'm here to be with Lissy Horowitz."

She leaned into him, trying to breathe in his easy perspective on the world, drink in his assurance that she was a whole person, not just a flailing actress. And thank god Noah was more interested in the person. She also reminded herself that she'd worked hard her entire life to make sure she had options, and she would use them.

At least that's what she told herself all the way to Rudy's office door.

"Greetings." Rudy walked around his desk and gestured to a pair of dilapidated chairs on the other side. "Sorry to interrupt the love nest this morning."

Lissy took a seat and decided to ignore his comment. The smoke drifting up from the ashtray on the desk tickled the back of her throat, and she wished she had taken his secretary up on her offer of tea. But she wanted to get this over with.

With previews ongoing, Zimmerman and Gray operated out of their small office on 55th Street, five floors up in a building that probably used to be white but was now various shades of brown and tan, the grit of the city streets smeared across the façade. An upright piano crowded one corner of Rudy's office below a poster of *Grandstand*, curled at the edges. His desk swayed beneath stacks of scores, scripts, and newspapers. And she'd considered Gray the tidy one.

"Listen, I'm sure you know our shaky run of previews has created certain challenges."

Lissy's eyes traced a rip in the carpet that snaked under the bookcase behind Rudy. She only partially took in his next words—that while the script had improved dramatically, it was increasingly difficult to overcome the rumblings around town that the show was in trouble. Ticket sales to the opening weeks were slow. Critics who'd already seen it needed a reason to come back. Critics who hadn't seen it needed a reason to come at all. More than anything, they needed droves of people to line up and hand over their hard-earned dollars for a ticket. The words *sold out*, more than anything else, were the secret to Broadway success, a self-fulfilling prophecy. Everyone wanted to get into the show they couldn't get into, and like a cat chasing its own tail around and around, audiences would scramble for months just trying to get in the door. But they needed to find a way to create an initial rush. They needed a wow factor, otherwise the show might not make it.

He finally paused to take a breath. Lissy gripped the arms of her chair.

"So I had an idea this morning as I was proofing the Playbill. What do you say we put your real name in there?"

Lissy snapped her eyes off the floor. He wanted to discuss the Play-bill? She wasn't sure she understood and forced herself to push past the scrim in her mind that was only registering shadows of ideas.

"What do you mean by my real name?"

"Okay, or stage name, whatever you want to call it. I hoped we wouldn't need it, quite frankly, but playing up the fact that you're Christopher Page's daughter? The missing Bella of the ball? People would be thrilled to see you onstage. And the people who buy tickets to Broadway are my generation, trust me. Your father's name means something to them. They'll come running."

The enormity of what he was asking created a new weight in her chest. She'd been raised with the understanding that she should neither give people cause to confuse who she was with any mention of her father's famous name nor try to gain any advantage from it. It warped reality. But she'd stupidly mentioned it in her audition materials. Had they intended to use it as a marketing ploy all along? Had that been enough to tip the scales in her favor? She would never know. That was her mother's point.

"I don't know if that is such a good idea."

"We need this for the show, Lissy. And it would be good for you. Raise your profile. Why not?"

Why not?

A sudden flare of anger surprised her. Why had she been burdened with the promise of keeping her father's identity hidden her whole life? Why couldn't she be proud of her origins, proud to share her father's legacy? Was there really any harm in that? Lissy's father was part of her, and the fact that her mother had forced such an important piece of her own identity into the shadows suddenly felt wrong. Why couldn't she be Christopher Page's daughter and be entirely herself at the same time? Why not be proud of the combination?

But something beyond the edges of her anger pulled on Lissy and tilted the room off-balance. Half of her mind understood this as a momentous decision, while the other half couldn't quite make sense of what she was choosing. She felt like she'd been tossed off a cliff with only a split second of float before free fall would begin. She could either pull a rip cord and glide to safety, or accept a nauseating dive toward destruction, and she wasn't sure which option represented which outcome. Was using her father's name the safety hatch or an accelerator toward doom? She forced herself to concentrate.

Rudy Gray, one half of Zimmerman and Gray, was asking her, Lissy Horowitz, to do them a simple favor to help make their show a success. If she could actually help, didn't she owe it to him? To the rest of the cast? Didn't she especially owe it to Bae? And was it really such a big deal? They just needed to get the audience into their seats. She would still have to deliver an impeccable performance to earn authentic accolades. The show would be judged on its merits.

"Okay. Sure." Her voice sounded small in her own head, and vertigo swirled the room again, making her unable to tell if she'd just flung herself off a small step or the edge of a canyon.

"Terrific." Relief spread across Rudy's face as he smiled. "Here's the printer's proof. Make any other edits to your bio you'd like, and I'll send it off."

Lissy looked at the words that would be printed in the yellow-and-black pamphlet handed to every person with a ticket, the publication that would mark the start of her professional career. After reading it over several times, she decided to make another edit. If she was going to do this, she was going to own it.

"Josh Allen from the *Village Voice* is coming in to interview me this morning." Rudy checked his watch. "In fact, he should be here in ten minutes. I'd like you to join us, okay? Tell him your story. It will make for great PR."

Lissy shifted in her chair. Ten minutes. Ten minutes to take off the persona of Lissy Horowitz and become someone else.

CHAPTER TWENTY-SEVEN

Lissy got off the subway two stops early to walk and think. The interview was an out-of-body experience, the reporter treating her like some kind of exotic bird. He was so eager to ask her which of her father's movies was her favorite, what it felt like watching him on the screen. Did she have any tics or tendencies she could ascribe to him? He was riveted by all her answers. Lissy was flattered until she realized he was less interested in her particular plumes than those of her more extravagant parent.

She told him about the time when she was ten and her mother showed her three newspaper clippings to help her understand who her father was—one of the elopement, one about him winning the Oscar for *Moonlight Sonata*, and one about his death. Lissy laughed as she recalled her initial amazement at seeing her own mother in a newspaper, how she almost missed the point.

She described how she religiously scoured the TV Guide from then on, hoping Saturday Night at the Movies on CBS would choose to feature him. She mentioned how it frustrated her not to be able to back up the film if she missed a line or slow it down so it would last longer than the ninety-minute time slot. She told him Dixon Grace was her favorite of his famous characters and admitted to crying every time she watched *The Last Tycoon*.

She didn't mention that those movies were her only memories of him. Or that her mother had otherwise erased him from the house. She didn't tell him there were no photographs of their little family from when she was a baby, no stories her mother liked to repeat. Just a kind of stony sadness walling her off whenever the TV flickered to black-and-white and he walked into the small box. Some nights her mother tried to pull Lissy away, saying, "You don't really want to watch this again, do you? Let's do something fun." Lissy always found that to be strange. Why would she want to deprive Lissy of any chance to see her father alive?

She also didn't mention to the reporter her odd desire to see a glimpse of her father's ankles on the screen, hoping to find her own. She was always on the hunt for a certain thickness above his shoe, the origin of her only feature bearing no resemblance to her mother, proof of her paternal connection. But all his characters wore long trousers, and even in a moment of real promise, when he put his feet up on his detective's desk in *Hawker*, the camera revealed nothing more than the bottoms of his black shoes.

Equally frustrating, no matter how close she scooched to the Trinitron TV to study his movements, it was impossible for her to tell who her father was underneath the guise of his many characters. Some actors, Lissy had learned over time, always played essentially the same person, pouring a lot of their own personality into every role. Her father became the characters he portrayed, each one entirely different. She hunted for reappearing intonations and gestures, any regular expressions or movements she could identify as belonging to the person behind the illusion, but she could never find any. This was why, she supposed, he was so revered as an actor.

The one photograph Lissy did have of her short time in LA was of just her and her mother. Her mother wore a terrycloth robe with Lissy on her lap, wrapped in a towel. Her mother's glamour—the perfect wave of her blond hair and her long legs peeking out from the robe—was less central to the scene than her obvious joy in the moment, the camera catching her midlaugh while Lissy patted her cheek. All of Lissy's memories were like this, just the two of them, a happy pair.

The thought slowed Lissy's steps. Would her mother be disappointed in her for using his stage name? Maybe even angry, considering it an attempt to snatch unearned acclaim, akin to asking for the heavyweight belt before stepping into the ring? She wondered what Noah would think. She hoped he would pull her into his arms, tell her it didn't matter one whit what name she used, that every ounce of recognition she was about to receive for the show would be fully deserved and would have nothing to do with her father; that they were creating two characters together who would stick in the minds of audiences for years to come; that their duets would long be hummed by young lovers, dreaming of the future. Hearing those declarations in her head filled her with renewed confidence, her excitement building for the promise of opening night.

By the time she climbed the stairs to Noah's apartment, she was practically laughing at herself for worrying about being fired. Anxiety put to rest, she would stretch out beside Noah for another hour or two, perhaps fall back to sleep. They deserved a day of lounging. In fact, she wanted to take advantage of every remaining day, to store up as much energy as possible, until *Happily* opened. She'd heard it said that starring in a Broadway show was as exhausting as running a marathon every day of the week. They had only completed their warm-ups. The official race hadn't even begun.

When Lissy flung open the door, Noah wasn't lying in bed but sitting on the edge of it, staring at the floor the way one might gaze at the linoleum in an emergency room, waiting to hear the fate of a patient. His obvious concern for her sent a new burst of warmth through her. She did love this man.

"Not dead yet!" She threw her arms up in a sign of victory. "But can we still crawl back into bed?" She pushed at him playfully to roll him back onto the comforter. He barely budged, bending only slightly before returning to his stoic position.

"That's great." He nodded his head as if trying to convince himself, or trying to remember where she'd gone and why. Something was wrong.

"What is it?" She settled next to him.

He took a deep breath and repositioned himself on the bed to look at her directly. Suddenly she felt like the one waiting for news from the doctor.

"Remember the band that wanted to record my song?"

"Of course." Lissy's mind raced. Maybe he'd decided to sell it to them after all?

"Their guitarist had a psychotic break. They want me to take his place."

"Holy shit!" Lissy bounced as she turned to him, then stopped. "Wait. When?"

"They have six weeks left on their tour. Then they're going into the studio to record their next album. They want my song on the album, Lissy. With me in the band." He sounded like he had practiced these words but didn't yet believe them to be true.

"Six weeks from now? You can't leave the show six weeks into the opening run." Lissy's confusion hardened into a flash of anger. He was talking nonsense.

"Lissy." He took her hands in his. "Their next concert is tomorrow night. I won't get this gig, including the recording, unless I join them on the road. Now."

"So you turned them down."

He didn't respond.

"I don't understand." She pulled her hands back. He couldn't walk out on *Happily*. They were a team. A duo. Costars. Nobody walked out on a Broadway show.

"You said it yourself this morning. A week is plenty of time. Jake knows the role cold."

She couldn't process his words. He was going to leave this to Jake? The understudy?

"You can't do this, Noah. The show's already in trouble. Everyone knows it. This will sink us." She needed him to understand the implications of leaving, to feel awful for even contemplating it, let alone going through with it. The show couldn't handle any more missteps, and her career hung in the balance. Being the lead in a failed show wasn't exactly the best way to get future work. An understudy in a successful show, as it turned out, was a much better path to success. She thought of Bae and winced.

"I told them I'd be in Philly by noon tomorrow."

He had already decided. She backed away from the bed.

"I half-hoped they'd fired you so you could come with me." He tried a smile, his eyes pleading with her.

That was what he thought of her career? It was so unimportant that he wished it had been cut short so she could—what? Become a groupie of some dumb band?

"You're leaving tomorrow?" The feeling of vertigo threatened to topple her again.

"They're opening for the Eagles." He allowed his excitement to take over for a moment, his dimples on full display, the energy back in his limbs.

"You can't do this. It's breach of contract."

"What are they going to do? Sue me?"

If he were anyone else, she'd tell him they would make sure he never got another part in the city, but she knew it wouldn't matter to him. But didn't he care about her enough not to yank out from under her feet the one thing keeping her steady onstage?

She thought back to their first night, how effortlessly they had come together. But she never did stand a chance against his guitar. She would never convince him to forgo this opportunity. It was what he'd been waiting for. She wished she could say she couldn't blame him. Like hell she couldn't.

"Rudy is about to send the Playbill out for printing. You better call him right now so he can take your name off it." She practically spit the words at him.

"Please understand, Lissy." He reached for her.

She dodged him and yanked open the door.

"Get your name off the show, Noah."

The hollow door of his apartment didn't provide the loud slam she'd hoped for. No satisfaction bloomed alongside her anger, no comfort arose from her abrupt departure, only a deep sadness that followed her down the stairwell and out onto the street.

When she got back to her apartment, she was relieved to find it empty. She needed to regroup. How did everything become such a mess? She'd just agreed to flaunt her famous lineage—which felt like opening up her underwear drawer to all of New York—in an attempt to save something she was no longer sure could be saved. Did she have it in her to conjure a memorable love story if Noah wasn't the one on the stage with her? Or was she about to become the most famous flop in Broadway history?

And what about Bae? She needed to pull herself together, if only for Bae. She had practically forced Bae to do this show. And now it was on death's door.

No. That was *not* how it would go. She'd faced major setbacks before. Like the time the black box theater at Vassar inadvertently printed the wrong date on the tickets for her one-woman performance of *The Music Café*. And when her costar in *Oklahoma!* couldn't hit his high notes thanks to a case of over-rehearsing laryngitis. She'd still found a way to make those shows a success. And *Happily* had evolved into something far superior to what the first preview audience had seen. Lissy's name and story attached to it would double ticket sales overnight—Gray had been certain about that—and Jake would make a fine Cassidy. *Happily After Ever* simply had to succeed. Anything else was unacceptable.

Lissy pulled herself off the couch and put Carole King on the turntable. It had a way of setting everything right in her heart. She carefully placed the needle on the sixth groove on the second side and belted out the words to "Tapestry" as if she was alone on a Vineyard beach with no one to listen for miles. Her life had always felt like a tapestry, rich with hues of love, secretly royal, just like King sang it. Now was the time for her to mine the magic woven into her bloodstream, to prove she was worthy of where she'd come from.

PART II

CHAPTER TWENTY-EIGHT

New York City
September 1975

Aster wove her way through the chattering crowd to the will call window and picked up the ticket Lissy had left for her. She followed the usher down the aisle as he walked closer and closer to the stage, the majesty of the theater enveloping her like a forest of velvet and brass. The hum of the orchestra coming to life in the pit vibrated in her chest, and as she settled into her seat, she tried to find calm in the murmur of the strings and the wind instruments all drawing out the same long note.

The couple seated next to her smiled in her direction, and the man held out his plate-sized paw.

"I think this row's just for family. Joe Callahan, and my wife, Elena. We're Bert's parents. He plays Sal."

"Lovely to meet you. My daughter plays Melanie."

"I don't think I've ever been so nervous in my life," Elena said, as all three of them turned their attention to their laps.

Aster caressed the cover of the Playbill, a time-honored tradition and clever ploy to cajole the audience into perusing ads for restaurants and tourist attractions amid paragraphs about the director, choreographer, cast, and crew—their collective experience meant to impress before the curtain rose.

Aster thought of the first time she brought Lissy to a professional show. They'd gone into Boston to see *Peter Pan*, Lissy in her bobby socks and Mary Janes. Lissy was astounded by the story unfolding beneath the lights, the boys and girls flying, the stage transformed from bedroom to pirate ship and back. Lissy carried the program all the way back to the Vineyard reverently, the ultimate souvenir. There was a teetering stack of them in her bedroom at home.

Despite Lissy's early appreciation for large-scale productions, Aster was still surprised by her draw toward theater as a serious pursuit. Her foray into musicals as a kid made sense given how much she loved to sing—Aster's friends would joke that they could hear Lissy on her bike before they could see her, her beautiful voice floating on the wind—but she never seemed entirely comfortable once the music stopped. Lissy kept at it anyway.

Lissy had always been accomplishment-oriented, and achieving something easily didn't count. First place in the potato sack contest had meant more to her than Mrs. Humphrey giving her yet another solo in school choir. Lissy had remarkable range—something not expected from the other children—and was Mrs. Humphrey's default choice. Lissy didn't consider those selections a win. Jumping past Bobby Keating for the blue ribbon on field day, on the other hand, was something to celebrate. He was the tallest kid in the class.

Aster had long suspected that all it took to spark Lissy's Broadway dream was a *Life* magazine profile of Mary Martin published during rehearsals for Lissy's first musical—maybe sixth grade? The piece detailed how Martin had to beat out two hundred actresses to win her debut role on Broadway even though her vocal talents were off the charts. Those were just the kinds of odds that revved Lissy up for a challenge. Aster couldn't help but smile at her daughter's perseverance.

Flipping through the pages of the Playbill, she searched for Lissy's bio, evidence of her acceptance into the pantheon of Broadway. The format was always the same—the alphabetical list of cast and crew, a small headshot of each actor, their name in bold, their role in the current production, followed by their prior theatrical achievements—as indelible as the list of seniors in a high school yearbook. Aster scanned the blocks of text, briefly wondering why she hadn't seen Lissy's photo before she came across Bae's—Horowitz should come before Kim. Then her eyes settled on two words she had never before seen combined: *Bella* and *Page. Bella Page.* An icy fist took hold of Aster's heart.

BELLA PAGE—making her Broadway debut in the role of MELANIE, the daughter of beloved Christopher Page has previously been seen in . . .

She read it again, confused by the words before her. Her vision blurred. Lissy never described herself as the daughter of a beloved movie star. She was an ordinary Vineyard kid who could read the tide with one sniff of the salty air, who refused to wear shoes from May through September, even when it poured rain. She drew people to the farmers market just to hear her rendition of "Angel of the Morning" or "Do You Believe in Magic?" None of those things had anything to do with Christopher Page. All of them belonged to Lissy alone. She'd worked hard for summer stock and took all those small roles in New York to get to this moment: Lissy Horowitz, starring on Broadway. Why would she want to detract from her own efforts?

Aster pressed her hands into her thighs to stop them from shaking, her mind reeling. They used to play a game called "ten words" when Lissy was younger—a friend of Aster's suggested it as an easy way to figure out what was going on with a child without asking too many probing questions. Aster thought it was genius. Lissy had to come up with ten words or phrases to describe herself in under a minute. *Vineyarder* and *only child* were always on the list, as was *fish*, because she swam like one. She never could get enough of the water. Other descriptors came and went. *Georgia's best friend, conqueror of striped bass*, or *corn-shucking champion* said one thing, where *too skinny, prisoner*—after being grounded—or *stinks at math* expressed another. Anything remotely close to *daughter of movie star* never made the list.

Aster had of course worried in the early years that Lissy might feel something was missing as she grew up, find their twosome to be incomplete, or worse, be haunted by the ghost of a lost father, a presence that turned everything dull and gray. But their home revolved around activity and laughter, light and music, friends and fun.

And Aster had prepared well for the inevitable questions. When Lissy asked, at the age of five, "Where is my daddy?" Aster was ready with a children's book called *Luna's Den* about a wolf pup who grew up to be strong and happy, loved by the whole pack, though its father had been killed.

Aster was also ready for the next question, which came when Lissy turned seven. This time, "*Who* was my daddy?" Aster simply told her he was a man named Benedict Horowitz who had been an actor in movies before he died. When Lissy asked, "Like *Sleeping Beauty*?" which they had recently seen together in Edgartown, Aster smiled and said yes, it was kind of like that. Lissy nodded and then jumped off Aster's lap to skip rocks in the pond.

Of course, Lissy finally came to understand that the world knew her father as Christopher Page, and his presence surfaced whenever one of his movies came on TV, but those evenings were infrequent. Aster would remind Lissy that the person she saw on the screen wasn't Benedict Horowitz. Christopher Page was an invented quantity. The truth of that, the truth that had been his undoing, inevitably stung Aster's eyes and sent her from the room. Once the movie ended and the television was turned off, he was gone again from their lives.

"Bert didn't tell us about this." Joe pointed to Lissy's bio in his own Playbill and leaned into Aster. "I was a huge fan. I'm so sorry. What a shame."

He appraised her with a look Aster hadn't experienced in years, like he had suddenly noticed a set of crowned jewels atop her head, his expression loaded with deference, apologetic for not realizing earlier his inferior standing in the world. She immediately became both invisible and a flashing beacon, exposed once again as Christopher Page's wife, the legend's widow.

A rush of heat crested over the back of her skull and turned moist behind her eyes. Reflexively, she slipped on her most polite smile, nodded at the man, and turned the page of her Playbill, pretending to read, determined not to lift her gaze until the applause of the audience signaled the entrance of the conductor. She welcomed the darkness as the houselights dimmed to black, so no one would see the tears streaming down her face.

CHAPTER TWENTY-NINE

New York City
September 1975

Lissy arrived at the Majestic early enough to give herself time alone at her makeup station before this particular show, the sixteenth performance since *Happily After Ever*'s official opening. An enormous bouquet of roses blocked her mirror. She assumed they were from Rudy and moved them aside, reluctant to open the card. The absence of Noah more than the presence of anyone else had lately defined the contours of her nights and mornings.

She'd let the answering machine screen all of Noah's calls over the last three weeks—her anger at him still made her jaw clench—and she hadn't called him back at any of the numbers he left in Philly, Atlanta, Detroit, or Chicago. But she listened to every message and detected the excitement in his voice even as he tried to infuse his words with concern for her, with pleas to call him back, and the consistent refrain of needing to hear her voice.

The messages stopped coming five days ago.

She missed Noah, the way he would gently wake her each morning, stroke her forehead with his thumb, smile at her as she blinked open her eyes. She missed seeing the ice-cream scoop in the sink as she made her coffee, a telltale sign he had quietly risen in the middle of the night for a sweet snack. She missed stretching out on his bed after a grueling day onstage and letting the deep resonance of his guitar flow over her like a hot bath, his lyrics a salve. Mostly she missed how he listened to her, his calm bearing suggesting he had all the time in the world to do nothing but talk to her, to really understand her thoughts. He'd taken it all with him.

At least the relentless schedule had kept her busy six days a week, with two shows on Wednesdays and Sundays, but now that would be gone too. The sixteenth performance of *Happily After Ever* would be the last. The show was officially closing.

The reviews after opening night were universally scathing. All the adoration Zimmerman and Gray had engendered over the years seemed to round on them with collective fury. The kings of Broadway had duped their fans into blind reverence and then led them into the desert. The critics said the show made no sense. While an interesting idea, the script didn't successfully deliver the story in reverse, each jump back in time a jolt for the audience, the "barely-could-be-considered costumes" a lame attempt to fix glaring holes. What should have been emotional high notes were lost in the confusion of what had come before.

Worse, there was consensus that while the script was flawed, the show might have been saved by stronger performances. In particular, the reviews claimed, "There is no spark between these two leads. We are made to watch Melanie and Cassidy go through the motions rather than be swept up in what might have potential to be a grand love story." If that wasn't bad enough—Lissy hardly needed public scorn for Noah's abandonment—nothing could compare to the brutal analysis of Clive Barnes himself. "While she has a singular voice, Bella Page is no substitute for her father's former greatness. Her performance fell flat for this critic and fan."

Lissy read those lines over and over. There it was in black-and-white, for all to see.

The only bright spot was the clear praise for Bae. "The scenes featuring BaeJin Kim as Trudy are worth the price of admission. She is one to watch." Lissy was truly pleased for Bae. For once in her life, the measuring stick Lissy normally used to compare herself against the world felt irrelevant, like trying to compare the length of a fish to the speed of a horse. Bae's rare trio of talents had been discovered, vaulting her into a different category. Bae deserved it. And it brought Lissy a certain amount of relief. Single-handedly tanking Bae's career on top of everything else might have done her in. Of course, a positive review offered no guarantee of future employment. And even if Bae did score the next big part, she still might never forgive her.

Lissy circled the empty dressing room, running her fingers over the discolored counter, the mug holding her makeup brushes. She examined Bae's station, her bowl of hair clips, the curled family photo taped to her mirror, a young Bae in a tutu and ballet shoes with her parents and brother at her side, all grinning. She picked up the shawl from JoJo's chair, the velour and satin swath of blue she wore around her shoulders as she applied rouge and eyeshadow each night. She eyed the costume rack, anemic with its row of T-shirts. She would miss all of it. For now, she had one more chance to make her performance shine, to raise the elusive "Brava!" from an appreciative onlooker.

She reluctantly pulled the envelope off the bouquet and opened the note:

Lissy,

I'm so sorry Happily is shutting down. Whatever you do tonight, just sing with everything you've got. They will love you.

I still hope you can forgive me. And if you can do that, maybe you'd be game to join me on tour? I've included the schedule and the phone number of our manager. He can always track me down.

Please come find me. Let me properly apologize for being such a jerk, and then "stay with me."

Noah

The wad of sorrow in her throat she'd sung around for the last three weeks swelled again. *Stay with me.* The first time she hit the high notes of that song, the first time she and Noah effortlessly harmonized, her future had held so much promise. She put her nose into the velvet center of one of the roses and breathed in deeply. They were intoxicating, perfect. And yet she knew their splendor to be temporary, each flower suspended somewhere between bloom and decay. She considered where on that spectrum her relationship with Noah lived. It had been such a whirlwind, undeniably linked to the excitement and challenges of the show. Could she imagine it surviving outside that context? She wasn't even sure where she existed outside that context anymore. Who was Lissy Horowitz now? And what about Bella Page?

If her mother was upset by her decision to use her father's stage name, she'd chosen not to pile her anger on everything else. It was pretty clear, even on opening night, that the show was missing something fundamental. The cast had failed to conjure the kind of magic that transports the audience to an imaginary world, that gently untethers them from reality and allows them to slip into a story different from their own. Lissy's mother went through the motions of showering her with praise afterward, but her enthusiasm was strained.

Thankfully, she realized Lissy didn't need a personal confrontation on top of it all. She got enough of it from Bae.

After the curtain dropped on opening night, Bae seethed.

"When were you going to mention this?" She slapped the Playbill. "I thought we were friends, Lissy. All this time you gave me the poor struggling artist routine, as if we were in the same boat. And you just happen to be Hollywood royalty?"

"It's not like that. It's never been important."

Bae looked incredulous.

"And next you're going to tell me you're not rolling in dough, not living in some huge mansion up on Martha's Vineyard while you pretend to need a waitressing job."

"I did need the job, just like you." Sadness ballooned in Lissy's chest. How could she explain?

"No. Our experiences are nothing alike, but you'll never understand that, will you?" Bae walked out before Lissy could respond. They'd barely spoken since.

"Still have adoring fans, I see." Rudy leaned against the doorjamb behind her.

Lissy wondered how long he'd been standing there. She folded up Noah's note and spun on her stool to face him.

"Surprised?"

"Listen, we still plan to record the cast album tomorrow." He pushed off the wall.

She nodded. It was the only thing she'd been looking forward to since opening night. The producers had booked the studio time before previews and decided not to cancel. Rudy's songs still deserved to be recorded. It would be a relief for her to sing without having to act out the bits in between. It would feel more like rehearsals than a stage performance, more natural, more fun. She could imagine a day, years from now, when she would wonder if the show had ever really happened at all. The album would give her a living imprint of it, as imperfect as it was. She only wished Noah would be standing next to her in the studio, etching a shared groove into the vinyl. She slipped the note into her makeup bag.

"And then I was thinking we should take a break." Rudy pulled her off the stool and brushed his lips along the side of her neck. "Come with me up to the Berkshires. Just you and me."

He ran his hands over her hips. She'd hoped from the beginning that his attraction to her was proof of her promise. Men like him were turned on by talent, weren't they? Or maybe he needed distraction as badly as she did.

She pulled back from him and looked into his eyes. She saw urgency, confidence, desire. She couldn't bring herself to ask him what she most wanted to know: if he thought her career might still have a chance. Nor did she ask if a trip to the Berkshires was meant to be one last fling, or the first step toward a relationship outside the trappings of the show. She was pretty sure what her own answer to that question would be.

One week after Noah left, Rudy had told her he had a surprise and whisked her off to his apartment before she could protest. He owned a sixteen-millimeter projector and had somehow managed to secure a copy of *Moonlight Sonata*. As the film flickered to life, Lissy was both thrilled and discomfited by watching her father on the screen with Rudy sitting beside her, smiling back and forth between her and the black-and-white light. His hands were on her by the time Dixon Grace—her father's most famous character—first donned a top hat and tails to woo a waitress at a diner.

She instinctively pulled Rudy from the room, cringing at the idea of having a man touch her in the glow of her father's own flirtations. She should have turned off the projector instead, realizing too late that the only other room in the apartment was the bedroom. As soon as they stumbled through the door, time accelerated. She gave into his urgent caresses and the strange power he held over her, an assumption of inevitability she found impossible to resist.

After that, their occasional postperformance romps served as an escape for her, a way to pretend her career wasn't careening off a cliff. And she found it surprisingly exhilarating to transform her raw anger into a kind of dangerous pleasure. She wasn't good at sitting alone and contemplating her own shortcomings, especially not when she still had to go onstage every night. Choosing to be with Rudy gave her a way to exert some level of control over her life. But she had no idea if he thought of her as Bella Page or as Lissy Horowitz. She had known exactly who she was to Noah.

She looked over Rudy's shoulder at the roses on her station, long on youth, soft and sharp.

"First, I have a show to do," she said, shooing him away.

"Bring your bag to the recording studio tomorrow. I want to leave straight from there." He hummed the chorus of "Stay with Me" as he left the dressing room.

She bristled at the sound of the song on his lips. Of course, it was his song. And he was here. Noah was the one who didn't stay.

CHAPTER THIRTY

Martha's Vineyard
October 1975

Aster set down her tea, the blue sheen of the mug streaked with dried clay, and turned her attention back to the sculpture taking shape on her workbench: a Labrador running full speed at the edge of the ocean, foam kicking up at its paws. She'd been focused on the dog's ears all morning, molding them to express freedom and movement while still appearing relaxed and floppy. She loved the challenge of communicating fluidity and tenderness in a medium that eventually turned hard—the rounded cheek of a child, a horse's velvety nose.

Her studio crouched out of sight behind the Haven. Two windows let in just enough light without causing distraction, and the small shack managed to fit everything she needed inside: crates with various types of clay, a small sink, canisters full of scrapers, sponges, and modeling tools, and a slate-topped work surface in the middle of it all, the place where things came to life.

The studio was within earshot of the store, making it possible for her to sculpt on slow days—which described almost every day in the off-season—and still hear the jangle of the bell announcing customers at the front door. They'd come to this arrangement at the gallery after the first few open off-seasons proved successful, more than twenty years ago now. Graham decided to expand, and the new lease included two small buildings behind the larger shop, one he used for storage and one he offered to Aster. Her sculptures consistently sold well—the more sculpting she did, the better for both of them—and she could be on hand to cover for Graham if he needed to attend to something away from the gallery.

Graham's store and her studio truly were her haven, sanctuaries of color and shape, of life held still long enough to be properly appreciated. Working there allowed her to be surrounded by seascapes and landscapes, enjoy interesting conversations with whoever swung through the door—all locals in the off-season—and listen to their stories about a particular place on the island an artist had captured in oil or charcoal, each personal anecdote adding new depth to a piece. It was the place where she felt most herself, a place where she could let her hands fly into the creation of whatever stirred her.

Like so many things, she owed the discovery of her love of clay to Graham. Not long after moving to the island, she showed him the sketches she'd drawn for her interview at Parsons, and he suggested she try sculpture. He said she had an eye for the human form, for movement that needed to extend beyond the page, for weight and substance that longed to be expressed in three dimensions. It wasn't easy to find clay on the island back then, but he offered her access to the high school art room on the weekends, just to see if she liked it. Lissy played with finger paints while Aster explored the clay.

Aster found solace in the feel of it, how the heat of her hands softened a block as she kneaded. Once pliable, she began to transform it into recognizable shapes—an elbow, a shoulder. She then taught herself how to turn the clay into various fabrics, the twill of a girl's skirt, the flannel of a fisherman's jacket. She knew the texture of each one intimately, how it moved, where it bunched up, how much it pilled. She discovered as much enjoyment in the process of creation as she did in the thrill of the finished product. The smell of wet clay grounded her to the earth, and the metallic taste of the air brought her comfort. Mastery arrived as if unbidden. The thread and needle required for clothing tangled all her ideas. But the clay responded to her touch, made the images in her mind tangible, beautiful.

She'd come to believe over the years that art was a handshake with the viewer—only made whole through such a bond—but a true artist must define the size, shape, and motion of the hand they wanted to hold out to the world first, without a view to what anyone else might want. Then they had to trust there would be someone, even if only one person, who would reach through the void and grasp the outstretched offering. That connection made every ounce of energy and emotion poured into a piece more than worth it.

She'd been spending more time buried in her clay lately than she normally did, if that was possible. So much of the past had come rushing back to her after seeing the Page name stamped onto her daughter's life in that Playbill, and she needed to work the clay to think it all through. After the initial shock subsided, she realized how foolish she'd been to ever think it would be enough to offer Lissy the unadorned fact of a famous father and leave it at that. She'd chosen to treat Christopher Page's place in their life like one of an imaginary friend. Acknowledging its presence would only give credence to something not actually there, would only add color and depth to an illusion. And so, she'd chosen to ignore the ghost of him, encouraged it to fade from memory, to let it become as inconsequential to Lissy's life as the name of the hospital on her birth certificate.

How absurd to think she had successfully minimized the impact of the specter of Christopher Page on Lissy's life. Of course Lissy craved more, wanted to make him part of her life somehow. How could Aster have missed it all this time? She'd been so willfully blind, in fact, that even after Lissy declared her desire to be a star like Mary Martin, it never occurred to Aster that it had anything to do with who she believed her father to be. After all, it was well known in Hollywood that Christopher Page couldn't carry a tune, and Lissy was a prodigy. Of course Lissy liked to sing onstage, and Aster had assumed her interest had simply escalated from there. Besides, Lissy was still a child then and regularly declared her intention to be the best at anything she tried. Just like when she announced she wanted to be the youngest winner ever of the Vineyard fishing derby. It didn't mean she was likely to become a professional fisherman, did it?

The more leading roles Lissy got, the more logical pursuing theater as a profession became. But it still never occurred to Aster that Lissy might want to brand herself as Christopher Page's daughter. She had no right to tell Lissy she shouldn't—after all, she'd been the one to make Lissy believe he was her father—but why would Lissy want to introduce herself to the world as secondary to someone else? And why had Lissy kept such a monumental decision from her? Aster couldn't deny how much that hurt, as if Lissy's entire childhood was an asterisk on a more important story, much like Martha's Vineyard might be seen from the air, as the afterthought of a more impressive body of land.

Aster should have realized that his tragic death would transform the idea of Christopher Page into something mythical in Lissy's eyes. Had they divorced as originally planned, Lissy would have thought of her father as a heartless man, a bad guy. A resilient child, she would have adjusted to the unfortunate circumstance. But Aster saw clearly now that downplaying a dead superstar was like trying to catch smoke in your fist.

And Aster worried deeply for Lissy now. Lissy didn't have much experience with failure and had called only twice since closing night. Lissy said there was nothing to talk about, and Aster didn't know what to say anyway. While Lissy had been transcendent when she sang—an ethereal being capable of floating off the stage and taking the whole audience with her—she hadn't brought the same command to her lines. Aster hoped it was a subtle shortcoming, something only a nervous mother would notice, but she'd been wrong about that too.

She leaned back on her stool, her eye catching the old postcard she'd tacked above one of her drying shelves so long ago, its edges curled with humidity, the photo of a diner on Route 66 faded to a wash of bluish gray. Fernando had enclosed the card with a letter he'd sent to Aster at Greta's apartment in New York. Thankfully it arrived before Greta packed up and moved to Hudson Valley so she could forward it on.

It was clear from his letter that he'd left LA before receiving Aster's note telling him of her move to the Vineyard. He'd written from the road to say he'd shut down his boutique and left with no destination in mind. He said he couldn't take the oozing greed and ambition of LA anymore, the constant posing, the cold calculation needed to get ahead. He told her he'd started many postcards to her but never finished any, giving up each time he realized anew how little space the small rectangle offered, nowhere near enough room to hold all he needed to say. He enclosed the blank postcard with the letter, as if to prove his previous attempts.

Gulps of sadness clogged Aster's throat again as she remembered the words in his letter—how much he missed her and Lissy, how the absence of their gentle love had torn another hole in his life. But mostly, he wrote about Benny, how much he missed his tenderness, his touch, his spirit, his food, all selflessly offered up as nourishment. Fernando was starving, unsure how he mustered the will to get out of bed each day. He had no idea where he would end up but intended to wander until he found "anyone or anything worth loving again."

They had no way to reach each other after that, another cruel twist in their friendship. It felt akin to losing her brother all over again, a sudden severing of a tie not ready to be cut. At least Fernando was out there in the world somewhere. She could only hope he'd found someone deserving of him.

Aster sensed the air shifting behind her and swiveled on her stool.

"That's going to sell as soon as we put it in the gallery," Graham said, leaning against the doorway, smiling. "You might have to make a series of them."

He still was her biggest artistic champion. And closest confidant. It was Graham she'd told about the Playbill after getting back from New York. He knew all too well the circumstances behind their move to the Vineyard—or at least the invented story, though even that was something she rarely discussed with anyone else. He'd witnessed Lissy's remarkably normal childhood. More importantly, Graham knew Lissy almost as well as she did, her determination, her earnestness. He was one of the only people who could get away with teasing Lissy about her competitive drive, like the time he tapped her nose repeatedly with dollops of whipped cream to distract her from the Olympic level decorating she poured into her entry for the Oak Bluffs gingerbread cottage competition one year. They ended up in a food fight, laughing until their sides ached. Lissy almost didn't finish perfecting her entry. Almost.

Aster's appreciation for Graham had only increased over the years. While she occasionally imagined what might have happened if she'd admitted her love for him that first day on the island, she took solace in not having allowed another rash or selfish decision to disrupt any more lives. Graham and Marcia had been married for more than twenty years now and had three beautiful daughters. Lissy had babysat all three girls over the years and had evolved in their eyes into a cross between a big sister and a rock star they were lucky to know. Clearly, this was how it was meant to be. They were as close to siblings as Lissy would get, the one thing Aster could not give her. She and Lissy had maintained their own keel, Lissy had thrived, and her friendship with Graham had never wavered. It was the most constant thing in her life next to Lissy, and she cherished it.

Aster considered the Labrador skipping along the water's edge she had just created.

"I'm not sure I've quite captured the ocean spray yet. What do you think?"

"If you can find a way to show the water coming off his back leg, I think you'll have it."

She rolled over to see it from his angle.

"I see that. Yes, yes."

He did have a great eye.

She grasped her ribboning tool and bent over the left side of the dog. She didn't look up for another forty minutes. It was another thing she adored about Graham. He respected the process, quietly taking his leave when she slipped into the flow of her work. No need for explanation or a word of goodbye. The unspoken between them said it all.

CHAPTER THIRTY-ONE

Martha's Vineyard
October 1975

The string of bells on the Haven Art Gallery door rang out as Lissy pushed through. She'd come straight from the ferry, hoping to find her mother.

Graham popped out from behind the counter and wrapped Lissy in a warm embrace.

"Your mother didn't tell me you were coming."

"She doesn't know."

Lissy realized how much she missed familiar comforts. Graham had been in Lissy's life since before she could remember. She'd spent many an afternoon sprawled out on the floor beneath the shelf of art books in the back of the Haven, half doing her homework and half watching her mother and Graham walk customers around the space to discuss various paintings and sculptures. The normalcy of her mother's friendship with Graham always made Lissy feel safe—the way they finished each other's sentences, the time they took for kind gestures, Graham delivering Aster fresh honey when she was sick, Aster bringing him the first tomatoes of the season from her garden. Theirs was a reliable relationship that Lissy counted on like salt in the ocean breeze.

"She just left for the farmers market ten minutes ago. You know how she always wants to be first in line for the granary cider."

A sculpture in the middle of the room caught Lissy's eye, clearly one of her mother's—a swimmer, a girl, popping through the surface with an expression of pure joy. Her mother had perfectly captured the movement of the ripples around her and had managed to suggest water dripping down her face without diluting her features.

"A beauty, isn't she? A real labor of love, that one," Graham said.

It struck Lissy how little she had asked her mother about her work lately. She used to hear about the progress of every sculpture of her mother's—the boy clasping a frog in his little hands, the goat munching on poison ivy—and could picture them before seeing them herself. She knew nothing of this girl.

"How long are you staying?"

"I'm not sure. I have some things to figure out." That was an understatement. Lissy didn't like operating without a plan, but she honestly had no idea if she would go back to the theater or even back to New York. And then there was her love life.

Graham nodded. "I'm sorry the play didn't work out."

"Yeah, thanks." She swallowed, wondering if she would ever be able to talk about it without wanting to burst into tears. She felt childish but knew she had lost a piece of her future.

"Skedaddle, kid. Your mother will kill me if I delay you a second longer."

Lissy smiled. At least she'd gotten one thing right. She had come home.

꧁꧂

October was Lissy's favorite time on the Vineyard. Each falling leaf cleared a wider view out her bedroom window to Lake Tashmoo. The scrubby pines along the shore would never give up their needles, and she considered them an essential part of what drew her to this place. The white sand mixed with evergreens ensured that one season never forgot about the last.

Lissy had been home for almost a week, and thanks to several beach walks, long meals, and after-dinner fires in the post-and-beam living room, Lissy and her mom had covered most topics on at least a cursory level, her mother first testing Lissy's willingness to go deeper on each one before diving in too fast.

She told her mother all about Bae—how she'd pushed Bae toward *Happily After Ever,* how guilty she felt when *A Chorus Line* ended up being such a smash hit, how she wasn't sure Bae would ever forgive her. Lissy went by herself to a matinee of *A Chorus Line* after *Happily* closed, grabbing a last-minute ticket at the discount booth in Central Park. It eclipsed Barnes's review. The cast flawlessly delivered an emotional wallop with every line, every song, each mini-story its own masterpiece. She silently wept throughout most of the performance—for its power, for all she had lost, for what she'd ripped away from Bae. Lissy could only hope Bae hadn't missed her one chance at Broadway stardom, but what if she had?

She also told her mother about Rudy. He didn't deserve the position of a secret. She was embarrassed for being sucked in by him, for falling under whatever strange power he'd been able to wield over her. Talking about it slowly untangled her confusing emotions, like picking at a knot in a necklace until the jumble was loose enough to pull apart. Her mother seemed to understand the allure some men have, even when they clearly aren't the right guy. She didn't chide Lissy for making the mistake, only applauded her for pushing Rudy to the side.

And of course they discussed Noah. Lissy's mother listened carefully but understood this story less. She asked Lissy several times what was holding her back from going to him. Lissy wasn't quite sure herself. She longed for him in a way she hadn't experienced before with other men. But her yearning was still edged with anger. She felt like a toddler with plenty of stomping and wailing left in her, even if she could barely remember what had upset her in the first place.

"I've told you this all your life," her mom said, "but we don't get the chance for a great love many times in our lives, and maybe never more than once. Don't take that for granted."

Lissy recognized the familiar sadness in her mother's eyes, the ever-lingering grief.

"I'm sorry, Mom. I should have told you I was going to use his name. It was a last-minute decision."

There she had said it, finally.

Her mother looked surprised. She moved to the bright blue couch and huddled next to Lissy. She didn't say anything for a few long minutes.

"How did it feel to have the world judge you as Christopher Page's daughter?"

Lissy thought about that. She'd only pictured the triumph of it, a successful Broadway run cementing a father-daughter legacy. The failure of the show was too intermingled with the double disappointment of having fallen short of his prowess to separate one from the other.

"Something about revealing it felt right. Why can't I be proud to be his daughter?" This was the one question Lissy had been wanting to ask her entire life. "And now I don't have to carry this massive secret anymore, constantly wondering if I should or shouldn't tell someone about him. Now it's just out there."

"I had no idea you felt that way."

"Mom. How could I not?" Didn't her mother feel that way too? The thought always hovering in the back of her mind: *Oh, by the way, the love of my life was Christopher Page?*

Her mother leaned back on the couch and pulled a pillow onto her lap. She stared into the fire for a long time before responding.

"Your life can't be about the past. It has to be about you. It has to be about what you want."

"I wish I knew what that was." Lissy slumped over and put her head in her mother's lap. The embers in the fireplace glowed, warming Lissy's face as her mother stroked her hair, touching the same soothing spot on her temple Noah had so quickly found.

Several possibilities ran through her mind, each one more exhausting than the last. She could go back to New York and get back on the audition wagon again, stand and smile for casting directors and pretend she hadn't just stubbed her face on a very public stage. She could put plan B into motion and look for a job on the management side of theater, such as logistics or promotion. Her friends at Vassar nominated her countless times to run things like the Booster Club or the Spring Fling. She had a knack for creating events and getting the word out about them. Or she could hide on Martha's Vineyard, give kids voice lessons, maybe direct a school play or two if they'd let her. Of course, none of those options included Noah.

She still didn't understand how he so easily packed his bags and walked away from her, from the show, possibly dealing *Happily* its fatal blow, leaving her to face total failure on her own. Just thinking about it was like poking at a raw wound with a rusty nail, tempting infection and ensuring a nasty scar. Could she ever move past her resentment and be happy for Noah, excited that his dream was still alive? She wasn't sure.

The embers in the hearth gave up a final burst of smoke as they faded to black. They could have revived the fire with a jab of the poker and a puff or two of oxygen, but neither of them moved, allowing the steady light of the moon to replace the flicker of orange flames.

CHAPTER THIRTY-TWO

Martha's Vineyard
October 1975

A ster pulled off her wool sweater as the day warmed. The sun skipped off the lake and winked through the trees. By the time the guests arrived at noon, it would be the ideal temperature for al fresco dining, the radiating light smoothing the sharpest edges off the chill in the air. She wanted the day to be perfect for Lissy.

She'd decided to host a twenty-sixth birthday party for Lissy even though it was seven months late. Lissy was too busy to come home in March, but she was here now, and Aster wanted to recognize the milestone, to celebrate her daughter. She hoped it would remind Lissy how many people loved her, regardless of Broadway success or failure.

After dipping her ladle into the cioppino base and tasting the broth, she added more red pepper flakes and oregano. She thought of it as

Benny's dish, one of the many he'd cooked for her and Fernando. She'd recently begun to revive some of his old recipes.

Memories of Fernando and Benny were interrupting her daily routines lately in ways they hadn't for years, as if the Playbill had jarred loose a marble that had been stuck for ages in a crack in the floor. Now it reappeared at the strangest moments, rolling across her waking thoughts, clacking through her dreams. She'd been tempted on a few occasions to tell Lissy everything, and almost did on the night they'd lingered by the fire, when Lissy admitted what an enormous presence Christopher Page—his ghost, really—had always been in her life. But telling Lissy the truth, informing her she had no biological legacy to uphold, meant unveiling a far more uncomfortable reality: that Lissy had a different father, a fifty-eight-year-old man who was still very much alive. It had been easy enough for Aster to keep track of him from afar. His name still showed up in the production credits of movies, his photograph occasionally appearing in a Hollywood roundup in *Life* magazine.

Aster had originally planned to tell Lissy everything after she turned eighteen. Any sooner would have been too risky. She couldn't have stopped Lissy from reaching out to Sam and had no idea how he would react. Sam Sawyer was a powerful man. He might have tried to lure her to him with money or Hollywood glamour. He might have launched a custody battle.

But by the time Lissy turned eighteen, Aster couldn't bring herself to reveal the truth. She cherished the honest and uncomplicated relationship she and Lissy shared, unlike so many mother-daughter duos she'd seen disintegrate during the teen years. Why disrupt her world? What would be the point? She believed it had no bearing on who Lissy had become and would only add unnecessary emotional turmoil to an otherwise wonderful life, boundless in its simplicity. And so, she set the truth aside for good.

Standing at the kitchen sink, she scrubbed the mussel shells to rid them of their barnacles and reveal their glossy surfaces. As she moved on to the clams, she glimpsed Lissy's bike coming up the lane, her long legs pumping over the sandy ruts, just like when she was a young girl.

Lissy was now twenty-six. By that age, Aster already had a five-year-old daughter. Thankfully Lissy didn't yet have to worry about the needs of a child. She could still make decisions based on what she alone wanted from life.

Aster washed her hands and pushed through the screen door.

"How was the ride?"

"Beautiful. I found these at Lambert's Cove." Lissy pulled a fistful of sunflowers out of her basket.

"Gorgeous." Aster took the proud flowers into the kitchen and settled them into a ceramic jug.

"Before you hop in the shower, there's something I want to talk to you about." Aster let the screen door gently slap closed behind her again.

She took Lissy's hand and led her to the little bench between the scrub pines and the lake, the site of countless important conversations, everything from discussing the birds and the bees, to mulling what to do about Lissy's eighth grade crush on Billy Wallace, to her attempt to give Lissy her best motherly advice on the responsibilities of adulthood before Lissy moved to New York. Even though Lissy had already been away for four years, those absences always felt temporary to Aster, small blips between vacations, her return for the summer always just over the horizon. Moving away as an adult, to another city, required a different level of independence and resilience. Today would mark yet another milestone in Lissy's life.

"You know that movie royalties have been helpful to us here and there." Aster had used some of the money for the down payment on their house on the island—one fact she hadn't hidden from Lissy—but they lived frugally. Aster paid for living expenses from her own earnings. The income from her art and working at the gallery was modest, but they managed to live within the means she could provide. It was the deal Aster made with herself, and Lissy had never questioned it.

The fact that their finances were more substantial surfaced only once, when Aster informed Lissy she didn't need to limit her college choices to schools with available scholarships. Money from her father's estate had been saved for just such a purpose. Lissy was thrilled to know she could seriously consider Vassar despite the relatively low monetary scholarship offer compared to Smith, and she began to weigh in earnest the pros and cons of the two programs. She never asked if there was more money beyond those funds. But there was more, much more. And Aster had always intended it for Lissy.

"There have been additional royalties through the years, and I put it all in a trust for you a long time ago. It's now going to be released to you."

Aster carefully watched her daughter's face as it registered surprise and confusion.

"Why haven't you told me this before?"

"I wanted to make sure you found your own motivation, learned to work hard for what you wanted in the world. There's nothing more satisfying. Of course, I never did have to worry about that with you." Aster stroked Lissy's hair and smiled at her daughter, thinking back on how many times she'd counseled her to slow down, to stop pushing herself so hard. "I think the bigger challenge, though, is figuring out what you really want to do with your life. I know firsthand how difficult that can be. It takes time."

"You're telling me."

Aster realized how similar their paths were in a way, how much she had stumbled at first. Eager to escape the burdens of modeling, she'd latched onto the idea of clothing design as a logical extension of her fashion experience and a good use of her artistic eye. Aspiring to a coveted apprenticeship gave her purpose. Thank god she'd realized she didn't love the work as soon as she had. It wasn't what she was meant to do with her life.

"This will give you a little cushion while you figure things out."

"But I didn't earn it." Lissy looked stricken.

Aster smiled. This was pure Lissy. Always wanting to prove her own worth.

"This isn't about you living off the money forever. That's not the idea. The important thing is that you don't need to rush into anything for financial survival. Not a job, or a relationship, or anything else. You have time."

Time. That's what she was really giving Lissy, the one thing she herself had lacked back then. Everything had moved too fast, doors opening and swinging shut overnight thanks to the ticking time bomb of her own body, the choices she'd made, the consequences of them looming so much larger than she ever thought possible. But at least she could give Lissy this.

"You don't need to have all the answers right now. And you don't have to get everything right the first time. You're allowed mistakes, Lissy. And I'm as sure as I've ever been that you will find the path that's right for you."

"You have no idea how much I needed to hear that." Lissy leaned into her mother as tears built into deep sobs. Aster felt them reverberate in her own chest.

I think I know exactly how much you needed to hear it, Aster thought. *I think I do.*

CHAPTER THIRTY-THREE

San Francisco
November 1975

Lissy checked the address one more time before turning down Hyde Street. She'd been in San Francisco for less than seventy-two hours but already felt connected to the current of the city's energy, a combination of carefree and propulsive that quickened her pulse. In the park by her hotel, tie-dyed groups danced in the sunshine next to artisans selling their wares. Remnants of war protest signs and concert flyers littered the ground. Near Lombard Street a group of half-dressed women wove in and out of traffic on roller skates. It felt like a place where anything was possible, whether it was a good idea or not. Unlike New York, where individual freedom felt synonymous with danger, the entire metropolis slipping into decline, San Francisco thrummed with potential, a city moving toward a colorful and welcoming horizon.

The number 245 was stenciled on a dented gray metal door that looked more like the entrance to a warehouse than a recording studio. As Lissy pushed through the door, a young woman glanced up from a folding table where she was sticking hand-written labels onto a stack of reels.

"Hey, can I help?" She wore long braids that disappeared past her waist.

Lissy referenced the piece of paper in her hand, creased and smudged from her worrying.

"I'm looking for Marcus Manfred?"

"You've got the right place. Booth A. Down the hall to your left. Make sure you go into the booth, not the studio. Marcus is in there."

Lissy headed down the hall, the walls lined with brown veneer, her heart flopping like a fish on a dock. She'd spent two days in San Francisco trying to work up the nerve to come here and hadn't sent advance notice of her arrival in case she changed her mind.

The small birthday party on the Vineyard had encouraged her to take this leap, reminding her how much runway remained in front of her. Most of her friends had moved off island, and Graham's daughters—almost cousins to Lissy even though they were significantly younger—worked weekend jobs, so the afternoon get-together consisted mostly of the adults in Lissy's life she thought of as aunts and uncles. Like Gloria and Bob Franklin, their next-door neighbors, who arrived through the hedge at noon sharp, barefoot as always. Gleason, who ran a bait shop in Menemsha, reminisced about his own twenty-sixth birthday, which coincided with D-Day, and how the postwar party went on for a week. Verna, who made yarn from her sheep on Stonewall Farm, said she could barely remember turning twenty-six through the fog of having two toddlers by then. "Live it up while you can," she told Lissy. The only person at the get-together close to Lissy's age was Alfred, Gleason's son, who had moved back in with his father after returning from Vietnam. Two years younger than Lissy, he was a tall oak tree of a boy who came home a hollowed-out version of himself, as if his limbs were too heavy to hold up anymore. She knew to allow him his silences.

It all felt comfortable and warm to Lissy, especially watching her mother in her element, happily serving her fantastic fish stew with fresh-from-the-oven sourdough rolls. Then came a salad of baby lettuce, peppers, and tomatoes, all harvested from her own garden, outdone only by the flaming Baked Alaska—not exactly a traditional birthday cake, but Lissy's favorite since seeing it at the Crab and Claw restaurant in second grade. Her mother had made the delicious, melty mess for her on every birthday from then on.

Graham, as usual, served as Aster's third and fourth hands all afternoon—bringing an extra chair outside, fetching paper napkins, running out for more Michelob, shuttling empty dishes to the kitchen—all without ever being asked. Their movements were seamless, their banter continual, exactly how they operated in the gallery. Graham's wife, Marcia, on the other hand, spent much of the party looking beyond the perimeter of the table, watching gulls land on the water. She had often seemed lonely when not with her girls. It wasn't unusual for Marcia to come home early when Lissy was babysitting over the years, saying she wanted to tuck the girls in after all. When Lissy asked once how Graham would get home, Marica looked confused. "He went to a concert in Tisbury. I was just out with a friend." After that, Lissy noticed that their nights out involved two cars more often than not. Sitting on the lawn now, Marcia managed a wan smile as the rest of the group laughed wildly at Gleason's story about one of the cameramen for *Jaws* getting seasick on his beloved boat, *Flounda*.

Everyone had a story about being an extra in the movie, or meeting Roy Scheider, or predicting the weather for the director—which no one got right—or offering up a sunfish or an old buoy to make a particular scene look more authentic. Everyone except her mother, who had avoided it all like the plague.

"Wasn't the *Flounda* a beauty on the big screen, Lissy?"

She did a poor job of hiding her sheepish expression.

"Don't tell me you haven't seen the movie?" Gleason's mouth hung open.

How to explain that she was so wrapped up in auditions and then rehearsals, so involved in her own life, that she hadn't managed to set aside two hours to see the blockbuster everyone else in the country couldn't stop talking about, the movie that just happened to be filmed in her hometown? The truth was, she'd barely noticed it come and go from the theaters in New York. Everyone stared at Lissy in disbelief, waiting for her to respond.

"The soundtrack wouldn't really be Lissy's thing. It's just *dun, dun, dun, dun . . . dun, dun, dun, dun*. She can do better than that." Alfred's voice rang with confidence.

Collective surprise at his participation in the conversation melted into quiet laughter at the truth of his comment. Lissy glowed at him with appreciation for saving her from further scrutiny on the topic.

After the guests had all left, the tablecloths and Chinese lanterns put away, Lissy noticed the emptiness of the place in a way she hadn't before. Her mother placed the jug of sunflowers in front of the kitchen window and paused, making Lissy wonder if she was truly happy on her own or if she ever longed to share her life with someone who would wrap his arms around her, content to watch the sun set on an empty lawn.

Her mother had long touted the benefits of single life, joking with her married friends about the comfort of stretching out across the entire bed, how she had no snoring to contend with, no quilt hog to interrupt her sleep. But she had also taught Lissy how much easier it was for two people to make a bed—laundry Sundays were a ritual of

Lissy's childhood—and Aster never brought home a scallop shell for her collection unless both sides were intact and still attached. She said a single shell was only half of the whole, missing its partner. It saddened Lissy that her mother hadn't found love again after her father died.

It was then, as her mother rearranged the sunflowers, that Lissy decided she shouldn't throw away her first real chance at love. She booked her ticket to San Francisco the next day.

Standing now in front of the door marked Booth A, she ticked through her list of worries. She was afraid Noah had already moved on, put her out of his mind. She was afraid of the opposite, that he would pull her into his life, and in her state of flux, she would let her uncertain future be swept up by the current of his. She feared the band wasn't everything Noah had hoped for, leaving him as rudderless as her. And she feared that he'd found the ultimate group of players and formed a brotherhood she would always be on the outside of, looking in.

The only thing she knew for sure was that she needed to face all those fears in person. A letter or even a phone call wouldn't tell her what she would know simply by looking into Noah's eyes. And her mother thought it would be a perfect opportunity for a change of scenery. No matter what happened with Noah, her mother encouraged her to experience new perspectives, go where the young people were taking charge and doing their best to change the world.

Lissy steadied herself and opened the door. One of the two men sitting in front of a large glass window held up a finger to let her know he would be a minute. She nodded and stood against the wall, trying to make herself take up as little room as possible. The duo slid levers up and down a huge soundboard while metal-faced components blinked red and yellow. On the other side of the glass the band was jamming. Noah's band. They all wore bell-bottom jeans, the drummer in a tie-dyed T-shirt, the bassist in an unbuttoned denim shirt, his beard hanging down to his chest. Noah stood at the mic with an electric guitar Lissy didn't recognize, his hair long enough to tuck behind his ears. A woman in a paisley skirt skimming the floor swayed in rhythm beside him. Lissy was struck less by her beauty—her long black hair flowed over her bronzed shoulders—than by her proximity to Noah, how they sang in sync and shared the same mic. And the song soared, probably another one of his.

Her heart sank. Noah had found someone else to harmonize with, someone else to share his bed. He no longer needed her. She felt foolish for coming all this way, for imagining that after going silent for three months she might still be anywhere near the forefront of his mind. She was about to back out the door when one of the men at the controls apprised her.

"You waiting on Noah?"

Caught staring. She nodded before she could stop herself. She should have feigned being in the wrong place. No one would ever have known she was there.

"Have a seat. We're going to break after we lay this down."

Lissy reluctantly sat on a folding chair and became increasingly miserable by the minute. Had Noah gotten more gorgeous since she last saw him? He riffed a lead and nodded at his bassist. He was the new member of the band but was clearly the magnetic center around which everything else revolved. Watching them answered one of her questions, at least. He had found a groove here, and she was no part of it.

She thought of all the casual lies she could make up, how she'd come to San Francisco to visit a friend from Vassar—she did know someone who lived in Marin—and thought she'd stop by to say hello, no big deal. She practiced the words in her head a few times as the song wound down. Noah closed his eyes as he sang the final stanza, his mouth almost grazing the mic.

After a few beats of silence vibrated through the booth, the men at the controls high-fived. One of them pressed a button and his voice crackled through the studio.

"That's another wrap, guys. Spectacular. Let's take fifteen and then we'll fire up 'Mystic Valley.' Oh, and Noah, you have a visitor."

Noah froze midway through pulling his guitar off and peered through the glass. In an instant his whole being shifted from artist at ease, submerged in his work, confident of his next move, to someone who'd lost his bearings and had surfaced in an entirely different spot than expected.

Lissy's heart sputtered, caught between beats. Noah handed his guitar to the woman in the skirt and pushed through the door to his left. Lissy mirrored his movements and they spilled out into the hall at the same time, ten feet apart. She stopped moving, almost afraid to walk toward him lest he be some kind of mirage.

"You sound good. Great, actually." Currents of nervous energy coursed through her body.

"What are you doing here?"

Lissy swallowed as heat rushed up her face. She'd stupidly hoped for "I've missed you," "I was hoping you'd come," or no words at all. Just an embrace, a kiss, a coming together that would tell her everything she needed to know. What was she doing there? What was the right answer? The idea of saying she was just passing through town sounded ridiculous in her head now, but the truth suddenly struck her as equally absurd, that she'd travelled all the way across the country to find out what they were to each other, if whatever they had was still alive, if it had staying power, if she wanted him to become central to her life, if he wanted her to be central to his.

"I mean, you never called me back. I thought—" He left the sentence unfinished.

"I don't want to be angry at you anymore."

His dimple appeared as his face broke into a huge grin. In an instant, he closed the distance between them and spun Lissy off her feet.

Lissy didn't see much of Noah over the next two weeks as his band worked to complete the album, but she didn't mind. She happily traded in the anxiety and confusion that had plagued her for the comfort of knowing he would slip into bed next to her every night. During the days, she explored the city, trying to clear her head enough to make sense of her own professional desires, whether she would climb back into the never-ending maze of the theater world or exit it for good.

As she wandered by day, she took in the constant partylike state of Haight-Ashbury, the colorful personality of the Castro, the incredible views of the Golden Gate Bridge from Russian Hill. Her favorite spot quickly became the beach at Sea Cliff where she enjoyed afternoon picnics as the surf rolled in, sometimes taking her shoes off and digging her toes into the sand even though it was November. Occasionally she stayed until dusk, mesmerized by the sun setting over the open ocean with no land in sight.

Lissy had gotten to know Noah's bandmates, Max and Esau, a bit—easygoing guys who were earnest about their music, albeit almost as serious about smoking weed and dropping acid. She was grateful Noah had chosen not to move into their house in the Haight with its rotating cast of musicians, groupies, and homeless kids looking for the next summer of love, all sprawled out like a horde of travelers stuck between cancelled flights. The girl at the mic, it turned out, was hired for backup vocals on one song and now flopped there too, possibly sleeping in Esau's bed, although it was hard to keep track of that revolving door.

Needing solo time to compose his songs—the band was hungry for more—Noah found a tiny apartment on 19th Street in the Castro, a location Lissy was surprised to learn he had apparently chosen because of her. He took the name of the restaurant on the corner as a sign, and said he wanted to bring her there for a celebratory dinner once he finished the album.

"It's called Tivoli's?" Lissy was surprised Noah even remembered her middle name—he really did listen to her during their many hours of winding conversation after rehearsals. She chuckled at how deep Noah's romantic streak ran, believing the name of the restaurant might somehow bring her to him. Of course, she couldn't argue the point considering she'd come. Mostly she was relieved and touched that the heady rush of success barreling toward Noah hadn't pushed her from his mind. He had missed her as much as she had missed him.

On the day Noah's band wrapped the album, they both put on the closest thing either of them owned to finery and headed out for Tivoli's. It was a sweet Italian place complete with bistro tables dressed in checkered linen, breadsticks at every table, and a mural of the Amalfi Coast along the wall. Noah asked the elegant man at the front for a table for two for a special occasion. He checked his list of reservations, said he had the perfect table, picked up two menus, and gestured for them to follow all in one grand motion. But when he looked at them, he paused as if he'd forgotten what to do next. After a beat, he gathered himself and showed them to a table in the front window.

Noah ordered a bottle of champagne from the waiter, but the gentleman from the podium brought it to the table.

"Celebrating something special tonight?" He expertly wrapped a linen napkin over the cork and opened it with a muffled pop.

He nodded when Noah told him he'd completed an important project, but his focus remained on Lissy. She shifted in her seat and elaborated about the album, if only to fill in the awkward silence. He offered his congratulations and smiled but didn't seem overly interested.

"And you, *mia signorina?*" He filled both glasses, his movements exaggerated but assured, as if he were a marionette being pulled by exacting strings.

"I'm actually visiting from New York."

"Something else to celebrate." Noah raised his glass.

Lissy tilted her glass toward Noah's, assuming the man would take the hint and leave them to their celebration, but he stayed put, his dark eyes still examining her.

"You grew up in New York then?"

Lissy thought it an odd line of questioning but didn't want to be rude.

"I moved there after college."

"I see." He looked strangely disappointed and finally left the table.

After toasting to Noah's success, they ordered two pasta dishes and settled into the cozy room, the candlelight of their table reflecting off the dark window. Noah raised his glass again to toast his luck at having her back. The bubbles playing on Lissy's tongue made her giddy, and she clinked and sipped and thought she might never stop smiling.

Before long, the gentleman returned to the table with focaccia and oil and retrieved the champagne from the bucket to refill their glasses. A customer donning his coat at the front door called out a farewell with a wave.

"Thanks, Fernando. See you next week!"

"Grazie mille. Ciao!"

Lissy gasped.

"Lissy, what's wrong?" Noah asked.

Fernando looked from Noah to Lissy and set the bottle on the table with a thud.

"*Mio Dio, Bellissima!* I knew it was you." Fernando dropped to one knee like a proposal, his eyes misty, his hand on hers. *Bellissima.* Her mother used to call her that when she was little, but she hadn't heard it in years.

"You look exactly like your mother." Fernando leaned in to kiss both of her cheeks.

Lissy felt disoriented. This man radiated pure adoration, as if he already knew her, as if he'd been waiting his entire life for her to walk through the door.

"Pardon my manners. I'm Fernando Tivoli. I'm an old friend of Lissy's mother." He was back on his feet, shaking Noah's hand enthusiastically. He turned back to Lissy. "How is she?"

Lissy knew her middle name came from one of her mother's closest friends in California, but like everything else about her mother's life in Hollywood, she knew little about him other than his name. Her mother described him once as a kind and loving person, one of her favorite people in the world. But when Lissy pressed for more—asking why they never heard from him—her mother said only that they'd lost touch. Then she'd shrunk into herself, the way she did when her father's old movies came on TV. Lissy understood it as another topic to be avoided.

The only detail Lissy managed to surmise was that her mother worked for Fernando at one point. She could have sworn he owned the store where her mother modeled, but had she misunderstood?

"Did you know my father too?" Maybe this man could fill in some of the detail her mother never would.

"Of course." Color momentarily drained from his face. "Is your mother well?"

"Yes, she's wonderful. I was just with her two weeks ago."

"*Grazie Dio*, I'm so glad to hear that. Let me bring some wine and we can talk!"

The evening became an enjoyable sprawl of celebration as Lissy and Noah's modest order turned into tastes of seemingly everything on the menu. Whenever he wasn't seating, serving, or clearing other tables, Fernando pulled over a chair and sat with them.

"I tried many times to find your mother but couldn't find any listing for her in New York." Fernando grated cheese onto spinach ravioli.

"We live on Martha's Vineyard."

"Ah, she moved there after design school?"

Confusion again.

"My mother didn't go to design school."

"Does she make clothes on Martha's Vineyard, then?"

"My mother?" Lissy's mother was hopeless in her choice of clothes, never moving much beyond overalls and denim shorts. Maybe this man didn't know her mother very well after all.

"She's a sculptor, known for her renderings of islanders," Noah said helpfully.

Fernando smiled and nodded his head. "*Magnifico.* That makes sense. She always understood forms, the power of body language."

"Didn't she used to work for you?"

"I suppose she did, yes." Something dark passed over his face. "It was a long time ago."

When Fernando left them to attend to other guests, Lissy watched him with interest. He had an easy way about him, was quick to laugh, and his customers obviously adored him. The evening played like a happy song he conducted, his arms and hands gracefully guiding the rhythm. It wasn't difficult to imagine Fernando as a good friend of her mother's, and yet their time working together seemed like an afterthought to him.

"I think there's a lyric in here somewhere," Noah said. Lissy smiled at him, the poet at heart, always mining life for material. "It's pretty crazy, right? What are the chances I would lead you to your mom's old friend?"

"And the man who named me."

"You mean the man your mother named you after."

"Not *Tivoli*. I mean *Lissy*. It's short for *Bellissima*. She used to call me that when I was little. I never thought to ask her where it came from."

Noah leaned across the table and spoke in a hushed voice. "Do you think there was something more between them?"

Lissy let out a cackle and then put her hand on Noah's cheek, not wanting him to think she was making fun of him. "You're adorable, but I think it's pretty obvious he's not the type to be interested in my mother. And besides, my parents were very much in love."

"Like you and me." He was definitely a little drunk, but she beamed at him.

After enjoying cappuccinos with biscotti—Fernando insisted they have the biscotti for dipping—Noah asked for the check, but Fernando refused to let them pay for a thing. He kissed Lissy again on both cheeks as they said goodbye.

"I still can't believe it. Tell me, will your mother visit you here? When might she come?"

"No, well, I only just arrived—" Lissy stopped herself.

"She thinks she's just visiting, but I have other ideas." Noah put his arm around her shoulder.

"Please, will you call her and tell her you met me?" Fernando swallowed, his expression oddly mimicking the strained look Lissy associated with her mother's memories of California.

"Tell her I very much would like to see her." His tone sounded more like someone who had just lost a friend than someone who had rediscovered one. The glow of the evening threatened to fade the way the warmth of the summer sun suddenly succumbed to the chill of afternoon shadows.

"I'll tell her."

Lissy leaned into Noah as they walked home. Turning down Noah's street, hushed laughter wafted onto the sidewalk. Lissy watched the glow of two cigarettes, close together, sharing a front stoop and the night air. Something about it warmed her inside, the calm of the scene, the pleasure of having another person to share in simple moments.

She could have walked for hours with Noah's arm around her. New York had never been a strolling city for her. Life outside her apartment or the theater consisted of pushing through crowds to get to her destination as quickly as possible, a form of individual combat that kept her on high alert until she locked a door behind her. San Francisco was the opposite. The fun, the creativity, the energy lived out on the streets, in the parks, on front stoops. She could imagine getting comfortable here. If only she knew what she was meant to do with her life.

The money her mother gave her was a shocking windfall, something she never expected. As much as it loosened the knots of panic that had seized her the moment she found out the show would close, it could do nothing to rewire her brain. She was meant to excel, put her energy toward something of consequence. And she needed to earn any success she enjoyed, otherwise it wouldn't matter. Her mother had been right about that all along. Now she just had to figure out what she wanted her path to be.

"You're quiet." Noah leaned his head into hers.

"I wonder what my mother will think about us meeting Fernando. She's always been so uncomfortable talking about that part of her life. It's like when my father died her whole life there just disappeared."

"Well, it seems it's reappeared." Noah unlocked the door to the apartment. "Want to give her a call?"

Lissy glanced at her watch. "Way too late on the East Coast. I'll call her tomorrow."

After Noah fell asleep, his arm swung over her belly, his breathing soft and steady, Lissy lay awake. She tried to imagine what her mother's reaction to her news might be. Fernando seemed nothing short of thrilled to have a new connection with his old friend, but there was a familiar sadness not far from the surface. Would telling her mother about Fernando undo her, unleash the tide of sorrow she had struggled to blink back all these years?

Something else worried Lissy. She couldn't get out of her mind the look on Fernando's face when she mentioned her father, how he blanched, as if hiding something he didn't want her to know. Was her father not the upstanding man she'd always assumed? Had there been trouble between her parents? Lissy stiffened at the thought. Could that be the real reason her mother never talked about him? Good god, she hoped not. She'd had enough disappointment of late without learning that the father she'd revered wasn't worthy of it. That just might do her in.

CHAPTER THIRTY-FOUR

San Francisco
November 1975

A ster boarded a plane to San Francisco five days later, the first flight available without paying triple the normal fare. Lissy had found Fernando! She made Lissy repeat every word of their evening several times. How did he end up running a restaurant? Why San Francisco? How long ago did he try to find her? Lissy didn't have the answer to many of her questions, and Aster couldn't wait to ask them all herself. She desperately hoped she'd find a happy man, maybe even one who had found love again.

She was doubly pleased to visit Lissy so soon and finally meet Noah. Lissy had sounded increasingly calm with each phone call, nothing but pleased to be with Noah again, content in her surroundings. She was toying with auditioning for some shows in town, but Aster heard the hesitancy in her voice and encouraged her to take her time. Once Lissy opened that door, she was likely to get caught up in the forward motion of it all. There was no need to rush it.

Aster was jumpy with nerves about the trip. She hadn't traveled farther than New York City since moving back from California those many years ago. Nor had she thought quite so much about her wardrobe since then—she obviously couldn't see Fernando for the first time in over twenty years wearing her sculpting overalls. Fortunately, Lissy had cajoled her into buying two new pairs of hip-huggers during her last visit, and she'd matched them with several pretty flowered blouses. While not the finery Fernando had known her to wear, at least she had maintained her figure all these years.

The moment Aster saw Fernando, she felt twenty years old again. Other than a slight peppering of his hair, he looked exactly the same: elegantly dressed in a fine suit, one of his own making she assumed, and he still carefully arranged his limbs, this time to stop his gesticulations from knocking over all the glassware in the restaurant. The way he hugged her felt like coming home. This man who had been more of a father to Lissy than she would ever comprehend, and the only person who fully understood the truth of Aster's life stood right before her. The joy of it almost crowded out all the air in her lungs.

After they embraced and he kissed Lissy hello, she couldn't help but notice a tinge of nervous energy at the edges of his trademark warmth. He had a restaurant to run after all, and while he sat with them as much as possible, he popped up whenever a new customer arrived, as attentive to all his diners as he had been to his clients at the boutique. But it was a strain to have to tap dance around the one topic at the forefront of both of their minds. Aster couldn't ask him how he really was, if he'd managed to finally recover from the loss of Benny. He couldn't ask her how much Lissy knew about any of it.

Fortunately, the conversation flowed easily anyway thanks to Noah and Lissy, and whenever Fernando left the table, there was much she wanted to talk to them about too. She immediately liked Noah. He reminded her of the kind of musicians she preferred at the Barn on the Vineyard. While some came there for the applause, the recognition, or a chance at fame, she could tell which ones were sincerely invested in their music and just grateful to play, not expecting a throne and crown to come along with every gig. And Lissy seemed at ease with him, her essence shining through effortlessly. Lucky kids. As much as the idea of possibly losing Lissy to the West Coast pained Aster, she understood the draw completely and hoped for Lissy that if Noah was the great love of her life, she would find a way to make it work—something she herself had never managed.

When they stood to leave, Fernando pulled Aster aside.

"We don't open tomorrow until five. You must come to my apartment. For lunch? Just you," he said gently. "There's so much we must discuss."

Aster accepted without hesitation. She would finally be able to pore over the emotions of the last two decades with the only other person who could possibly understand.

Fernando didn't live very far from Noah's apartment, so Aster walked there. She hadn't been to San Francisco since her Fashion Guild tour and was fascinated by the changes. The young people filling the streets were uninhibited, clearly experimenting with various lifestyles, pushing all sorts of boundaries. While it suggested a kind of freedom Aster had craved in her youth, she also noticed a level of dinginess she hadn't expected: collarless street dogs with no happy marker of the home that claimed them, kids wearing frayed denim shorts with rips at the pockets, their stringy hair badly in need of a wash, sallow skin sapped of proper nutrition. She missed the Vineyard already.

She laughed a little at herself, realizing how much her life on the island sheltered her from the revolution still rocking the country. She and Graham would often talk about how stuffy Boston was compared to their free-flowing, forward-thinking, relaxed lifestyle on the Vineyard. But they had nothing on these kids.

Standing at Fernando's door, memories of the day she came to say goodbye to him in LA crashed through her, making her momentarily wobbly. It had all been so devastating, so awful. And she felt more than a little guilty for managing to live an entire second life since then, a happy life complete with new friends, new joys, the simple pleasures of motherhood, not to mention the creative outlet that sustained her. Was the restaurant a true source of happiness for him now? Was it enough, or was his life still defined by all he had lost?

Fernando opened the door, his usual suit swapped out for jeans and a T-shirt, his feet bare. The T-shirt showed the definition of his chest, still muscular, and the jeans hung loosely at his hips. He had kept himself in good shape. The apartment looked far bigger than the one in LA where she had seen him last. They stepped into a large living room with an attached study on one side and a kitchen beyond. Down a long hall, a staircase spiraled up to an additional floor. Fernando led her through French doors to a lanai. Two lounge chairs faced the sun while a striped awning shaded a small dining table, set for lunch. The courtyard below brimmed with oleander bushes and four tall palm trees. It was all very beautiful.

"I thought we could eat out here." He pulled out a chair for her.

As they sat at the table, Fernando dove right in. "Tell me, are you happy? You never married?"

Aster thought about the best way to describe it without sounding pitiful.

"I dated some. But the topic of my first marriage would come up pretty quickly, impossible to hide given I had a child. It was always too soon for the truth—I couldn't trust just anyone with that information." Aster remembered too well the dread lingering at the edges of each date, like a shadow she couldn't shake. The more she tried to skirt the topic ("I'm widowed," "I was married to an actor," or "I prefer to leave it in the past"), the larger the specter of having to eventually admit she'd been married to Christopher Page loomed. Given how little she could tell them without inventing stories, they read her circumspection as proof of his indelible place in her heart. Of course, the men who didn't worry about their ability to live up to Christopher Page were the ones who should have. Like Bob Halifax. He came to the island one summer and bought three of Aster's sculptures in one fell swoop, as if such a magnanimous gesture should endear her to him forever. "The longer I stayed single, the more everyone just assumed my heart was forever broken. I think I became a bit untouchable."

Being able to talk about it after so many years was like taking off a too-tight and too-warm jacket and allowing a summer breeze to wash over her skin for the first time. Complete relief.

"But yes, I'm happy. I've built a fulfilling life on the Vineyard. It was a wonderful place for Lissy to grow up."

"She's lovely. She reminds me so much of you in every way."

Aster relished the compliment coming from her old friend.

"Have you completely given up fashion?" She couldn't imagine giving up sculpting. "How did you end up running a restaurant?"

"I was going to ask the same of you. What happened to design school?"

"Oh, gosh. That feels like a different person. I realized it wasn't for me. I think I was just trying to get out of modeling, get off the stage, you know? And I thought clothes were something I knew enough about to try my hand at. I guess I craved a deep connection to my work. But with everything that happened, I don't know . . . I think I began to question the importance of clothing. I found I enjoyed studying people and capturing the moments in life that mean something."

"I understand. Feeding people, hosting special occasions, it all feels better to me now than dressing people for them."

"And you? Do you have anyone in your life?" She had noticed pairs of things in his home right away: two leather chairs in front of the television, two stools at the bar in the living room. While she supposed most people decorated in twos, she also noticed two slickers on the hooks in the hall. No one needed two raincoats.

"That's what I wanted to talk to you about."

Fernando gave a slight tilt of his head toward the French doors, a gesture she had seen him make at the restaurant when he finished pouring the wine, signaling the waiter to deliver the next course.

A man with an apron around his waist came to the table with two bowls of soup, steam swirling above the rims. He had a bushy beard the same espresso color as his hair and looked at Fernando tentatively after placing the dishes on the table. She wondered briefly why they were being served in Fernando's own home.

"Thank you." She picked up her spoon.

The man didn't move, and Fernando reached for his hand. Aster looked at him more closely, sensing his importance. She almost didn't see it at first—his nearly black eyes, the lean six-foot-two frame under a little more muscle than before.

"Aster," he said.

She dropped her spoon. That voice. Everything tilted, and she grabbed the edges of the table. She must have been losing her mind. The emotions of seeing Fernando again had gotten the best of her, and now she was going to faint right there, or vomit, she wasn't sure which.

"Aster," he said again, and knelt at her side.

Aster's hand flew up to her mouth, the tears coming so fast she couldn't breathe.

"Benny?" She was misunderstanding somehow.

"I know it's a lot to take in, believe me." Fernando was at her other side.

Aster felt herself slipping through a break in reality. She became unbearably light-headed, her sight blurring, her lungs straining for air. Her fingers struggled to firmly clutch the table, to find some kind of tangible connection to the world. Was she going insane? Closing her eyes made it all worse, her banging pulse a dangerous warning that her heart might burst.

Through the roiling chaos, she sensed warmth on her back. Fernando's hand was holding her steady, calming her as he had done so many years before, patiently coaxing full breaths into her lungs. She had no idea how long he silently waited for her to come back into herself.

When she could finally move again, Aster put her hand to Benny's face. Perfect. Not a scratch. The tears started again, gentle this time. Here she was between these two men again, as if a time machine had picked her up and deposited her back in 1949. Her friends, her family, reunited.

And then the reality of it all pushed its way through the haze. Another lie. Her shock flared with anger.

"Why didn't you tell me? You let me believe I ruined both your lives." She hated the petulance in her own voice, but she had no control over the torrent of emotions swamping her.

"Fernando didn't know. The only way I could get the studio to agree was if I swore I'd disappear and tell no one. You and Fernando couldn't have faked that kind of grief. They were watching both of you closely. I'm so sorry."

"Sam knew?" The implications hit her like a second rogue wave, smashing into her while she was still struggling beneath the first. She remembered her last meeting with Sam so clearly, his smug expression, his treatment of their interaction as nothing more than a transaction. Once again, Sam knew the inner workings of her life before she did. He'd let her believe she'd bested him, that she'd gotten some small slice of what she wanted, but he'd been the conductor of her misery.

"Benny waited a full year to find me. We disappeared for a long time. In Crete, mostly. We couldn't risk anyone recognizing him. We eventually tried to contact you, but I had no idea where to find you."

"But don't people realize who you are?" Her head swam with the impossibility of it all.

"In our community here, so many of our friends have something in their background they don't want to discuss," Benny said. "An ex-wife left behind, an abusive parent they don't want to ever find them . . . We don't ask a lot of questions. There's an unspoken agreement to accept each other for who we are now, whatever that means."

"And at the restaurant, people see what you tell them to see. Benny's a chef now. A damn good one." Fernando beamed at him, just like he used to.

Aster thought back to the meatballs she'd ordered the night before and how familiar they tasted. He always did make brilliant meatballs.

She looked at him closely again, trying to assure herself this was actually happening. She saw a man who was familiar but used different gestures than she remembered—he touched one earlobe when he talked rather than crossing his arms over his chest, he pursed his lips in concentration instead of letting that brow furrow like it used to. He'd always been able to transform himself fully into whatever character he played, so it probably wasn't that difficult for him to disappear behind the façade of another man. He managed to hide in plain sight by leaving behind the bright shock of blond hair the studio had invented, growing a beard, adopting new mannerisms and an entirely different profession. Aster wouldn't have thought it possible if she hadn't known him to be a gifted actor. The best there ever was.

"Does Sam know you're together now?"

"If he does, he'd never bring any attention to it. You saw what happened after the car crash. There's nothing like the death of a young star to vault them into the pantheon and ensure the success of their movies forever—no offense, Benny. Sam has just as much at stake in keeping this quiet as we do. Obviously, the public can never know."

Aster sat back in her chair, numbness beginning to overtake her as if the circuit breaker to her heart had been tripped. She still couldn't quite make sense of it. Her friend was alive. Fernando hadn't been suffering all these years. There was so much to be grateful for. She could have these two wonderful men back in her life.

But Lissy.

"She was supposed to hate you," Aster said.

"What?"

"Remember? We were going to get divorced. You were going to be the absentee father. The 'lowlife' who deserted his child. After you . . . after I thought you died, I thought it would be better to tell her you were a wonderful man who'd adored her." She looked squarely at Benny as she spoke. "She idolizes you."

"Is that such a bad thing?"

"You have no idea." Aster put her head in her hands.

What was she supposed to do with this information now? Lissy's "father" wasn't actually dead. And yet, Lissy obviously couldn't meet this man while still thinking he *was* her father. That would require a varnish of lies thicker than the original coat. But if Aster told Lissy the full truth, she would also have to tell her she was born from someone else—a man Aster had kept from her her entire life.

Of course, Aster could say nothing and go on as before. But Lissy knew Fernando now, knew him as an important person to her. Aster had jumped on a plane to see him again, after all—and Lissy was possibly about to take up residence not only in the same city as him, but in the same neighborhood. Could Aster really be in the same room with all of them and pretend she had just met Fernando's Benny for the first time? Lissy would see her discomfort immediately. Not to mention that Lissy was one of the few people on the planet who knew that Christopher Page's real name was Benedict Horowitz. What if she pieced it all together herself?

It was a riptide of treacherous choices, and telling Lissy none of it felt impossible, like failing to mention that the sky had changed from blue to fuchsia. How could Aster ever hide such a sea change? Reciting a rehearsed story from the time Lissy was a baby was one thing—by the time Lissy was old enough to ask any questions or interpret her mother's emotions, it was accepted as fact. But Aster was no Christopher Page—she didn't have an acting bone in her body. Lissy would know something dramatic had shifted the moment she laid eyes on her.

"What in god's name do I do now?" Not that she expected either of these men to have the answer.

CHAPTER THIRTY-FIVE

San Francisco
November 1975

M y whole life is a fucking lie?" Lissy paced Noah's tiny living room.

"No sweetheart, it's not. You're still who you've always been—"

"Stop saying that. I still don't understand why you had to lie to me."

"Because it's the story the world knew. And a child can't understand everything I just told you. And before I knew it, you were a fully grown person and it didn't seem to matter." Her own words sounded ridiculous, but Aster had no other explanation. She was finally telling the truth. She'd taken every one of Lissy's fulfilled dreams as proof that a missing father hadn't made an impact, regardless of who he was.

"Didn't matter? Are you joking? You let me throw myself onstage because I thought I had a heritage in acting somehow. You let me put myself out there, on Broadway, as Christopher Page's fucking daughter."

Lissy never swore, and now she couldn't seem to come up with any other words. Aster hadn't seen Lissy this angry since her friend Georgia borrowed the ten-speed Lissy'd bought herself with a summer's worth of waitressing tips only to leave it unlocked in front of Aggie's General Store, where it was stolen in under five minutes. And her anger then was a summer breeze in comparison to this storm.

"Your talents don't have anything to do with either of your parents. Haven't I always told you that?"

Lissy sat down and put her face in her hands.

"Do you want to meet Benny?" Aster asked gently.

Lissy looked up, incredulous.

"What's the point? He's nothing to me."

"He and Fernando helped me raise you in the beginning. They were both fathers to you in a way." In the last twenty-four hours, Aster had been flooded with memories of Fernando playing with Lissy in the pool, Benny holding her tiny hand as she teetered across the living room, both of them taking turns rocking her to sleep whenever Aster hit her limit.

"Great, my two gay dads." Lissy threw her hands in the air.

"Lissy! Don't talk that way." She had raised Lissy better than that.

"Can I be upset, Mom? Would that be all right with you? Can you not understand why I am going a little bit crazy right now?" She was back on her feet, pacing.

Aster never had been good at letting anger loose in the world. As much as she logically knew trapping it inside wasn't helpful—Graham always said it was easier to extinguish negative thoughts if you could see the fire—she'd been raised to bottle up the bad stuff. She and her father never talked about her mother's disappearances or drinking. They just drove the streets together, poured her mother into the car once they found her, and tiptoed around the house for however many days it took her to shake off her blues. Once her mother showered and put her house clothes back on, Aster preferred to take comfort in the mopped kitchen floor and freshly made beds rather than allow the images of the back alleys, lecherous bartenders, and smudged mascara on her mother's face invade their home.

Aster had been determined to be the kind of mother to Lissy that she'd never known—reliable, trustworthy, deeply interested in her daughter's life. She wanted Lissy to experience unconditional love and for them to be honest with each other about everything—except, of course, the one thing she'd never before revealed. And now she'd put it all at risk.

Lissy was quiet for some time. She stopped pacing and stared out the window above Noah's guitar stand. Aster didn't think more explanation would be helpful, so she waited for Lissy to sort through her thoughts, process all she'd just learned.

Finally, Lissy spoke again. She was calm now, eerily so.

"Then who is my father?"

Aster knew this question was coming and had already decided there would be no more lies.

"His name is Sam Sawyer. He runs Galaxy Studios."

"Does he know about me?"

"I don't know. Maybe." Aster had asked herself the same question many times. She supposed he must know at some level, unless he thought Benny played it both ways, but the timing was more than a little suspicious. But if he did suspect the truth, Aster still couldn't fathom how he so easily turned his back on his own daughter, pretending she didn't exist. Then again, Aster had spent more of her life living a lie than not. She understood the power of an invented narrative, especially a convenient one. It could reshape reality when given the chance.

"Why didn't you stay with him?" Fear suddenly darkened Lissy's eyes. "He didn't force himself on you, did he?"

"No. Absolutely not. I was with him willingly. He was charming in many ways. But I wasn't in love with him. And I wasn't ready to sign up to be a glorified housekeeper."

"So instead you signed up to be the wife of a megastar? How did that help?"

"It was on my own terms. We always planned to divorce. Until I became a widow instead."

"By his choice. How are you not furious?"

Aster had been thinking about that too. Benny took all their lives into his own hands when he orchestrated the crash. But it was likely the only way he could imagine exiting the business and choosing Fernando. He would never have been comfortable coming out to the entire world, and he wouldn't have been able to explain walking away from Hollywood otherwise. The press would have hounded him until they discovered the truth, which would have been a mess for all of them.

"I know it's hard for you to imagine how awful it was to be found out as a homosexual back then. Things are starting to change now, but it felt desperate then, and I wanted to protect them. They were so in love. They still are. So no, I'm relieved, not angry. And don't forget, having a baby out of wedlock wasn't done back then either. If I wanted to keep you, which I desperately wanted to do, I had to pick a husband. So, I picked." Aster needed Lissy to understand, to forgive her. She couldn't live with the alternative.

"There's something else that makes no sense." Lissy came and sat next to Aster on the couch. "You always talked about my father—shit, I can't even say that anymore—you've always talked about the pain of losing a soul mate. I've seen the tears in your eyes. But now you're saying you never loved my real father. And you certainly weren't in love with Christopher Page." She said his name with a bitterness now that made

Aster wince. "All the weepy looks, telling me about the magic of true love, how rare and special it is, how it shouldn't be taken for granted. Was that all bullshit too?"

Aster froze. Of all the difficult questions she expected, this was not one of them. She looked down at her hands. She craved the feel of cold clay in her fingers, the satisfaction of kneading it until it became pliable, the ability to control what took shape.

"Mom?"

Aster couldn't look at her.

"Oh my god. Have you been having an affair with Graham?"

"No! Of course not!" Her voice sounded tinny in her ears, too high-pitched.

"Mom?"

Aster wasn't sure how much Lissy could absorb in one sitting—Graham was like an uncle to Lissy—but she was done hiding the truth.

"There was something between us once, but it was a long time ago."

"What happened?" Lissy's voice softened.

"I thought keeping our family to just the two of us was best."

"So let me get this straight." Lissy was on her feet again, her voice rising. "My existence forced you into a fake marriage then kept you from the one person you really loved?"

"No, Lissy, it's not like that." She was making a mess of this. "Those are choices I made. It might all sound crazy now, but I was just—" Aster struggled to find the right words. "It's so hard to explain it in a way that makes any sense. I was just doing the best I knew how." Aster swiped at the tears on her face. This wasn't about her. She had to stay composed for Lissy.

"Anything else you want to share? Any other bombshells I need to know about? I swear I feel like I don't know who you are."

"Please don't say that." A fissure cracked open inside Aster and threatened to tear her apart.

Lissy strode across the living room toward the door.

"Where are you going?" Aster needed Lissy to keep talking to her, give them time to process everything together and figure out how to move on.

"I need to talk to Noah."

"But you can't tell him—"

"Don't tell me what I can and can't tell him," Lissy interrupted, seething. "I need at least one relationship in my life not to be based on lies."

"Lissy—" Aster could barely get the word out before Lissy cut her off her again.

"Please don't be here when I get back. I don't think I can see you for a while."

Lissy slammed the door and was gone.

Back in her hotel room, Aster couldn't remember exactly how she'd gotten there, the entire afternoon a blur. The one clear image in her mind was the look on Lissy's face before she'd walked out. A deep foreboding told Aster she'd made the wrong choice once again. She should have told Fernando and Benny goodbye, flown home, and let that be that. Fernando said it himself. Everyone saw Benny as Tivoli's chef, nothing more. Maybe Lissy would never have guessed the truth.

Aster called Noah's apartment repeatedly but got no answer. She thought about going to Tivoli's to ask Fernando for his advice, but he didn't know Lissy as an adult—her stubborn streak, how humor could break her out of a funk but would backfire unless you'd taken her issue seriously first, how her lifelong desire to excel drove all her decisions, something Aster now realized might have been in an attempt to find common ground with her exceptional father. No, the only person who could help her think through what to do next was Graham. As much as the truth of her past would shock him too, he could be trusted with it. And she desperately needed a friend.

Aster almost never called Graham at his house, but it was already past dinnertime on the East Coast. Aster hoped Marcia didn't answer. They'd never become close, and she wasn't in any state for a forced conversation. To her relief, Graham picked up.

"Oh, Graham." She barely formed the words over the tears in her throat.

"I'm so glad it's you. How'd you find out so fast?"

"Find out what?" She sat up straight, her frayed nerves at attention once again. "Graham?"

"Marcia's leaving me." He said this the way he might tell her someone had purchased his favorite painting in the gallery and taken it away, an inevitable outcome that was nonetheless tinged with loss.

"Leaving you? What happened?"

He let out a long sigh. She pictured him sitting at his kitchen table, spinning the lazy Susan slowly, watching the salt, syrup, sugar, and a stack of paper napkins go by.

"She said she was tired of competing for my attention, tired of feeling like second fiddle. She's fallen in love with someone else."

Second fiddle? To the Haven? Aster didn't know Marcia very well—she managed to avoid Graham's life at the gallery almost completely—and the state of Graham's marriage wasn't a topic they discussed. It wasn't any of her business.

"Oh my god, Graham. I'm so sorry."

He told her everything. How Marcia had fallen for their youngest daughter's sixth-grade teacher, which meant it had been going on for almost two years—Bindi was now in eighth grade. Marcia had already planned it all out. She was going to move into his house in West Tisbury. Bindi and Jan could go back and forth between the two houses, easy enough now that Jan had a license, and Chrissy could do the same whenever she came home from college. Graham said all three girls were crushed, furious with their mother, and they refused to pack up and move anywhere, which gave him comfort and broke his heart all at the same time. Aster could picture the girls' anger all too clearly. Graham went on, his voice laden with exhaustion.

"The truth is, things haven't been good between us for a long time. But I guess I didn't realize how miserable she was, how overlooked she's always felt. How overlooked she deserved to feel."

Second fiddle.

"Wait. If you didn't know, what were you calling about?"

Aster hesitated. Did he just hint that he'd never stopped loving her? Throughout his marriage? She gave him up those many years ago so he could get on with his life, have the children he wanted. And he'd perceived her rejection as coming from a grieving widow who couldn't give her heart to anyone else. Would he turn on her if she told him the truth now, just as Lissy had?

Aster ached to see his expression, watch his body language to understand the feelings buried in his words. He always rubbed his left arm when he was upset, scratched behind his ear when he was nervous. Instead, she stared at the hexagonal shapes on the hotel quilt, willing them to show her a pattern that might mean something.

"Aster?"

He listened quietly as she unfolded for him the layers of her past without any neatly constructed stories or half-truths. She admitted the mistakes she made, described the trap she'd created for herself. More than anything, she needed him to understand why she'd never fully extracted herself from the tangles of lies.

After she'd said as little as she thought necessary and as much as she could handle in one sitting, she waited for him to react. She hugged a pillow against her body as if it would protect her from an incoming blow.

Graham cleared his throat, a muffled sound. She clutched the telephone's cord to keep him tethered to her. Could he understand?

"It's late. I need to go, Aster." The connection went dead.

More than a week later, Lissy still refused to see Aster. At least Noah started to answer the phone, but he told Aster the same thing every night, that Lissy didn't want to talk to her. She was reeling. His voice was kind but firm.

Aster spent most days sitting at one café or another, the activity around her rendered gray and ashen, flat figures with no interesting definition. When she tired of half-empty coffee cups, she shuffled down one street or another, looking for a sign that her miserable purgatory might come to an end that night when she called Lissy again, only to have all hope extinguished by Noah in less than a minute.

"Please tell her I'm here when she's ready," she would say, not knowing if the message ever got to Lissy. And then she would dial Graham's number.

He did answer his phone the second night, and every night after. He asked her questions carefully, like a person unsure where his foot might break through a floorboard and create further damage. As he attempted to make sense of all he didn't know throughout the quarter century of their friendship, every conversation came around to the same question: Why hadn't Aster trusted him with the truth sooner, a question he asked with varying amounts of anger and sadness. All Aster could say was that she wished she had.

Eventually, Graham told her more about his failed marriage, how early on it had disintegrated, how much they relied on their children as connective tissue. How the love between them had evaporated in such small increments that no particular day was dramatically different from the one before, until they found themselves cohabitating in a parched place, too hardened to absorb any attempt at new sustenance.

Aster and Graham spoke for hours most nights, after his girls were tucked into bed, her room service dinner gone cold and pushed to the side, conversations full of grief for time and relationships lost, and worry about a fractured future. What they didn't talk about was what, if anything, might still be possible between them. The only hint came when Graham said, in almost a whisper, almost to himself, "I would have taken care of Lissy like she was my own."

Aster's throat constricted, knowing he'd done just that, all her life.

She saw Fernando and Benny every few days for coffee or lunch. Their company was an oasis for her, their trio still soft and pliable, unlike the cracked clay of the rest of her life. They were fascinated by her life on the Vineyard, her sculpting, and Lissy. They couldn't get enough of hearing about Lissy. Aster loved their stories of living in Crete, how they'd befriended the fishermen who caught their dinner by day, and their penchant for practicing new salt rubs and sauces by night. They spoke with satisfaction about the process of getting the restaurant up and running from its roots as a shuttered bakery, its rapid ascension to neighborhood favorite, the details of menu design and finding the perfect fabric for the tablecloths. The day the *San Francisco Examiner* dubbed them "the newest taste of Old Italy," they knew they had a hit on their hands.

Aster surveyed the apartment, the Giacometti coffee table, the four Ansel Adams prints she hadn't noticed on her first visit.

"By the looks of it, the restaurant has done quite well for you."

Fernando laughed.

"It holds its own, but we have you to thank for this lifestyle," Benny said. "Giving so much of the money to Fernando, that was incredibly generous."

"It allowed me to get out of LA. Staying there might have killed me," Fernando said.

"It was never meant to be mine. And our piece of it—well, Lissy's—was more than enough. Getting royalties out of Galaxy was quite a coup, by the way." She raised her mug in Benny's direction.

"That was Sam's idea. Obviously, I had to take a chunk of money out of my account before disappearing to give me enough to live on. So Sam suggested a new contract to include royalties."

"I don't understand. That's money out of Galaxy's pockets. Why would he do that?" Aster's mug drifted slowly back down to the table.

"Maybe he was trying to take care of you in the only way he knew how."

And Lissy, Aster thought. What had Sam said that last day in his office? *"You have a daughter to think about now."* Or was it merely a clever way to ensure her silence? After all, he made clear that if the truth ever got out about Christopher Page, he'd make sure the royalty payments stopped. But wouldn't he have understood that she had more compelling reasons than money for keeping the truth from the world?

"When are you coming home?" Graham asked ten days into their ritual of evening calls. "I need you here."

Aster understood how much support Graham needed while he dealt with a dissolving marriage and three unhappy girls. She should be there to handle closing time at the gallery so he could get home to make Bindi's favorite sweet potato pie and cover the weekends so he could keep an extra eye on Jan, a hormone-riddled teen with a wild streak.

She badly wanted to be a steadying force for him and wished she could say she was headed back East the next day. She longed to be with him in person, to calibrate what they were to each other now, but it was too treacherous to discuss it on the phone, too ripe for misunderstanding and missed connection.

"I can't leave until I work things out with Lissy. What would it tell her if she's ready to talk and I'm not here?" She would wait forever if that was what it would take.

"If there's one thing I've learned by this mess with Marcia, it's that we can't put our lives on hold for our kids, as hard as that sounds. Marcia and I have both been unhappy for a long time, but we were afraid to do anything to upset the girls. It doesn't work in the end. You've sacrificed so much for Lissy already. She'll come around."

Aster didn't consider anything she'd done for Lissy a sacrifice. Motherhood was sacred, a state of giving as natural as a tree sending the water it drinks from the ground up to the tiny shoots in the sky.

"I don't know if I can get through Thanksgiving without you."

"I'm sorry, Graham. But I can't leave."

It was the only thing Aster knew for sure. She wouldn't budge until Lissy agreed to see her again. All she could do was hope Graham would understand. And wait.

A week later, Noah said something she didn't expect when he picked up the phone.

"She's gone to LA, Aster. She decided she needs to meet her father."

CHAPTER THIRTY-SIX

Los Angeles
December 1975

Lissy wasn't at all sure what one should wear to meet her father for the first time. She didn't want him to think she was intent on impressing him or wanted something from him. She had no idea what she wanted; she only knew she had to meet him. In the end, she decided to go casual, bell-bottoms and a Bad Company T-shirt. She wasn't a huge fan herself, but Noah had shrunk the shirt in the dryer by mistake and it fit her perfectly. She wanted a piece of him with her for this.

Lissy had never gone as long as ten days without speaking with her mother. But every time she thought about her, she felt nothing but anger. She pictured herself huddled close to the TV as a child, gazing at the man on the screen. How did her mother allow her to believe she was connected to him, to grow up imagining she had something special running through her blood because of it?

Lissy pictured herself sitting in Rudy's office and wanted to cry. What an idiot she'd been, thinking she might save the show by finally revealing the great secret of her family tree to the world. As if it proved she deserved to be onstage in the first place. Her mother had let her stack her professional ambitions on top of a foundation of feathers. What a joke.

Lissy forced herself to pull it together as the taxi rolled up to the entrance of the studio. She needed to prepare herself for her meeting with—her father? Sam? Mr. Sawyer? She didn't even know what to call him. She was surprised how quickly she'd secured an appointment with him but should have realized that the name Horowitz worked like a secret handshake in this particular corner of the world. His secretary called back later the same day with several possible times to meet. Lissy didn't take the soonest one—not wanting to appear too eager—and agreed to a time the following week. While she thought scheduling it out a few days would give her needed time to prepare, in truth she'd done nothing but worry about what the interaction might feel like. Now she just wanted to get it over with.

A guard picked her up in a golf cart on the other side of the security gate and tried to make polite conversation while he drove. She barely responded, not knowing exactly how to explain what she was doing there—"I have an appointment with Sam Sawyer" was all she offered—and took in the chaos of the Galaxy Studios lot. It seemed to be in constant motion, like a gargantuan machine that sorted people and equipment and dropped them in their proper spots. A sausage factory of fame.

After parking in front of a faded white building, the guard opened a large door and pointed out the way to Sam's office. A poster for *Midnight Sonata* assaulted her, the same one that used to bring a sly smile to her face, her secret carefully tucked away. How strange that the man in the top hat and tails was no longer her father.

An older woman behind a desk asked her to take a seat. Mr. Sawyer would be with her shortly. Lissy ran through some of her pre-audition exercises as quietly as possible to try to calm her breathing and maintain her composure. Mostly she tried to visualize an easy conversation, a light interaction leaving them both smiling.

When she finally entered his office, the recognition on his face was immediate.

"Wow, you look just like your mother."

"That's what I hear." She sat in one of the chairs facing the island-sized desk between them. Nothing about him struck her as familiar, but she did see the outlines of a man who had once been attractive. He was tall and still lean. She guessed him to be ten years older than her mother, maybe more. He had disarming eyes, but the creases on his forehead and between his brows marked a life of deep concentration or perhaps disappointment. He didn't have the sunshine lines that fanned out next to Graham's eyes every time he smiled. She had the bizarre urge to ask him if she could see his ankles, to confirm their association through the one body part she hadn't inherited from her mother.

"So what brings you to my door? Trying to break into film? Looking for a screen test?"

Did he honestly not know who she was? Or did he think she didn't know?

"No, I'm not an actress." That much had been become painfully clear.

"I see. What is it you do, if I may ask?" He began to fiddle with a silver letter opener even though there was no mail to be seen on the gleaming expanse of his desk.

"I'm a singer." Lissy had never described herself as such before, no matter how many times she sang in public, no matter how often her teachers told her she had an exceptional voice. Using the moniker of *singer* surprised her even as she said the word, and in the same breath she knew it was true. That's what she wanted to do with her life.

"No kidding. Fred Allen's an old friend of mine."

"Fred Allen?"

He pointed to her T-shirt. "He heads their label. Want me to give him a call? Put in a good word?"

He flipped through his Rolodex. How could he "put in a good word"? He hadn't even heard her sing. She should have been touched by his reflex to try to help her, but she only found herself annoyed. What made him think she needed his help?

"I think I'll go this one on my own, thanks," she said.

He sat back in his chair. "That's a hard road in this business, you know."

"Yeah, I know."

Lissy began to wonder what she'd come for exactly. Had she expected him to wrap her in his arms, tell her he'd been waiting her whole life to meet her? He could have found her if he'd wanted to.

"The resemblance is truly uncanny." He leaned forward, resting his elbows on the desk. "How is your mother? It's been a long time."

Lissy heard real interest in his voice. He wanted to know how everything had turned out for a girl tossed up and spit out by the Hollywood machine. His machine.

"She's great. She's a well-respected sculptor on the East Coast."

"Really? Did she ever marry again?"

Again. As if her first marriage had been legitimate. Lissy didn't want this man to pity her mother, nor was she here to talk about her. Instead, she blurted out the question she most wanted to ask, the question she realized was the purpose of her visit.

"Do you have any kids?"

Ever since her mother told her the truth of her provenance, she'd tried to picture herself inside another family with a living father and siblings. While her mother would never be in that family portrait, was there room somewhere in it for her?

"I had two children with my first wife, Jean. Three more with my second wife. I don't see much of them anymore."

Five human beings sharing half of her bloodline, two incomplete families she was connected to. Or was she?

"So what can I help you with today?" He put down the opener, ready for business.

She studied him carefully, trying to gauge if this was a game they were playing, or if he really didn't know why she was there. And if he didn't know, she wondered what she might unleash by telling him.

"I thought we should meet each other, considering—" Lissy tried to find the right words. "Considering the circumstances." She sat on her hands to stop them from shaking and did her best to look at him directly.

He studied her for a moment before responding.

"I'm not sure what circumstances you refer to. This may come as a shock to you, but women like your mother were known to play the field, if you know what I mean. I thought she was different, but her relationship with your father came as a complete surprise to me."

"My father? Can we stop this? You and I both know that marriage was a fabrication, a Hollywood lie created to protect your precious star."

He stiffened. "She and I made a deal that she would never reveal anything about him to anyone."

"Well, things get a little more complicated when there's another human involved—a daughter who's attached to a dead father who's not really her father and turns out isn't even dead."

His face turned white, and she could tell he was working hard to hide his discomfort. He probably staked his business on his ability to keep a neutral expression, but he wasn't entirely succeeding.

"I trust you understand that the image of Christopher Page belongs to his audience. He's a symbol of a different time. You don't want to damage that."

"Because he has more value as a straight dead person than who he really is?"

"Your mother's bank account depends on it." His voice cooled.

"Is it only about the money with you?" Lissy had had just about enough.

His gaze shifted somewhere Lissy couldn't follow, as if he was in a murky a part of his mind he hadn't visited in a long time.

"I tried to do my best by her." He said this to no one in particular.

And then Lissy saw it. Sadness. And a whole new understanding washed over her. At a time when most women had no choice but to marry the father of their child, her mother had chosen otherwise. It had wounded him, maybe even devastated him. It wasn't Lissy's place to explain to him her mother's unwillingness to commit herself to a man she didn't love—something no one should have to do—or her fear of giving up her ambitions, her independence, by submitting herself to tradition and becoming an uninteresting wife. She was only beginning to understand it herself.

Lissy was also starting to appreciate the power of the stories people create for themselves. The idea of being shunted by the mother of his child, by a woman he may have genuinely loved, was too painful to accept and absorb. So he changed the story. He told himself Lissy belonged to someone else—maybe Christopher Page, maybe one of a supposedly long line of men her mother had slept with. It didn't matter which one. There was no point in trying to disavow him of his version of things; it might prove costly for both of them.

Whatever he knew deep in his bones, and despite what Lissy knew to be true, neither of them had yet to speak the two words that had the power to disrupt everything if they were uttered and connected. Father. Daughter. Those words didn't apply to them.

"Thank you for seeing me. I'm sorry to have taken so much time." She stood and held out her hand.

"Please give your mother my best, will you?" He returned her firm shake.

Lissy nodded, left his office, and got off the lot as quickly as possible. She cried the entire way back to her hotel, hot tears and endless snuffles that left her a mess. She couldn't explain what was so upsetting exactly, what she had expected, why the encounter had so utterly wrecked her. But she couldn't stop sobbing. Her taxi driver pulled over at a Rite Aid in West Hollywood and bought her a packet of Kleenex himself. The kindness of the gesture set her to crying all over again.

When she got back to her hotel room, she lay on her bed until she was completely wrung out, her eyes still stinging but her breath finally under control. She considered trying to reach Noah, but there was only one person she needed to talk to.

She picked up the phone and called her mother.

CHAPTER THIRTY-SEVEN

Martha's Vineyard
September 1976

Lissy got ready in her childhood bedroom, loving the feel of the dress on her hips. Fernando had made it, of course, fawning over her in his apartment, making her model it for Benny. They regaled her with stories of her mother on the runway, how much Lissy looked like her now. It made Lissy smile, thinking of the woman her mother used to be. She'd learned a lot about her mother's life in California over the past several months.

Aster told her all about working in LA, from the shock of being asked to work as Lauren Bacall's stand in—Lauren Bacall! Lissy had no idea!—to the disappointment of learning about the underbelly of Hollywood, the brutal crush of fame and expectation. And she indulged Lissy with tales of her babyhood, how Benny made baby food from scratch when trying to relax before an important shoot, and how Fernando used to bounce her for hours in the pool. It finally explained her odd love of pools despite growing up so close to the ocean.

Lissy couldn't get enough of hearing her mother talk about that time, the old hesitancy and sadness replaced with genuine joy at remembering the love of their household, the family the four of them had been, if only for a short time. Lissy began to spend time with Fernando and Benny when she could, Benny always showering her with food, Fernando eager to tell her all about her mother as a young woman, how accomplished she was on the runway, how all his clients wanted to be her. "She didn't need any marriage to Christopher Page for that. No offense, darling," he would say.

Big band music played in the background of all those conversations. She loved the easy feel of it despite its emphasis on the trumpets and clarinets over the vocals. Fernando made her dance with him to "Tuxedo Junction," like he used to do with her mother. And Glenn Miller's "It's Always You" was in steady rotation, Fernando never missing a chance to hold Benny's hand while it played. Lissy found herself humming it sometimes, the lyrics stuck in her head, her thoughts turning to Noah.

Lissy reached for the small blanket she'd brought home with her, a steady companion through her entire life. She caressed the three small daisies needlepointed there, the yellow of their centers faded to a buttery white. She had often rubbed the threads under her thumb for comfort as a child, even as a teen, and now she knew those three flowers represented the triad who'd been there at the beginning.

And now she owned another memento of her early days. Her mother had presented her the night before with the emerald ring given to her by Benny as a token of their friendship, a symbol of their chosen family.

"I'm so glad you know that family now. Whatever you do in your life, keep choosing the family that will love you unconditionally and support you for who you are."

The gems glittered with all the glamour of another era, and Lissy found herself amazed all over again by how much her mother had locked away all these years.

Lissy and Aster both wished Fernando and Benny could be there on this day, but it wasn't worth the risk. Their own private acknowledgement of the past and what they all meant to each other was more than enough.

Lissy's view to the lake was blocked by the top of the white tent. Nothing too big, but Lissy's mother insisted the day not be marred by rain or scorched by an unexpectedly hot September sun. Lissy couldn't wait to stand on the lawn, in her favorite place, next to Noah, glasses of champagne in their hands.

He'd been a pillar for her through the entire ordeal with her mother, through the pain of losing two fathers in one breath, and then the joy of discovering she had two fathers after all. And Noah loved the idea of her trying her hand at becoming a bona fide professional singer. He surprised her with a small keyboard and set it up in the corner of the apartment so she could create music of her own. He taught her how to make demo tapes. He even wrote a song for her to record, insisting it would work much better in her vocal range than his.

She recorded five songs for a demo tape, three of them with Noah accompanying her on the guitar, and slowly sent them out to a few labels. She hadn't gotten any bites yet, but unlike when she auditioned for musicals, the process didn't leave her feeling the need to compensate for something lacking or push herself to deliver a performance that didn't feel natural. Instead, she embraced a style of vocals all her own. Finding a label to sign her would mean connecting with a producer who appreciated the stories she wanted to tell, who found her sound appealing. It would take time, and she was happy to wait. There would be no more shortcuts for her.

In the meantime, she'd gone on the road with Noah. It was a crazy life of late nights and blurry bus rides from city to city, but it gave her a front row seat to what professional music entailed, and she loved all of it.

Their travels even brought them all the way back to New York, where Lissy was able to watch Bae up on stage in a revival of *The King and I* that had once again captured the attention of theatergoers far and wide. Yul Brynner was back in the role of the king, and Bae played Tuptim, a woman gifted to him as a secondary wife who tries to escape for real love.

Lissy joined the crowd at the stage door afterward and watched Bae as she weaved her way past the clump of bodies and outstretched arms on the sidewalk trying to snag an autograph from Brynner or the lead of the show, Constance Towers. Lissy managed to position herself at the end of the row to catch Bae before she slipped away.

"Any chance I could get your autograph, Miss Kim?"

Bae looked up with surprise, and Lissy held out her copy of the *Happily After Ever* album. "I just loved you in this show."

Bae laughed and took the record from Lissy's hands. "If only more than ten people had seen it."

"I knew you'd make it to the big time, Bae. It doesn't get any bigger than this."

"Playing a slave wife in a white woman's story? You're probably right," Bae said, rolling her eyes. Bae always did cut straight to the point, but Lissy was relieved to no longer detect anger in her voice.

"Fair enough. But Yul Brynner?" Lissy leaned in. "Is he amazing to work with?"

"I'll tell you who's amazing. Yuriko is an incredible director. If I play my cards right, maybe I'll get to work with her again."

"She'd be crazy not to. You were amazing up there." Lissy felt immediately foolish for offering such a bland compliment when there were so many other things she needed to say. "Do you have time for a drink?"

"Two shows tomorrow, so I have to get to bed, but call next time you're headed to town, okay? Maybe lunch at Al's," she said with a smile.

Bae handed back the record before leaving the still-shrieking throngs behind and walking down West 51st like any other patron headed home after a show.

Lissy looked at the album in her hands. Bae had pulled out the liner notes and circled the title of Trudy's one solo, "Back in Time." She wrote, *Here's to the future, for both of us. With Love, BaeJin Kim.*

Lissy smiled to herself. It wasn't complete absolution, but perhaps an invitation to start over. She was grateful for it.

Lissy felt like she'd learned something about forgiveness over the past year, how much relationships can be deepened by it, how much courage it requires from both sides—one person willing to hand over their deepest regrets and mistakes, and the other able to hold and examine them without judgment before finally setting them aside. As soon as Lissy had found the ability to hear her mother's version of the story, she could find nothing more to blame her for. A tremendous relief for them both. Of course, it had first required her mother's bravery, her ability to recognize her own blind spots, her willingness to admit the false assumptions and missteps she had made. Lissy owed Bae that too.

The last year had also taught Lissy not to take anything for granted, especially the chance for the kind of relationship her mother had always talked about, one strong enough to last. She thought she just might have found that in Noah.

Lissy walked across the hall to her mother's room and knocked.

"You look so beautiful," they both said at the same time.

Lissy's mother had never looked more stunning. Fernando had made her the dress from afar, and it fit perfectly, the white linen cut on a bias with tiny pearls at the neckline and sequins running the length of each sleeve. Lissy promised herself she wouldn't cry.

"Ready?"

Mother and daughter walked out onto the lawn, arm in arm, and Lissy couldn't remember ever feeling happier, even in this favorite place of hers. She spotted Noah near the front and winked at him before smiling at Chrissy, Jan, and Bindi, the other three bridesmaids. Gleason stood next to Graham. It had taken her mother more than twenty-five years to get here, but she was finally getting the chance to indulge her one great love.

Lissy held her mother's arm as they glided toward the rose arbor the Franklins had set up on the lawn to frame the ceremony, toward Graham. Lissy heard her mother sniffle and glanced sideways as a tear the size of a pearl slipped into her mother's broad smile. Graham beamed too, and Lissy finally understood that the fan of lines next to his eyes she adored had been etched there by her mother, by the joy they had brought to each other for decades.

Graham's daughters looked happy too. After the horrible shock of their parents' breakup, and once their anger at their mother dissipated, they seemed relieved to see their father happy. And they had always adored Aster and Lissy, two pieces of a puzzle that so naturally fit. Lissy hoped that once they were ready to see things from their mother's point of view, they'd be happy for her too.

The ceremony went by too fast, the toasts on the lawn, the local oysters shucked and slurped, and by eight o'clock, the guests were all gone. Noah and Lissy did their best to clean up, picking up stray glasses, folding tablecloths, and putting plates and serving trays away. As Lissy carefully arranged her mother's bouquet in the ceramic jug over the sink, she looked out the window and caught sight of Aster and Graham sharing a quiet glass of champagne on the little bench between the scrub pines, the same place her mother had spent so much time with her over the years patiently answering burning questions and listening to all of her grand plans. It was a comforting and happy spot, and it looked so natural to Lissy to see the two of them there, Graham's arm wrapped tightly around her mother, Aster leaning into him, Graham turning to kiss the top of her head as if wanting to reassure himself that she was really there. Lissy pictured them walking hand in hand across the lawn and into the little cottage after the last light had left the sky, and felt supreme contentment in knowing that her mother would never again stand at that screen door alone.

Lissy found Noah stuffing the last of the garbage into the bin by the back door. "Let's get out of here, give them some space," she said.

She told him to grab his guitar, then took him up island to the Barn. It was their last open mic night of the season, and Lissy thought they might have some fun.

The venue was a converted barn surrounded by enough farmland to provide ample parking and a buffer of sound, the nearest neighbors being at least ten acres away in all directions. Lissy's mother had brought her there on countless occasions, for puppet shows and story time as a kid, and later to introduce her to folk musicians who somehow found Martha's Vineyard on their way to or from Boston and New York. Open mic nights were traditionally the time for islanders to flex their vocal cords. Lissy hadn't taken part since her college days.

She grabbed two beers—chatting briefly with one of her high school chums who manned the bar—and hopped up on the tall crate Noah scored with a good view of the stage. The crowd felt like an extension of the wedding reception, everyone in good spirits and eager for a celebration. Each performer was greeted with cheers upon arrival and sent off with enough applause to be encouraging, with hoots and whistles added when particularly deserving. Noah leaned against Lissy as they enjoyed the music, giving each musician his full attention, sometimes tapping on Lissy's leg to the beat or nodding his head in approval. She was grateful his newfound fame didn't render the scene too provincial for him. Music was still just music, something sacred, a gift to be shared.

After the twelfth performer wound down, it was Noah's turn—Lissy had put his name on the list ahead of hers—and she chuckled watching the emcee's eyes go wide as Noah stepped onto the stage.

"Well, ladies and gentlemen, we have a very special surprise. I give you Noah Hoyt, yes, that Noah Hoyt of the Treetop Flyers!"

Whoops and applause filled the place as a sea of hands thrust beer bottles and BIC lighters into the air. Noah played an acoustic version of "Resurrection" as the crowd sang along with every word. He left the stage after just the one song—that was always the deal at the Barn—even though the audience stomped and cheered for more.

Lissy jumped onstage next, and as hard an act as Noah was to follow, she felt surprisingly calm, like she had found her way to the other side of an unexpected riptide and was now floating under the sun with nothing else to fear.

The emcee put his hand over the mic. "Sorry, what's your name?" he asked, pointing to the chicken scratch barely legible in the dim light of the place.

She was about to say the name she'd written on the sign-up sheet, the label that had defined her for so much of her life, the name that had meant everything and then nothing. She changed her mind.

"It's just Lissy."

AUTHOR'S NOTE

Broadway aficionados may have noticed an uncanny resemblance between *Happily After Ever* and the Stephen Sondheim/Hal Prince production of *Merrily We Roll Along*, a musical that opened in 1981 and closed after only sixteen performances. I owe a deep debt of gratitude to Lonny Price and the producers of *The Best Worst Thing That Ever Could Have Happened* (Netflix) for introducing me to that story. Thank you to the entire original cast for so tenderly revealing what it felt like to experience the highs and lows of a failed production (albeit one that has become a cult classic). While there are many similarities between that musical and my invented one, none of my characters or their personal stories bear any resemblance to the actual individuals involved.

For those readers who enjoy exploring the line between what is real and what is imagined in fiction, the true story that inspired the character of Aster Kelly can be found within the pages of *Finding Home*, my family memoir.

ACKNOWLEDGMENTS

Publishing a novel is a team effort, and I am grateful to have so many wonderful people by my side on this journey.

It is a joy to once again be part of the Pegasus Books family. Thank you to Jessica Case for believing in this project and for your keen editorial eye. Your insights and suggestions rounded out this story in very important ways. Thanks also to Faceout Studio for the most beautiful cover I could have possibly imagined. As first impressions go, this is as good as it gets! And to Jocelyn Bailey for your laser-like copy edit, catching all the issues I could no longer see, and for your lovely notes to me snuck in along the way.

To the Four Points writing group, Susan Bernhard, Michele Ferrari, and Jessie Manchester Lubitz. Getting this book from first draft to something whole was a heavy lift. Your close readings of that early manuscript, your unvarnished feedback, and your excellent ideas opened up pathways of character and story development that made all the difference. Your love and support on this journey is worth as much as your editorial advice. I cherish you all dearly.

To Pam Loring and the Salty Quill Writers Retreat for creating space and such a supportive atmosphere in which to write. That precious week always seems to arrive just when I need it most. Special thanks to Deborah Good, Barbara Sheehan, and Leslie Teel for staying up late after my reading fell flat and helping me tease through the issues. That conversation was like wiping fog from glass and allowed me to finally see Aster clearly. You'll notice that the first chapter that poured out of me the next day is pretty darn close to the opening pages here. And as we all know, if we don't get those first pages right, game over. Thank you.

To Eve Bridburg and GrubStreet. My writing journey started within those walls and continues to be deeply entwined with the wonderful community of writers you have created. None of this would be possible without all I have learned at Grub.

To my trusted reading crew, Nancy Bewlay, Nora Speer, and Lynn Tetrault. Your insights into a manuscript I thought was pretty close to "done" were instrumental. I made several key changes based on your collective feedback, three in particular I can attribute directly to ideas that came from each of you. I hope you noticed.

To Megan Beatie at MB Communications, thank you for your tireless work to create excitement for this book. Fingers crossed that it finds the widest possible audience. To Michael Carlisle at InkWell Management Literary Agency for being there from the beginning and Michael Mungiello for your continued support of my writing career.

Finally, deep gratitude to my husband, Patrick, for your unending belief in my literary ambitions, your willingness to listen to my endless fretting, and for always being at the ready to pop a bottle of champagne at the slightest hint of good news. I love you. May we keep those corks flying!